the christmas you crash

PIPER HALE

a note from piper

While I have tried to stay as true to the rules and realities of professional hockey as I can, I may change or adapt some things to better serve the story. Please also note that while the story takes place in actual towns and cities, the vast majority of the places and businesses described are fictional. My hope with doing this is that you won't be pulled out of the story if you read it five years from now. If the places and businesses are fictional, they can't change or disappear.

Ultimately, this is a work of fiction, and I hope it will provide a temporary escape from the real world. And a new book boyfriend to swoon over.

Happy reading!

one

LEXI

If I have to listen to Bing Crosby guilt-trip me about being home for Christmas one more time, I'm going to chuck my phone out the car window.

"Sorry, Bing, but I'm guessing you never had to choose between spending Christmas with your mom, and her awkward new boyfriend, or your dad, who could list hockey stats for days but probably can't remember your middle name," I mutter as I switch from holiday music to my favorite true-crime podcast.

It's Genevieve, by the way. My middle name.

The episode starts from the beginning, instead of where I left off, but I keep my eyes on the road and my hands on the wheel rather than trying to find my place. My Civic has new tires, and the snow is only beginning to fall, but the last thing I want is to end up stuck in a ditch out in Middle-Of-Nowhere, Minnesota. I've got an emergency kit in my trunk—including one of those uncomfortable Mylar blankets—but I have no desire to test it out today.

Plus, with my luck, it would be some backwoods serial killer that comes to my aid. So, as my favorite podcaster always admonishes, I decide to *make good choices* and keep my hands on the wheel.

Two Harbors, Minnesota, and my family's cabin are so close, I can practically taste the fresh lake air. I can't wait to unpack my car and settle in for a week of peace, quiet, and hot tub skinny-dipping. My parents' cabin hides in a nice private patch of forest. Thick swaths of evergreen and birch trees surround three sides, while a black sand beach butts up against the fourth. It's not so isolated that I'm worried about being stuck there for weeks if the snow is heavier than forecasted, but it's private enough that I won't see anyone unless I actively seek them out.

It's one of the last remaining assets my parents share, post-divorce. Honestly, I think the only reason my mom hasn't let my dad buy her out is purely out of spite. Whatever. It works in my favor because neither one will allow the other to claim it over major holidays. That means it's just sitting there, empty, waiting for me to fill it with winter-scented candles, a crackling fire, and the stack of books tucked carefully into my suitcase.

Neither will ever know I was here.

Plus, keeping my trip a secret means no one gets to use the cabin as leverage. I hate that I'm stuck in the middle of their drama, especially since I'm certain the only reason my dad is trying to guilt-trip me into taking his side is to make my mom pay. Not because he cares and is desperate to spend time with me.

No thanks.

Honestly, it would have been no contest. I would have sided with my mom, if not for her affair. I wasn't the only one my dad neglected in favor of his career as the head coach of the Minnesota Rogues. He'd never call it neglect, of course. He'd call it *doing his job and providing for his family*. But it's hard to make that distinction when you're sixteen years old and your dad doesn't show up to the opening night of the school musical you're starring in (or the three shows after that) because he's in some other state, parenting a bunch of grown-ass men. Sorry. *Coaching* a bunch of grown-ass men.

Neither of my parents is innocent in the demise of their marriage, so I refuse to pick sides. The cabin, though? That's neutral ground. That's a quiet refuge where I can hide away.

Will it be a little lonely to spend Christmas alone in the woods? Sure. But it means I won't have to suffer through Jeff—my mom's affair partner turned boyfriend—calling me *kiddo* and trying to weasel his way into a parental role he'll never have. It also means I won't have to don that too-familiar mask I only put on when my dad cancels our plans because some guy on his team needs him.

Case in point: we were supposed to get dinner last week. It was the first time in months he'd made any attempt to see me. I even felt hopeful he'd show up as I sat at my favorite restaurant, waiting. And when it was half an hour past the time we'd set, I still managed to look at the server with her pitying smile and tell her that, surely, he was just running late.

It wasn't until I was at home in my pajamas, nursing a bottle of rosé while watching an old episode of *Dateline* that he called to apologize. Well, sort of apologize. He never actually said *sorry*, just told me why he didn't show up. Apparently, one of his asshole players dropped his gloves in a brawl on the ice and ended up with a nasty gash through his palm. My dad told me it was his duty to make sure his player was going to be okay.

Must be nice for that guy. Dad was coaching practice when I broke my wrist in sixth grade. He didn't make it to the hospital.

It's fine. I'm over all of that. I'm a grown woman, and I'm used to being disappointed by my father. Which is why I'm not giving him the chance this time.

The soft *crunch* of gravel under my tires pulls me from my thoughts, and my face splits in a wide smile. Breaking through the tall pines and snow-dusted skeletons of dormant oaks and maples, the cabin's green metal roof and log peaks offer a welcome distraction. It's even more peaceful than normal in the growing quiet of the falling snow. A refuge. A sanctuary.

Still, as the podcaster describes the bloody murder scene central to the current episode, I'm thankful I'm arriving at lunchtime while the sun's still out. Even if swollen gray clouds shroud it in gloom. When the cabin is unoccupied, there's only one lone porch light to cut through the overwhelming darkness. And even though I've never felt unsafe here, I've listened to too many murder stories not to be wary of the dark.

Pressing the button on the garage door opener, I pull my car in, glad to have it out of the snow. There's nothing worse than trying to clean a foot of powder off your car, and it's coming down now. Big, fluffy flakes intermingle with the smaller flurries.

"Made it just in time," I say to myself as I unlock the door to the house and let myself in. Memories whisper their tales around me while I wander through the mudroom and into the kitchen. Ghostly images play across my mind's eye. Weekends with my parents when I was small, before my dad became head coach. My mom and dad kissing beneath the can lights that illuminate the kitchen as she made grilled cheese after a long day of swimming. Sleepovers with friends and secrets whispered to a chorus of girlish giggles. My mom shouting through the phone at my dad after he'd called to say he wouldn't make it. Again.

Shaking my head, I unload my car. It's a long process. There are two suitcases filled with oversized sweatshirts, leggings, and other cozy things. One has a stack of six paperbacks and my e-reader. Then there are the bags of groceries, the bottles of wine, and the extra blankets I couldn't bear to be snowed in without.

After I put everything in its place and crank the heat, I grab an apple, turn up the hot tub, then flop onto the over-sized L-shaped red microfiber sectional while I wait for the water to heat. My eyes trace the familiar space.

Despite the log cabin exterior, the inside is more lodge-like. The main living area has high, vaulted ceilings with exposed beams that run width-wise across the room. The long, red sectional I'm lounging on faces a floor-to-ceiling brick fireplace I can't wait to use. A seventy-inch TV is mounted above it. The walls are a warm off-white—drywall, not logs—and the floorboards are wide pine planks that don't quite shine the way they used to. Use has worn down the hardwood to a dull gleam that speaks of parties and barbecues and summers spent running from the house to the black sand beach at the edge of the backyard.

Faded Oriental rugs keep the hardwoods from feeling too cold in the winter months. The open-plan kitchen and dining room overlook the back porch, and I smile softly as fat snowflakes fall just outside the wall of windows above the countertops and the French doors leading to the porch.

My phone buzzes in my pocket, and I fish it out with a deep sigh.

DAD

Sure you don't want to come over for Christmas dinner?

Halfway through typing *Gee, I can tell you really want me there.* I catch myself and delete the snarky message. I've long since stopped trying to make my dad acknowledge the way his absence and lack of interest affect me. There's no point in starting back up. Instead, I type a simple, two-word response before leaving my phone on the couch and getting everything ready for a nice, long, naked soak in the hot tub.

ME

I'm sure.

I don't need to spend Christmas with my dad. I don't want to hear about hockey, his players, or his team's record so far this season. No part of me could handle watching his eyes light up with fatherly pride as he brags about his players' accomplishments or narrow with concern about players who are struggling.

No, I'm a big girl now. All I need is an empty house,

half a dozen good books, and enough snacks to make me gain a few pounds before I go back to my normal life and my grueling master's program. No dad, no hockey, no complications.

It's going to be the best Christmas ever.

two

RYDER

This is not how I planned to spend the week.

My wipers drag across the windshield of my sports car with a groan, smearing melting snowflakes and not helping all that much. I should be out with my teammates, having a beer, enjoying the post-game high, and preparing for our next match. But I'm not. I'm in my car in steadily worsening weather because I'm being punished. Like a kid in need of a timeout.

I almost started a fistfight in a bar last night. So what? I'm a hockey player. Fights come with the territory. Granted, we're only supposed to brawl on the ice, but Chase had it coming. He knew what he was doing when he showed up at Chasers. That's our home turf, and he had to stroll in with his dick swinging, chirping bullshit. What did he think was going to happen?

A growl rips itself from my throat. Goddamn Chase Bowen. I can't believe I considered him one of my closest friends back in college. There was a time when we were like brothers. I've never understood why he turned on me.

Not that it matters anymore.

Three weeks. I'm out for at least three weeks while this massive gash in my palm heals. I can't even fight them on it. It's my dominant hand and, according to my doctors, if I don't let it heal all the way and injure it again, not only could my hockey career be in jeopardy, but I could lose the full use of my hand. That would mean I could have trouble writing, driving, zipping up my pants. Hell, even eating a bowl of cereal.

Nope. Not going to risk it.

But damn. What am I supposed to do for a week, isolated from everyone I know? Normally, I'd say, at least I can spend some time jerking off, but I can't even do *that*. I tried with my left hand the other night and it was *not* the same.

I wonder if this place will have any bars or a few good restaurants? I didn't exactly research my destination, but every town has to have some kind of nightlife, right? If I can't play with my team, at least I can surround myself with cheering strangers and watch from afar.

The leather of my gloves creaks against the steering wheel.

"Take a deep breath, Ryder. This isn't the end of the world."

Except, it feels like it could be. The team is on a roll so far this year. And my game has been on fire.

This is my first season playing professional hockey, and while I didn't get as much time on the ice as I would have liked at the start of the season, things have changed in the last month. Coach bumped me up from a third string defensive pair to a second, which is huge. I won't give up that momentum for anything. Even Coach banning me for a week is a good sign. It means he doesn't want to lose me as a member of the team. If he didn't care, or if he didn't believe I bring value to the Rogues, he never would have tossed a set of keys at my chest and told me to get the hell out of Minneapolis while Chase and the Chicago Blizzard are still in town for a multi-game series leading up to Christmas.

So, here I am, cursing this stupid car and these garbage tires for being so shitty in the rapidly growing snow drifts blowing across the road, while I listen to Mariah Carey hit notes only a dog should be able to hear and convince myself it doesn't matter that I'll be spending Christmas alone. After all, it's not like I have anyone at home who will miss me. Even though the team captain, Maddox Graves, and his girlfriend, Isla, did invite me over for dinner.

But it's fine. This is fine. I've got *Die Hard* and a few other of my favorite holiday movies ready to go on my laptop, a bottle of expensive scotch to be savored, and several pairs of the most ridiculous Christmas-themed boxer briefs I could find. Because why not? There won't be anyone to see me walking around with Frosty's face on my crotch and my dick nestled in a pointed pouch that looks like his carrot nose. It's impossible not to laugh every time I wake up with morning wood and see the carrot standing tall and proud.

I wince as the stitches on my palm rub against the thin strip of gauze beneath my leather gloves. I'm lucky I didn't end up needing a sling or a massive bandage that would limit my mobility. Between that and Mariah's high-pitched vocal runs blasting in the car, I'm ready to get out of this icebox, order a pizza, and veg out in front of the TV. Except, now that I've been driving for two hours and the snow is really sticking, I wonder if I'll even be able to find some place willing to deliver.

Shit. Although I brought the scotch and some snacks for the road, I figured I'd go grocery shopping once I settled in. The last I heard, there was the possibility of some snow, but I'm worrying I've royally screwed myself over. What if I can't get this dumb car into town?

"Always using your head, aren't you, Ryder?" I chide myself.

I almost don't make it up the winding drive when I arrive at my destination. There's at least four inches of snow on the ground, and it's coming down hard. Here's hoping there's a few cans of lightly expired soup here, or this will be a really miserable getaway.

My eyes lifting to take in my accommodations, I square my shoulders. I can do this. I just need to stay out of trouble for one week to show Coach I'm not a loose cannon. I need to show him he can depend on me.

At least if I'm alone and bored, there won't be many ways for me to screw this up and lose his trust.

I grab the key out of my pocket and head inside.

three

LEXI

THIS IS THE LIFE.

Snow falls all around me, the bite of the frigid breeze over my neck and face eliciting a shiver, even as the rest of me almost overheats. I've probably been in this hot tub twenty minutes too long, but I can't seem to bring myself to go inside.

It's so *silent* out here. With every additional inch of snow, the world stills, and so does my heart. Between school and my parents' divorce, I've been so stressed, I swear my heart always feels like I've just finished an hour of cardio. There's so much pressure to have it all figured out right now. To be responsible and mature and perfect. I need to keep my grades up so I can get a good job after I finish my MBA.

Then there are things with my parents.

Dad has asked me to get together a couple of times since things with Mom imploded, even though he hasn't made any real effort to bridge the gap he created between us. I figure it's out of obligation, since he knows on some level that he should feel bad about everything that's happened. Not that he does.

My mom wants me to have this great relationship with Jeff, even though I want nothing to do with the man. Shitty marriage or not, nobody likes a home-wrecker, and Jeff knew my mom wasn't single when they started hooking up.

Everyone wants something different from me, but do any of them care about what I want?

Not likely. Hell, they didn't even bother asking what I might like for Christmas. Not that I expected them to. I'm an adult. I don't need presents. But it's nice to feel thought of and seen.

But all of that fades away as I turn into a human prune in this hot tub, surrounded by wintery magic. This is exactly the peace I was looking for.

My stomach growls, reminding me that all I've eaten today was a breakfast sandwich and a few snacks on the road. Not to mention way too much coffee. Tonight feels like the perfect night for bougie grilled cheese. I have gruyere, onions to caramelize, the perfect, soft sourdough, and this really yummy bacon jam I picked up from the indoor farmer's market last month. Time to get out of this gloriously hot water and run inside.

Grabbing my freezing cold towel from the lidded tub I brought out to keep the snow from covering it, I take a few deep breaths. "Get your ass out of the hot tub, Lexi. It's like ripping off a Band-Aid. You're going to freeze your tits off, but it'll be worse if you don't suck it up and run inside." I still can't seem to make myself get up. "One. Two. Three!"

Leaping out of the hot tub, I quickly wrap the fluffy towel around my body. I grip the cold cotton in one hand and my empty wineglass in the other before scampering over the snow-covered deck. It's so. Damned. Cold. Worth it, but geez. My nipples are hard enough to cut glass. The wine stem in my hand causes me to fumble with the door for a moment, then I rush inside with a shiver and a little squeal. I give the winter wonderland outside one last look as I shut the door. Beautiful. Now it's time to dry off and get dressed.

Turning, I take a step toward the counter to set down my glass when I stop dead in my tracks. All the peace and relaxation I just enjoyed is undone in spectacular fashion when my eyes land on the massive, well-over-six-foot form of an intruder standing mere feet away from me. My heart thunders in my chest as I quickly take him in. Black coat, black leather gloves, a black knit beanie tugged low over his eyebrows, drawing my attention to icy-blue eyes that flash with anger, a strong jawline that ticks and flexes, and full lips pursed into a severe line.

My heart thunders in my chest. I'm going to be murdered. This is how I die. Killed by a man who is way too hot to be a serial killer, and yet here we are.

Screaming, I do the only thing I can think of and chuck my empty wine glass right at his head. It connects with his jaw with a satisfying *thud*, and my would-be murderer shouts. The pain distracts him from pulling out his weapon. It's probably a jagged-edged knife or a garrote or something equally ominous. He rubs his jaw, his eyes furious as he stares at me like I'm going to pay for that.

But if I die here tonight, at least I'm going out with a fight. When my favorite true crime girl creates a podcast about my murder, she'll be able to tell her listeners I got in a few hits of my own.

"Get. Out!" I scream as I grab the half-full bottle of rosé and throw it at him. My aim isn't quite as solid this time, and the man swats it away with his hand, which makes him shout again with pain. I must have hit a knuckle or something, because he cradles the hand to his chest.

"What the fuck?" he shouts. "Bitch!"

Bitch? He's the one trying to murder me, and *I'm* the bitch? Mind spinning, I grab the only other potential weapon within reach. The corkscrew I used to open my wine. My fingers close around it, and despite the fear that makes me tremble, I stand straight, putting both hands out in front of me, ready to defend myself.

And then my towel drops to the floor in a wet *splat.*

Well, shit. In all my panic, I sorta forgot about the fact that I'm naked and the towel keeping me from using my left hand was the only thing covering my body.

Wide-eyed and nearly feral with panic, I lift my gaze to the intruder. He's still cradling his garroting hand to his chest, but his attention is now squarely on my nipples. My very hard, very pointy nipples.

At least he's distracted?

With few options left, I throw the corkscrew at him and run. If I can make it to the main bedroom, I can lock and barricade the door, then lock myself into the main bath. Two locked doors between us are better than none, and hopefully, it will give me time to call for help.

Putting on a burst of speed, I make it past the stunned axe murderer I've hypnotized with my nipples, and pound through the house on wet feet. I pray I don't slip, because I sure as hell can't afford to slow down. Not if I want to keep my blood in my body. And I do want that. Very much.

"Hey," the man shouts as the spell breaks and his heavy footsteps follow behind me. "Get back here!"

"Fuck you," I scream as I skid into the main bedroom, slam the door shut, and lock it. My heart tries to punch its way out of my rib cage, and I gulp down huge, ragged gasps of air. I press my forehead to the thick wood of the door for a moment as I try to catch my breath. But the relief is short-lived as the man in black pounds on the door.

My panic comes back full force.

RYDER

What in the fresh hell is happening?

My injured hand throbs beneath my glove after blocking that damned wine bottle from hitting my face, my jaw aches from where that little naked home invader hit me with a wineglass, and my stupid dick is hard from the sight of those perfect pink nipples and her smooth, curvy body.

Focus, Ryder.

Using my left hand, I pound on the door she's slammed shut between us after trying the knob and realizing she's locked herself in. This is not how I thought this trip would go.

"Hey. Come out here, right now."

There's a brittle bark of laughter on the other side of the door. "No fucking way."

"I'll have to call the cops, then," I tell her. If she won't leave on her own, I won't have another choice. This is Coach Cross's cabin, and he made me responsible for it. I can't let him down.

"*You're* calling the cops?" she screeches. There's rustling on the other side of the door as she moves around the room. "*I'm* calling the cops! You're the one breaking and entering, asshole. You think I'm going to fall for your shit? You've probably got a garrote gripped and ready in those murder-glove-covered hands of yours. I won't be strangled while I'm wet and naked and end up the subject of a true crime podcast. They'll title it something awful, like *Hot Tub Horrors* or *Ho-Ho-Homicide*. Not today, Satan. Not. To. Day."

It takes me a moment to compute what she's said. Garrotes? Murder gloves? *Ho-Ho-Homicide*? Wait. "What do you mean, *I'm* the one breaking and entering? I'm supposed to be here. I have a key."

And that's when the crazy, naked woman cries, "Oh my god. Did you murder my dad?" She's screeching now, her voice rising higher and higher in pitch with every new word she speaks. "Did someone hire you to kill my whole family? What, did his stupid hockey team make your mob boss lose some money on a bet or something? Because I haven't spoken more than a few words to my father in months!"

Oh. Shit.

I go completely still as my mind puts all the pieces together, and I ask a question I'm not sure I want to know the answer to. Because if this woman is who I think she is, then I just saw my coach's daughter completely buck-ass naked. "What's your name?"

"Shouldn't you know that already if you've been hired to kill me?"

Pinching the bridge of my nose, I inhale deeply, hoping it will bring patience to my tone that I'm not feeling. "No one hired me to kill you. Jesus. I think this is all one big misunderstanding. Why would you think this is about your dad?"

She scoffs, and I can picture her rolling her eyes behind the door. "Because this is our family's cabin, and he's the only one who's used it in the last year."

Fuck. I let my head fall forward and bang on the door. The woman shrieks and I sigh. "I'm not going to hurt you. You can open the door."

"Oh, yeah. You're not going to hurt me," she parrots. She's fiery—I'll give her that—but I don't miss the waver in her voice. She's also terrified. "I totally trust you now that you've said that. Let me just open the door so you can garrote me."

"What in the hell is with you and garroting?"

"What? It's a very common tool used by hitmen and mobsters. I've listened to like three separate true crime podcasts this month where that's how the victim died." Her voice is reedy and high-pitched, and I can hear her breathing rapidly, even through the door. I need to reassure her she's not in danger before she ends up hyperventilating and passes out.

Keeping my voice low and soothing, I say, "My name is Ryder Hanson. I'm a defenseman on the Minnesota Rogues. I'm here because Coach Cross banished me to the boonies, so I'd stop trying to pick fights with my former best friend on the Chicago Blizzard, who almost ended my hockey career." I pause, and when she doesn't respond, I add, "I'm not a hitman or a mafia guy."

The woman behind the door is so silent, I wonder for a moment if she's climbed out a window or something. But she finally speaks again, and this time, her voice sounds almost pained. "My dad is your coach?"

"Is your dad Arthur Cross?"

There's a pause, and then a quiet, "Yes."

"Then, yeah, he's my coach. What's your name?"

There's a rustling behind the door before it cracks open to reveal wide green eyes the color of emeralds, long, wet, golden-blonde hair, and full, pursed lips. She's dressed now in an oversized hoodie emblazoned with a college logo and black leggings that hug every inch of her toned legs. She's stunning.

"Lexi." She tucks a strand of wet hair behind her ear. "Lexi Cross."

I take a step back as she cracks the door open a little wider, not wanting to crowd her and make her feel uncomfortable or scared. I'm a hell of a lot bigger than she is. She's probably all of five-foot-six. Rubbing my uninjured hand across the back of my neck, I meet her guarded gaze. "Mind telling me what you're doing here, Lexi? Because I doubt very much that Coach would have banished me to this cabin if he knew you'd be here too."

"No," she agrees. "Probably not. Come on, I need some hot chocolate to warm up." She pads past me, the slipper socks she's wearing *snicking* across the floor like whispers. "Want some?"

"Sure," I reply. Hopefully, she's also got some Bailey's we can splash in there, because after the last ten minutes, I need a drink.

20

$$four$$

LEXI

STAY CALM, LEXI.

I repeat the mantra over and over in my head as I tromp down the hallway with one of my dad's players at my heels. Screaming won't get me anywhere, and neither will having a full-blown nervous breakdown. So, I'll make hot chocolate and come up with a nice way to tell Ryder Hanson that he doesn't have to go home, but he sure as h-e-double-hockey-sticks can't stay here.

I don't understand why my dad gave him the keys to the cabin. As far as I know, he's never done that, and this place is for our family. Not his players. They get enough of his time and resources, thank you very much. He doesn't need to let them encroach on my physical spaces too.

Acid churns in my gut as I wonder what else he's doing with his players that he should be doing with me. Does he invite them over for dinner? Do they have movie nights as a team? Are they just one big, dentally challenged family sitting around eating popcorn on his couches while he silently wishes he'd been given a hockey-god son, rather than a needy daughter he's never understood?

I don't realize I'm grumbling incoherently under my breath until Ryder's hesitant voice asks, "Um, are you okay?"

"Fine," I snap. Okay, then. Remaining civil may be more difficult than I'd hoped, but he saw my tits and bits, and all of this is awkward and frustrating.

Once we're in the kitchen, I ignore Ryder. Maybe if I can focus on the task at hand, it'll help me chill out. Because, logically, I know this isn't his fault. Unfortunately, I'm not working on logic right now. No, right now, I'm feeling an uncomfortable cocktail of hurt and anger. It doesn't matter that I should be used to my father showing more care and consideration for his players than he ever has for me. It still stings.

"Wait." I turn to Ryder, the realization hitting me hard. "Were you injured last week during an afternoon game?"

He appears confused, like my question is completely out of left field. And for him, it is. But I just put the pieces together. This is the guy my dad ditched dinner with me for.

"Uh, yeah." He tugs off his leather gloves, still favoring the hand I hit with the wine bottle. Which makes sense, once I see the bandage wrapped around it. Shit. "Yeah, I caught a blade to the hand. Not fun. Why do you ask?"

He looks so adorably confused, with his brow furrowed and his lips twisted to the side, as he eyes me speculatively. It's almost too bad that I don't date hockey players. Ever. And that this particular player has the added strike against him of having earned my dad's concern when I never have. Not that Ryder would want to date me. That would be crazy.

"He was supposed to have dinner with me that night and stood me up." I turn my back on him and grab a gallon of milk out of the fridge, pouring enough for a few mugs of hot chocolate into a saucepan. Next, I add a splash of heavy whipping cream, a couple tablespoons of powdered sugar, and just a pinch of powdered espresso and whisk them together. "Guess I know why, now."

"I'm sorry," Ryder says quietly. "I didn't know. Coach never said…"

My laugh is bitter, and I hate the sound of it as it forces its way out of my mouth, but it's been so many years of this shit. "Of course, he didn't. Why would he?"

The chocolate is next. I pull the bag of dark chocolate out, along with a cutting board and knife, and begin chopping it into fine pieces while the milk and cream slowly heat.

There's an awkward silence, followed by the shuffling of feet behind me. Ryder's voice is gentle when he speaks next. Or maybe that's just fear. He's not being considerate, he's afraid I'm a bomb that's about to detonate. Which is probably accurate.

"Can I help you with anything?"

"No. This isn't really a two-person job, and, unless my dad is giving out weekend getaways to our family cabin regularly without my knowledge, you don't know where anything is."

"As far as I know, no one else from the team has ever been here. Look, did I do something to offend you?"

He's trying to be nice. I know he is. But I still scoff

because I'm feeling a little tender right now, and I'm not exactly the best version of myself. "Yeah. You barged in on my nice, peaceful getaway, saw me naked, and chased me through the house."

"To be fair," he drawls, humor lacing his tone, "you flashed me. It's not like I was trying to see you naked."

"Not helping."

His low chuckle skates over my skin, and I'm glad I'm fully covered in an oversized hoodie because my nipples pebble at the sound and goosebumps break out along my flesh. Dammit. No, Lexi. You cannot be attracted to this guy. He's off-limits. Forbidden fruit. A hockey douchebag. Your dad's player.

When tiny bubbles form around the edges of the milk and cream mixture, I add the dark chocolate and stir with a wooden spoon. The smell is rich and heavenly. This recipe is thick and creamy comfort in a cup. I grab cinnamon out of the cabinet and shake a small amount in, then go back to stirring.

"Damn," Ryder says, "that smells amazing. Where'd you learn how to make it like that?"

"The internet," I reply. "It's not hard, and it tastes so much better than the powdered stuff." I turn to him. If he's offering to help, I guess I might as well take him up on it and make some whipped cream. "Would you mind gently stirring this?"

"Sure." Ryder's icy-blue eyes meet mine and he searches my face. Not that he'll find anything there. I've mostly locked down my emotions by now.

When he steps beside me to take over the stirring duties, I finally get a feel for just how massive he is. He's got to be around six-five with broad shoulders, muscular arms, and those thick hockey player thighs that strain against what I am just now realizing are gray sweats.

Shit. Do not look at the dick, Lexi. Do *not* look at the dick.

My eyes drop to his crotch, and the very sizable bulge hidden behind a layer of what can only be described as fleece-lined-lady-catnip, before I can stop myself. Cheeks and lower belly warm, I step away, hoping he didn't notice me checking out his crotch. His soft chuckle tells me I'm not so lucky, so I busy myself with making the whipped cream.

More heavy whipping cream and powdered sugar go into a bowl, then I grab a whisk and beat the hell out of the mixture. At least it will give me a reason to ignore Ryder and his bulge and get some frustration out at the same time.

"So, what happened to your hand?"

"Oh, uh, got into it with a guy on the opposing team. We used to be close friends in college, but he turned into a real piece of work, and now we end up brawling every time we play. I got shoved onto the ice, and Chase's skate sliced right through the center of my palm. Pretty fucking deep too. He says it was an accident, but I don't buy it. I know he did it on purpose." Though Ryder's voice is tinged with anger, I can hear the hurt as well. I should know, I'm a pro at masking my hurt with anger. "He could have cost me my career and the use of my dominant hand."

Ah, crap. Now I don't feel so smug about hurting him with the wine bottle. "I'm sorry. Are you okay? I hit you with the wine bottle, and it looked like you were in a lot of pain." I look over my shoulder to steal a glance at him and find Ryder frowning as he stirs the hot chocolate, his attention completely on the thick, dark mixture.

"Didn't feel great," he says with a shrug. "But you thought you were in danger, so I can't be mad at you for it."

My arm burns as I continue to whisk the whipped cream. "Still, I'm sorry."

He glances up at me, and my traitorous knees wobble when he gifts me with a melancholy sort of smile. "You're forgiven. I'm sorry for scaring you and seeing you naked and ruining your peaceful night. I'll head out as soon as we've had hot chocolate. This smells amazing, and I'd leave now, but I really want to try it."

That earns a chuckle from me as I switch hands to whisk with my left. The cream is getting thicker, but it's not as fluffy as I'd like. As we lapse into silence once again, it's less tension-filled. After a few more minutes of stirring, the whipped cream is done. Instructing Ryder to turn the stove off, I pull two mugs from the cabinet before doling out the hot chocolate, scooping a generous serving of whipped cream into both, then sprinkling some chocolate flakes on top.

"Cheers," I say, clinking my mug against his. "And here's to never *ever* telling my dad you saw my tits. Or even that I was here."

He smiles brilliantly at that little toast. "Cheers. And I definitely never will. I'd like to keep my balls attached to my body."

We both sip our hot chocolate and let out simultaneous groans of pleasure. Drinking hot cocoa with an attractive stranger isn't the worst way I could have spent an hour during this long week of solitude, but I can't forget he's a hockey player. One of my *dad's* hockey players. And an hour is all we'll ever have.

I'm ready to go back to the quiet of my regularly scheduled plans. Plans that definitely do not include Ryder Hanson.

five

RYDER

LEXI CROSS IS NOT A FAN OF HER DAD. Unfortunately, that also means she's not a big fan of me. I guess I can't blame her if he blew her off the day I got my injury, but I didn't ask him to stick around and check up on me. Hell, I'm a grown man. He should have gone out with his daughter.

As far as I know, Lexi's never been to a game since I've been on the team. We all know the coach has a daughter, but the photo on his desk has to be from when she was a teenager. Maybe fourteen or fifteen. She looks nothing like the woman sitting beside me, sipping hot chocolate. This woman is beautiful and tough, if a bit jaded. The girl in the photo had a wide-eyed innocence that the current iteration of Lexi seems to lack.

Sipping my drink beside her at the kitchen island, I'm so tempted to ask her what their deal is, but I won't. Though we're enjoying a ceasefire right now because I'm leaving, I doubt it would hold if I asked something so intensely personal. I mean, she packed up her shit and drove to an isolated cabin in a town of only three thousand people for Christmas, rather than spending it with her dad. There has to be a story there.

I don't understand it myself. My mom passed away when I was seven, and my dad died four years ago. I'd give anything to spend the holidays with them again. Anything.

"Are you sure your hand is okay?" Lexi asks, breaking our silence. "I can look at it and make sure your stitches didn't open."

"It would be bleeding through the gauze if they had," I reassure her. I'm confident everything is as it should be, even if it is throbbing.

She peers at me from beneath the long fringe of dark blonde lashes. "I'm really sorry. Again. I feel terrible."

"You don't need to apologize," I say with a chuckle. "After all, you were just trying to keep me from reaching for my garrote."

That makes her laugh, and the sound is like chimes on a late spring day. It warms my chest. She's gorgeous, even frowning, but a smiling Lexi? Damn. If she wasn't Coach's daughter, I might try to charm my way into an invitation for the night. I'm not usually a one-night-stand kind of guy, but I'd happily enjoy a night or two with this woman if the situation was different. Hell, there wouldn't even need to be any sex involved. We could sit around and talk about the weather, and she'd probably make it sound like a revelation.

"Are you in criminal justice or something?"

She nearly spits out her cocoa. "Me? Oh, god, no. I'm working on my MBA. I just really love true crime stuff."

"I've never really understood women's fascination with brutal murders."

"We're full of rage," she says with a shrug, as if that explains it. "Plus, my favorite girl has a podcast and a YouTube channel where she goes over the details of crimes while putting on her makeup. It's fun and she's hilarious."

"Sure," I say with a shake of my head. "Murder *is* fun and hilarious."

"We all have our things." She shrugs again before tipping her mug back and draining the last of her cocoa. She stands, bottom lip tucked between her teeth. "Do you want more?"

Damn. I think that's my cue to leave. "Oh, no. Thanks though. I should get going. I don't want to impose on you any more than I already have."

Lexi's voice is soft as she tucks a strand of damp hair behind her ear. "Yeah. And we're supposed to get a lot of snow, so you probably don't want to wait any longer."

My attention swings to the now-dark wall of windows. I can see the flakes falling, thanks to the light mounted on the back of the house, but I can't tell how deep it's getting. With all the mayhem that's gone down in the last hour, I completely forgot that the snow was already becoming an issue for my car on the drive in. Maybe I should find a hotel or a bed-and-breakfast nearby to hole up in until this passes.

"Yeah. I think you're probably right." It's my turn to stand. I bring my mug to the sink, where I wash it, before excusing myself to use the bathroom. I don't want to be stuck in my car with a full bladder. Been there, done that.

It's not fun. Once I'm done, I grab my duffel bag, pull on my layers, and walk toward the front door.

Lexi and I stand there, staring at each other for a moment, before she shakes her head and says, "Well, drive safe, Ryder."

I'm tempted to hug her, but I don't think she'd accept one from me. Not knowing what I do about her dad and the fact that I'm the reason he bailed on her last week. But I am worried that she's out here alone. And if her dad doesn't know she's here, does anyone? I can't leave until I confirm she's going to be okay. "Thanks. Hey, does anyone know you're out here? It's just, if the weather gets bad and you need help, does anyone know to check on you?"

"My best friend, Rachel, knows I'm here," she says.

"She's nearby, in case you need her?"

"Uh, well, no. She's in Chicago. But it's fine. I have everything I need. I won't need help."

I don't like that. I don't know Lexi, and I'm perfectly aware that she doesn't need a white knight to ride in and save the day, but my dad raised me right, and I won't be able to sleep tonight unless I know she has more than one person to call if she needs help. "Here," I say, holding out my hand. "Let me give you my number. I'm planning to get a hotel nearby, anyway. Then, if you have my info and you need help, you can call someone closer."

She hesitates for a moment, studying me. Like she thinks this is some kind of trick.

"I promise I won't call you or bother you. This is just in case of an emergency."

After waging an intense inner struggle that plays out vividly across her features, Lexi finally unlocks her phone and hands it to me. I punch in my number and send a text to myself that simply says my name, then hand it back. She pockets it with a grin. "Thanks. But if you stalk me, I'll tell my dad you saw my nipples."

I bark out a laugh. "I sure as hell don't want that. Don't worry, though. I'm not the stalking type. I don't even own a pair of binoculars."

"Whew. Crisis averted, then." Lexi offers me a genuine smile that I have no problem returning.

I wish she wasn't the coach's daughter. I wish she didn't have obvious issues with hockey players. I wish we had more than this one hour that will live rent-free in my mind forever.

"Merry Christmas, Lexi. I hope it's exactly what you need it to be." I open the front door a crack, and a blast of arctic air whips past my legs. Damn. The temperature is really dropping.

"Merry Christmas, Ryder. Sorry about flashing you and stuff. Drive safe, okay? Maybe text me when you get to where you're going?" She sucks her bottom lip between her teeth again, worrying at it.

God, she's sweet. "Aw, Lexi Cross, I didn't know you cared."

"I don't," she says lightly. "But if you end up dead in a ditch somewhere, my dad would be so pissed. He'd probably never speak to me again, and I'd miss our quarterly conversations."

Fuck. Rubbing my chest, I don't feel quite as light after that little quip, but I let it go. "Coach would have my ass if I ended up dead in a ditch," I agree. "Good night."

"Night."

With that, I pull the door open, and my stomach lurches. There's so much more snow on the ground than when I arrived. Hell, there must be at least another inch or two covering my car. I'd better figure out somewhere close I can stay and then hightail it out of here, or I really will end up in a ditch.

I'm not the only one who looks concerned. Lexi's brow furrows, a deep groove appearing between her eyebrows. But before she can say anything, I tip my beanie at her and head out into the night. The only reason I don't eat it as I waddle to my car is because I've got years of practice on the ice. Not that penguin-walking through slick, fluffy snow is quite the same as ice skating, but it's close enough that I make it to my car in one piece.

Once I've loaded my bag, I start the engine, brush the snow off my little sports car, blast the heat, and Google the nearest hotel. There's one about five miles away, and their website says they have vacancies, so I don't even bother calling. I need to get on the road as quickly as possible.

Lexi watches from the front porch, her arms wrapped around herself to keep warm. I wave, flash my headlights, then throw the car in drive so I can turn around. The last thing I want to do is try to back out of this long, winding driveway in this much snow. She waves in return before heading back inside, shutting the door behind her.

It's stupid, but I feel the loss of her immediately.

"She's not for you," I tell myself as I lift my foot off the brake. Nothing happens. The car doesn't move. "Okay. That's not ideal." I press gently on the gas. Although the car moves, the tires spin, unable to find traction. Careful not to press too hard on the pedal, I urge it forward, wishing I'd bought a truck or something more practical for Minnesota winters. But no, I had to buy something fancy and cool when I signed that contract with more zeros than I'd ever dreamed of.

Finally, the car starts to move, and I give a little cheer. I can do this. I manage to turn it around and begin my trip along the winding gravel drive. It's slightly downhill, so I keep my foot on the brake, ready to slow myself down if I pick up too much speed.

I make it all of thirty feet, and when I try to take the first gentle curve, my stupid car drifts.

"No, no, no, no, no." The antilock brakes vibrate and pump, but there's too much snow on the ground. It's a slow slide into the ditch—of course—and my impractical car comes to a stop with a dull *thud* and a spray of snow.

Great. Just. Freaking. Great.

I put the cursed thing in park, cut the ignition, count to ten to calm myself down, then get out of the car. A quick look tells me there's no way in hell I'm getting this thing out of the ditch without a tow, so I won't even try. I strap my duffel bag to my back and begin the short trek back up to the cabin. Except, when I try to climb out of the ditch, I slip and fall on my ass. Three separate times. My sneakers are soggy, my ass is soaked and starting to freeze, and it takes almost ten minutes of slipping and sliding before I'm, once again, standing in front of my coach's cabin.

Lexi may be pissed, but I'll call a tow truck as soon as I get changed out of these wet clothes so I don't lose a testicle.

Picking my way up the stairs, careful not to fall and land on my face, I let out a sigh of relief when I make it without wiping out. And then, despite having a key, I take a deep breath, raise my fist, and knock on the door.

six

LEXI

I'M ALONE AGAIN, WHICH IS A RELIEF. RYDER seemed nice—and he's certainly pleasant to look at—but that doesn't mean I'd want to spend a week with him. Back to my regularly scheduled program of romance novels, chick flicks, serial killer documentaries, and blissful solitude.

And bougie grilled cheese. Because I'm stupidly hungry, now.

I watch the snow fall through the windows as I chop onions. Hopefully, Ryder will make it safely to whatever hotel he's found. If I were nicer, I would have offered to let him stay because I'm sure the roads are treacherous. But I'm not. Especially when it comes to hockey players.

The scent of butter melting in the pan distracts me from thoughts of Ryder, and my stomach growls when I drop the onions in with a sizzle. Cooking is relaxing for me. I'm no chef, but I love trying new recipes and changing up classics to make them more interesting. Like grilled cheese. It's so good, even in its most basic form. But add some fixings, and it becomes something elevated and unexpected.

And maybe that's why I love tinkering with old staples. Because if you tell someone you're serving grilled cheese, they've got this image in their head of what it will look and taste like. Then you slide a gooey sandwich packed with surprises on their plate, and the moment they take their first bite, you see the realization that they've underestimated the meal, and by extension, you.

I'm in the middle of spreading a generous amount of mayonnaise on the first slice of sourdough—mayo helps the bread get extra crispy—when there's a knock on the front door.

"You imagined it," I tell myself as I reach for the second piece of bread. Except, there's more knocking, and I can't lie to myself twice. Crap. *Crap.* There's only one person it could be, and I have a sinking feeling I celebrated the return of my solitude entirely too soon.

Sure enough, a bedraggled-looking Ryder stands at the door, shivering. The bottom of his sweats are drenched, and snow clings to his legs and ass. Concern momentarily overshadows my annoyance.

"Oh my god, are you okay? What happened?" I move aside and wave him in. Maybe I should have started a fire before I began cooking. It looks like he could have used it.

"S-sorry," he says, his teeth chattering. "My car slid into the d-ditch, and I fell on my ass a few t-times trying to get myself out of it. I'm going to call a tow, but I need to change out of my wet clothes. If that's okay."

"Of course, it is. I think there's still some hot cocoa left. I'll warm it back up while you change."

"T-thanks, Lexi." Ryder flashes me a grateful smile before toeing off his sneakers and heading down the hall.

Guess I'm making two sandwiches. I can't eat in front of him while he waits for a tow truck. I turn the burner beneath the hot chocolate back on before setting to work spreading mayonnaise over two more pieces of bread. I'm assembling the sandwiches when Ryder pads back into the kitchen.

"Hot cocoa should be ready in a minute," I tell him as I spread bacon jam generously across the inside of two pieces of bread. Then I portion out the grilled onions atop the waiting bottom halves of the sandwiches and start the stove. "You hungry?"

"I'm a hockey player. I'm always hungry."

Having grown up around hockey players, I know all too well how much food those guys can put away. I should probably make him two sandwiches, but the pan won't fit three, so for now, we'll each start with one. It'll have to be good enough.

"What are you making?" he asks hesitantly as I pour some pre-made tomato bisque into a saucepan and turn on the heat.

"Bougie grilled cheese and tomato soup. It's one of my favorite things to make when it's cold and snowy out."

He chuckles. "Bougie grilled cheese? What, exactly, makes it bougie?"

"You'll see," I say.

"You didn't have to make any for me, you know." Ryder shifts his weight from one foot to the other. He's got his chin tucked close to his chest, and he doesn't meet my eyes right away.

"It's really no big deal," I tell him. And it's not. However, I appreciate that he doesn't just assume I'll cater to him now that he's here. There are plenty of pro athletes that would have expected me to roll out the red carpet in this situation. At least he doesn't seem like one of them.

"Well, thanks." He gifts me a blinding smile when he finally meets my gaze. "I'm going to see if I can get someone out here to drag my car out of the ditch." He wanders into the living room in a new pair of sweatpants and hoodie, with his phone in his hands. He taps away on it for a minute before lifting it to his ear.

"Hey, I was hoping you had a driver available tonight. My car doesn't do too well in the snow, and I kinda ended up in a ditch after leaving a friend's house. I don't think there's any damage or anything, so we should be able to just tow it to a hotel nearby." Ryder listens to the person on the other end of the line, his face quickly pulling into a frown. "Are you sure? Don't your trucks have all-wheel drive and stuff? I really need to get to a hotel tonight."

My stomach sinks as he goes silent again. He's pacing, now, and his jaw ticks.

"No, I get that it's snowing and I'm not the first person to get stuck tonight. I'd be happy to pay a premium fee, if that makes a difference." He pauses before sighing deeply. "No, no, of course. No, it's not an emergency. Yeah, let me give you the address and my number. And I'll be the first person on your list once the snow clears?"

Shit. *Shit.*

Ryder rubs a hand over his dark, tousled hair. Hair that I can now tell is just a bit wavy on the top. "Yeah. Okay, great. Yeah, I understand." He rattles off the address of the cabin and his number before sighing again. "All right, thanks, man. Happy holidays."

I don't like the sound of that conversation. Not one bit. I flip the sandwiches before returning my attention to the massive man in my living room. His shoulders slump, and he looks like a toddler about to get in trouble for drawing on the walls. He takes a deep, fortifying breath, rubs the back of his neck, and meets my eyes.

"So, uh, there's only one tow company in town, and they're not taking any more non-emergency calls until the snow stops and the plows have had a chance to clear the roads. Since they're calling for snow for at least the next four days, they said it could be almost a week until they can get me out."

"Oh." I don't know what else to say. I mean, we don't really have any options here. Either I kick him out to freeze to death in his vehicle, or my solitude is no more. I only consider banishing him to his car for all of thirty seconds before I plaster a fake-ass smile on my face and say, "Well, looks like you're staying here, after all."

Blowing out a breath, Ryder eyes me cautiously. "I'm really sorry, Lexi. I swear, I'll do my best to stay out of your way. You won't even know I'm here."

I doubt that very much, but it's a nice sentiment.

"Don't worry about it. You don't have to tiptoe around me all week. That would be miserable." I want to say, *Yes. Please do stay out of my way.* But my mom raised me better than that. And it's not Ryder's fault I hate hockey players. So, despite my inner Grinch shouting about hating noise and Christmas and general merriment, my outer Cindy Lou Who can admit no one should be alone for Christmas. Especially not alone in a frozen car.

"Well, thanks, Lexi." Ryder looks visibly relieved. "I'll, uh, I guess I'll just toss my bag in a bedroom so no one trips over it. Got a preference for which one I should take?"

None, I say in my head. "Any of them are fine. I already unpacked in the main bedroom at the end of the hall, but there are three others. They all have their own bathrooms, so take your pick."

"Okay. Thanks." Ryder rubs the back of his neck. "I'll just be right back."

With a sigh, I turn the burners off and grab two bowls, plates, and spoons. I dole out the soup and plate the grilled cheese, and by the time Ryder's back, I have everything laid out on the table. I pour us both another mug of hot cocoa, and then we take a seat.

The atmosphere is decidedly less comfortable than it was when we were just drinking hot chocolate, expecting to spend an hour, tops, together. But faced with the reality of being snowed in with a complete stranger for at least a few days, we're both stuck in our own heads. I'm mourning the loss of my peace and quiet, and who the hell knows what Ryder's thinking? He's probably cursing my dad for putting him in such an awkward position. I know I am.

"Wow," Ryder says after taking his first bite of the grilled cheese. "This is amazing."

"Oh, thanks. I'm glad you like it."

"Thanks for making it."

"Of course."

We lapse back into silence, only the soft, wet sounds of

chewing filling the air. He's halfway through his sandwich when he clears his throat. "So, uh, you're getting your MBA, huh? That must be hard."

I chuckle. God, this is awkward. "Yeah, it can be. It'll be worth it, though."

After another few minutes of silence, Ryder asks, "What do you want to do once you graduate?"

"I'm not totally sure," I admit. I've spent so many nights waffling between a job that will make me a lot of money or a job that fulfills me, even if it doesn't pay the big bucks. "There's always finance or business development, but I'm also considering non-profit work."

Ryder's eyebrows rise. "Oh, yeah? What kind of non-profit?"

"Ideally, something that would have a direct impact on the local community. Maybe something with kids. I'm still trying to narrow down what moves me most."

"Well, I think that's awesome." He watches me while he takes a few sips of his soup. "I bet your dad is proud of you."

I scoff before I can stop myself but manage to keep my true thoughts about that inside. "I'm sure he is."

In truth, I doubt my dad ever thinks about what I'm doing with my life. It's not hockey, so it's not important. The extent of his involvement is paying my tuition and living expenses until I graduate. Don't get me wrong, I appreciate that he's footing the bill, and I know how lucky I am that I'll graduate without a cent of school debt. But that doesn't mean I don't wish he'd take an interest.

I can't stand the weight of Ryder's gaze, so I focus on my soup and sandwich. This turn in the conversation has significantly lowered my enjoyment of it. "So, how come you're not spending Christmas with your family?"

Ryder's spoon is halfway to his mouth when he goes completely still. Crap. Does he have a poor relationship with his parents like I currently have with mine?

Way to step in it, Lexi.

His gaze goes distant for a few beats as his chest rises and falls slowly. Like he's taking in deep, measured breaths to calm himself. I'm practically squirming in my chair when he finally says, "Unfortunately, it's not possible to spend Christmas with my family." He sets his spoon in his bowl and pushes away from the table, grabbing his now-empty plate and almost-empty bowl, bringing them to the sink. "Are you done? I'll do the dishes."

Well. I *definitely* stepped in it, somehow, but I'm not dumb enough to ask any sort of follow-up question after that reaction. "Uh, yeah. I'm done. You don't have to do the dishes, Ryder. You're a guest."

"I pull my own weight," he replies with his back to me. "I'm sure as hell not going to expect you to wait on me when I'm the one intruding on your vacation."

I finish my food in uncomfortable silence. Ryder's movements are jerky as he washes his dishes and the pot and pan, but he's still careful. I don't know why my question set him off like that, but I make a mental note not to bring up his family again. Once I'm done, I set my dishes in the sink for him to wash. He doesn't even acknowledge me. It shouldn't bother me—shouldn't affect me at all—but my chest tightens at the slight, and I rub my sternum as I busy myself building a fire. Anything to keep from dissecting why even the smallest dismissal from a complete stranger can undo me in spectacular fashion.

Ryder isn't my dad. He isn't anyone to me. Plus, he's clearly upset, which is somehow my fault.

I've just ignited the kindling when Ryder's dull voice makes me pause.

"Thanks again for dinner, Lexi. I'm beat. If it's okay with you, I'm going to head to bed."

My chest squeezes tighter. "Oh, yeah. Of course. Good night, Ryder. Let me know if you need anything."

"Night, Lexi."

For some reason, I hold my breath as he walks away. Only when his footsteps grow quiet and the soft *snick* of a door shutting breaks the silence, do I breathe again.

I have the room to myself for the night. That should be a relief, but I can't seem to muster any excitement about it.

seven

LEXI

I WAKE TO A WORLD FILLED WITH WHITE. IT'S almost enough to banish the early-dawn darkness. Snow still falls outside the massive wall of windows in the main bedroom. The trees are heavy with it, their branches sagging beneath the weight of the magical fluff, twisting their forms into something otherworldly. It's also quite cold. Putting a wall of windows in a bedroom like this is gorgeous, but man, can it make getting out of bed in the winter a nearly impossible task. Especially when the floors are gleaming oak wood, with only area rugs to break up the chilly surface.

My phone tells me it's only six a.m., and I consider going back to sleep. Except, I promised my best friend, Rachel, I'd text her once I got here, and I haven't. By my best guess, I've got two more hours before she FaceTimes me to check for proof of life. I'll text her. But first, I decide to do a bit of internet stalking to learn about my unexpected cabinmate.

The first thing I check out is Ryder's Instagram account. You can tell a lot about a professional athlete based on what they post. Are they focused on their sport? Or is every third photo of them drinking and partying? Is there a half-naked woman clinging to them in every frame?

Ryder's account is surprisingly wholesome. At least, the stuff he posts. I click on a photo of him training at the gym, and holy crap. The women in his comments are *thirsty*. The clip of Ryder sailing a wrist shot through the five-hole is impressive as hell, but again, the comments are filled with women telling him he can shoot his puck into their goal or commenting on how well he handles his massive stick. It's cringey as hell, and I wonder how anyone can post crap like that without dying of embarrassment.

The comments lead me down a rabbit hole, and soon, I'm trawling Ryder Hanson social media fan groups and contemplating the life choices that brought me there. I want to unsee some of the gross things people have said about him.

When I can't stand to read a single additional comment objectifying the man who was nothing but polite to me last night, despite the awkwardness of our situation, I close out of my browser. Still nestled under my blankets, I open my messages app and shoot off a text.

ME

Hey. Sorry I didn't text last night. I'm here, safe and sound, but there were some

complications.

Immediately, the ellipsis that tells me Rachel is responding flashes across the screen. I should have guessed she'd be up already. She has a marketing internship that doesn't break for Christmas. Knowing my best friend, she's probably already power walking through downtown Chicago on the more than mile-long hike between her apartment and her work. I don't know how she does it, but Rachel wakes up at four in the morning five days a week for her internship.

RACH

Thank god you're all right. I was worried a yeti got you or something. They have those in MN, right? LOL.

ME

Ha ha.

Complications? Spill it, Alexis.

She must have been worried. Rachel only calls me Alexis when she's pissed or exasperated.

ME

Well, there's no yeti, but there is a hockey player. And I did think he was going to murder me for a minute there.

Those three little dots flash across the screen, disappear, then flash again.

RACH

WHAT? Explain. Now.

ME

Well, seems Dear Old Dad gave his set of keys to the cabin to one of his players. My dad must have a real interest in this one, because he banished Ryder to the cabin when he almost got into a fight with some rival who injured him on the ice. I walked inside after a naked dip in the hot tub and found a massive stranger wearing leather gloves standing there.

You accused him of being a serial killer, didn't you?

In my defense, he LOOKED like a serial killer.

You have got to stop listening to so many true-crime podcasts.

Never. But that's not the worst of it.

Oh, god. Do I want to know?

He saw me naked.

WHAT?

I threw my wineglass and bottle at him, and when he didn't run away, I got ready to fight for my life and accidentally dropped my towel.

Is he hot?

What difference does that make? I tell you this complete stranger I thought was going to garrote me saw me naked, and your first question is if he's hot?

I think it's a totally valid question. I'm trying to decide if this is the plot of a holiday rom-com or a holiday slasher flick.

Neither. God, you suck.

So, what happened? Did he leave?

I wish. His car got stuck. We're snowed in together.

He's hot, isn't he?

Fine. Yes. He's hot. Are you happy?

Very. Because you're living a rom-com. Which is great, because it's been way too long since you cut loose and got some dick.

I've dated plenty of guys.

Not since you started your master's.

Whatever. That doesn't matter, because I'm sure as hell not doing anything with my dad's player.

Maybe the best way to get your dad's attention is by banging one of his players. It's pretty much the only angle you haven't tried.

No. There will be no banging.

Famous last words. Listen, Lex, I gotta go, but I want updates. At least twice daily. I love you. Be safe.

Love you too. Talk soon.

Locking my phone, I stare at the ceiling. I should get up, but I don't want to leave the comfort of the blankets I've been nesting under. Unfortunately, my bladder has other plans. A minute later, I almost leave the bathroom without washing my face or dragging a comb through my tangled hair before remembering my uninvited guest. Guess I should at least look somewhat presentable. I don't want to care what Ryder thinks about me, but I also don't want to scare him half to death by walking out of here looking like some grouchy yeti. Stupid Rachel, putting yetis in my head.

And I am grouchy. The moment I remember the too-attractive, hockey-playing interloper sleeping down the hall, my mood sours. Although he said he'd stay out of my way, I'm going to feel obligated to include him. I might not like it, but that's just who I am. A reluctant people pleaser. Thanks, Dad.

Yoga. I need to start off my day with some yoga. Tugging on a pair of leggings, a long-line sports bra, and an oversized sweatshirt, I quietly open the bedroom door and peer down the hall. Why? I don't know. It's not like I'm expecting Ryder to be standing, unblinking, outside my door like some weirdo. But I'm uncomfortable after the way the evening ended last night, and I have no idea what to expect when I see him today.

The house is silent, and I make sure it stays that way as I creep down the hall to the closet in the mudroom that holds my yoga mat. Carrying it out to the living room, I start a quick fire to banish the chill, then get set up. The snow falling outside is even more beautiful as the barest hint of warmth from the sunrise tints the swollen clouds a delicate pastel peach.

My anxiety fades as I take deep, steadying breaths and move through my favorite poses. The stretch of my muscles and the familiar routine of the movements help quiet my mind.

So this trip isn't turning out the way I had hoped. So my father has, once again, done something that led to my disappointment. None of that is new. I can overcome my anxiety and frustration. Throughout the years, I've learned to center myself and cope with unforeseen changes.

Deep breath in.

Hold it for a count of four.

Slow breath out.

Soon, I'm completely in the zone. Nothing exists outside of my breath and my body. Nothing matters except for the familiar strain of my muscles as I flatten my palms on the mat, pull my knees and legs off the floor, and move into Crow Pose.

I'm okay.

Everything will be fine.

You are strong and resilient.

"Mornin', Lexi."

Zone obliterated, I fall on my face, narrowly avoiding smashing my nose into the floor. "Ow."

"Shit." Ryder's feet move into my line of sight as I groan. And then his hands are untangling my limbs and lifting me easily off the floor, where I'd wanted to stay so I could melt into it in a puddle of shame and embarrassment. His voice is low and so close to my ear when he asks, "Are you okay?"

I groan again, this time less from the pain and more from shame as he sets me down on the couch and settles in next to me. "I'm fine. My pride stings more than my face."

Ryder's low chuckle rolls through my body in a way that should be illegal. Especially since I cannot like him. Not even as a friend. It would be highly inconvenient. He's already got that damned dark-haired, blue-eyed thing going for him. Plus, he's annoyingly polite. It would be really great if the universe would stop stacking this guy up with all my favorite *yums* and throw some *yucks* in there to balance things out.

"Don't laugh at me," I grumble.

Of course, that just makes him laugh harder.

"Sorry, Lexi," he says once he gets himself under control. That's when I allow myself to look up at him. Which, I quickly realize, is a mistake.

Ryder Hanson is hot as hell. There's no denying that. But *morning* Ryder? He's adorable. His blue eyes are squinty and just the slightest bit puffy as he blinks at the world, attempting to acclimate to the sun. His dark hair has more pronounced waves this morning, and they're sticking up at all angles. But it's his sleepy, lazy smile that gets me. Which is how I find myself returning said smile against my will.

"Why are you up so early? Shouldn't you be sleeping in? I know you guys don't get time off very often." The question is gruff, but he pretends not to notice.

"Force of habit. I have a hard time sleeping in, even during the off-season. I'm too used to early mornings. Why are you awake?"

"Same reason," I say, staring at the fire, so I'm not tempted to look at Ryder. "I go to an early yoga class most mornings at home."

Silence stretches between us, and I'm unsure whether I should apologize for whatever I said that shut him down last night or just pretend it never happened and hope I don't ask something stupid again. I get not wanting to talk about your family. Besides distancing myself from my dad, because I'm not actually sure he gives a rat's ass about me, I've also distanced myself from him because this is Minnesota. As soon as people find out that I'm Coach Cross's daughter, they stop seeing *me* and start seeing a way to get free Rogues tickets or to meet the team.

Nothing is more demoralizing than finding a guy you really vibe with, dating, and then having to break up with him because his eyes glaze over any time you speak and it doesn't have to do with hockey. Hell, there were a few times guys stopped being interested in sex with me because they didn't want to piss off my dad. Just in case they ever met him. Which they never would.

So, yeah. I get it. Family can be a sore subject, and I won't ask again.

After another few minutes of silence, I can't take it anymore. "Listen, I—"

"I wanted to apologize—" Ryder says at the same time. We look at each other, laughing awkwardly. "Go ahead," he says with a reserved smile.

"Oh, I just wanted to say I'm sorry for last night. Whatever I said that pissed you off, I'm sorry."

Ryder runs a hand through his sleep-mussed hair and grimaces. "You didn't piss me off, Lexi. There's no need to apologize. It's just... It's a sore spot for me, that's all. I shouldn't have reacted like that."

I shrug. "I'm not offended." The rejection had stung a bit, but it obviously wasn't about me. I can respect that. "Want some coffee?"

Coffee is part of my morning ritual, especially on days I don't do yoga. Not because I like the taste, because I don't, really. At least, not unless there's a metric ton of sugar and cream in it, or it's one of those fancy drinks that cost way too much at a coffee shop. But I developed a pretty intense caffeine habit in college, and graduate school doesn't seem like the time to detox. Nor does a week trapped in a cabin with an attractive stranger. Not unless *I* want to become the serial killer.

Ryder's attention stays glued to my back as I push off the couch and stride into the kitchen. Hopefully, I brought enough coffee beans for this trip. There's enough for one person, but two? We shall see.

The smell is rich and eye-opening as I pour a decent amount into the grinder. Even the little *tink, tink, tink* of the beans hitting the blade has me anticipating the jolt of energy they'll bring. I glance over at Ryder to see him watching me.

"Well?" I say, arching one eyebrow. "Speak now, or be forever sad and tired."

He laughs at that, and it erases the frown that was marring his striking features. "Sure. I'll have a cup."

I prep the drip machine and press start. It's not long before the cabin fills with the energizing scent of freshly brewed coffee, and I hum my approval. My ass does a little wiggle before I can stop it, causing my cheeks to warm when Ryder lets out another one of those low chuckles that vibrate through my body and somehow end at my clit.

Down, girl. We are not going anywhere near the hockey player.

The problem is, we haven't gone anywhere near *anyone* in way too long, so my body doesn't really care that Ryder is on my dad's team and therefore completely off-limits. Nope. My body just sees a glorious specimen of a man with thick thighs, a round ass, and a sexy-as-hell laugh, and that's all she needs to know. She can only think about ending this prolonged dry streak. Because, between school and my shitty part-time job waiting tables on campus, it's not like I've had the time. Things are probably looking a little dusty down there.

"So," I say, needing to fill the silence. "What were you planning to do while you're here?"

Ryder chuckles. "Uh, well, I guess I didn't really have a plan. Coach..." He glances at me, his hands rubbing up and down his thighs. Thighs that are again encased in a pair of those damned gray sweatpants. "Your dad sort of sprang this on me last minute. I was hoping there was a bar in town and some decent takeout places. But that's clearly not an option." He motions to the still-falling snow.

"Wait." I turn to look at him fully. "Did you bring groceries and stuff with you?"

The pink that creeps up Ryder's cheeks is the cutest thing I've ever seen. He grimaces, rubbing his hand across the back of his neck. "Uh, no? I was planning to find a store once I got here."

He was planning to find a store once he got here.

"Did you even check the forecast before you started driving?"

"I meant to," he says, ducking his head, so he doesn't

have to meet my gaze. "But I guess I got distracted."

"Seriously? You drove almost three hours up to a town you'd never been to before for a week-long trip, and you didn't even check the weather or pack food? What would you have done if I wasn't here?" There are always some cans of soup and some snacks that have a long shelf life stocked in the pantry. My dad pays someone to stock it up every six months just in case of emergencies. But Ryder doesn't know that. He could have ended up stranded and starving.

His cheeks flame brighter as he shifts on the couch. "I, uh, I'm not really much of a planner. I..." He glances up at me, and my heart does a funny squeeze. Ryder looks ashamed. Like he's a child who was just scolded for the hundredth time about something he knows he did wrong. I don't enjoy being the one to make him feel that way. I know all too well what it feels like to disappoint someone.

With a bright smile, I wave off his explanation. He doesn't owe me one, and besides, I'm always overly prepared. What would be the point in making him feel bad? "Well, never mind that, now. I brought plenty of food for both of us. And if, for some reason, we run out, my dad keeps the pantry well stocked." The coffee maker hisses and burbles as the pot fills. "Do you like cream and sugar in your coffee? I also have peppermint mocha creamer. It's so good."

The tension of the moment melts off of Ryder as he gifts me a brilliant smile. "I normally drink it black because creamer isn't really a part of our nutrition plan." He chuckles as I make a face.

"Seriously? Only serial killers drink their coffee black. Everyone knows that coffee is simply a vehicle for flavored sugar."

He laughs as he rises from the couch and wanders into the kitchen, where he leans against the counter less than a foot away from me. "Flavored sugar?"

"I like a little coffee with my sugar. What can I say?"

"Well, I guess I am out for a few weeks. No one will know if I cheat on my plan."

"That's the spirit. Creamer's in the fridge. Can you grab it?"

Ryder flashes me a lopsided smile that makes my belly flip. While he grabs that, I pull two mugs out of the cabinet and fill them three-quarters of the way up. After he hands me the creamer, he watches me pour enough to turn my coffee from a dark umber to a light tan.

"Jesus, woman. You weren't kidding."

"Don't yuck my yum," I tease, bumping him with my shoulder. His responding chuckle vibrates through me.

"I'm not the one who equated your coffee preference with serial killers." He spears me with an arched eyebrow and a crooked smirk. He probably has puck bunnies falling at his feet, with looks like that.

Another reason I can't and won't like him. You never know what's an act and what's real with these guys. Something I've learned the hard way. Still, I can banter and tease without dropping my panties, right?

"Yeah, but that's a proven fact. A university in Austria did a study that found a correlation between preferring black coffee and being a sadistic psycho." I grin at him over the lip of my favorite mug. It has an illustration of a hedgehog that says *I'm prickly without my coffee.*

"I call bullshit," Ryder says, laughing.

"Google it, then. You can't make stuff like this up."

Don't ask me what possessed me to do a search for that little tidbit, but I suppose it all comes down to my slightly unhealthy obsession with true crime stories.

Dark, messy waves bouncing, Ryder shakes his head but does as I suggest. His long fingers tap a steady rhythm across his phone screen, and I watch with a smirk as one eyebrow rises. He barks out a laugh, side-eyeing his still-black coffee. "I swear I'm not a psycho. I just have to watch my intake."

"Suuuure." I tease. "That's what all the serial killers say."

"Would a serial killer like the movie, *Elf?*" he asks.

Elf? "I don't know, why?"

"Because I've been itching to watch it all month and haven't had a chance. Why don't I make us some breakfast and we eat on the couch while we watch it?"

He's lucky that *Elf* is one of my all-time favorite Christmas movies. The offer to cook breakfast doesn't hurt, either.

"There's pancake mix and chocolate chips in the pantry. Or is that too much of a cheat for a big, muscly hockey player?"

A slow grin creeps across Ryder's face. "Big and muscly, huh?"

It's my turn for pink cheeks. I roll my eyes. "Shut up. All of you are big and muscly. Isn't that basically a requirement of the job?"

He shrugs, still grinning. "Sure, Lexi. But to answer your question, yes, it's probably too much of a cheat. But I'm going to have one, anyway. I'm going to make some eggs too. How do you like them?"

When was the last time someone made me breakfast

that wasn't being paid to do so by a restaurant? I can't even remember. It's nice.

"Over easy?"

Ryder nods. "You got it." He grabs the creamer from the counter and pours a small amount into his coffee. "And now that I've proven I'm not a psycho, I'll get started on that."

God, he's charming. Not good.

"Want some help?"

"Nope. Go shower, if you want to. I've got this."

Chewing on my bottom lip, I study him for a few moments while he putters around the kitchen, opening cabinets and searching for supplies. I don't know how to feel about any of this. I'm still annoyed that my plans for the week were shot to hell, but I also can't deny that it could have been much worse. Ryder is sweet and charming, and he doesn't seem to carry an ego the size of a jet plane, like so many other pro hockey players I've had the misfortune of meeting. I'm still not sure if that's a good thing, or if it's going to spell trouble for me.

I guess, for now, all I can do is take it as it comes and hope this snow stops falling.

eight

RYDER

MY MIND IS IN THE GUTTER.

Here I am, making chocolate chip pancakes and eggs, and all I can think about is Lexi showering a few rooms away. It makes me feel like a creep, but shit. Lexi's ass in those tight green leggings as she twisted into impressive yoga poses will be burned in my brain forever.

Her body is perfection. She's strong. Toned, but still curvy. It's obvious she takes care of herself. I'd gotten a quick glimpse of her naked body when she thought I was trying to murder her, of course, but my eyes were glued to her perfect tits, so I didn't really see much of the rest of her.

She's a bit of a contradiction. Prickly and sweet, fiery and sad... I'm not sure which is the real Lexi and which is the mask. I'd like to find out, though. I'd also like to wrap my fist in her pretty blonde hair, press her full breasts into the shower wall, and explore every inch of her. But that can't happen.

Even if Lexi was interested, she's off-limits—something I'll need to keep reminding myself.

By the time she reappears in the kitchen, wearing another pair of ass-hugging red leggings with snowmen all over them and an oversized white Henley that slides off one shoulder, I've got a huge stack of pancakes and a pan of eggs ready to go. Lexi closes her eyes and inhales, giving me a moment to study her face. She doesn't seem to be wearing any makeup, except for maybe a light coat of mascara. Her pale skin is dewy and smattered with freckles across the bridge of her nose and her cheeks. Cheeks which are stained with pink as they're pushed up with a smile.

"That smells so good," she practically moans. I have to adjust myself.

"Good." Hopefully, I don't sound as turned on as I feel, but I know my voice is a bit more gravelly than usual. "Want to get the movie queued up and ready? I'll get all of this plated."

"Sure." The scent of orange and vanilla overwhelms even the sweetness of the pancakes as she flits past me to grab the bottle of maple syrup and a few napkins. She smells amazing.

Ass swaying as she walks, Lexi sets the syrup and napkins on the coffee table in front of the couch, carefully adds a few more logs to the fire, and turns on the TV. I remind myself to focus as I plate up our breakfast. After bringing our coffee and the salt and pepper grinders over, I grab our plates.

We settle down on opposite sides of the couch. The soft *clink* of silverware hitting ceramic punctuates the opening narration of *Elf*. I can't help stealing glances at Lexi as she chuckles around a mouthful of pancakes. A small smudge of chocolate dots her lower lip, and I have to tell myself not to reach over and wipe it away with my thumb.

That would be weird. It would cross a line.

It's all I can think about.

So, I look past Lexi and focus on the snow-white world outside the French doors leading to the back porch. It's really coming down now. Heavier than it was yesterday, even. As if it's noticed my attention, a gust of wind whips the falling snow into a little snow-nado.

Lexi notices the direction of my gaze and sucks in a breath. "Wow. I hope the wind doesn't pick up any more than this. We definitely don't want to lose power when it's this cold outside."

Eyes wide, I turn to her. "Do you think that's a possibility?"

"Nah." She waves a hand dismissively. "I'm sure we'll be fine."

I'm not as convinced. And when I pull my phone out of my pocket to check my weather app, my chest constricts. We're under a blizzard advisory. It could still shift, so we miss the worst of it, but it could also leave us smack-dab in the middle of a shitstorm.

Worst-case scenarios tumble through my head in quick succession. "Where does your dad keep the firewood?"

"He's got some in the garage," she says, like she's not worried at all. "And then there's a big pile on the side of the house."

Lexi gives me a funny look when I set my half-eaten plate on the couch and stand. But now that I'm thinking about it, I need to check how much wood is being stored in the garage. If we lose power, we'll need to ensure we have plenty of dry wood on hand. Right now, having a fire lit is cozy and gives off extra heat. But if the wind kicks up and knocks out our electricity, it will be the only way to keep warm.

She catches my hand. "Hey. What are you doing?"

"Just checking the garage," I tell her. "I'll be right back."

"Ryder." She tugs at my hand, and I stumble, my ass hitting the couch. "Hey, it's going to be fine. Eat your breakfast, and then we can check, okay? You spent all that time making yummy food. At least eat it while it's hot." She gifts me a soft, encouraging smile, and some of the tightness in my chest eases. "Seriously. We're good. Eat your food and watch the movie with me. Then we'll both get dressed in something warmer and make sure we're well stocked."

I'm still itching to get up and take care of it right this second, but I also don't want to disappoint Lexi. Especially since we're getting along. "Okay, yeah. You're right. It'll be fine."

She smiles broadly at me when I settle back into the cushions and grab my plate. "This is great. Thanks again for making breakfast."

"It's the least I could do," I reply. We stare at each other for another moment before returning our attention to Will Ferrell and his yellow tights. It takes a bit, but eventually, I relax and laugh along with Lexi. The sound is loud enough that I don't even notice the wind picking up outside.

"I'M STUFFED." LEXI PATS HER FLAT STOMACH before grabbing our plates and bringing them to the kitchen. She turns the water on hot and squirts some dish soap onto a scrub brush. It's all so easy and domestic, and something about it hits me right in the chest. "Oh, wow. That's a lot of snow."

The thick, white powder has created a drift that would reach above mid-calf against the back door. It has to be at least seven or eight inches of snow, and that's under an overhang. Without the movie to distract me, I'm right back to worst-case scenarios. Checking the weather app doesn't help. That blizzard advisory has turned into a blizzard watch. Still not as ominous as a warning, but it tells me we're in for some serious accumulation.

"I'm going to get dressed in something warm and check on the wood."

Lexi's lips pinch into a straight line. "Yeah, I'll come with you." She's no longer feeling so unconcerned.

Five minutes later, we're both wearing several layers of pants, shirts, and heavy coats. Lexi has a pair of snow boots on, but I only packed my stupid sneakers. She frowns when she notices my footwear.

"I think my dad left a pair of boots here. What size shoe do you wear?"

"A thirteen."

Her brow rises. "Damn. Okay, well, hopefully, you two are close in size. Be right back." She disappears into the room off the kitchen. There's some rustling, a few curses, and the slamming of a closet door, and then she's pushing a pair of boots into my waiting hands. "They're twelve and a half, but they'll have to do. You can't wear those sneakers outside in this. You'll get frostbite."

"Thanks." I wince when I shove my feet into the boots. They pinch my toes, and they're not very comfortable, but they'll do for now. Hopefully, all of this is unnecessary. If we're lucky, we'll walk into the garage and find a wall of cut wood waiting to be burned.

"Come on, then."

We're not that lucky.

"Shit," Lexi mutters. Her eyebrows pull together as she twists her lips to the side in frustration. "This is barely enough for the next two days, even if we just wanted to keep the fire going for ambiance."

Flexing my injured hand, I can only hope Coach Cross has a massive pile of pre-cut wood out there, because chopping firewood is the last thing I should be doing right now. "Where does your dad keep the rest of it?"

Lexi worries at her bottom lip, nodding her head toward an exterior door. "This way."

Icy wind smacks me in the face as soon as we exit the shelter of the garage. This is no longer the idyllic snowfall of the night before, and I'm glad neither of us had to navigate this weather yesterday on the drive up. The little Civic in the garage that must be Lexi's wouldn't have fared any better than my ridiculous sports car.

"Oh my god," she says, her teeth chattering.

"We should bring in as much wood as we can," I say to Lexi's back as I follow her around the side of the cabin. "We don't want to come out here again tonight after the temperatures drop."

"No kidding."

We come to a stop in front of a blue tarp draped over a stack of wood. It's a large pile—plenty to get us through the week—and I mutter a prayer to the hockey gods that it's already split before tugging the tarp off.

"That'll be enough, right?" Lexi looks between me and the wood. Less than a third of it is pre-split. The rest are thick enough pieces that they'll need to be quartered, at least.

"I hope so," I say, trying to do the math. There's not as much split as I'd like, but with my injured hand, cutting more is out of the question, absent an emergency scenario. As long as we don't lose power for more than a few hours, we should be fine. And hockey gods help us if that happens. I doubt either of us is prepared for something like that.

When I return my attention to Lexi, she's staring at the wood with a troubled expression. My anxiety has bled into her, and I kick myself.

Keep your shit together, Ryder. Don't freak Lexi out.

I press a gloved hand to her shoulder. She looks up at me, blinking owlishly, and I fight the urge to wrap her in a hug. I want her to know that everything will be okay, but she doesn't know me. I don't think that would go over well. Instead, I say, "I saw a wheelbarrow in the garage. I'm going to drag it out here. We can stack the wood in it, so we're not making a bunch of trips."

"Okay." She nods. She's still worrying at her full lower lip, and it's killing me. "Thanks, Ryder."

Pushing a wheelbarrow through eight inches of snow sucks. I'm sweating, swearing, and grumbling under my breath by the time I make it to Lexi. Her eyes widen as she watches me struggle, and I can tell she's fighting a smile. Those full lips of hers twitch and curve before she schools her expression into something neutral.

"Do you need help?" She hurries over to me, ready to help me drag the thing, when she loses her footing. Her emerald eyes go wide, her arms flail in a futile attempt to regain her balance, and her lips pop open in an *O* shape. "Shit!"

I close the distance between us without thinking. My hands grab her hips as Lexi's latch on to my shoulders, and her face smashes into the puffy down of my coat with a soft *oomph*. The impact is enough to cause me to slip, and there's a split second of clarity as her wide eyes lift to mine. We're going down, and there's nothing either of us can do to stop it.

Lexi's not tiny. She seems to be somewhere around average height. She's thin, but in a fit sort of way. I know she's strong after watching her do her yoga this morning. But I'm six-foot-five. She's a pixie compared to me. If I land on her, it'll hurt. So, I do the only thing I can. I wrap my arms around her and twist my body.

The snow cushions our fall, but Lexi still lets out a little squeak of worry as she lands on top of me. Her hands grip my shoulders, and she's tucked her face into my neck, so we don't crack our skulls together. Every single inch of her body is pressed against mine, and for a moment, I don't feel the snow. The cold doesn't seem to touch me. All I can feel is her warmth, the rapid puffs of her breath against my neck, and her thigh pressing against the hardening length of my dick.

Shit.

"You okay?" I ask. Hopefully, she doesn't notice the raspy quality my voice has taken on.

Her lips feather ever so slightly over my neck as she sucks in a few deep breaths, and fuck, if I don't want to switch our positions, throw her onto her back, and cage her in with my body. If it wasn't for the snow—and the fact that she's Coach's daughter and therefore completely forbidden—I'm not sure I'd be able to restrain myself.

"Lex?"

"I'm okay," she finally whispers. "I'm okay. Are you? I landed on you. Did I hurt you?"

"I've had two-hundred-pound guys land on me in brawls on the ice," I reassure her with a grin. "You didn't hurt me."

"But your hand..."

"Is fine." I flex it against her back. As we stare into each other's eyes for a beat, it's like the world takes a deep breath. There's a moment of utter silence where Lexi's attention drops to my lips. Her pink tongue flicks out and wets hers. I don't think she's even conscious of the movement. When she meets my gaze again, her cheeks flush a deep pink, and she wiggles in my hold.

"Sorry. I'm sorry." She pushes off my chest and stumbles to her feet. Losing her warmth knocks the breath from my chest, and I rub my sternum. She tracks the movement before giving me her back. "We should load this up. It's freezing out here."

She grabs an armful of firewood. They make a hollow *clang* when she drops them onto the rusted metal of the wheelbarrow. Normally, the sound would reverberate through the trees. But not in this weather. The snow and wind swallow the noise completely.

I wonder if it would swallow her moans if I pushed her up against the wall of the cabin and fucked her with my fingers?

Not going to happen, I remind myself. She's off-limits. And she wouldn't want me, even if she wasn't.

This is going to be the longest week of my life.

nine

LEXI

THE WIND IS HOWLING.

I was prepared for some snow on this trip, but the weather has quickly taken a far more serious turn than originally forecasted. As annoyed as I am at Ryder's presence, part of me is relieved not to be alone in this. I'd be panicking if I was by myself.

After hauling a wheelbarrow full of logs into the garage, Ryder and I slipped into a mutual silence. To call it comfortable would oversell it, but it's also not painfully awkward. Still, there's a tension between us. We can't seem to shake it ever since Ryder saved me from falling on my ass in the snow. The last thing I want to do is evaluate said tension, so I'm sticking with a tried-and-true method of disassociation.

Reading.

I'm halfway through my spicy book (and trying not to blush when the characters get frisky), while Ryder flips through his third sports magazine of the afternoon. Pine logs crackle away in the fireplace, and the occasional bit of sap snaps loudly as it burns. The late-afternoon sun is low in the sky, not that we can see it. We've officially moved past a simple snowstorm and into blizzard territory.

A loud ringtone blaring through the otherwise silent room has me nearly jumping out of my skin. Ryder gives me a sheepish look.

"Sorry. Didn't realize that was set so high. Guess I'm used to being around a bunch of loud guys." He digs under the blanket he's wrapped himself in to free the phone. His face blanches when he sees the name on the screen.

"What?" I ask, suddenly nervous. Which makes no sense. I don't care who's calling Ryder. It's none of my business. "Do you need me to go into the other room?"

Ryder's jaw flexes as he turns the phone around so I can see the name on the screen. "No, it's not that. It's just... Well, it's..."

My dad. The word *Coach* flashes across the display, and my body goes through a wild array of responses. My stomach drops, my cheeks heat, and my chest twists painfully. Why is my dad calling Ryder?

"Well, answer it," I whisper, as though my father can hear me.

"Are you sure? You didn't tell him about being stuck here together, right?"

"God, no," I hiss. "And you'd better not, either."

"Shit. Right." Ryder answers, then presses the *speaker* button, so I can hear the conversation. Every muscle in my body tenses. "Hello? Coach?"

"Ryder, how're you doing, son?"

Son? What the fuck?

My dad's voice is warm and colored with familiarity. "I saw the weather report and wanted to check on you. We're getting dumped on here in the city, but when the meteorologist said the words blizzard and Two Harbors in the same sentence, I got worried."

When my teeth grind together, Ryder notices, his brow creasing. No doubt he's confused by my visceral reaction to my father's voice, but I can't help it. When was the last time my dad felt this level of concern for me? Hell, when's the last time he picked up the phone to call me just to check in? Arthur Cross only calls me when he feels obligated to do so. The twisting sensation in my chest worsens.

Keep your shit together, Lexi.

Ryder rubs the back of his neck with his free hand, his attention still on me. "Oh, uh, yeah. It's coming down pretty hard up here. The visibility is next to nothing."

"Do you have everything you need to make it through?"

"Yeah," Ryder says. He gives me a grateful smile. He would have been screwed if not for me and my haul of groceries, and we both know it. The guy would have been subsisting on a diet of canned soup and rice for the entire week. "Yeah, I'll be just fine. Thanks."

"I'm sorry for getting you stranded out there. I should have just had you stay with me for Christmas or something. Kept you out of trouble without banishing you to the middle of nowhere in a blizzard."

The casual way my dad speaks about offering to have Ryder stay over the holiday straightens my spine. It sounds so easy and natural. When he'd asked me to spend Christmas with him, he'd hemmed and hawed about how my mom shouldn't expect me to travel to Wisconsin, where Jeff's extended family lives, so I should just spend the holiday with him. He barely put up a fight when I said no and didn't even bother asking what my plans were. He made the obligatory offer, and that was that.

Like asking was his duty. Because that's what I am to my father—a duty.

Maybe if I'd been born with a penis and an inclination to play hockey, he'd have asked me with the same warmth he just used with Ryder. A man he's known for less than a year.

Ryder clears his throat. I can feel his gaze on me, but I can't look at him anymore. I'm too busy staring at my hands as I twist my fingers together. My book is long forgotten.

"That's okay, Coach. Christmas hasn't really been a big deal for me for the last few years."

My dad clucks his tongue in disapproval. "Well, you're part of the Rogues now. We're a family. Family supports each other. They're there for one another."

Oh, that's rich.

Pushing off the couch, I stride into the kitchen. With my back to Ryder, I press my palms hard into the cold marble countertops and stare out the window at the falling snow. The snow that's trapping me in this cabin with a man I don't know. And the conversation he's having with my dad is a great reminder of why I don't want to know him.

Ryder Hanson plays for my father, and I've done everything I can to put boundaries in place to protect myself from being hurt by my dad. Boundaries I'll have to work to rebuild because, after listening to one awkward minute of their conversation, I've been reduced back down to that devastated sixteen-year-old girl whose father couldn't bother to show up for her first starring role. Not even for four hours. Not even for something she'd been over-the-moon excited about.

Family supports each other.

What a joke. The man didn't even bother to show up for my high school graduation, let alone college.

"Well, listen, son, if the weather clears in time, feel free to join me for Christmas. I'll be having a small get-together with some players and staff who don't have family in town. I'm hoping it'll be a new tradition. It would be great to have you."

Ryder's silent for a beat before he asks, "You're not going to spend the holiday with your family?"

My dad chuckles. "Sure, I am. Like I said, the Rogues are a family."

The words deflate me. My spine curves and my shoulders hunch because, not only does my dad sound completely unbothered that he won't see me this Christmas, but he's already happily planning on not seeing me next Christmas too?

"Well, sure," Ryder says awkwardly, "but don't you have a daughter? I doubt she'd want to spend Christmas surrounded by a bunch of obnoxious hockey players."

Jesus, Ryder. Could you be more obvious?

Dad hums a noncommittal sound. "Alexis has her own life and traditions. I don't worry much about her. She's probably off, partying with her friends and having the time of her life right now." He chuckles. "Who knows with that one? I haven't understood her since she went through puberty."

A scream of frustration tries to push up my throat, but

I tamp it down. The edge of the counter bites into my palms. He hasn't understood me since I went through puberty? I doubt he even remembered when that was or noticed in the first place.

I was twelve, for the record.

And whose fault is it he doesn't understand me?

Understanding takes effort. And I've sure as hell put in the effort over the years. I made my mom take me to every Rogues home game until I finally woke up at fourteen to the fact that my dad loved hockey more than me. How many conversations did I redirect to hockey when his eyes glazed over because I tried talking to him about my life and interests, just so I could enjoy a few moments of his attention and a handful of bright smiles?

And off with my friends, partying? That's never been me.

My dad doesn't know me at all.

There's a long beat of silence, and I'm sure Ryder's staring at the back of my head. I can practically feel it. So, I decide to distract myself. I don't need his pity or his judgment. After all, I've been just fine without my dad's lackluster presence in my life for the last seven years. No need to pine for it now. Silently, so my dad doesn't suspect Ryder isn't alone at the cabin, I grab two mugs from the cabinet and measure coffee grounds out into the machine.

"Right," Ryder says. His voice is rougher than it was at the start of the conversation. Part of me is desperate to turn around and see his expression, but I don't. It'll either piss me off more or make me cry. "Well, thanks for the offer, Coach, but I think I'll stay here at the cabin for Christmas. It's growing on me."

Dad chuckles. "It has its charms."

"It does," Ryder replies softly.

A little thrill goes through me. Is Ryder talking about me? No, surely not. And I don't want him to be. All of this is complicated enough. I don't need to add in some stupid secret hope that Ryder has any feelings or regard for me. Because I don't have any for him. At least, not outside of base physical attraction, and I challenge anyone who likes men *not* to be attracted to Ryder Hanson.

But that's all this is. And that's all it ever will be.

"Well." Dad blows out a breath. The sound is fuzzy over the phone. "Have a good week. Feel free to stop by on Christmas if you change your mind. Stay safe, son."

"Thanks, Coach. Merry Christmas."

"Merry Christmas."

The line goes silent, as does the cabin. It's heavier than the snow-covered silence outside. Though the cold of this one is more oppressive, and it freezes my heart straight through.

ten

RYDER

Lexi Cross hasn't moved for almost a minute. She's just standing in front of the coffee machine, watching it. Except she hasn't pressed the start button. And I'm sitting here on the couch, staring at her like an idiot.

She's upset, that much is clear. After the way Coach brushed off my question about her, I can't say I blame her. Some of her comments when we first met repeat in my head. I wondered why she didn't seem close to her dad—he's a great coach and mostly a solid guy—and I just couldn't wrap my head around choosing to spend Christmas away from my family. But my mom was an angel, and my dad was always present and interested in my life. He showed up, cheered me on, and always did his best to meet me where I was at.

I'm not so sure Coach does the same with Lexi. The

way he brushed aside her absence this week like it was no big deal... But maybe he's simply hiding his true feelings about all of it. It's not like I'd expect him to open up and tell me how much he misses her. That's not something a coach would share with one of his rookie players, right?

Still, I didn't miss the way Lexi shrank in on herself with every new word he spoke. I'm surprised by how much I hate it. Sure, Lexi's a little prickly and she's definitely got her quirks, but she has a fire I can't help but admire. Hell, even when she thought I was an axe murderer, she stood her ground, squared her shoulders, and let me have it. She's a fighter. Which begs the question, how many times has she lost the battle for her dad's affection? Because this—the stooped shoulders and the slight shake of her hands—isn't the posture of a fighter. It's the posture of someone who has accepted defeat.

After a few more silent moments, I rise quietly from my spot on the couch and make my way into the kitchen. I have no clue what I'm doing. Am I planning to pull her into a hug? Give her a friendly punch on the shoulder and tell her everything will work out? I've learned better than most that's not guaranteed.

What I do know is that Lexi Cross and I are going to be stuck in this cabin together for days—maybe longer—and despite my arrival throwing a six-foot wrench into her plans, she's been gracious to me. Annoyed, sure, but gracious. Hell, she's shared her food without uttering a single complaint. And I know she didn't plan on feeding two people for a week. I'm an interloper. But outside of being happy to push me out the door before my car got stuck, she hasn't treated me like one. I'd say kudos to

Coach for raising her right, but I'm thinking he doesn't have much to do with the woman she is today.

"Are you okay?" My hands twitch at my sides as I stop a foot behind Lexi. I want to pull her into a hug, but I don't think she'd appreciate that.

There's a sharp intake of breath and I watch Lexi inflate. Her spine straightens, her shoulders pull back, and her hands leave the counter and drop to her sides. She spins around with a painfully fake smile plastered to her too-pale face.

"Totally. Why wouldn't I be?"

Oh, I don't know. Because you just heard your father refer to you as that one *and admit he doesn't worry about you?*

Despite the fake-ass smile, Lexi can't make eye contact with me, and I don't miss the way her lower lip quivers ever so slightly.

"Lex…"

"So," she says, cutting me off in a too-cheerful voice, "what should we make for dinner? I brought stuff to make chicken cacciatore. Or hamburger stroganoff. Both are some of my favorite cold-weather comfort foods from when I was a kid. What are you more in the mood for? Chicken or beef?"

I open my mouth again to check on her, but she practically runs away from me and buries her head in the fridge, as if she needs a reminder of what ingredients she brought. She obviously doesn't want to talk about any of this. And why would she? I'm a stranger and the guy her dad seems to have taken under his wing. In her shoes, I probably wouldn't want to talk to me, either.

Sighing, I hold myself back from overstepping her boundaries. "Beef, I guess. But both sound great. Can I help you?"

"Sure." She's entirely too chipper. "Can you grab a few things from the pantry? I'll need some cream of mushroom soup, a box of rotini noodles, and garlic powder. Oh, and two cans of sliced mushrooms." She flashes me a smile that doesn't meet her eyes. "I hope you like mushrooms because that's my favorite part."

Even if I hated mushrooms, I'd never tell her. Not when that smile on her face is so damn brittle.

"Love mushrooms. I'll grab that stuff, then you can put me to work."

"THIS IS REALLY GOOD," I SAY FOR THE THIRD TIME. Anything to break up this god-awful silence.

One corner of Lexi's lips twitch. At least she's finding some small measure of amusement in my awkward attempts to bridge this chasm that's opened between us.

For better or for worse, we're stuck here together with no buffers, except for Lexi's books, my sports magazines, which I've already read, the internet, and the television. I suspect Lexi is perfectly capable of sitting in silence and reading through every single one of those books she brought, but I'm going out of my mind.

Ever since my dad died, I've tried my hardest not to be alone. I spend most of my time with the guys on my team. But when I'm not with them, I'm out at a sports bar or coffee shop, where at least I'm surrounded by people, even if I don't know them. It's a compulsion—my need to fill the silence. When I don't, I'm left with my thoughts, and that can be a dark and lonely place.

"Did you learn how to cook from your mom?" I ask.

Lexi chews on her bottom lip and shrugs. "Sort of. My mom's an okay cook, but she's never enjoyed the act of it. I think it got old, making all these elaborate meals, only to have my dad waltz in hours la—" She stops herself too late. As those green eyes of hers lift to meet mine, I can tell she didn't mean to reveal something so personal. But she's still raw after the phone call with Coach.

I never should have put the damned thing on speaker.

"Anyway"—she tucks a strand of hair behind her ear, which only draws attention to the flush of pink overtaking her cheeks—"when I went away to school in Chicago, I hated the cafeteria food. It was *awful.* So, when my best friend and I got an apartment together my junior year, I made it my mission to learn how to cook whatever we wanted. I watched a lot of YouTube tutorials and botched my share of recipes before I felt like I knew what I was doing."

"I can cook the basics." My mom died before she could teach me much, and my dad...well, taking care of a household and a kid who spends most days at hockey practice meant there were a finite number of available hours in a day, and some things had to fall by the wayside. Cooking was one of them. We ate a lot of takeout and frozen food. Not that I'm complaining. My dad was there for me when it would have been completely understand-able for him to shut down. So what if we ate pizza at least once a week? Like Lexi, everything I've learned was through tutorials or trial and error. There are a handful of things I feel confident making. Breakfast, for instance, is pretty easy.

Lexi opens her mouth to say something, then apparently thinks better of it. Her lips purse as she studies me. She's probably remembering the way I shut down last night when she asked about my family.

"My mom died when I was young," I reveal. I just put her in a position where she was forced to air some of her family's dirty laundry in front of me, so it's only fair I reciprocate. Besides, as much as my mom's death still stings, she's been gone a long time. That wound isn't nearly as fresh as my dad's death. It's easier to talk about her in the past tense.

Lexi's face softens, but to my relief, I don't see the syrupy look of sympathy I loathe whenever I tell someone new about my parents. "How old were you?"

"Seven. She had cancer. We knew it was coming."

She frowns as she nods. "Sure, but that doesn't make it any less painful."

"True. It doesn't." I suck in a deep breath. "She was a great cook. I wish I could have learned more from her. When I started college, the only thing I was proficient at making was Easy Mac."

For the first time since her father called, Lexi laughs. Some of the tension in my chest eases with it. "That's sad, Ryder. Easy Mac? Really?"

"Don't knock it until you've tried it. That stuff is addicting."

She giggles. The sound reminds me of summer nights, and I'm becoming addicted. "Oh, I have. Rachel and I had a huge stash of it in our dorm room freshman and sophomore year. Pretty sure it's a trigger for me."

God, she's adorable.

"Well, I can cook more than that now, but I lived off it for a while."

We laugh and chat through the rest of the meal. Lexi is mostly back to her normal self, but there's still a wall between us that wasn't there this morning. Though I hate it, I can't say I blame her. I'll just have to earn her trust so she can let the walls fall.

I clean up and do the dishes, since Lexi did ninety percent of the cooking, even though she tries to fight me on it. But once she realizes that trapping me in the kitchen gives her the freedom to pick what to watch tonight, she lets me have at it.

"Do you want some tea?" I ask as Lexi flips through different streaming apps. I'm not sure what she's looking for, but her nose crinkles in concentration.

"Uh, yeah, sure. Mint, please." She doesn't even look at me, too absorbed in her search.

Grinning, I fill the kettle and put it on the stove before preparing two mugs and choosing spiced orange tea for myself. My phone buzzes in my pocket. After the call from Coach, I learned my lesson and switched it to vibrate. A text from my teammate and our team captain, Maddox, flashes across the screen.

MADDOX

Hey, rookie. I know you're spending some time at Coach's cabin, but I wanted to extend the offer to come to New Year's Eve dinner at my place. Isla's bummed you declined our offer for Christmas. She's going all out for our first New Year's

as a couple.

ME

Thanks, man. I really appreciate that. Think I may be snowed in, still. But if I'm not, I'll let you know.

I glance at Lexi again. Does she really want to spend Christmas alone here, or does she just not have anywhere else to go? I haven't seen her on her phone. Does she even have friends in town? I know she went to college out of state. Maybe I could at least convince her to spend New Year's Eve with the guys? I'll have to swear them to secrecy, so no one tells Coach, but that shouldn't be a problem.

ME

If the roads clear, would it be cool if I bring a guest?

MADDOX

A guest? You got a girl, rookie?

It's not like that. I mean, yeah, she's a woman, but we're not together.

Isla wants to know why not.

> LOL. She's great, but we just met. And it's complicated. Anyway, would that be okay?

> Of course, man. The more the merrier.

> Thanks. You're a good captain.

> Now you're just sucking up. Stay safe, rookie. Let me know if you're going to make it.

> I will. Later.

Pocketing my phone with a grin, I wonder if Lexi would agree to having New Year's dinner with a bunch of hockey players on her dad's team. It's not like everyone will be there, and they'd be cool, but she might not even go for it. And, at this point, there's no way I'm leaving her alone on the holiday.

The kettle whistles, and I prepare our tea.

"Here you go. Careful, it's hot." I hand Lexi the mug, enjoying the soft smile she gives me in return.

"Thanks, Ryder."

"Don't mention it." I settle down on the couch, leaving a good foot of room between us. "So, what are we watching?"

"Well," she begins, her eyes sparkling, "There's this series I've been meaning to watch. It's called *Homicide for the Holidays*. It's the perfect thing to watch during a blizzard."

Reading the synopsis of the true-crime docuseries, I turn to Lexi with one incredulous eyebrow raised. "Seriously? You want to watch a show about holiday murders?"

She nods enthusiastically.

"I just need you to tell me one thing first."

Her brow wrinkles. "Yeah?"

"Who hurt you, Lexi Cross?"

The adorably macabre woman beside me just laughs and laughs. Without bothering to offer me an answer, she simply presses play before burrowing deeper into the blanket wrapped around her and sipping her tea. She grins like a kid in a candy store as the opening sequence plays, promising murder, mayhem, and holiday fear.

Shaking my head, I can't help my answering smile as I settle in for an evening full of murder mysteries. Whatever it takes to ensure that defeated look from earlier doesn't reappear.

"Oh my god, I'm so excited," she squeals.

Her excitement must be infectious, because even though true crime isn't my jam, I'm excited too.

eleven

LEXI

I'M SO TIRED THAT NOT EVEN BRUTAL MURDERS CAN keep my eyes open. A glance at Ryder tells me he's in the same boat. His chin is pressed into his chest as his eyes blink slowly at the TV.

"Hey," I whisper. "I'm going to head to bed. I'm beat. Thanks for watching this with me."

The lazy grin Ryder offers me makes my heart thud heavy in my chest. "Course, Lex. Thanks again for making dinner. It was a good night."

It was. After I stopped thinking about Ryder's conversation with my dad and let myself enjoy it, it was a really nice night. I'm sure Ryder would rather be out doing something more active, but I'm a homebody. This was basically my idea of a perfect evening: books, good food, a crackling fire, and true crime. The company didn't hurt, either.

"You going to stay up a little later? Otherwise, I'll put the fire out."

Ryder runs his hand through his messy, dark hair, and it makes him look adorably rumpled. "I'll take care of it. I think I'm going to finish this episode. Unless you want me to wait and finish it with you tomorrow?"

Why does he have to be so sweet and thoughtful? It would be a lot easier to keep my distance if Ryder Hanson was a self-important asshole, like so many other hockey players I've known. All I can do is remind myself of my *no hockey players* rule. It's there for a reason, and not just because of my dad. I can't forget that. Even though I don't think Ryder is anything like Garrett Trace.

"That's okay. You can finish it if you want." I twist my fingers together, unsure of how to end the night. Somehow, a simple *good night* doesn't feel like enough, but what am I going to do? Hug him? I want to. He dragged me out of my funk. But that's stupid. I'm overthinking this. Tucking my hair behind my ear, I offer him a sleepy smile. "Night, Ryder."

"Good night, Lexi."

My mind is a muddled mess as I go through my nighttime routine in the bathroom. Thoughts of my dad and Ryder and all the things I wish I could say to my father swirl around in my head with the same ferocity as the snow whipping around outside. Utilizing my yoga training, I slow my breathing, making it deliberate and deep. My reflection's tension noticeably ebbs. This is fine. All of this is fine.

The lights flicker as a loud hum surges through the walls, and then I'm plunged into darkness.

"Shit," I shriek as thick, oppressive black pushes in on me from all sides. I'm not afraid of the dark, per se, but who in the hell feels great about being shut in a small, windowless room without a speck of light? No one, I'd argue.

I need to get out of here. With my hands in front of my face, I make my way to where the door should be. Then I trip on the corner of the fuzzy rug in the middle of the floor and fall sideways, bashing my hip into the corner of the vanity. "Ouch! Oh my god, that hurt."

Thundering footsteps draw close from outside the door. "Lexi? Lexi, are you okay?"

"Fine," I lie. My hip is throbbing. No doubt, there's already a nasty bruise forming. "Just tripped. I can't see a damned thing in here."

The knob jiggles. "Are you decent?"

"Yeah."

The door swings open a moment later, and I'm blinded by the flashlight on Ryder's phone. Shrinking away from it, like some deep-sea creature who's never seen the light, I throw my hand in front of my eyes. "Ow."

"Sorry," he says with a chuckle. The light dips to the floor as Ryder takes a step into the bathroom. "Are you all right?" His attention drops to where I'm rubbing my hip, and his mouth pulls into a frown as he reaches for me.

I suck in a breath as Ryder's long fingers trace gently over my hip. The sound seems to break him out of whatever trance-like state he's in, and he shakes his head as if to clear it and pulls his hand away. Pink floods his cheeks as he meets my gaze.

"I'm okay. Just bumped into the corner of the vanity with my hip."

"Ouch." He winces sympathetically.

"Did the power go out in the whole cabin?" It's a stupid question, and I know it, but I need to get the subject off my minor injury. Plus, I'm trying not to freak out. It's freezing, we're in the middle of nowhere, and there's a full-fledged blizzard happening outside. Losing power isn't good.

We leave the bathroom and move into the bedroom, so we're not in total darkness.

Ryder nods. "Yeah. Sounded like a power surge, so my guess is, whatever transformer is feeding power to the cabin blew."

Well, shit.

"Hopefully, they'll get it fixed quickly."

We both turn to stare out the wall of windows. The howling of the wind is even more pronounced now that we've been plunged into complete silence, not even the hum of electricity to break up the night. Snow whips through the air outside in a violent dance. It's heavy and wet, and there's over a foot of it by now. I know very well it won't get fixed quickly. Not in this weather.

It's going to be a long, cold night.

"Are you going to be warm enough in here? It's already chilly with this many windows, and the heat just turned off." Ryder's attention moves from the wintry wonderland outside to my bed, which is piled with blankets.

Will they be enough to keep me warm? I guess they'll have to be, because what other options are there? "I'll be fine. We can always steal some blankets off the beds in the unused rooms if we need to. Or I could switch rooms, though I doubt the others will end up being all that much warmer."

Ryder's jaw ticks, but he just nods. "All right. I may sleep on the couch tonight and keep the fire going."

It's probably the smart thing to do. "Okay. Will you be comfortable?"

He shrugs. "It's a pretty big couch. It'll do for one night." We stand there looking at one another for a few beats before he runs a hand through his dark waves. "Well, I'll get out of your hair and let you get some sleep."

"Thanks for coming to my rescue with your flashlight." I grin, and he returns it.

"Any time, Lex. Night."

"Night." I can't drag my eyes from Ryder's big form as he retreats from my room. Even in sweats, I can see his body flexing and rippling with each step. When the door closes behind him, I let out a sigh, and a shiver ripples down my spine. Time to get into bed and burrow under the covers before all the heat leaches from the room.

MY TEETH WON'T STOP CHATTERING. GLANCING AT my phone, I groan when it only reads two a.m. This is going to be the longest, coldest night of my life. The power's been out for three hours. Just three hours. And, already, I'm freezing my tits off. Stupid wall of windows.

A soft knock on my door makes me jump.

"Lex?" Ryder's raspy voice filters through the wood. "I can hear your teeth knocking together all the way in the living room. Can I come in?"

"Yeah," I croak. Why not? It's not like I'm sleeping.

Ryder looks adorably sleep-rumpled as he peeks his

head around the door before pushing inside. His lips twitch like he's fighting a grin when he sees me.

I'm cocooned in blankets. The only part of me that's visible is the top half of my face. Everything below my nose is covered. I'm sure I look ridiculous, but it's too cold for me to care.

"Hey. Why don't you come sleep on the couch? It's a hell of a lot warmer in front of the fire than it is in here. I feel like I'm getting frostbite just from standing on this floor."

Sleep on the couch with Ryder? I mean, there's plenty of room for both of us on the L-shaped sectional, so it's not like we'd be touching, but still. I barely know him. Sleeping in the same room is…intimate. He watches me roll my bottom lip between my teeth but says nothing. And that's what allows me to make my decision. Because Ryder's not pushing me to do anything. He's waiting for me to choose for myself. It's the same gentle thoughtfulness he's shown me since he realized I wasn't breaking and entering, and I stopped accusing him of being a murderer.

I may not know Ryder Hanson all that well, but I know I'm safe with him.

Blowing out a deep breath, I struggle to untangle myself from my cocoon. He chuckles as he watches me, but when I'm finally free, I climb out of the bed with a shiver. "Okay, yeah. That's probably a good idea."

"Come on, then." Ryder helps me gather up the pile of blankets and my pillow, then we tread silently down the dark hallway. He adds a few more logs to the fireplace while I arrange my blankets on the shorter side of the sectional. The movement, combined with the heat of the fire, finally helps my teeth stop chattering. It's still way too cold to be called comfortable, but I won't freeze to death.

"You good?" he asks after I've tucked the corners of the last blanket under the couch cushions. I don't want any cold air sneaking under the edges.

"Yeah. I'm good."

We both burrow under our blankets. Though the wind still howls outside, the cozy crackling of the fire drowns some of it out. Once we're settled and my eyes are finally drooping, I let out a sigh.

"I'm glad you're here," I admit to Ryder with a whisper. "This would have been scary by myself." And it would have been.

I'm used to being alone. Even grown to like it. But I miss my friends from college. I miss having people to lean on and confide in who aren't on the other end of a phone. I told myself that I was looking forward to a quiet Christmas with no one else around, but now, I'm not so sure I wasn't lying to avoid facing how lonely this week would be.

Ryder's presence has been more comforting than I'd like to acknowledge. But with the power out and the snow piling up all around us? I can admit that his presence is likely the only thing that's kept me from absolutely losing my shit.

"I'm glad too," he answers. "For the company and that you had the foresight to bring groceries when I didn't."

I laugh at that. "Yeah. If I hadn't, we might have had a Donner family Christmas."

"Jesus," he chuckles. "You and your murders."

"You like it," I tease, a yawn warping the words.

There's a soft huff of laughter as Ryder shifts on the couch. "Yeah. I really do."

We lapse into silence after that, and everything grows hazy around the edges. I'm barely clinging to consciousness when I hear Ryder's soft words.

"Sweet dreams, Lexi."

And maybe he has some kind of magic because I sleep better than I have in years.

twelve

LEXI

"I'D KILL FOR SOME COFFEE RIGHT NOW," I GRUMBLE from beneath several layers of blankets. Ryder kept the fire going all night, and even though it helped, I'm still cold. Plus, I have a headache developing. I really need to cut back on my caffeine consumption, because withdrawal is a bitch. I made it through most of the morning, but it's hitting now.

Ryder grins at my pissy grumbling like he thinks it's adorable. Weirdo. I am *not* adorable right now. I'm cold, my hair is a tangled mess, and I have the disposition of a bridge troll. He should be running away, screaming.

But I like that he's not. Not that I'll tell him.

"The stove's gas powered, right? It should still work. How about I make us some tea?"

"You don't have to do that," I say. "You're a guest. I'll do it." The problem is, I'm wrapped up in so many blankets that I almost fall on my face when I stand and try to untangle myself. "Oh, shit!"

Strong arms wrap around me and pull me into a hard chest. He smells like expensive cologne and raw male musk. Despite knowing it's creepy, I breathe him in, hoping he doesn't notice.

"You're kinda clumsy, aren't you?" When Ryder smiles —really smiles—he has dimples. It makes his handsome face look boyish and impish, and I like it more than I should.

"No," I say. The words come out breathy, and I swear his eyes darken. "I'm not usually clumsy."

Those damnable dimples deepen. "I just have that effect on you, huh?"

It takes a second to register what he's said because I'm too busy staring at his mouth. Jesus, how can one be grumpy and horny at the same time? Am I grumpy because I'm horny? *Get it together, vagina. We are* not *going there.* I roll my eyes at him. "Sure, sure. Whatever you want to tell yourself."

His deep chuckle rolls through my chest as he rights me and helps untangle me from the mess of blankets. "Just sit your cute ass down, Oscar. I'll make the tea."

Spluttering like an idiot, I blink owlishly at Ryder. "Oscar?" *Cute?*

"Yeah," he says, laughing. "Because you're a grouch in the morning without coffee."

"I am not!"

He doesn't even look at me as he strides into the kitchen, shivering now that he's discarded his blankets on the couch. "Are your arms crossed right now? And do you have a pouty little frown happening?" He turns the knob for a burner on the stove, letting out a relieved little sigh when it clicks on and lights.

Meanwhile, I look down at myself. Sure enough, my arms are crossed over my chest, and I'm definitely scowling. Damn him. Letting my arms fall, I say, "I don't have my arms crossed."

The man laughs, as if he knows I just dropped them. "It's okay, Lexi the grouch. I get that way at the end of the day sometimes." He glances at me out of the corner of his eye while moving to the cabinet that holds the tea bags. "Earl Grey, rooibos chai, mint, or green tea?" he asks.

"Rooibos, please." I pull the blankets over my head and wrap them back around my body. The power needs to come back on because it's unbearably cold in here.

A few minutes later, Ryder sets two steaming mugs of tea on the coffee table. "Here, let's pull the couch closer to the fire, and then we can watch movies on my laptop. I have a power bank, and my computer has a long battery life, so we should be able to watch a few movies at least."

"That sounds nice," I agree. We push the couch closer to the fire, and then Ryder grabs his gear from his room.

"I hope you like *Die Hard* and *National Lampoon's Christmas Vacation*. I have those and a few other random movies downloaded." He sets his laptop on the coffee table and taps away at it.

"Either of those sound good to me. But so we're clear, *Die Hard* is not a Christmas movie." I take a tentative sip of my tea and smirk when Ryder's face morphs into one of shock and disgust.

"Excuse me, Oscar, but it is *so* a Christmas movie."

"Oh my god," I say with a sigh. "Don't call me Oscar."

He smirks. "OTG?"

"What? *No!* You suck." I refuse to have my nickname be OTG. Oscar the Grouch? Come on.

Ryder starts bopping his head along to some phantom beat, and then he raps under his breath. *"OTG, yeah, you know me."*

That has me bursting with laughter. "Oh. My. God. You are such a dork."

"You like it," he says, parroting my words from the night before.

I can't deny it, so I say nothing. Because I do like it. A little too much. And that's dangerous.

"All right. Here we go." Ryder starts the movie on his computer and settles down on the couch next to me. We're both bundled up in blankets, the fire is roaring, and the tea is steaming hot, but I'm still chilled.

At the halfway point of the movie, while John McClane realizes no one will be able to help him, and he'll have to deal with the terrorists on his own, I'm shivering.

"Come here," Ryder says after glancing at me half a dozen times over the course of the scene.

"Hm?"

"You're shivering, OTG. Come here. We'll share body heat." Ryder stands and unwraps himself from his blankets. Meanwhile, I'm staring at him like he spoke in a foreign language.

With a quirked brow and the reappearance of those damned dimples, Ryder guides me to my feet. He waits for me to pull the blankets away from my body, but when I just stand there like an idiot, blinking up at him, he chuckles and pries the edges of them from my fingers. "Let go, Lex. We need to get you warm. I promise I won't bite."

Great. Now I'm picturing him biting me. In a sexy way. This isn't good.

The sound of gunfire plays through the laptop speakers as Ryder tugs me down beside him on the couch. Pressed against my side, he arranges our blankets around us. He's so warm. I melt against him, despite myself. It's hard not to when my whole body is stiff from the cold. As I thaw, I can't stop myself from letting out a happy hum.

Ryder wraps his arm around me and pulls me closer. "That's it. Just relax, Lexi. I'll keep you warm." He gently applies the slightest pressure to the top of my head, encouraging me to rest my head on his shoulder. I should protest. I should sit up straight and put space between us. But I don't. Because this is the first time I've felt warm in about twelve hours. So, ignoring my better judgment, I let Ryder guide my head to his shoulder and sigh happily.

"You're so warm."

His arm slips down around my waist, and he squeezes. "So are you."

We fall into a thick silence. I don't know what's running through Ryder's mind, but mine is a stormy sea. This isn't me. I don't melt into hockey players or random guys I met two days ago. I'm strong and independent. And hockey players? Of all the men I could be interested in, hockey players are the worst for my heart.

My mind wanders to my ex, Garrett. To the sweet lies he told me. To the imperious way he looked down on me the day he broke things off.

But Ryder isn't Garrett, and nothing will ever happen between us, so what's the point of dwelling on this? He's right. We're just sharing body heat. That's all this is for both of us. So, I try to tell my brain to shut up and enjoy the feeling of his arm around me and his strong body beside mine. We're only sharing heat, but that doesn't mean I can't secretly enjoy the feeling of having a massive man hold me. I'll tuck this away as something to look back on when I need self-care material to get me going.

We only break apart when Ryder adds more logs to the fire. Halfway through our second movie of the day, my legs are draped over Ryder's thighs, and he has one arm around my waist while his other hand rests on my knee. His thumb rubs slow circles over my leggings, and I'm so relaxed, I doze off for a few minutes with my face pressed into the crook of his neck. At least I think it's only a few minutes, because the movie is still playing and Ryder startles me awake when he barks out a laugh at the Griswolds' hijinks.

"Oh, shit. Sorry, Lexi. Didn't mean to wake you." He chuckles when I jolt upright.

"Hm? I wasn't sleeping."

"Right. And you don't snore." He gives me a shit-eating grin. I level him with a scowl in return.

"I do *not* snore." *I don't, right? I would know if I snore.*

His grin widens as he reaches over and wipes some drool from the corner of my mouth. I suck in a breath as his thumb brushes over the side of my lower lip. He leans in close. So close, our noses almost touch. "Do too. It's cute."

"How is snoring cute?" I'm completely mortified, and I try to push away from Ryder's side, but he grips my hip and holds me in place.

"It is the way you do it. Your mouth hangs open slightly and you make these soft little snores. You sound like a kitten purring."

He's got to be shitting me. I do not sound like a kitten purring. I don't snore. Narrowing my eyes at him, I cross my arms over my chest. "You're full of shit."

"I'll take a video next time, if you don't believe me," he says with a twinkle in his eye. His smile grows wide, and he flashes straight white teeth at me. I bet a few of them are fake. Stupid hockey players and their missing teeth. No way all of those pearly whites are originals.

"There won't be a next time," I growl.

"Unless the power comes back on in the next few hours, I think there will be. In fact, I was going to suggest we drag a mattress out here tonight and sleep closer to the fire."

My mind skips like a scratched record. "I'm sorry, what? You want me to sleep next to you tonight?" Oh, that is a bad idea. Bad, bad, bad. I'm already too comfortable with him. I fell asleep with my legs in his lap, for crying out loud. Who does that with a man they just met? Not Lexi Cross. Lexi Cross has learned her lesson. Men like Ryder Hanson cannot be trusted.

I blame my hussy of a vagina.

"I want us to share body heat," he says, rolling his pretty blue eyes.

Wait, what? No. Not pretty. Stupid. His stupid blue eyes.

"It's really not a big deal. Are you worried your dad will find out and get mad?"

Well, I wasn't worried about that, but I am now. "No. Of course not."

"Then, what's the problem, OTG? We're both adults and nothing's going to happen. It's survival 101 when you're stuck in freezing temperatures." He shrugs. Like this is just the way it is. Like he's some survivalist who has casually shared body heat with a virtual stranger millions of times.

He's probably not attracted to me the way I am to him. That's why this is such a non-issue for him. He looks at me and sees his coach's daughter. An average-looking woman with an unhealthy obsession with murder podcasts who left a little drool stain on his sweatshirt. Obviously, he's not thinking about getting in my leggings. He's only snuggling with me now to share body heat. This will be fine. I can keep my wandering vagina under control. This is fine.

I do my best to look nonchalant when I shrug, but if his quiet snicker is anything to go by, I don't succeed. "Sure. Totally. Survival 101. We'll just drag a mattress in here if we have to."

"You're being weird," he says, smirking.

"You don't even know me," I retort. "Maybe this is me being normal."

Ryder's lips press into a hard line and his nostrils flare as he tries to hold in his laughter. I know he's trying not to laugh, because his stupidly hard body shakes and his stupidly pretty eyes dance. "Whatever you say, OTG."

"Stop calling me that!" I shout, throwing my hands into the air in exasperation.

"So cute and grouchy," he says, chuckling.

I try to growl again but end up sounding more like a pissed-off kitten than a ferocious beast. "I hate you."

"No, you don't."

No. I don't.

thirteen

RYDER

Being snowed in with Lexi Cross is pure and utter torture.

She's off-limits. I know this. Although Coach seems like he's not the best father, he'd still kick my ass if I crossed the line with his daughter. When push comes to shove, all dads are protective of their little girls, right? And even though Lexi clearly doesn't need anyone to fight her battles, I'm still fairly certain Coach would punch me in the face if he found her wrapped in my arms with her ass pressed against my very hard dick.

It took some convincing to get her to pull a mattress into the main room with me last night, but after twenty-four hours of no heat or power to the cabin, she eventually caved. Besides, we'd spent most of the day cuddled together for warmth, so what's the big deal about sleeping next to each other for the same reason?

Turns out, the big deal is that Lexi has zero inhibitions

while she's sleeping. She was like a heat-seeking missile. As soon as she started snoring away, her body pressed itself to mine. Her legs tangled with my legs, her hand found its way beneath the hem of my hoodie, and she nuzzled against my neck. Her lips were practically pressed to my skin as her warm breath fanned across my collarbone. She must have turned over during the night, because now I'm the big spoon, and it's impossible not to notice how perfectly she fits in my arms.

It doesn't matter that she fits perfectly in my arms. It doesn't matter that she's funny and sweet or that being so close to her yesterday nearly drove me to madness. None of that changes the fact that Lexi Cross is forbidden fruit and I don't think she's into me.

The woman in my arms lets out a soft groan and shifts in her sleep. Her round, perfect ass grinds against my dick, and it's all I can do to hold myself still. Biting my lip, I keep my own groan contained. I want to press myself into the curve of her ass. I want to slip my fingers beneath her shirt and play with her pretty, perky breasts.

Fuck. This is torture.

"Mnff," she mumbles incoherently. Then her ass does a little wiggle.

Lexi's head is pillowed on my left arm, but I use my right hand to grip her hips and hold her still. She grumbles something else, still half asleep, and tries to wiggle again. This time, when I grip her hip to hold her still, she ends up pressed against my hard-on. Lexi stops moving and her body goes rigid.

"Quit squirming," I murmur in her ear. My voice comes out raspy and thick, and Lexi shivers against me. *It's probably just from the cold.*

"Um..." She giggles, but it sounds nervous. "Could you let me go?"

I could, but I don't want to. My fingers release her, and I lift my hand away from her hip. "Sorry. You were..." There's no good way to finish that sentence.

Lexi lets out another nervous laugh and scoots away from me before turning around. Her cheeks are flushed, her eyes are hooded, and she's pulled her bottom lip taut between her teeth.

She looks like sex and bad decisions.

We stare at each other for a moment, both lost in our heads. Me, thinking about how this must be close to what Lexi looks like when she's freshly fucked. With her tangled hair, pink cheeks, and hooded eyes. Lexi is likely thinking about how she wishes she was tangled up with someone else.

"Morning," she finally says. She sounds shy, and her voice is slightly raspy from sleep. She's cute as hell. Which means I need to distract myself before I do something I regret.

"Good morning," I reply. Then my stupid hand reaches out to tuck a strand of blonde hair behind her ear without my brain's permission. *Right. Time to get up.* "Uh, looks like our fire died. I'll get another one started."

Her chest rises and falls heavily as she watches me leave the comfort of our stack of blankets and the warmth of her touch. "Right. Thanks. I'm going to go to the bathroom and brush my teeth." She gives me one last look before fleeing to the bathroom.

I watch her delicious ass sway as she retreats, then berate myself for it. *She's off-limits, idiot. It doesn't matter if she's beautiful and driving you crazy. You can't do anything about it. You need your spot on the team.*

After throwing the last few logs we'd brought inside on the fire and carefully stoking it, I shove my feet into Coach's boots and pull on my coat. My stomach drops when I see how few cut logs we have left. It won't even be enough to get us fully through the day, let alone another night without power. My attention goes to the door leading outside. It's still snowing, but it seems the worst of the blizzard is over. Fat, lazy flakes float down from the sky in haphazard trajectories. At least two feet of snow covers the ground, though it might be more.

I'll have to go out there and cut more wood for us.

My injured hand flexes, as if preparing for the discomfort that will accompany the chore. I'll have to pad my palm with some fabric to minimize the impact the blows will have on my wound. Even then, it's still going to suck.

"Ryder?" Lexi's soft voice floats through the house.

"In the garage," I call back.

Her hair is brushed and pulled back into a low ponytail when she peeks her head around the door. Lexi takes in the way I'm running my uninjured hand through my hair and the tight set of my jaw, then asks, "Everything okay?"

"Everything's fine," I tell her. "I'm just psyching myself up for cutting firewood this morning. We're running low."

Those beguiling green eyes of hers go wide as she takes in the dwindling pile of cut logs and the snowy outside world. "Crap."

"It's okay. I've been lazy since getting here. It's about time I did something close to a workout."

Lexi narrows her eyes. "You're injured, Ryder."

"I'll make sure most of the impact goes to my left

hand." I try to sound nonchalant, but I'm dreading chopping these stupid logs.

Her full lips purse, then she turns on her heel and heads back inside. "Just wait, okay?" she calls over her shoulder. Amused, I do as she says, and a few minutes later, Lexi strides back into the garage, all decked out in jeans, her boots, her puffy pink coat, a hat, gloves, and a long scarf that's looped several times around her neck. It makes me feel unprepared for the weather in my jeans, coat, hat, and gloves. "You can help if I need it, but I'll be chopping the wood this morning."

My eyebrows have a mind of their own, and they're inching up my forehead before I can school my expression. Of course, she notices and glares at me.

"I know how to chop wood." She snatches the axe with a cute little noise that's probably supposed to be a growl of frustration, but once again, she sounds like a kitten purring.

Grabbing the wheelbarrow, I follow her out into the frigid morning air as we struggle to trudge through the snow to the tarp-covered stack of logs on the side of the house. The snow is taller than my boots, and it's not long before I'm shivering and glad I pulled my pants down over the boots, rather than tucking them into the top. "What, do you watch that lumberjack guy on social media or something? Is that how you learned to chop wood?"

She makes another annoyed sound as she hefts a large, unsplit log on top of the stump that's clearly used for this purpose. Her fingers barely wrap around the entire width of the handle, but Lexi doesn't let that stop her. All of her focus is on the log before her as she lifts the axe, inhales deeply, then lets it swing downward in a perfect arc. The sharp blade embeds deep into the log, but it doesn't split. I watch, surprised and kind of turned on as she wiggles the axe and dislodges it before swinging it again. A sharp *crack* cuts through the silence of the snowy morning as Lexi's perfect aim brings the blade down on the same spot as before and the log cleaves in two.

"Damn," I whisper, more to myself than her.

She doesn't look at me, just repositions the two halves of the log before repeating the motions and quartering them. "The lumberjack guy is hot," she finally says. "But my dad taught me when I was younger. Then, when I got older, cutting the firewood always fell on me because he couldn't be bothered to take time off work and come to the cabin with my mom and me."

Lexi moves to grab another log from the pile, but I beat her to it. When I try to catch her gaze, she avoids meeting my eyes. Clearly, I've hit a sore spot. I wish Coach were here so I could shake him. If I were lucky enough to have a daughter like Lexi, I'd drop everything to spend time with her.

"He's an idiot," I say before she brings the axe down once again.

The unaffected shrug she gives me in response doesn't fool me one bit. She may be used to her dad's absence, but it still stings. "It is what it is. Anyway, that's how I learned how to do this." Another *crack* slices through the muted morning. "But I'm not sure I'll be able to cut as many logs as we need. All the yoga in the world doesn't really build the muscle groups used for chopping wood."

"I think you're stronger than you realize." I put another unsplit log on the tree stump for her and toss the quartered logs into the wheelbarrow.

"Maybe."

We slip into a silent dance as Lexi continues to split another six logs, and I continue to stack them for her. By the time she's done quartering the tenth log, she's breathing heavily and her arms begin to shake. She goes to lift the axe once more, but I stop her.

"Hey. You're going to hurt yourself. Let me do a few."

Green eyes blink up at me. "I can do it."

Carefully peeling her fingers away from the axe's handle, I crowd her when her lower lip trembles slightly. Setting the axe down, I do something incredibly stupid. I lift my hands to cup her cold, pink-tinged cheeks. My words are soft and low as I brush a thumb over her quivering lip. "I know you can. But you're not alone this time."

A single tear slips down Lexi's cheek, and I break. Forget that she's off-limits. That she's Coach's daughter. Forget that she could do so much better than me. Dipping my head, I press my lips to hers with desperate need.

Lexi is stiff for only a moment before she melts into me with a sweet little gasp. It's all the invitation I need to sweep my tongue inside her mouth. She tastes like wintergreen and possibilities, and her body feels like heaven pressed against mine. With my hands still gently gripping her face, I walk her backward until she's pressed against the house. The breathy mewl she makes when I cage her body in with mine drives me wild, and our kisses grow more desperate.

One of Lexi's hands fists my coat, while the other snakes up my body and over my shoulder. Her gloved fingers scrabble to grab hold of my short hair. When she finally gets a good enough grip to tug on it and send a jolt of slight pain down my spine, I groan into her mouth and press a knee between her tempting thighs.

"Be a good girl," I demand against her swollen lips before nipping at the bottom one.

She moans at that, and I grin against her mouth. When I press her harder against the wall, Lexi's hips buck, and she grinds herself against my thigh. I don't think she meant to do it, but the little whimper she lets out tells me it felt good. Emboldened, I press my thigh harder against her jean-covered core, earning another whimper. Lexi's hips roll as she grinds her hot little center against my leg again and again while I kiss the hell out of her.

I'm hard as steel, lost in this woman as we dry hump each other in the still-falling snow. My brain is blissfully empty of everything, save the taste of her lips and the feeling of her body flush against mine. Dropping her face with one hand, I grip her hip and encourage her to ride my thigh. I need to know what she sounds like when she shatters. I need to show her she's not alone, and since burying myself in her wet heat isn't an option, I can at least bring her pleasure this way.

"That's it, baby. Ride my leg. Make yourself feel good."

Lexi gasps and whimpers as I guide her to rub her center against me. She's almost there. Her back arches and her grip on me grows painful. She's so close to her release, so blissed-out from the friction between us, that her head falls back against the house with a soft *thud.*

Leaning down, I pepper the column of her throat with kisses and gentle nips. Her hips move faster, her movements urgent with her impending release. "That's my good girl. Take what you need."

Those words tip her over the edge, and I watch with

deep satisfaction as Lexi shatters. Her eyelids flutter, her body shakes, her breathing is ragged, and she comes with a strangled cry. Gripping both of her hips, I press her harder over my thigh. She cries out again as I draw out her orgasm for as long as I can.

When she sags against me, I wrap her up in my arms and hold her tight.

That was the hottest thing I've ever done, and we didn't even get naked. In fact, we're both fully covered in several layers of clothing. I didn't even touch her pussy or kiss across her breasts. All it would have taken was another of those sexy moans of hers, and I would have come in my pants like a teenage boy.

When Lexi's breathing evens out, I take her lips with mine in a slow, sensual kiss. It's too cold to stay out here. I need to get her warm. "Come on, OTG. Let's get you inside."

fourteen

LEXI

I JUST HUMPED RYDER'S LEG LIKE A BITCH IN HEAT.

Lost in my head, I don't speak as Ryder takes my hand in his and leads me back inside the house. I can't believe I did that.

What the hell, Lexi?

He leads me through the garage and into the mudroom, where he studies my dazed expression. His long fingers unzip my coat and peel it off my body before he removes my hat and gloves, then drops to his knees to untie my boots and tug them off my feet. When he rises, he scans my face once more before gently gripping my cheeks and forcing my head back so my eyes meet his. Ryder's lips twitch. His swollen, sexy-as-sin lips.

My eyes flutter shut when he leans down and presses a long, gentle kiss on my forehead before whispering, "Go warm up in front of the fire, beautiful. I'll bring the wood into the garage."

It's all I can do to nod mutely. Ryder Hanson kissed the words right out of me. His thumb traces my lower lip, and I hold my breath while I wait to see if he'll kiss me again. For a moment, I think he's going to, but then he shakes his head slightly, as if to clear it, before stepping back.

"Go on, baby. You're shivering."

I am, I realize as the door snicks shut behind him. Dazed, I make my way into the main part of the house. But before I settle in front of the fire, I need to change my panties and clean myself up. I'm soaked and uncomfortable. My pussy still throbs from my orgasm.

Did that really just happen?

My feet barely touch the floor as I float through the house. I change into an entirely new outfit because I'm wet in more ways than one. Between the snow and exerting myself while I chopped wood, my clothes are damp and uncomfortable. Then, of course, there are my soaked panties.

God, I can't believe I just did that. I must be out of my damned mind. If my father ever found out about what we did... No. Nope. Not going to think about my dad right now.

Every nerve ending in my body is still lit up like a Christmas tree, and all my traitorous mind can focus on is how I want more. I want to know what it feels like to have Ryder Hanson between my thighs for real. To have him whisper dirty, filthy things in my ear as he pounds into my pussy like a man possessed. To scream his name as he fills me with his cum.

Wait, what? Down, girl. No one is filling anyone with cum.

Banging my head against the wall is all I can think to

do to change the direction of my wayward thoughts. With a groan, I listen for Ryder, to see if he heard me knocking some sense into myself. But the house is still silent.

Should it be taking him this long to drag the wheel-barrow into the garage? What if some desperate drifter was watching us outside, just waiting for his chance to slit Ryder's throat, and I'm next?

On tiptoes, I make my way through the cabin and toward the garage. There are no sounds of a struggle, no gurgle of life's blood leaving Ryder's jugular as he bleeds out and dies.

Jesus. That's dark for a girl who just got off.

"Ryder?" I call, poking my head into the garage. "Do you need help?" *Or something to staunch the bleeding?*

"I'm good, Lex. I'll be right in." He grunts as he wrestles the wheelbarrow into the garage. "Think you could make us some more of that hot chocolate?"

Satisfied that all of his blood is, indeed, still in his body, I nod. "Yeah. Of course."

Despite wearing several layers of clothes, I still shiver as I heat milk in a saucepan and chop up the chocolate. At least this kind of chopping isn't nearly as strenuous. I try not to stare at Ryder's muscular form as he hauls a few armfuls of wood into the cabin, but he catches me a few times and rewards me with a sinful smirk.

Should we talk about what happened? Ignore it? Pretend that aliens momentarily took over our bodies and forced us to hump like horny teenagers?

Probably the second option. Ignoring is usually the way to go. Especially since whatever that was between us can never be repeated. Ryder and I have no future. There's no world in which this works out for us if we keep playing such a dangerous game.

"That smells amazing," he says after changing into dry clothes. He stands behind me, mere inches between our bodies. It's all I can do to keep myself still. What I really want is to turn around, tug his sweatpants down to his ankles, and choke myself on the massive cock that pressed into my butt when we woke up this morning.

Oh my god, Lexi. Get a freaking grip already!

"Should be done in a minute," I squeak out instead.

Ryder's low chuckle vibrates through me and travels straight to my clit. When he walks away to add another log to the fire, I sigh with relief. Stupid blizzard, causing a stupid power outage, which caused us to sleep together so we didn't turn into stupid human icicles.

All of this has gotten way too complicated.

"We should play a board game," I blurt out. Because board games are the least sexy thing I can come up with right now. Which makes them the perfect distraction from my raging horniness.

"Sure," he says. Amusement colors his tone. "What game?"

There's only one game that can go on forever and is so boring that my libido can't possibly outlast it. "Monopoly sound good?"

"I can't guarantee my attention span will allow me to finish an entire game, but yeah. Monopoly works."

Perfect. We'll be so bored, it will be impossible to get turned on.

"CHEATER!" I SHOUT AS RYDER PULLS A GET OUT OF jail free card on his first try.

He scoffs. "Excuse me? How am I supposed to cheat at Monopoly? That was just lucky."

"Lucky, my ass," I grumble. He rolls the die and lands on the property I've been itching to buy for the last thirty minutes. "Don't even think about it."

Dark eyebrows rise and his dumb dimples make an appearance. "Think about what? Buying this lovely piece of property? Why, yes, I think I will." He counts out his money and hands it to me with a flourish.

"You knew I wanted to buy that."

He chuckles. "Sorry, OTG. That's the way the cookie crumbles, sometimes."

I slam his money down. "Stop calling me that!"

"Aww," he coos, turning his lips down in an exaggerated pout. "Are you feeling grumpy because you're losing, Oscar?"

"I'm not losing. I'm still going to kick your ass."

He throws his head back and laughs at that. So much for choosing a boring game. Turns out, both Ryder and I are way too competitive to allow even Monopoly to be boring. From the moment the die hit the board for the first time, it was on.

"Your pathetic stack of money would say otherwise," he taunts in a lyrical voice. "Someone is about to go bankrupt. And then how will you pay your rent when you land on my properties? Accepting sexual favors in lieu of money is illegal, you know."

I screech in frustration and launch myself across the board, grabbing for his money. "I'll show you illegal, you pompous ass."

Ryder barks out a laugh as my fingers wrap around his monopoly money. "You little shit. I'll teach you not to steal from me." And then his fingers dance along my sides as he wrestles me onto my back and away from the board and his money. "You'll pay for that."

I squeal as he tickles me, still clutching the colorful paper bills to my chest like they're real currency. "What are you going to do, huh?"

Ryder's long fingers wrap around my wrists. My hands are clasped together to keep him from getting the money. It allows him to maneuver both of my arms above my head with his left hand while he continues to torture me with his right. "I'm going to make you beg for mercy," he says with a laugh. His face is mere inches from mine, and his big, muscular body covers my own, pressing me to the floor. "And maybe if you're a very good girl, and you ask very nicely, I won't punish you."

Oh, shit. Heat floods my core, and my eyes are wide as saucers. It's at that moment that I know my plan to bore the sexual tension between us to death has failed. Because Ryder's pupils blow when he notices my breathing has gone ragged and his attention goes to my chest. Despite the layers, I'm certain he can see my peaked nipples.

"Lexi," he whispers. He's utterly still, and I know that if I lift my head even the slightest bit and close the gap between us, that will be it. We'll cross the invisible line in the snow, and there'll be no taking it back. And I want that. *God,* do I want that.

But I can't. I can't risk my heart for a man who is contractually obligated to be loyal to my father above me. I can't fool myself into thinking that this would be nothing more than a meaningless fling. A hot, snowed-in hookup.

Because I don't do meaningless flings and no-strings-attached hookups. I crave something real. A connection that will help me believe in love again. I always have.

And whatever this is with Ryder Hanson, it can never be that.

So, I suck in a breath, embrace a moment of searing regret, and open my mouth. "We can't do this."

It takes him a moment to register what I said, and then he's scrambling off me. "Of course. I'm sorry, I didn't mean to—"

"Ryder," I say, cutting off his panicked words. "It's okay. You didn't do anything I didn't want, we just can't... I just can't do this."

"With me, you mean," he says softly. "You can't do this with me."

I hate the way his eyes dull and his dimples disappear. Hate myself for the change that washes over him like an icy wave. But it's better for both of us this way. We've already taken things too far, and I don't know if I could come out of this week unscathed if I let this go any further.

"My dad," I say by way of an explanation.

"Right. Yeah. Your dad. Totally. You're absolutely right." He stands, extending a hand to help me up. A smile curves his lips, but it's disingenuous. I can tell, because mine is too. "How 'bout we watch a movie?"

My heart clenches when he puts space between us and throws another log onto the fire. But this is what I wanted. This is how it has to be. "A movie sounds perfect."

When the film ends, I don't remember a single scene.

fifteen

LEXI

THE DISTANCE BETWEEN RYDER AND ME disappeared once again as we slept. My logical brain may know that nothing can happen between the two of us, but my subconscious holds no such qualms.

My subconscious wants Ryder Hanson. And if the way I woke up, once again tangled up in him, is any indication, my subconscious is damned needy.

We politely disentangled ourselves with as little eye contact as possible, and he very kindly didn't call me on my closeness. After all, I'd been the one to pull away yesterday. But I'm pretty sure I was also the one to close the distance between us on the mattress last night and shove my hand beneath the hem of his hoodie, so my heat-seeking fingers ended up spread over his hard abs.

Luckily, by the time breakfast was over, we both shook off the awkwardness hanging between us like sharp, dangerous icicles. We passed an hour watching John Wick on his laptop. Both of us ignored the battery icon, which was slowly draining.

"Man, Keanu is fantastic at killing people. I just don't think it's fair that he looks so hot doing it."

Ryder levels me with an arched brow. "That's what you're getting out of this? That Keanu looks hot while killing people?"

"I mean, that's one of the things, yeah. I also said he was great at murdering. I'm giving credit where it's due, okay?" Stretching my back, my shoulder brushes against Ryder's. He's so warm. So solid. I bet he has just as many muscles as John Wick. Hell, I know he does because my traitorous fingers were feeling up the ridges of his abs when I woke up this morning. But as hot as a murderous Keanu is, I'm glad Ryder is something more innocuous. Even if that thing is a hockey player. Which is unfortunate.

Ryder's smooth laugh washes over me, and I shiver. I'm starting to crave that sound. It's deep and rich and so free from bullshit. "You're ridiculous, OTG."

Despite the way I roll my eyes, there's no hiding my grin. "Oh my god. Stop calling me that." I shiver again, this time from the chill that never quite leaves my bones, despite the fire blazing in front of us, the blankets we huddle beneath, and Ryder's body beside me. The power needs to come back on, and it needs to be soon.

"Cold?" Ryder asks, his brow pinched.

"Aren't you?"

His grimace says it all. "Come here."

The feeling of his arms around me is becoming too familiar and comforting. I don't even resist him when he wraps one around my back and tugs me closer to his body. With a sigh, I lean my head against his shoulder. "You're so warm," I murmur as his cheek comes to rest on my head.

"So are you."

"Think the power will come on soon? I'm starting to worry." And I am. We're going through wood fast. We can cut more, of course, but it's all the other things. I need a hot shower, and we're running through batteries for the two lanterns I found far too quickly in this cold. I haven't been able to find more.

Ryder's thumb rubs a lazy, comforting circle against my hip. "Yeah, Lex. I'm sure it'll come back on soon. They've gotta have people working on it now that the snow has stopped."

"Yeah. I'm sure you're right." With a sigh, I burrow into Ryder more, desperate to soak up his heat. It doesn't escape me that I've only known this man for a few days. Normally, I'm not so open and forward with people. It takes a while for me to be comfortable with someone new, especially a guy. I have no problem admiring someone who's physically attractive, but to feel truly comfortable and develop an attraction that's more than skin deep takes longer for me.

I feel like I've always known Ryder. I feel safe with him. And with every passing moment, my attraction to him grows.

Which is really inconvenient, since I can't develop feelings for him.

"We'll be okay, Lex. I'll keep you safe and warm." He says it so softly, so genuinely, that my heart squeezes. There's no posturing or macho male B.S. behind the words. Just a quiet promise. "You're not alone."

It's not the first time he's said those words, but they

still strike me right in the chest. Because I have felt alone this year. More alone than ever. During college, I had Rachel and our other best friend, Adam. I had classes and activities and a dorm full of noisy students nearby. But since moving home and working on my master's degree, I haven't had any of that. Rachel and Adam are still in Chicago. They have an apartment together and see each other daily, while I only see them when we FaceTime. I'm not living in a dorm this year—and thank god for that— but the small apartment I share with another student is too quiet.

I suppose I could reach out to some of my high school friends, but we've all moved on to these new phases in our lives, and I'm not sure we had much in common in the first place. I've made a few acquaintances in my master's classes, but that's as far as it's gone. My roommate and I cohabitate easily, though we never hang out. We have nothing in common. A couple of guys have asked me out, but the dates never go anywhere. And I'm too busy to get on any apps and really give dating a shot.

As a strong, independent woman, I've been fine with all of it. Or, at least, that's what I've been telling myself. Do I wish my best friends were close by? Yes. Do I wish I had at least a few good friends here so that we could sit together at coffee shops or browse bookstores together? Absolutely. Hell, do I wish my parents weren't such colossal, selfish messes, so I could spend time with them without being subjected to awkward boyfriends or obvious disregard? Also, yes. But I've been telling myself that all of this is simply temporary. This is just a side quest.

Still, I have been alone. I have been lonely.

"I'm glad you're here," I whisper.

Ryder's thumb stills on my hip for a moment before resuming its lazy rhythm. "Yeah, Lex. Me too."

We slip back into silence as Keanu kills another bad guy. The battery on his laptop is almost at the end of its life. The fire could use another log or two. But I don't want to move. There's a fragile beauty to this moment that almost has me holding my breath.

The unfortunate truth is that Ryder Hanson is a genuinely good man. And the more time I spend with him, the easier the walls I've erected around my heart seem to crumble. Plus, he's stupidly hot. Leaning into him the way I am now, it's taking all of my willpower not to slip my fingers beneath his hoodie and press my hand to his chest again.

"What would you be doing today if this was a normal Christmas Eve?" he asks me softly.

"Like, when I was a kid?" I ask. "Before my parents split?" Because the last time I had a relatively normal Christmas was probably my senior year of high school. Back then, my parents were still trying to convince me—and themselves—that their marriage was in a good place. It all fell apart once I left for college.

"If that's the last time you felt like you had a normal Christmas Eve, sure."

Humming, I think back to all the things that made the holiday feel special when I was younger. All those magical things that lost their luster as I got older and saw how dysfunctional my family was. For all her faults, my mom has always done an amazing job of making Christmas—and every other holiday, really—full of magic and wonder.

"Well…" I blow out a breath, shifting my body to lean against Ryder's chest. I still need his warmth, but I can't look him in the eye if we're going to talk about stuff like this. "We made cookies every year. Those sugar cookies with the royal icing, so you can create all sorts of designs and patterns. No matter how terrible they looked, my mom would gush over them and tell me they were incredible. She'd also give me some money and take me to the mall, so I could pick out gifts for her and my dad. We'd make a day of it and get lunch at the food court, some hot chocolate from a coffee shop, that kind of thing."

Ryder's fingers drop to my leg, where he traces a line back and forth from my thigh to my hip. "That sounds fun."

"It was. That wasn't what we did on Christmas Eve, necessarily, but the whole month leading up to Christmas was fun. We'd decorate the house and go all out. I think there are even some bins full of decorations in the garage. We spent a few Christmases here when I was a kid, and my mom would make my dad hang these garlands and lights everywhere." I grin, remembering. "She'd hang mistletoe all over the cabin so he'd have to stop and kiss her."

"That sounds fun."

"Yeah. And the Christmases we spent here, we'd go to this cute little tree lot in town and pick out the perfect one and put it up in front of the windows there." I point to the two large windows that overlook the front yard and the driveway. "It was this whole thing. I had to find the perfect tree. It couldn't be too skinny, couldn't be too short, and of course, it couldn't have any weird bare spots." I chuckle. "My dad would get so annoyed with me. It would take an hour just to pick out the tree."

"I'm sure he was having just as much fun as you were,"

Ryder says. His voice is soft and full of warmth. "I bet you were cute, marching around the tree lot like a tiny blonde dictator."

It's impossible not to laugh. "Not sure my dad ever thought that. Whenever we were together, I mostly felt like he couldn't wait to get back to his team and the ice."

"Lexi," Ryder starts.

I cut him off. "But it was so fun. They have this hot chocolate stand, and we'd get one after Dad loaded the tree onto the car. Then we'd go home, get it up, and decorate it. My mom gave me a new ornament every year on Christmas Eve. It was the one gift I was allowed to open before Christmas morning. She always picked something cute that had to do with what I liked or did that year."

"My mom did that too," he tells me. So softly. Like he hasn't spoken about the things his mom did for him for Christmas in a long time. "When she died, my dad picked up the tradition, but it just wasn't the same without her. I don't know. That probably sounds silly."

"Not at all," I say, sitting up so I can look at him. Old pain is etched into the lines that appear along his brow. "I get it. It's like, as soon as something puts that first chip in the facade of Christmas magic, everything loses some of its shine."

I hate the way Ryder's eyes grow unfocused. Like he's losing himself in the memories, and they aren't all good ones. So, I suck in a deep breath, grab his hand, and quietly ask, "What were your favorite Christmas traditions with her?"

His eyes meet mine, and for a moment, I don't see the big, sweet hockey player who's confident and capable. I see a little boy who lost his mom too young. A little boy who still misses her, even after all these years. "We'd watch *It's a Wonderful Life* every Christmas Eve night. She'd make us these fancy appetizers, and the three of us would snuggle up on the couch while we ate and watched. I'd lay my head in her lap, and she'd run her fingers through my hair until I fell asleep. Then she'd carry me to my room, tuck me in, kiss my forehead, and tell me I was the best gift of all."

Oh, my heart.

"She sounds lovely," I murmur.

His smile is melancholic. "She was. I miss her."

"I'm sorry. I'm sorry she's gone." I squeeze Ryder's hand. I want to wrap him in a hug. I want to run my fingers through his hair the way his mom did to comfort him.

He squeezes my fingers back. "Thanks, Lex." Ryder searches my face before he says, "I know this Christmas Eve isn't exactly what either of us were expecting, but I'm glad I'm spending it with you. Despite the cold and everything else, this has been kind of perfect."

My chest warms. "Yeah, I mean, once I realized you weren't going to murder me, I've had fun too. More fun than the last couple of Christmases."

Tension crackles in the air between us as we stare at each other. When was the last time I've been this vulnerable with a man? Or felt so drawn to someone else? I don't even realize it at first, but we're drifting together. Our faces are so much closer than they were moments ago. He's going to kiss me. Or I'm going to kiss him. Either way, after the things we just shared, I'm not as convinced as I was last night that I need to stay far away from Ryder. My body heats with remembrance of the way he made me come from riding his leg. My lips tingle as I recall the way he claimed them outside the day before. Why did I pull away from him last night, again?

I want to kiss him. I want to do far more than just kiss him. I'll deal with the consequences later.

His lips mere centimeters from mine, Ryder cups my jaw. "Lexi…" He breathes out my name like a prayer.

Tilting my head, I lick my lips. "Ryder…"

Something beeps in the house, followed by another beep, and then all the lights roar back to life. The television lights up, the landing page for the holiday murder series we'd been watching the night the power went out filling the screen. The house gives a shudder and a groan as the heat kicks on. But I don't care about any of that. I don't care, because Ryder's lips are so close to mine.

His eyes flash with some unreadable emotion before he presses his forehead to mine and sighs deeply. He pulls back, kisses the spot his forehead just touched, and sits up straight. "How 'bout I make us some coffee? Warm us up while the heat does its thing?"

My fingers flutter to my lips. Lips which are not kissing Ryder Hanson. With a little effort, I'm able to curve them into some semblance of a smile. "Sure. That sounds great."

sixteen

LEXI

GOD, THIS IS THE BEST SHOWER I'VE EVER TAKEN. IT won't last as long as I'd like, because I have to save some hot water for Ryder, but I've never enjoyed anything more. Well, except maybe the way Ryder's body felt against mine. And his lips.

Gah. I'm so wound up from the last couple of days with him that my fingers flutter down to the apex of my thighs. I could probably come from just remembering the look on his face when he helped me ride his leg. But then I think about Ryder sitting in the living room down the hall, and I can't do it. What if he hears me?

Maybe he'd barge in and help me finish?

The thought is ridiculous, but it's enough. Lifting one foot, I balance it on the edge of the tub and drag my fingers through my slick folds. Have I ever been this horny? I hiss when my fingers slide over my clit before I press them to my pussy and begin to fuck myself.

I think about Ryder as the pads of my fingers graze along my inner walls. What would he feel like inside of me? Fingers coated in my arousal, I draw them back out and circle my sensitive bud of nerves. My stomach clenches, and the first hints of that euphoric tightening start in my core. This won't take long at all.

In my mind, it's not me circling my clit with ever-faster movements. It's Ryder's tongue. I picture him kneeling before me, his fingers digging into my ass as he draws me closer, his face buried between my thighs. My touches become more urgent as I imagine how he'd eat me. He'd be ravenous. Desperate for the taste of me. Feral in the way his tongue would plunge between my folds as he fucked me with his mouth.

A quiet whimper escapes my lips as the muscles in my body tighten and warmth floods my core. I have to press a hand against the shower wall to steady myself as my legs tremble. My fingers move, as if of their own accord. They circle my swollen clit, then plunge as deep into my pussy as I can manage. But it's not enough. God, what I wouldn't give to have Ryder's fingers pushing inside me right now. Or better yet, his dick.

I groan. *What is wrong with me?* Ryder is off-limits. I silently chant the words as my fingers circle my clit faster and faster. I'm so close to coming. My skin feels tight, my stomach feels hollow. I'm warm and tingly and achy.

Ryder's off-limits.

Ryder's off-limits.

My fantasy switches from Ryder's face between my thighs to his powerful hips. With my eyes closed to block out reality, I picture him pushing into me. That perfect, round ass of his flexing with every thrust. His muscular thighs barely straining to hold me up against the shower wall as he pounds into my core. I've woken with his dick pressed against my ass for the last two mornings, so I have a pretty good idea of how big it is. And it feels big. I bet he'd stretch me so good. Make me feel so full.

My whole body tightens as I whimper. I'm so close. I press my shoulder against the cool tile wall to free up my other hand. Desperate for release, I twist and pinch my peaked nipples as I rub my clit. My fingers are slippery with my arousal, and my body nearly crackles with electricity. I replay Ryder's dirty words from when we were dry humping like teenagers outside.

That's it, baby. Ride my leg. Make yourself feel good.

That's my good girl. Take what you need.

Those sinful words rumble through my mind, pushing me over the edge. I gasp as my orgasm washes over me. It's sharp and intense, and my knees wobble as it overtakes me. As my pussy tightens around nothing, I kick myself for pushing Ryder away last night. He could have been filling me right now. My core could be pulsing around his impressive cock, instead of being empty. Would it be a bad idea? The worst. But I'm starting to not care about any of that. We're snowed in, for goodness' sake. Steamy hookups don't count when you're snowed in, right?

I sag against the shower wall as I come down from the high of my orgasm.

I need to get my head on straight. I need to remember that I would never be Ryder's priority. No matter how sweet he seems and how different I want him to be.

After I'm done washing my hair, scrubbing my body, and shaving everything *just in case*, I step out of the shower and shout to Ryder that he can take one now. My mind wanders as I blow dry my hair. I can't help imagining what it would be like to share every Christmas Eve and Christmas with him. Despite how the week started, the blizzard, and the stupid power outage, being with Ryder has been so nice. More than nice. He makes me feel seen and listened to and...not alone. I wonder what his dad is doing this year that Ryder's not spending the holiday with him? Maybe he lives out of state and couldn't travel. From the stories Ryder's told, they seem close. Not like me and my dad.

The thought of my father brings his conversation with Ryder to mind. Why doesn't my dad give a crap about me? He hasn't been that excited to talk or make plans with me since I was a little girl. I know I'm not all that sporty, and my dad and I don't have much in common, but when has he ever tried to meet me where I'm at, rather than expecting me to love the things he loves?

It's been that way for as long as I can remember. I'd be excited about a book I was reading, or a new toy Mom got me, and he'd give me one of those smiles that let me know he was humoring me and say something like *that's nice.* When I was old enough to pursue hobbies and do extracurriculars, he could barely muster even the smallest level of fake interest. The day I found out I got my first lead role in a high school play, all he said was, *Make sure your mother can pick you up from school if you can't take the bus. I have work.*

It's been like this for so long that none of it surprises me, which means it shouldn't bother me. But it does. And hearing the way he speaks to his team is somehow so much worse than simply imagining it.

But whatever. Screw my dad. He doesn't care, and

that's why I'm here at the cabin and not spending the holiday with him and the guys on his team who he loves more than me.

Dressed in clean clothes with my hair dried and smooth, I swipe on a couple coats of mascara, some blush, and tinted lip gloss before heading out into the living room. Now that getting clean is an option and Ryder and I won't have to hibernate, I want to look cute.

Because I'm a sucker, and I'm totally crushing on the hot hockey player.

Obviously, I'm a glutton for punishment.

I'm scrolling through my now-charged phone when Ryder strolls down the hallway, looking chipper and sexy as hell with his dark hair damp and kissing his forehead. He stops in front of me with his hands propped on his hips and a mischievous smile tugging at his lips.

"On a scale of one to jail time, how pissed would your dad be if there was one less tree on the property the next time he visits?"

My fingers stall on my phone screen, and I look up at him with a pinched brow. "What?"

He flops down next to me on the couch, grinning. "Let's say we went out in the yard and happened to find a small enough pine tree to fit in the cabin. Then let's say we took the axe out there and chopped it down so we could bring it inside. How pissed would Coach be?"

My mouth gapes open like a fish, which makes Ryder chuckle. "You want to cut down a tree?"

"Yeah, Lex. I was thinking about our conversation earlier. About our Christmas Eve traditions. And, well, we may not be able to make it to the tree lot because of the snow, but I'm pretty sure I can handle chopping one down for you." His crystalline eyes sparkle like gems, and it makes my heart flutter wildly.

"You want to decorate a tree with me?"

His smile is soft as he tucks a rogue strand of blonde hair behind my ear. "Yeah, I really do. If you're up for it."

Up for it? Now that he's suggested it, I can't imagine a better way to spend the afternoon. And as for my dad? Who gives a crap if he'd be mad? Not that I'm going to tell Ryder that.

"I doubt my dad would even notice. Especially if we found one that wasn't right up against the house." That's the truth. The property is big enough that he'll probably never even come across the stump if we can find a tree small enough for the cabin.

Ryder's smile grows. It's contagious. "Then, what do you say, Oscar? Get bundled up and kill a tree with me?"

Rolling my eyes at the stupid nickname that is absolutely *not* growing on me, I shrug. "Can't think of anything else I'd rather do."

Ryder slaps his hands to his knees as he stands, his face boyish and adorable with excitement. "Hell, yeah. Make sure you wear a bunch of layers. This is going to be cold."

I demand he use my hair dryer so his hair doesn't freeze, then hurry to do as he says, even though the warmth spreading through my chest is bound to keep the worst of the chill away.

seventeen

RYDER

Hopefully Coach doesn't kick my ass for this, but even if he does, the bright smile on Lexi's face will make it worthwhile.

She hasn't stopped grinning since we grabbed the axe from the garage and started tromping through the yard toward the more wooded areas. The majority of these trees look like they'll be far too tall to bring inside the cabin, but if worse comes to worst, I'll just cut the top half of a pine tree down and make it work.

All our talk about Christmas traditions earlier made me want to do something to bring a little magic back into the holidays for Lexi. I don't know too much about Coach's divorce, but the guys say he was a raging beast last season. Supposedly, he's not quite as bad this year, but he's still grumpier than normal. I'd guess it's been at least a few years since Lexi's had a Christmas she can look back on fondly.

I'm determined to change that.

"It's so beautiful," she says breathlessly. "It was hard to enjoy the snow when it was the reason I was freezing my ass off, but now that the power's back on, I feel much more benevolent."

She sighs as we push through the deep drifts, but it's a happy sigh. Her high cheekbones are flushed pink from the wind nipping at them, her green eyes sparkle in the bright wintery light bouncing off the snow, and her lips part just enough to let little puffs of mist swirl around her face as her warm breath meets the icy air. "The most beautiful thing I've ever seen," I admit. Though I'm not talking about the snow.

Lexi glances my way, and the flush of her cheeks deepens when she catches my meaning. "You sure you should be chopping anything with your bum hand? I can do it, you know."

She could, too, but I also know she's sore from cutting all that firewood. She keeps rolling her shoulders when she doesn't think I'm looking.

"I think I can handle it. But I promise I'll tell you if it starts to hurt."

"Does it bother you?" she asks, her attention dipping to my gloved hand. Those pretty lips of hers pull into a grimace as she looks back up at me. "Especially after I threw that wine bottle at you?"

I shake my head. "Nah. I'm good. I promise."

She hums but doesn't fight me about it. "Do you get into a lot of fights on the ice?"

Fighting is a part of hockey. I've gotten into my fair share of brawls, but I don't actively seek them out like some guys do. For some reason, I always picture my mom when a fight breaks out. She has that look on her face that she'd give me when I was a kid and getting into trouble. "Not really. I won't back down if someone else starts one, but I don't go around picking fights on the ice."

That seems to be the right answer, because Lexi grimaces again. "Good. I can't stand guys who go around starting fights because they think it makes them look cool."

The tone of her voice tells me there's a story here. "Know someone like that?"

"Yeah," she scoffs. "My ex."

Her ex? Alexis Cross dated a hockey player? Well, shit. Didn't see that one coming. "Oh? Did you date someone on your dad's team?"

"What? God, no."

Ouch.

"My college boyfriend. He loved to start fights. I think it's because it made all the girls drool over him."

He sounds like a winner.

"Does he still play?" I want to know who this guy is. Because if he plays pro hockey, that means I may have the chance to check his ass into the boards for getting to touch Lexi. And for being a dick of a boyfriend, if her tone is anything to go by.

She smirks. "Not that I know of. Not for lack of trying on his part. He thought he was hot shit when we were dating, but he never put in the work he would have needed to go pro."

"Lazy?"

"Entitled. He thought he could get into the NHL with his good looks, social media presence, and connections."

The emphasis she puts on the word *connections* has me bristling. I'm not sure I'll like where this is going.

"Did he know people in the NHL?" I ask casually.

"Yeah," she says bitterly. "My dad."

Damn. That was what I was afraid she'd say. I want to ask her to tell me more, but I remain silent. Maybe if I don't say anything, she'll keep talking.

Lexi sighs. "Turns out, Garrett was more into my dad than me, and when that relationship didn't work out the way he'd hoped, there wasn't much reason to stick it out with me."

"I'm sorry, OTG," I say, reaching out to grab her hand. "He's an idiot."

"I don't know. Pretty sure I was the idiot in that scenario. After all, I was the one who thought he was interested in me, not my dad. Should have seen it coming from a mile away." Lexi squeezes my hand before dropping it, her tone growing brighter, even if it's forced. "But enough about Garret, the ass. I want to know how many times you've been injured. You guys really get beat up out there."

"I've been pretty lucky," I tell her. "I never sustained any serious injuries when I was a kid or during college. A few sprains and bruises, like everyone else, but nothing too bad. This is my most serious injury. Which sucks, because I had a great start to the season before this. Now I'm worried I'll go back and have lost my mojo."

"That's ridiculous." I glance at Lexi in time to see her roll her eyes. "It's not mojo, it's skill. You hockey players and your superstitions. I swear."

"All I'm saying is that I had finally started earning my place on the team, and I'm worried that, by the time my stupid hand heals, Coach'll have replaced me with someone else." That's always the fear. Guys get traded, let go, bumped down into lower lines that don't see as much time on the ice. It sucks, but it's just the way it is.

"I wouldn't worry about that," she says. "Pretty sure he likes you, from the sound of it."

I need to turn this conversation around because we're skating into dangerous territory. "I don't want to worry about it. You're right." We make our way into a copse of trees. I let the axe fall from my left shoulder and rest the head on the ground while I survey the nearby evergreens. "Right now, I just want to focus on finding the perfect tree."

That brings a smile to Lexi's face. "It has to be fat and fluffy."

"Right. Fat and fluffy. Let's see if any of these fit the bill." Together, we pick our way through the snow-covered forest. We occasionally shake the heavy white powder from branches to judge a tree's shape and beauty. But they're all too tall for the cabin. Looks like I'll be chopping down half a tree, rather than a whole one.

"What about this one?" Lexi asks. Her eyes are bright when she turns to me, and the way the sun hits her face makes it look like her fair skin is glowing. "It's a little tall, but it's fluffy, doesn't have any bare spots, and the branches seem nice and sturdy."

She could be pointing to the ugliest tree in the forest, and I'd tell her it's perfect. Because I don't care about the tree. Not really. I care about the way Lexi has completely forgotten about her shitty ex and her crappy dad because of a snow-covered tree in the forest and the prospect of decorating it.

"I think it's perfect. Looks like it's maybe twelve feet, so I'll need to cut it down to size a bit, but that just means we'll have some extra firewood, right?"

"Exactly!" Lexi claps her gloved hands as she looks at me expectantly. Hopefully this doesn't mess up my hand too badly, because I'm committed now. I can't let this woman down. Not after everything I've learned about her.

"Okay. Stand back so I don't hurt you."

She salutes me with a smirk. "Aye aye, Lumberjack Ryder."

There's a stupid grin stretched across my face as I lift the axe, making sure to grip it tighter with my uninjured hand, and let it swing. The first hit makes me hiss as the impact jars my wound, but with a minor tweak to my grip, it should be doable. The second swing still stings, but it's not nearly as bad. By the tenth swing, I'm sore but almost through the trunk.

Lexi watches me with wide eyes. They're filled with excitement and pleasure and maybe even a little hunger. The realization gives some extra power to my next two swings, and the tree groans as the trunk teeters, then falls.

"That's so much hotter in person than social media," I hear Lexi murmur to herself. Social media? Oh, she must be talking about that guy who makes thirst traps splitting huge logs. She thinks I'm hotter? Forget the pain in my hand. Worth it to hear her say stuff like that.

Giving my tingling palms a good shake, I eye the fallen tree. If I cut it to about seven-feet tall, it should be manageable enough to get inside the cabin. The real trick will be dragging it through the woods. Luckily, we didn't get too deep in before Lexi found *the one*.

"You okay?" she asks when she notices what I'm doing.

Her jubilant expression shifts into one of concern. "Did you hurt your hand?"

I shake my head. "Nah, I'm good. It's just a lot of vibrations, and my palms are all tingly." Though that's not a lie, it's not the whole truth. My palms are tingling, but my injured hand is also throbbing. Luckily, it doesn't feel like I've split any of the stitches, and I made sure to shove some extra padding into my glove over my palm.

"Are you sure?"

Her nose wrinkles and her lips purse as she studies me. It's adorable, so I can't help myself. I boop her nose. "I'm sure, Oscar. But it's sweet that you're worried about me."

She rolls her eyes at the use of the nickname—or maybe the boop on the nose—but lets it drop. "I'm not worried about you. I'm worried about dragging this tree to the cabin if you drop dead. It's huge."

With a bark of laughter, I turn my attention back to the task at hand. "It is huge. I need to cut it down more." After eyeballing it, I point to a spot on the tree with the axe and turn to Lexi. "Think that looks about right?"

She squints, cocking her head to the side. Those lips of hers twist adorably as she thinks about it. "Hell if I know."

"Right," I say with a deep laugh. "We're just going to go with it and hope it fits."

"That's what she said," Lexi whispers under her breath. She jumps a little when I laugh at that, and her pink, winter-kissed cheeks flush a deeper shade of rose. "What? I like re-watching *The Office* in between murder mysteries."

"I didn't say anything," I reassure her. Except, I can't hide my smirk.

She folds her arms over her chest and taps her booted foot. "Whatever. You gonna cut that, or what?"

With a tip of my beanie and a bow at the waist, I say, "As you wish, Oscar."

The *thwack* of the blade hitting the tree drowns out her half-hearted grumbles. All I can think about is kissing the sass right out of her mouth.

eighteen

LEXI

"Oh. My. God." Ryder and I flop down onto the couch beside each other. We're both sweaty and panting. The freaking tree is way bigger than it looked outside. That, and even though we shook off as much of the snow as we could, it's still dripping onto the floor in a massive puddle as the rest of it melts. We've already mopped twice. I throw an arm over my face and groan. "Remind me why we thought this was a good idea?"

"Oh, come on, OTG," Ryder teases, nudging me with his foot. "It's Christmas Eve, the snow has finally stopped falling, and the power's back on. We're celebrating."

I run my hand through my hair and groan when I realize I just rubbed sap into my sweaty locks. "We should celebrate in the hot tub after all of this." My muscles are screaming at me. After chopping all that firewood, then helping Ryder drag the tree through the yard and into the house, I'm exhausted and sore.

"Think it'll be hot?"

"Should be. I never turned it off after that first night, so it's been re-heating since the power was restored. So, hot enough, anyway. Did you bring a suit?"

He chuckles. "Nope. That would have required foresight. Not my strong suit. But I can just swim in a pair of boxers."

My face flushes at the suggestion. God, what am I? Some virginal high school girl? "Sure. That works. Same thing, right?"

"Oh, shit." Ryder groans. I force my head to flop in his direction so I can see him. He rubs a hand over his face, which is all scrunched up. "I'm a dumbass."

"What?"

"I thought I was going to be alone all week, and I brought these Christmas boxers that..." He groans again while covering his face with his hands. A few seconds later, one sky-blue eye peeks out at me from between his fingers. "I'll go in the hot tub with you if you promise not to laugh at me, and if you swear on pain of garroting that you will never, *ever* tell anyone about what you see."

Well, that sure has me curious. Despite the pain radiating through my entire body, I sit up, energized. What in the world could have Ryder so embarrassed that he feels the need to swear me to secrecy? I watch him expectantly.

He narrows his eyes. "Swear it, Alexis."

Oh, damn. He brought out my full first name. No Lexi, no Lex, no Oscar, or OTG. I guess this is serious. "I swear I won't tell a soul." I make an *X* over my heart. "Cross my heart and hope to be garroted."

"I'm going to regret this," Ryder mumbles to himself.

Still peeking at me from between his fingers, he lets out a deep sigh before saying, "I don't know how it started or why the hell I do this, but I have this collection of Christmas boxers."

I wait for him to say more, and after a moment of silence, I nudge him with my foot. "Okay. I don't really see why that's an issue."

Another groan. "Fuck my life. You will."

"Are you going to tell me what makes them so bad?" I am so curious now, I'm tempted to race into his room and root through his duffel bag until I find his stash of boxers. But that seems like a bridge slightly too far. Just slightly.

"No. I can't even bring myself to say it. Just…promise you won't laugh, okay?"

He looks so adorably pathetic that, even though I'm not sure I can uphold a promise not to laugh when whatever the issue is makes Ryder look this embarrassed, but I'll sure as hell try. "I promise."

"I'm so going to regret this," he mumbles again. "Fine. Let's take a dip. My muscles will need a rest after decorating this tree. Everything hurts and I'm dying."

"All right, you big baby. Let's decorate the tree. And pray there are no woodland creatures hiding in the branches."

Ryder's eyes go wide, and he turns slowly to me. "Wait, is that a thing? Did we just chop down some poor squirrel family's home?"

I try to stifle my laughter, because he looks so horrified by the idea, but it doesn't work. "I'm sure we didn't. And I guess if they were brave enough to stick around, at least they have a nice, warm tree now."

"Not funny, Lex." He scrubs a hand over his face.

I shrug as I push my tired butt off the couch and stand. "I thought it was. Come on, I think the ornaments are in the garage."

It doesn't take long to find the bin full of baubles and ornaments. The one stuffed with tangled lights is right beneath it. Both of us groan as we lug the boxes into the living room, then get to work untangling the strings. After working in silence for a few minutes, Ryder grabs his phone, connects it to the wireless speaker in the kitchen, and plays festive Christmas music. After that, we both get a second wind. The lights are up in no time.

"Okay," I say, admiring the twinkling lights. "I remember why we did this."

Even without ornaments, the tree and the strings of twinkling white lights lend instant magic to the cabin. It's like the cozy meter spikes straight up to one hundred percent. A jolt of childlike awe shoots straight into my heart. Once we get the ornaments on, it will be even more beautiful. Maybe I should start putting a tree up in my apartment for Christmas. Even if my roommate and I are the only ones who will ever see it.

Ryder has this big smile on his face, palms braced on his hips as he surveys our handiwork. "It's a great tree, OTG. Good choice."

I gently hip check him. "Told you I was a master tree-picker. I can't believe you doubted me."

"Doubt you? Never." He bumps my hip right back. "I'd never bet against you, Lexi Cross. I know a winner when I see one."

My heart pulses with a glow similar to the lights on the tree. "Yeah, yeah, yeah. Enough with the sweet talking.

Let's decorate this baby, so I can see those boxers of yours. I need to know what all the fuss is about."

The groan Ryder lets out fills the room, but he digs through the bin full of ornaments with me. He picks out one of the silly homemade ones I created in grade school. His big, strong fingers handle it carefully as he twists it around to admire every angle. "This is cute. You had a real gift with elbow macaroni."

Hand on my chest, I gasp in faux outrage. "Had? I'll have you know, I'm still a wiz with the macaroni. I just tend to cook it these days."

"Sure, sure. A likely story, Miss Cross. A likely story." He hangs my little macaroni rainbow front and center before pulling a red frosted glass bauble out of the bin. "I bet you have a whole craft room at your place with different colored pasta and shelves lined with Elmer's glue."

"You've got me all figured out."

I pull a pretty framed wedding photo ornament out of the bin, and my chest squeezes. My parents. It's difficult to remember that they were happy once. The arguing and contention of the last decade seems to have overwritten all the happier memories that came before. Noticing my gaze, Ryder's big body appears behind me. His broad chest brushes against my back as he looks over my shoulder.

"Wow. Hard to believe Coach was ever that young."

Harder to believe he ever looked that carefree and happy.

"Yeah. I guess it's a good thing we're putting these up. If one of my parents had come across this, they probably would have thrown it away." I debate keeping it in the bin but finally hook the ribbon loop around a branch. "Maybe I'll take it with me when we leave."

I'll probably just shove the ornament in a box or a drawer myself, but even though I'm pissed at both of my parents for the way their marriage ended, I can't bear the thought of all their memories being discarded like trash. As though they never meant anything.

"Do you have a favorite ornament?" Ryder asks cheerily. He's trying to keep me from spiraling, and I appreciate it. He's much more observant than I would have guessed. It's hard to get much past him.

"I do," I tell him. "But it's not here. It's in the box of ornaments at my mom's house. I don't know if she put up a tree this year." Imagining her decorating a tree with Jeff while they play house makes me feel a little nauseated. Don't get me wrong, I want my mom to be happy, but does it have to be with Jeff?

"Tell me about it." Ryder hangs another bauble. He's cute. While I would have expected him to place the ornaments randomly on the tree, that's not what he does. He studies the area and makes sure there's enough space between ornaments, so they don't look crowded. I'm starting to suspect he shows the same care with all the fragile things in his life.

The girls he dates are lucky.

Pushing that depressing thought straight off the cliff of my subconscious, I picture the cute little ceramic ornament my grandma bought for my first Christmas. She's gone now, so it holds even more sentimental value. "My grandma gave me this adorable little bear hugging a candy cane for my first Christmas. The colors are muted and soft, and it's just so sweet and pure, you know? Plus, she wrote my name and the year I was born on the bottom of it, so that's special. Every time I put it up, I trace her shaky writing and remember her."

"That's sweet," Ryder says, offering me a gentle smile as he hangs another ornament.

"What about you?"

He's quiet for a moment. His sky-blue eyes go hazy, as though he's seeing something a million miles away. "My mom liked to crochet. I have a few hats and blankets she made, but my favorite project she ever did was this silly little ornament. I was obsessed with the Ninja Turtles as a kid. Michelangelo was my favorite. I had this orange strip of fabric with eyeholes cut out of it, and I'd wear it everywhere. I tried to wear the thing to kindergarten a few times, but she caught me before I could leave the house in it." He chuckles at that, and my heart squeezes. There's an achingly soft quality to his expression and tone. Like the memories of his mother are precious secrets he doesn't reveal to anyone. They're jewels he hoards like a dragon.

I want to hear everything he'll tell me.

"Anyway." He shakes his head, dislodging the memories. "That year, she crocheted an ornament of Michelangelo's face for me. It was amazing. I have no idea how she shaped it and captured his expression so well, but she did. Every time I hang it on the tree, it feels like she's giving me a hug. Like she's standing there beside me, telling me she loves me." He peeks at me from the corner of his eye. "It's silly."

"No," I say gently. "That's not silly. Not at all."

We stare at each other for what feels like several minutes before his lips quirk into a thoughtful smile. He looses a gust of breath between his pursed lips and shakes his head. "How do you get me to spill my guts like that? It's a spell, isn't it?"

He's not the only one spilling his guts this week. I've opened up to Ryder more than I've opened up to anyone, outside of my best friends, Rachel and Adam, in a long time. I'm not sure how to feel about that. On the one hand, I feel inexplicably comfortable around Ryder. There's this sense of safety he exudes. It's rare to experience that with someone, and I want to explore it more. On the other hand, if I indulge this, I'm setting myself up for pain and disappointment.

Right now, we exist in an icy, untouchable bubble. But bubbles always pop. The plows will come through, the roads will once again be passable, and this week will end. I'm not delusional enough to believe that whatever this is will survive those plows. It can't.

But I'm tired of fighting myself and these damned conflicted feelings. How often do you get snowed in with an incredibly handsome man who makes you forget the rest of the world? Never, that's how often. Which means I'd be an idiot to ignore this strange little gift fate has given me. It's the moment I decide I'm going to enjoy the rest of my week with Ryder Hanson. I'll try not to think about the future or what might happen if I allow myself to give in to temptation. I won't dwell on how much it will hurt when Ryder inevitably prioritizes hockey over me. I won't harbor a secret hope he'll pick me. Because that way lies madness.

Maybe he's right. There's some kind of spell in the air, but it's not of my doing. I'm just as enchanted as he is.

Hoping it comes off as flirty and mysterious and not just weirdly demented, I flash Ryder a coquettish smile and bat my eyelashes. "A spell? Are you saying I'm magical?"

"Yeah," he says after a beat. "You're definitely magical. Now, let's finish this tree. I'm ready to get in that hot tub."

My dirty mind supplies an image of Ryder and me in the hot tub. Naked. Somehow, I resist the urge to fan myself. "Yeah. Me too."

nineteen

RYDER

Damn me for packing these stupid boxers. Why on earth did I ever think collecting them was funny? You go out shopping one time with your buddies in college, laugh at a pair of boxer briefs with a decorated dick pouch, and suddenly that's your new *thing*.

None of these are good options. There's Frosty the Snowman with the carrot dick pouch, Rudolph with the red pom-pom nose on the crotch, the pair with a Santa hat pouch, complete with white fur pom-pom on the tip, and more along those lines. The least embarrassing pair is one with mistletoe on the crotch, and I'm pretty sure that's going to send the wrong idea. I don't want Lexi to think I'm trying to get her to suck my cock. Obviously, I wouldn't be *opposed* to that, but I'm fairly certain that won't happen.

The second least embarrassing pair of boxer briefs is one with a present on the crotch and a big red ribbon bow.

Guess that's what I'm wearing in the hot tub. I certainly can't wear any of the ones with a fabric cone over my penis. I lightly bang my head on the wall a few times and vow never to go on another trip without packing at least a couple pairs of normal boxer briefs.

Oh, well. Can't be helped, now.

Once I've slipped into the mortifying boxers, I grab a towel from the bathroom, wrap it around my waist, and head for the back deck and the hot tub. The cabin is quiet. Lexi must already be outside.

Cold air envelops me as soon as I step outside, and I shiver. The arena is always chilly, but it's nothing compared to this. When I play, I've got padding and layers of clothes on. My feet are covered in socks and skates. My helmet keeps all the heat from escaping my head. But right now, I'm hopping through the snow in bare feet and nothing but underwear and a towel, and it's a lot, even for me.

But then I see Lexi, and all thoughts of the cold flee.

God, she's stunning. Submerged to her chin in the steaming water, Lexi has her head tipped back against the headrest behind her. Her eyes are closed, letting her long lashes fan out across high cheekbones. A small smile plays at her lips.

I've never been so attracted to a woman in my life.

"Just gonna stand there and stare, stalker?" she asks without opening her eyes.

Clearing my throat, I unwrap the towel and drop it with hers. And as I'm dipping my first toe into the water that's plenty warm but not quite hot enough to be considered *hot* after the days of snow and a power outage, Lexi's eyes pop open.

The way she drinks in the sight of me would be enough to make me hard if my balls hadn't already shriveled up inside my body from the cold and my dick hadn't tried to tuck tail to conserve heat. Her half-lidded stare starts at my shoulders before sliding down my chest and abs. Those pretty green eyes linger on the dark trail of hair that starts below my navel and disappears beneath the waistband of my boxers.

And then her gaze dips to my dick. My dick, which is behind a printed present and a big red ribbon bow.

Just like that, her half-lidded eyes widen, and her lips twitch before splitting into a broad smile, then opening with laughter. She tries to stifle it, but she can't.

With a sigh, I hurry to lower myself into the water and hide my *package*. The water feels blisteringly hot compared to the outside temps, even though I know it's cooler than normal. "You swore you wouldn't laugh."

Lexi covers her mouth with her hand. Her eyes dance. "I'm sorry, it's just...I wasn't sure what to expect, but that is..." She stares at my crotch through the bubbly water. Her shoulders shake with silent laughter. "There's a big bow on your dick."

I'm sure my cheeks are bright red with embarrassment, but I try to play it off like I'm unaffected. "This is the least offensive pair," I admit. That has Lexi bursting with laughter.

"No way. I need to see the others if this one is the tamest option."

"Hell, no, OTG. Not happening."

She bats her eyelashes at me and pulls her lips into an exaggerated pout. "Oh, come on, Ryder. Don't be such a grinch."

"No. Nope. I don't care how much you pout. That's going to be a no from me." I shouldn't want Lexi to want me, but I do. And, somehow, I don't think showing her my ridiculous boxers will help. Not that I think much of anything would, at this point. The frustrating thing is, I know she wants me. But she won't let herself go there. I can respect that. I don't *like* it, but I can respect it. Hell, I shouldn't be entertaining the thought of her, either, let alone dry humping her against an exterior wall. At least one of us has some self-control, because as far as Lexi Cross is concerned, I seem to be fresh out.

"You're no fun, Hanson." That damned pout. Her lower lip juts out, and I want to nip at it. Suck it in between mine. I want to make those lips swollen and bee stung.

"Agree to disagree," I say. My eyes drop to her chest as she sits up in the water, and I catch a glimpse of her bathing suit. It's a black string bikini with silvery screen-printed flowers all over the fabric. The triangular pieces hug perky breasts with peaked nipples. The top is tied tight enough that it helps push her breasts together and up, and my dick hardens as I watch small rivulets of water forge paths down her chest and cleavage. From what I can see, the bottoms sit low on her hips with bows tied on each side.

She's a goddess. Stunning. I can't look away.

"My eyes are up here," Lexi teases. Her chest rises and falls faster. Her voice is low and sexy. She's just as affected as I am.

Good.

Looking up, I don't deny that I was staring. I don't apologize. I don't even smile. Completely serious and utterly honest, I give in to my urges and surge toward her in the hot water. "You're beautiful," I say. She shivers when I trace my thumb across her jaw. "Absolutely stunning."

Pink floods Lexi's cheeks. It's more than the bite of the cold. This is a flush that starts at her chest and climbs up her neck before spreading across her cheekbones. It just makes me harder. She has to know how beautiful she is. Has to. But her chin dips to her chest, and she can't make eye contact as she whispers her thanks.

That just won't do.

With gentle pressure, I grip Lexi's chin between my thumb and pointer finger and tip her head up, silently asking her to look at me. "You're so beautiful, Lexi," I say when she finally does.

"Thank you." Her attention falls to my lips. Her pink tongue snakes out and wets hers.

"Lexi?"

Her attention remains on my lips. "Hmm?"

"I'm going to kiss you now." Her breath catches, and I surge forward, capturing her lips with mine. They're soft and pliant, while mine are demanding. My hands go to her waist, and I grip her, pressing her to my chest as I flip our positions. My back is where hers just was, and Lexi settles in my lap, straddling me. Whatever hesitation held her back after the Monopoly game has fled. She doesn't hesitate to return my kisses. Her hands grapple with my shoulders as she holds on to me.

When I nip her bottom lip, she mewls. Fucking mewls. Instantly hard, I try to shift myself, so I'm not pressing into her center. I don't want to scare her away. Not when she's meeting me stroke for stroke. Her movements become more intense, frantic.

"The way you kiss..." she murmurs against my lips. "No one's ever kissed me the way you do."

How is that even possible? What idiots has she been dating? I can't get enough of her. "No one's ever made me as hard as you do."

She chuckles against my mouth. The feeling of her mostly bare skin pressed against mine is everything. She's driving me wild. Water sloshes around us as we make out, both of our bodies starting to move against each other.

"Ryder"—she pulls back just long enough to meet my gaze—"I know this can't go anywhere, but what if we give ourselves a snowed-in-pass?"

My damned heart stutters, but I hide it. "What do you mean?"

Her fingers trace across my shoulders and map the planes of my back. "Well, it's like Vegas. What happens in the cabin, stays in the cabin. We can do whatever we want, and it stays here. My dad never has to find out. We never have to do the awkward *can we make this work* thing, and neither of us will have to try to alter our busy schedules, only to realize there's just not enough time in the week. We can be together while we're here, and when we leave, we go back to our lives. What do you think?"

What do I think? I fucking hate everything about that idea. A few days with Lexi won't be enough, and I know it. But she's determined to put a wall between us. Do I agree with what she's asking, or do I pull back now and put a stop to all of this? Can I leave whatever this is here when the week is up and the snow is plowed?

I should tell her no. I should tell her I think it's a terrible idea. That I don't want to pretend I don't know her when we leave. But she's so eager. It's written all over her face. I don't want to deny her, and if I'm being honest, I don't want to deny myself, either. If she was proposing we give this thing a shot and see where it goes, I'd agree in a heartbeat. But this? I've had a few casual flings with women, but none of them has made me feel half of what Lexi Cross does.

"What do I think?" The words hang between us. I cup her cheek in my palm and run my thumb along her chilled skin. "I think, if that's all you can give me, I'll take it."

Green irises study me, bouncing back and forth as she surveys my face. She drags her lower lip between her teeth. "Ryder...I think you're a great guy, and if circumstances were different, I'd..."

"Hey, it's okay," I say, stopping her.

"It's just that, with my master's program and everything, I really don't have time to date. There's so much going on, and I'm not really in the right place for a relationship, you know?" She stares at me, wide eyed and expectant while gnawing on her lower lip. Water sloshes around her hands as she wrings them in her lap.

She's probably right. She doesn't have time for a relationship, and neither will I, once my stupid hand heals. And sure, Lexi Cross is beautiful and smart, and hilarious, but how much of my attraction to her is proximity-based? After all, we're stuck here together with no one else around. Of *course*, she's going to seem like the most amazing woman ever. There's no one around to compare her to.

That has to be it.

So, why doesn't it feel that way?

"I get it," I say, pasting a smile on my face. "I vote yes

on the snow-pass." She sighs as I press my lips to hers. "I can't seem to say no to you."

"Are you sure?"

No. "Yes. Now, as fun as this hot tub is, I want to get you naked and eat your pussy. And it's a little cold to lay you out on the deck for that."

She shifts on my lap, her pupils blown wide.

"What do you say we bring this inside?"

"I say yes," she says, breathless.

That's all I need to hear. Ignoring our towels, I scoop her up out of the water and carry her inside. She squeals and holds on tight to my neck, but her laughter tells me she's not afraid. Lexi Cross trusts me not to drop her, and I won't betray that.

"The towels," she says through her giggles. "We're going to track water all over the cabin."

"That's what mops are for."

"We're going to soak the bed."

I smirk. "That's the plan, OTG."

We're both laughing as I get us inside. Water drips off our bodies, leaving a trail through the cabin as I make my way to the bedroom I've claimed as mine while we're here. The little minx in my arms peppers kisses across my jaw, my neck, my shoulders. Her warm skin against mine makes me desperate to remove every last stitch of fabric between us. I want to know what it feels like to be completely skin to skin. To feel her under me, on top of me. I want to be inside her. I need to be.

The door to my room bangs against the wall as I carry her in and toss her onto the bed. Her squeal as she bounces on the soft mattress makes me smile. The sight of her, breathless and flushed on her back, makes me hard.

Lexi notices, too. Her eyes widen as she stares at my bow-clad package. A package that is growing by the second.

"Merry Christmas to me," she whispers to herself.

Damn, she's cute.

"Come on, beautiful. Let's get you out of those wet clothes before you get cold." I climb onto the bed and make my way toward her. She watches me with rapt attention. Her chest heaves, her plump lower lip slips between her teeth, and her jewel eyes are hooded as I reach her. My fingers toy with the bows tied at her hips. "Look at you. All wrapped up for me. You're the perfect present."

A sweet little gasp meets my words as my fingers tug on one of the ties, and the side of her bikini bottoms falls open. Goose bumps cover her skin, and I can't tell if it's from the cold or her arousal. I untie the other bow in the same way, watching her expression the entire time.

"You sure about this?"

She nods.

"Words, Lexi. I need your words, or this can't go any further."

Her lips part. "Yes. I'm sure. Fuck me, Ryder."

All my blood rushes straight to my dick as I grip her bikini bottoms and tug them off. They land on the wood floor with a wet *splat*. "Jesus, Lex."

Her sweet little pussy glistens with arousal already. She's neatly trimmed and groomed, and perfect. I skim my fingertips through her dark curls. Lexi gasps, her back arching off the bed, and my attention goes to her chest. To the hard nipples begging to be played with. Slowly, I run my fingers up her lower belly, her stomach, and up to her sternum. I palm her left breast. A perfect handful. Lexi moans. The fabric is cold, and I waste no time untying her top and throwing it on the floor with the bottoms.

"Lexi. Fuck. You're perfect." And she is. Her skin is soft and warm, her body strong and elegantly curved. Everything about her is inviting. The fullness of her breasts, the dip of her waist, the swell of her hips; all of it is as close to human perfection as I've ever seen.

Her body flushes pink. She closes her eyes for just a moment before recovering and fixing her attention on me. "Ryder. I want to unwrap my gift." Slim fingers tug at the bow on my boxers, and I chuckle.

"You want my cock, baby?"

She nods. "Very much."

Far be it from me to leave a lady wanting. Without another word, I hook my thumbs in the waistband of my boxers and drag the wet cotton down my hips. The fabric catches on my ass, clinging to me, but after a few more moments of struggle, they're off, and my dick is free.

"Damn," Lexi murmurs, staring at it. She looks up at me sheepishly when I laugh, but she doesn't need to be embarrassed. I'm glad she likes my dick. And I'm going to make sure she craves it by the time the night is done. But first...

"Before you get to play with your present, I want to taste you." She squeals as I grip her hips and drag her toward me. With a wicked smirk, I drop to my stomach and wrap my arms around her thighs, spreading them for me. Her center glistens with arousal, and I hum with pleasure when I drag my tongue through her folds.

She tastes like ambrosia. Like sin and salvation.

Lexi's back arches off the bed as I groan low against her pussy before I unleash myself and feast on her. She cries out as my tongue parts her lower lips and lap at her. She's so responsive. Her cries fill my room as I press a finger into her tight heat.

"Oh, god, Ryder. Fuck!" Her hand tangles in my hair as I devour her. She hangs on for dear life. Unintelligible cries fall from her lips in a symphony of pleasure as I circle her clit with my tongue. Her hips move as I eat her. They're soft movements at first. Slow rolls that grind her pussy against my lips. But as I bring her closer and closer to the edge, she loses control, and they buck against me.

"That's it, baby." I cease my assault just long enough to place a kiss on her inner thigh. "Fuck my face. Take what you need."

Her pupils blow wide, mouth open and panting, and her chest heaves. It's quite a sight. I could get used to this. Maybe if I'm lucky, another blizzard will roll in and strand us here for a few weeks straight. Maybe a month.

Who am I kidding? Even that wouldn't be enough.

"Ryder," she whimpers. "Please." Her hips continue to roll, desperate for friction and seeking release. And who am I to keep that from her?

"Don't worry, Lex. I got you."

She cries out when I flatten my tongue against her clit before suckling on it lightly. "Please, please, please," she chants. Both hands run through my hair. I hiss against her pussy when she threads her fingers through my strands and tugs on them. My dick is aching. I'm rock hard. Hell, if I'm not careful, I'll end up coming just from the sounds Lexi makes and the pressure of her fingers gripping my hair.

I need to make her come, so I can bury myself in her wet pussy. I need to make her scream my name.

Thrusting two fingers inside of her, I curve them. She gasps. Lexi's stomach tightens and hollows out and her thighs shake. She's so close to the edge. It won't take much to push her over it.

"Come for me, Lexi," I order. The words vibrate against her clit as I speak them. I drag my fingers along her inner walls faster and faster, pumping them in and out more erratically. Her breathy pleas fill the room, and she thrashes her head back and forth on the bed. "Come for me." I suck hard on her clit, and her body goes rigid. A scream tears from her throat as her back arches off the bed. I don't stop pumping my fingers, but I release her clit, only to lap at it with my tongue.

"Fuck, fuck, fuck," she chants. When she starts to pull away from me, I wrap my arms around her thighs, pinning her in place. I'm determined to drag this orgasm out as long as I can. "Oh god, Ryder. It's too much. Please, it's too much."

With a last, lazy lick, I release her before surging up her body and claiming her mouth with mine. The taste of her pleasure coats my lips, and I want her to know how delicious she is. And she is delicious. I'm tempted to ignore my throbbing dick and go down on her again.

"How do you feel?" I ask against her lips. Her hooded eyes and slow smile say plenty.

"So good. You're quite talented with your tongue."

"I'm even better with my dick." I roll my hips, grinding my erection against her hip. "Why don't you let me show you just how talented I am?"

When her slender fingers wrap around my shaft and give it a lazy stroke, it's my turn to moan.

"I'd like nothing more."

twenty

LEXI

WHEN I FIRST MET RYDER HANSON, I THOUGHT HE was going to kill me. Now I *know* he will.

Death by orgasm. Impaled by dick. Croaked from the cock.

What a way to go.

"You're so big," I whisper as I draw my fingers up and down his silky, hard shaft. They don't even touch. He's too big. I mean, I don't have super long piano-player fingers or anything, but they're not tiny little doll hands, either. Ryder's penis is just...girthy.

Ew.

Why does that word gross me out? It's *accurate*, but still. *Ew.*

Thick. Ryder's dick is thick. I wonder if it will fit in my mouth. Or my vagina. It might just split me right in half. My tombstone will read *Here lies both halves of Lexi Cross. She died doing what she loved. Riding an impressive cock.*

Worth it.

"Lexi? Lex?" Ryder's amused voice pulls me out of my head. I give it a little shake and force my eyes to focus on his smiling face. His lips twitch before flashing straight, white teeth. I wonder if they're all his? "Lexi, where did you go?"

"Huh?"

Ryder's laughter vibrates through my body, making my nipples tighten painfully. "I said your name like five times, and you were off in your own little world."

I give his dick another stroke. "Just imagining what my headstone will say when I die."

Dark brown eyebrows climb to Ryder's hairline as his lips continue to twitch. "I'm sorry, what?"

"Don't worry about it," I say, rolling my eyes. "Are you going to fuck me sometime tonight?"

The way he stares at me with massive, round eyes that crinkle more and more at the corners makes me grin. Then he buries his face in my neck and laughs. "Eager, baby?"

Hell, yes. "You have condoms, right? Please tell me you have condoms, because it's not like one of us can run out to the gas station with all this snow on the roads."

"Yeah, baby." His crystalline blue eyes sparkle. "I have condoms. Pretty sure Griffin stuffed a box in my bag when Coach said he was banishing me. The guy had like three unopened boxes in his locker."

I let out a little whine when he climbs off me. It's impossible not to miss the heat and weight of him. He crosses to his duffel bag and crouches down to paw through it. Damn. Ryder's ass is a thing of beauty. His thighs are thick and strong, and his butt is round and firm. I want to sink my teeth into it, but I'd be afraid to chip one.

I enjoy the view while he finds his toiletry bag and pulls out a strip of condoms. Then my jaw drops.

"Are you planning on using all of those tonight?" I'm trying to sound sexy, but my voice comes out in an undignified squeak.

Ryder chuckles, and my eyes drink in the sight of him as he crosses the room. His long, thick dick bobs as he walks, jutting out proudly. I'm not ashamed to admit that I salivate at the sight of it.

"If all we have is a snow-pass, I'm sure as hell going to take advantage of it, Lexi."

I swallow hard, my eyes riveted on him as he climbs back onto the bed. The way his muscles ripple is hypnotic. God, I can't wait to have all that power focused on me. "Oh."

Ryder's hooded eyes scan my flushed, naked body. My arousal pools at my thighs. He licks his lips. "Hmm. Maybe I want to taste you again first."

Squirming, I press my thighs together. "No," I whine. "Please fuck me, Ryder. Please."

"Well, when you ask so nicely..." Ryder comes to a halt with his knees beside my hip. With one fluid motion, he rips one of the little foil packets from the strip, tears it open, and sheaths himself in the condom. His strong hand grips his impressive length and gives it a few lazy pumps while he watches me shift on the bed. It doesn't matter that he just made me come, I'm already aching again. I want him to fill me up and push me over the edge at least once more.

"Are you sure about this?" His voice is rough, but oh so soft. I'm pinned by his stare, flayed open by his blatant desire. Still, I know if I said no—if I changed my mind—he'd stop all of this without hesitation or complaint.

It makes me want him more.

"I'm sure," I say while I spread my thighs. "So sure."

The way he groans as I open myself to him has goose bumps erupting over my flesh. There's so much need, so much desire in the sound. I'm not sure anyone has ever made me feel so *wanted*.

"I'm going to take it slow, at first." He crawls forward, caging me in with his strong body. His gaze never leaves mine. "Gonna make you feel so good, Lex."

When his cock drags along my dripping pussy, it's like heaven. Ryder must agree, because he curses before rocking his hips to do it again. Every roll of his pelvis makes his shaft drag across my clit, and if he doesn't stop soon, I'm going to come again from that alone.

"God, Ryder," I moan. "If you don't push your big cock into my pussy in the next five seconds, I'm going to scream." I'm desperate. Empty. I need him. I've never been so eager to be fucked.

"So bossy, baby." He smirks and drags his length across my folds again. "But don't worry. I'll give you what you need."

I'm about to tell him I need him to stop talking and start fucking when the head of his dick pushes against my entrance. He's big. Wider than anyone else I've been with. I don't realize I'm doing it, but my body tenses.

"Relax, Lex," Ryder croons, kissing my neck and the tops of my breasts. "Just relax. I promise to take it slow. Tell me to stop if it's too much, okay? This is only enjoyable if you feel good."

Well, now I'm swooning. Because I can tell he means

every word. Realizing that is enough to help my body relax. My muscles loosen, and he pushes in another inch. I feel the ridges of his crown drag along my walls as he rocks back out a bit before slowly surging forward another inch. It's such a heady sensation that I'm clawing at his back by the time he's halfway in.

"Holy shit. Holy shit."

"You okay, baby?" Ryder studies my face, checking in. All I can do is nod. It earns me a deep kiss, and then Ryder's hips roll, and he thrusts himself all the way in. I gasp when he's fully seated inside of me. Never have I felt so very full. "God, Lexi. You're so tight." He presses his forehead to mine. "You feel like heaven."

I can't even manage an intelligent response. All I'm capable of is little gasps and mewls as he moves. He starts with shallow thrusts, so I have a chance to adjust to his size. It's maddening. When I no longer feel so full I might burst, I squirm beneath him.

"I've got you, Lexi," he murmurs against my lips. Then he destroys my world before piecing it back together in his image.

Deep, powerful rolls of Ryder's hips replace the torturously slow pace. It's amazing, but when he slides one of his huge hands beneath my ass and adjusts the angle of my hips, I'm a goner. Not only does it make the thick head of his dick drag across that sensitive spot inside of me, but it allows his pubic bone and the root of his shaft to press against my clit with every thrust. Despite having already orgasmed once, my body tightens again. The deep heat of impending pleasure ignites in my lower belly and spreads through my body.

While Ryder has one hand supporting my ass, his other

is braced beside my head. His fingers twist in the sheets as he fills me. Those beautiful blue eyes study my face and catalog every reaction. When I gasp at a particularly deep thrust, Ryder angles my hips a bit more before doing it again. This time, my gasp is accompanied by my eyes rolling back in my head, and a pleased sound rumbles through his chest.

"Yes, Lexi. Look at you. So beautiful when you let yourself go. So pretty filled with my cock."

Scratches probably line Ryder's back, but if he minds, he doesn't let on. No, it seems to spur him on. Each new drag of my fingers over his shoulders and back makes him buck into me even harder, and soon, his grunts and ragged breaths join my gasps and moans.

"Ryder." I pant his name, my breathing ragged. "Ryder, oh my god. Never stop fucking me."

Nipping at my lips, he pistons his hips harder, faster. "Never. I'm going to fuck you so good and deep, Lexi. I'm going to ruin you, baby. You'll dream about taking my cock deep inside you when this week is over and you're at home in your bed. You'll feel the phantom ache for me months from now."

Oh, god. My body tightens as he rolls his hips and drags his pubic bone against my clit again and again, and I worry he's right. I worry that I will always chase this feeling. In my dreams, in every relationship I have after him.

"I'm going to ruin you, Lexi. Gonna make you come so hard, you scream yourself hoarse. They'll hear your pleasure all the way in town." Ryder's relentless rhythm slips as I gasp and arch into him. His hips pound against mine and he grinds himself against me. My stomach hollows out, my body tightens, and the warmth in my core ignites into an inferno. Wild, desperate sounds drip from my lips, and he drinks them down like wine. "That's it, baby. You're so close, aren't you?"

"Yes," I choke out. It's all I can manage to say as my body coils tighter.

"Good. Me too, Lexi. Fuck, I'm so close. I need you to come for me, baby. Come for me right now."

And, as if my body was made to obey him, I do. My head arches back and my spine bows off the bed as a strangled cry rips from my chest. That tightness of my body pulls taut as a bowstring before releasing and sending the most intense vibrations through me. I scream, and Ryder holds my hip tight as he pounds my pussy again and again before coming with a guttural moan. His cock pulses inside of me as my pussy flutters and squeezes him. We both still, breathing hard. His forehead presses to my chest as he thrusts lazily inside of me a few more times, dragging out our pleasure as long as he can.

"Shit." Ryder sags, breathless and sweaty, on top of me, wrapping his arms around my body and pulling me tight to his chest. He presses slow, sweet kisses to my lips, my forehead, and my neck. "Lexi, that was..."

I giggle. "Yeah. Yeah, it was."

We lay like that until he's soft inside of me and the sweat on our bodies cools. Still, I don't want to get up. I don't want to move, afraid that if I do, this spell will break. I know this is a stolen moment. I know this won't last. I made sure of that.

But right now? I let myself pretend there's a future for Ryder and me. One with more of the best sex I've ever had. Relishing in the contentedness and safety that comes from being held in his strong, capable arms, I let myself pretend that I'm more important to him than hockey. That he chooses me.

I let myself pretend, even though it's dangerous to my heart.

A soft brush of fingers across my cheekbone pulls me from my reverie. "I'll be right back. I'm going to get rid of this condom and grab a washcloth to clean you up, okay?" Ryder presses a lingering kiss to my forehead, then, without waiting for my response, lets go of me and climbs out of the bed.

I miss his heat immediately.

When he pads back into the bedroom and gently drags the warm cloth over my skin, I think that's going to be it. He's gotten what he wanted, and he'll tell me he's tired and hint that I should go back to my room.

Except, he doesn't. He tosses the washcloth into the bathroom, pulls back the covers, and drags me beneath them before wrapping his naked body around mine. With my head pillowed on his shoulder and my face pressed into his neck, Ryder slips one of his legs between mine. He shifts and adjusts us until we're both comfortable and pulls the covers over us.

"This okay?" he asks quietly.

I take a moment to answer because my throat is so tight. "Perfect."

He hums and kisses my forehead. "I agree. Happy Christmas Eve, Lexi. I had the best day."

"Me too," I whisper. "Happy Christmas Eve."

It doesn't take long for Ryder's breathing to grow slow and even. But his arms never loosen around me. He holds me tight to his chest like he's afraid I'll leave. And despite how heavy my eyes are, despite how exhausted my body is,

I stay awake for as long as I can manage. Because I want to commit this moment to memory. To etch it into my heart, in case I'm never lucky enough to be held like this again.

As sleep makes my thoughts grow fuzzy, I find myself wishing this thing with Ryder didn't have to end. But I know where I stand. I'll never come before hockey. Never have. Not even with my own dad. Not even when I was a kid. And if I can't come first with the man who helped create me, I sure as hell won't come first with a man I just met. No matter how sweet and perfect he seems.

I'm used to coming in second to hockey. But it's made me ache. It's hollowed me out more times than I'd like to admit. I can't do it again. I won't.

For once in my life, I want to come first. And that's why this can never work.

twenty-one

LEXI

THERE ARE NO ARMS AROUND ME WHEN I WAKE UP. Ryder's side of the bed is cold, and I have to take a few deep breaths when my chest lurches.

This isn't unexpected. In fact, this is what I wanted, right? I put restrictions on this. He's just following my lead. It's fine.

Still, the bitter sting of disappointment pokes at me as I hurry into my room to use the bathroom, shower, brush my teeth, and get dressed for the day. It's Christmas morning. We had the most amazing sex last night, and then he held me for hours. That should be enough.

But my heart is a masochist, and the honest part of me can admit I want more. Not that I'd ever reveal that to anyone else.

"This was never supposed to last," I tell my reflection as I blow dry my blonde hair. "This was a snow-pass. You have no right to be upset or hold any expectations in a situation like this, Lexi. This was your idea, so stop being an idiot." Even my reflection looks at me like I'm stupid.

So, I put on some light makeup, pick out my cutest pair of leggings and a Christmas sweater that is somehow both incredibly cozy but also sexy, and suck in a deep breath. I'm going to walk out there and act completely unbothered. Pretend this isn't my first casual hookup. I'm going to prove to myself that this wasn't a mistake and that I can handle it.

The salty scent of bacon hits me the moment I emerge from my room. Following it toward the kitchen, I hear Ryder moving around. Pans scrape and clatter against the stove burners, the coffee pot gurgles and hisses, and he's humming "White Christmas." I pause at the end of the hallway, entranced by the sight of him. The spot allows me to watch him without being seen myself, and I'm not ashamed of taking advantage of that fact. Watching such a big man move around the kitchen with easy grace is hypnotic. He appears confident, even cracking an egg with one hand.

Ryder is shirtless, and his gray sweats hang low around his hips. The muscles of his arms and back flex as he whisks a couple of eggs. His face is set into a mask of concentration, and his tongue peeks out from the corner of his mouth. I don't think he even realizes he's doing it. I'm so busy taking in all of him that it takes me a minute to notice the decorations.

When we went to bed last night, the only sign of Christmas was the tree we'd chopped and decorated. But now? It looks like the North Pole exploded in here.

Twinkle lights stretch across the mantel, snaking around a fake evergreen garland, which drapes along the length of it. My mom's nutcracker collection stands sentry on the coffee table, the side table, and even the windowsill. Battery-powered candles wink at me in the corners of the room, reflecting off tinsel and festive glass knick-knacks and baubles. It's a little chaotic, but it's beautiful. And now I know why Ryder's side of the bed was cold.

He must have been up for hours.

"Morning, Lex," Ryder says with a grin from his spot in the kitchen. He must have known I was here the whole time. "Merry Christmas."

Shuffling out of the hallway, I tuck a strand of hair behind my ear and smile back. Why do I suddenly feel so shy? "Merry Christmas, Ryder. This..." I wave my hand around to encompass the decorations and breakfast. "You didn't have to do all this."

He flips the eggs before switching off the burner and turning his attention my way. While I hesitate to close the distance between us, Ryder doesn't. He stalks toward me with slow, measured steps. His attention never leaves my face. And when he's right there in front of me, his hands reach out and cup my cheeks, tipping my head back so I'm forced to look at him. "It's Christmas, and I had nothing to give you. I wish I had a gift for you to open this morning, but this will have to do." A featherlight kiss plays across my lips, and that's all it takes. I melt into him.

"God, you're sweet. I'm so happy you turned out not to be a serial killer." My arms wrap around his waist, and I kiss him again while he chuckles against my lips. "Merry Christmas, Ryder. Thank you for all of this. It's beautiful." My stomach rumbles. "And it smells amazing."

He chuckles before pulling back, one hand still cupping my cheek. "I may not know how to cook as many fun things as you do, but I make a mean egg." His hand slips down and wraps around mine, tugging me toward the dining table. "Come on, baby. Let's have some breakfast."

Despite my protests, Ryder doesn't let me help. He turns on some Christmas music before serving me coffee and delicious food. Only once I have everything I need does he sit across from me with his own overflowing plate. We sneak loaded glances at each other while eating in comfortable silence. Only the sounds of long-dead singers and the soft clinking of silverware on plates break through the stillness.

"This is so good," I finally say. "Thank you."

Ryder's cheeks pinken. "I'm glad you like it."

"I was thinking..." Not entirely sure this is a good idea, I suck in a slow breath. I was going to suggest it last night, but then we fell into bed together. "Even though it's not Christmas Eve anymore, I thought we could watch *It's a Wonderful Life* this morning. I can make some more hot cocoa. You already made us a big breakfast, so there's probably no point in making fancy appetizers, but we totally can."

His blue eyes are glassy as they pin me in place. And when he speaks, his voice is rough. "Yeah. Yeah, I'd really like that."

Conversation flows more naturally after that, and soon, we're laughing and joking around as we work in tandem to clean the kitchen and wash the dishes. There's something so *easy* about it. So domestic.

People make a big deal about the obvious perks of being in a relationship. The romance, the dates, the late nights and special moments. And all of those are fun. But to me, they're not what makes a relationship special. Any jerk can be decent for a few blips in time and take you on a date. They can even romance you and create special little moments that burrow into your brain and your heart until you think you're in love.

But in my experience? The special parts of a relationship are quieter. They're hidden. Like doing dishes together while you talk about your day. Or hurrying to clean up as much as you can so your partner has less to worry about. The moments when there's no glory or notoriety or kudos on the line are the moments when people show you who they really are.

And, unfortunately for me, Ryder keeps showing me he'd be the kind of man who shows up for the woman he loves. He'd be down in the trenches, fighting the mundane battles that make or break a couple so effectively.

But he can't be mine.

"How long did you spend doing all this?" I ask him as we settle down on the couch and search the streaming services for *It's a Wonderful Life*. "You put up a lot of decorations."

Ryder shrugs, his eyes crinkling in the corners as he suppresses a smile. "Not that much time."

Right. Not that much time. The yawn that splits his face would say otherwise. He woke up early to do all this for me. Really early. And now he's exhausted. So, twenty minutes into the movie, when he yawns for the tenth time, I wrap my fingers around his and give him a tug.

"Why don't you relax?" Patting my thighs, I watch his eyes widen adorably. "Come on. Lay your head in my lap. Sleep if you need to."

His muscles twitch as he starts to move, but he thinks better of it. "Are you sure?"

"Of course," I say with a roll of my eyes. "Ryder, we fucked last night. This is nothing."

He chuckles, and his body loosens, but his gaze is still so intense. This isn't *nothing* to him. We both know that. And maybe I'm playing with fire, here. Maybe I'm pushing this too far past the point of a snow-pass fling and into emotional territory, but damn me, I can't seem to stop. He studies me for another moment until, satisfied with whatever he finds, he lays his dark head on my lap. There's something so intimate about this moment. My fingers twitch with the need to run through Ryder's coarse hair, and it's not long before I give in.

His bare shoulders tense at the first featherlight touch, but soon, his whole body relaxes and a deep sigh floats out of him. I love the feel of his thick hair as it slips through my fingers. The way the soft waves tickle my palms. It's just as soothing for me as it is for Ryder.

I don't even notice it at first. How his breathing grows slow and steady. That his body is completely relaxed and devoid of tension. Two-thirds of the way into the movie, and Ryder Hanson is asleep with his head pillowed on my lap. It's another of those quiet moments. The kind I value so deeply. Another checkmark in his favor.

Which is inconvenient.

With George Bailey's breakdown providing background noise, my mind wanders. This week has been nothing like I expected. It hasn't been quiet or peaceful or alone. It's been one adjustment after another. At first, I assumed it would mean my week was ruined. That all the things I'd told myself I was looking forward to would go up in smoke.

But maybe, just like good ole George, I was so focused

on what I thought I wanted that I missed what I truly needed.

I thought I wanted a week alone. No family. No fuss or obligations. I thought I *needed* that, actually. Because I'm mad at my mom for challenging the status quo. We've always been together for Christmas. And so often, it was just the two of us. Dad spent so many Christmases on the road or coaching home games or dealing with some other stupid, made-up obligation to avoid spending the day facing the fact that he didn't know his wife or daughter anymore. We were supposed to spend Christmas the same way we always have. Together. Just the two of us.

Not with Jeff. Not with some rando she's sleeping with calling me *kiddo,* like I'm not a grown-ass adult. Not watching her make googly eyes at another guy who isn't good enough for her.

And my dad? Well, I thought I needed him to maintain the status quo too. And that's not giving a shit. I was okay with spending Christmas apart. I didn't even want him to ask to see me. Had no idea what to say when he did. Not that he tried very hard to get me to agree or seemed all that disappointed when I didn't. And that was fine. That was what I wanted because I don't want to want him anymore. Not his time or attention or love.

But then he called Ryder, and I realized that wasn't actually what I wanted or needed, either. I want to be loved. What little girl—or girl at heart—doesn't want her dad to love her? The thing is, we all learn to protect ourselves as we're wounded along the way. And not wanting to be close with my dad is how I protect myself.

So, I went into this week wanting—needing—to be alone. But the universe had other plans. And as Ryder's massive body warms my lap and my fingers brush through his hair, I can almost admit that the universe knew better this time. I'd be depressed if he wasn't here. And really, really lonely. And, quite possibly, frozen to death.

But, unlike George Bailey, there's no happily ever after in my future. There's no moment of epiphany when I realize I already have everything I need. This is real life, not the movies. And in real life, you're way more likely to be murdered than saved by some well-intentioned stranger.

Bells ringing and angels getting their wings? You've garrote to be kidding me.

Doesn't mean I don't cry when the Baileys are all hugging and saved and *happy*. I do have a heart, after all. This *is* Christmas. We're practically programmed to turn into sappy puddles of mush this time of year. I'm no different.

And that's why Ryder wakes up to a tear splashing onto his forehead.

twenty-two

RYDER

IS THERE A LEAK IN THE ROOF?

It takes a moment to remember where I am as water drops onto my face and draws me out of sleep.

I fell asleep on Lexi's lap. Her fingers still slip through my hair as the end of *It's a Wonderful Life* plays on the screen. It feels so good that I don't want to sit up and figure out where the water is coming from. I don't want to break whatever spell this is. I haven't felt this relaxed or content since my mom would run her fingers through my hair as I rested my head on her lap.

But then a sniffle breaks through my reminiscing, followed by a slight shuddering of Lexi's body, and the bubble I'm in pops. I sit up slowly, all my attention on the beautiful, teary-eyed woman beside me.

Shit. Why is she crying?

"Lexi? What's wrong? Are you okay?" Wiping another

tear away with the side of my finger, I wrap her in my arms and drag her onto my lap.

"N-nothing's wrong," she says through soft sobs.

I can't help it. I chuckle. This woman.

"It looks like something's wrong," I say, trying to keep my humor at bay. "Talk to me."

She sniffles again, then tries to dab discreetly at her face and nose with the sleeve of her sweater. "Seriously, I'm fine. It's this damned m-movie." Her breath hitches again before her face crumples and she sobs for real. Is she really this sad because of the movie? I mean, sure, it's moving, and the end is definitely on the emotional side, but she's *sobbing*. Even if it is just because of the film, I hate seeing her cry. It grates against the inside of my ribs and makes my stomach bottom out.

So, I do what I can and hold her tighter. I press slow kisses to her temple and rub circles on her skin with my thumbs.

"God, this movie is so sad. Seriously. Why does it have to be so sad?"

We've reached the end, where George Bailey and his family are surrounded by friends and family who've come together to save him from ruin. It's not a sad part. It's happy.

"They all love each other so much." She hiccups, another tear streaking down her cheek.

Ah. I get it now.

"And that's sad?"

Her slim fingers splay across my bare chest. "Obviously."

Fighting a chuckle, I hum low in my throat. "I get it. Sometimes I almost forget that I don't have any family left, and then some sappy-ass advertisement will play, showing big, happy families, and it's like I'm right back to the way I felt when my parents died."

Lexi's body goes completely still.

Shit. I did not mean to say that. I hate when people find out I've lost both of my parents. Hate it. The look of pity. The *what happened*-s. But with Lexi, those feelings are less oppressive. Maybe because she has her own familial crap to deal with. Maybe because we've been trapped in this cabin together for days and we're both feeling a bit raw. Or maybe she just puts me completely at ease. Whatever it is, the train's left the station and there's no backing it up.

Her voice is so soft, her eyes so wide. "Ryder."

I give her another squeeze and rest my cheek on her forehead. With a sigh, I explain. "My dad died four years ago. Heart attack. It was totally sudden, and they tell me it would have been quick and relatively painless." Her fingers stroke my chest slowly with featherlight touches. It's comforting, but my voice still sticks in my throat. "I was away at college."

"Shit," she whispers. No sorry, no pity, no platitudes. Just a quiet curse that somehow says it all.

Sighing, I slump against her, tightening my hold. "Yep. Shit is right. I wasn't there when he passed away. He was alone, and I was at some stupid party, thinking how great life was because a few girls were vying for my attention, and I felt like a big man, you know?" So stupid. All of it was so stupid. None of that ever mattered, but after losing my dad, it mattered even less.

"But that's what you're supposed to do in college," Lexi tells me with a soft certainty that nearly destroys me. "I don't think he'd blame you, Ryder. I bet he'd be happy knowing you were out there, living your life and figuring out who you were. Having some stupid fun."

She's probably right. My dad always worried I was too serious after my mom died. That I didn't laugh as much as I used to. That I worked too hard at hockey at too young an age. By the time I hit high school and college, I was still busting my ass to be the best, but I'd lightened up some too. I started allowing myself to have fun, go to parties, be a stupid kid every once in a while.

Still, the guilt eats me alive some nights. It's why I don't see the appeal when guys on the team go out to bars and clubs, night after night. They go with the goal of getting drunk and sleeping with a beautiful woman they'll never have to see again. It's fine if that's what works for them. I'm not one to judge. But all that stuff feels hollow to me. So, I never go. I'll hang out with them when they choose to do other things. Griffin Wright, our first-line left winger throws barbecues at his place sometimes, and I love hanging out with my teammates at those. Just like I'm looking forward to New Year's Eve at Maddox's place. Those guys are solid.

I'm searching for something real, I guess. Without my parents, I'm missing those deeper connections, and when Chase Bowen and I fell out in college, it wrecked me. I still don't understand what happened there. One minute, we're inseparable. Best friends. The next, my dad had died and Chase became a raging asshole. Now, every time I see him, we end up brawling instead of catching up. I hate it. Though, I suppose I owe him a thanks for injuring my hand. After all, I never would have met Lexi if he hadn't.

Scrubbing said hand through my hair, I give Lexi a bit

more of my truth. "He never got to see me play in the NHL. Didn't even know I'd gotten drafted. There was some talk among a few teams when I started college—a couple of them were vying pretty heavily for my attention—but I didn't sign with the Rogues until after he died."

Lexi's warm body presses into me, her arms wrapping around my waist to squeeze me tightly. I draw strength from it and continue.

"The Rogues were always his favorite team. He'd take me on weekend trips to see games whenever he could." God, those were some of my favorite times. Still are. He'd buy a ton of junk food from the concession stand, and we'd spend the whole game cheering and picking apart the best plays so I could try to replicate them at home.

"Where did you grow up?" Lexi asks.

"Milwaukee. So, not super far away or anything, but far enough that we'd make a weekend out of it."

She hums, and it vibrates against my chest, tickling slightly. "I bet that was fun."

I don't miss the melancholy in her tone. Did Coach Cross ever do anything like that with her? Did he take road trips with her to see a play or go to some concert she was excited about? I want to ask, but I don't. "It was. He worked so hard to pay for my hockey stuff, and I was old enough to realize it. So, when we went away for the weekend, it just felt like... Well, like I was the most important person in the world, you know?"

She hums again, and I almost miss her whispered *no*. It makes my chest ache.

"Do you have any other family?" she asks.

I nod against her head. "Yeah, I have an aunt and uncle and a couple cousins out in California. We're not really close, because they were my mom's family. When she died, we kind of lost contact, you know?"

"Yeah. My parents are both only children, so I never had any aunts or uncles. I guess I never thought about how much that might suck when they die..."

Well, this all got really dark. Time to turn it around. It's Christmas, after all. And I don't want to scare Lexi away. She's skittish enough. As if it's in on my plans to get us off the topic of parental death, my stomach chooses that moment to growl so loudly, it actually echoes around the arched ceiling. Lexi giggles, and the way her body shakes in my lap has me fighting a hard-on.

This is not the time.

"Guess I'm kinda hungry," I say sheepishly.

Lexi laughs. The sound is bright and vibrant, and I relax against her. "Come on. Let's figure out what to make."

Even though we're a tangle of limbs, we manage to get up without falling over. I instantly miss Lexi's warmth. I miss the soft yet solid feel of her in my arms. But she's letting herself touch me more. I doubt this will be the last time I get to hold Lexi Cross. Hell, I'll make sure it isn't.

"I wish we had stuff to make sugar cookies." They're not on our nutrition plan, but sugar cookies go with Christmas like peanut butter goes with jelly. "A couple of weeks ago, me and some of the other guys decorated a batch. They were the ugliest things you've ever seen, but they tasted so good." I chuckle, remembering. I tell her how Griffin made a snowman with a carrot dick instead of a carrot nose. Maddox whacked him upside the head when he saw it.

Lexi laughs so hard, she nearly chokes on her own

saliva. "You hockey players are such little boys sometimes."

"Yeah. Suppose we are," I say. No sense denying it. "Still, I'd kill for a cookie."

"Actually, we might have everything we need to make some," Lexi says once she's done choking. "I bet there's even stuff to make royal icing."

"Really?" Sugar cookies *and* an afternoon with the most beautiful woman I've ever met? Best Christmas ever.

She nods. "I'll check, but I think so."

Making Christmas cookies with the guys was fun. But making them with Lexi? I don't think there could be anything sweeter.

twenty-three

RYDER

"No, no, no!" Lexi's shout rings out as I flip the switch on the stand mixer and turn it on high. I'm so ready to eat some sugar cookies. Just gotta mix this flour in with the wet ingredients, and then I can sneak some dough.

Lexi shouts one more time, but it's muffled by the sudden cloud of flour plugging up my eyes, my nose, my mouth, and even my ears. Her shouts morph into sputtered laughter, and then she's howling from a few feet away. Once I wipe the flour from my eyelashes and turn to her, I find her doubled over, laughing so hard, she's clutching her belly and muttering something about trying not to pee her pants.

As I'm opening my mouth to tell her off, another puff of powder erupts from the mixer. I hurry to shut the damned thing off, but it seems the vast majority of the flour has already ended up all over me and the floor. There's barely any left in the big metal bowl.

"Oh my god," Lexi gasps, still clutching her stomach. Her green eyes dance as they survey me, lingering on my hair. She giggles, snorts, then wheezes as she laughs. "Oh, my god, Ryder. You look..." She laughs some more. "You look like an old man."

An old man? What the hell? When my fingers go to my hair, I understand. It's covered in white powder. Covered. My own lips twitch as I do my best to sound offended and menacing. "You think this is funny, OTG?"

Lexi's continued wheezing tells me she's not intimidated. Tears leak from the corners of her eyes as she nods emphatically. "Yes. I really, really do." She pulls out her phone to snap a picture of me. "This is so going to be your photo in my phone."

"Alexis," I growl, stalking forward. "Don't you dare show that picture to anyone." I reach for her phone, but she pulls her hand back and shoves it in between her breasts. Not sure that's the deterrent she thinks it is.

"Don't even think about it, mister," she shrieks as flour falls from my hands and arms, dusting the sleeves of her sweater. "I don't want to have to change."

My answering grin is wicked. I wasn't planning on getting her dirty. At least, not until she said that. But now?

As I lunge for her, flour creates a cloud around my body. I look like that stinky kid Charlie Brown is friends with. The one who doesn't seem to know how to take a bath. It floats down to the floor like a fine snowfall. Lexi tries to avoid my grip, but I'm so much taller than her, my arms are so much longer, it doesn't take much effort for me to capture her in a bear hug before she can fully escape the kitchen.

"Ryder!" Her shrieks turn into squeals as I curl my body around hers. And then I shake my head. "No! You asshole!" Lexi tries to push me away between bouts of laughter. Her whole body vibrates as she loses herself in a fit of uncontrollable giggles. I keep shaking the flour out of my hair and into hers.

We're both going to need a shower after this. *Damn.* I guess we'll just have to take one together.

When she's good and covered—though there's still way more flour all over me than there is covering Lexi—I tug my phone from my pocket. Flipping it to selfie mode, I keep Lexi wrapped in my arm and use my uninjured hand to take the photo. It's not as easy to use my non-dominant hand, so it's not framed as well as it could be, but I don't care. Because it's instantly one of my favorite photos of all time.

We're both laughing. Our eyes crinkle in the corners, and we're both smiling with all our teeth. I'm absolutely covered in flour, while it forms a fine layer over Lexi. But that's not the best part. The best part is that she's looking at me. Not the phone. Me. And her expression is so unguarded, so genuine and full of affection, that I fall for her right then and there. The *like* and attraction I've been feeling since day one shifts and coalesces into something much stronger. Not love—it's too soon for that, even for me and my sappy, romantic heart—but this is no longer just a crush.

I snap another photo, so I can remember this moment ten years from now. Because as much as Lexi talks about this thing between us being nothing more than a snow-pass, I know that's bullshit. There's no way I'm letting her leave this cabin and walk out of my life. Nope. My plans have changed. She thinks we can't work, but I think she's just scared to take a chance. And I get it. I really do. But I'm not scared. Right now, with a giggling Lexi pressed against my body and wrapped in my arms, I'm way more scared of letting this chance go.

It might not be easy, but I'm going to fight for Lexi Cross. I'm going to make her mine.

I turn, kissing her hard as I snap another photo and then another. And when we pull away, breathless and flushed, I take one of that too. "How about a silly one?" I request, brushing the tip of my nose across hers.

Her smile is so free, it solidifies my plan. She nods. "Okay."

Turning our flour-covered faces to the screen, she sticks out her tongue and crosses her eyes while I puff out my cheeks and arch one eyebrow. Then we make a different face and take another. And right as I'm about to tap the button a final time to take another photo, Coach's name flashes across the screen.

Lexi's body tenses in my arm. I don't need to look at her to know that all traces of the silly faces and the laughter in her expressive eyes are gone. My thumb hovers over the screen as my mind scrambles to change direction. I don't know what to do. I'm planning to ignore the call when Lexi speaks. I hate the brittleness in her voice, when it was filled with such freedom and joy moments ago.

"Answer it."

My throat is suddenly dry, and it has nothing to do with the flour. Turning to Lexi, I let her see how much I don't want to answer this call. "I don't need to, baby."

She bristles. Whether at the nickname or my tone, I can't tell, but I know we're taking two giant steps back, and I fucking hate it. Her lips press into a thin line. "Just answer it, Ryder."

I want to ask her if Coach called her yet today, but honestly, I'm afraid of her answer. If he had, she wouldn't look so grim, would she? Fuck. What is wrong with Coach? She's his daughter. She should have been the first person he called. The only person he *cares* about calling. I want to shout at him that he's a fool, and he's hurting the most precious woman in the world. But he's my boss, and she doesn't want him to know she's here. So, I suck in a deep breath and hit the answer button.

"Hello?"

"Hey, kid!" There's low-level chatter in the background as Coach practically shouts his greeting. He's not alone. Lexi folds her arms over her chest. When she starts to pull away, I tighten my grip around her waist. No way in hell am I letting her withdraw from me. As soon as this cursed phone call is over, I'm getting us back to where we were. Happy and carefree and enjoying our time together.

"Uh, hey, Coach. Merry Christmas."

"Merry Christmas, son. How're things going at the cabin? I wanted to check in on you and make sure you're doing all right."

"Yeah," I say, staring at Lexi. "W—" She elbows me in the ribs with wide eyes and makes a slashing motion with her hand over her throat.

Oh, shit. I almost just said *we're doing fine.*

I try to cover it up with a cough. "Uh, well, yeah. I'm doing all right. It got a bit hairy for a while there. The power went out for a couple days, but it's back on now."

Coach makes a worried sound in his throat. "Aw, shit, kid. Are you okay?"

"Only lost one toe," I reply as I make a silly face at Lexi. I need her to relax. I need her to stop trying to pull away from me.

Coach chuckles. "As long as it doesn't affect your skating. You managing to enjoy your quiet Christmas away from the rest of the world? I didn't plan on you getting stranded there."

This time, I look Lexi right in her eyes, so she sees the truth of what I'm about to say. "Yeah, Coach. I'm more than enjoying it, actually. It's the best Christmas I've had in years."

That thaws some of the ice building up around her. Lexi's emerald eyes soften, and she rests her forehead on my flour-coated chest. I hug her tight to me. I'm not lying. This is the best Christmas I've had since my dad passed. It's the first time in years I haven't felt crippled by the loss of my parents. The first time I've woken up excited for the day and everything it holds.

"That's great, Ryder. I'm glad to hear it. And don't worry, the company I pay to plow the drive should be out sometime tomorrow or the next day. They said the roads are still a mess, but as soon as they clear the main stretches, it shouldn't be long before they get to the side roads. Think you'll be okay to stay there a bit longer?"

"Yeah," I tell him, with my cheek resting on the crown of his daughter's head. "Yeah, I'll be more than okay."

There's a shout in the background, followed by a roar of laughter, and then Coach pulls away from the phone, and his muffled voice tells them to be quiet. "Sorry," he says. There's humor lacing his words. "It's a madhouse over here. I can't keep these hooligans in line. They're going to destroy my house. You good, kid?"

"Yeah, Coach. I'm good."

"Then, I'll let you go. Call if you need anything."

Call if you need anything. Lexi must hear the words, because she curls in on herself in my arms. Her shoulders hunch until they hit my chest. Does he tell her to call him if she needs anything?

"Will do. Merry Christmas."

"Merry Christmas." There's another wave of noise on the other end before it cuts off, leaving Lexi and I swaddled in thick silence.

Shoving my phone in my pocket, I wrap both arms around her still form and pull her tighter into my chest. Neither of us speaks for a few minutes, but the longer I keep her safe in my embrace, the more she melts. I don't know what's going through her head, but it can't be anything good. I always looked up to Coach Cross, but the last few days have been eye opening. How can he be such a great coach and such a shitty father? Doesn't he see how amazing Lexi is? Doesn't he understand how much he's missing out on?

I'm pissed, and without meaning to, I squeeze Lexi so tight to my chest that she lets out a squeak and then sneezes once, twice, three times. Chuckling, I move my hands to her shoulders and pull away. Her face is coated in flour and my chest has a face-shaped imprint on it. Lexi sneezes again.

"Sorry," I get out through bursts of laughter. "Didn't mean to choke you with the flour."

She scowls at me, but there's no real heat behind it. It's adorable and even more ridiculous than it would have normally been because it looks like Lexi has a flour mustache. It ruins the badass appearance she's going for. "Quit laughing at me, you giant shit."

God, I can't stop the laughter. "Chill, Oscar. You're just so adorable with your flour mustache." Using my thumb, I wipe it away from her upper lip. "I think you've found your signature look."

Her powdery eyebrows draw together as her gaze narrows on me. "I'll give you a signature look." And before I can stop her, she spins out of my arms, drops her hand into the mixing bowl, grabs the waistband of my sweats, and dumps the powder down my pants and onto my dick.

All I can do is stare at this maddeningly wonderful woman as her eyes go wide as saucers and her lips open in a little O. My expression probably mirrors it pretty closely. Her hand still grips my waistband, and she's still holding it away from my body. I peer down at my junk. It's almost completely coated in flour. Even my balls are covered. I glance up at her, then back down at my crotch. She looks too.

"You dredged my dick," I say with a stunned voice. She lets my waistband go with a squeaked little *eep*, and it bounces back against my skin with a *snap*. Slowly, so very slowly, I lift my chin and meet her wide gaze. "Oh, Oscar. This means war."

twenty-four

RYDER

"You better run," I growl at Lexi. She shrieks as she sprints away from me, but when she slips on flour, her shrieking turns to giggles. I lunge for her, confident in my ability to stay on my feet. Flour-covered hardwood floors can't be any more slippery than ice, right?

Wrong. Flour-covered floors are *definitely* slipperier. I go down like a sack of rocks. Somehow, I roll myself to avoid hitting my injured hand, but it means my butt takes the brunt of my weight. "Dammit. My ass."

Lexi's giggles morph into raucous laughter. If bruising my ass is all it takes to get her out of her dad-induced funk, I'll fall a million times over. We're right back to where we were before he called, and I love seeing her like this. She's so fun and silly and free. Lexi Cross is genuinely herself, and it's refreshing after the months of playing pro hockey and being surrounded by women chasing the clout and money that comes with dating a pro athlete. I can't stand that shit, which is probably why I haven't seriously dated anyone since college.

But Lexi isn't like them. She isn't impressed that I'm a hockey player. Hell, to her, that's a strike against me. Little does she know that makes her even more perfect. I'm hooked on this woman. Totally smitten.

"Want me to kiss your boo-boo and make it better?" Lexi teases as she struggles to her feet. She makes a ridiculous face and talks to me like I'm an infant.

I grab for her leg, but she dodges me. "Do I want you to kiss my ass? Hell, yeah, I do. You can kiss other things while you're down there too." Waggling my eyebrows at her, I get to my feet and we face off. Lexi glances at my crotch, and when I chuckle, her cheeks heat.

"You're awfully confident for a guy with a flour-covered dick." Her eyes dance, and I shimmy my ass to dislodge as much of the flour as I can. It tickles my thighs as it falls. What a weird feeling. I'm not a fan.

"You are so dead, Oscar." My muscles bunch as I prepare to pounce. "So dead."

This time, I don't miss her. Lexi squeals when my arms wrap around her waist, and I lift her in the air, spinning us in a circle. "Oh my god, Ryder, be careful!"

But I won't slip again. I'm too determined to pay her back. When she sees me headed for the flour, she flails and wiggles in my arms. She shouts empty threats at me, which I just laugh off. So, when I press her back against the counter and grab a handful of flour in my good hand, she changes tactics. Her dancing eyes melt into bedroom eyes, and she pushes her breasts out. Her nipples are hard in her bra, and I bite back a groan when she rubs them against my bare chest.

"Ryder, you don't want to do this. Why are we having a flour fight, when we could be fucking? Why don't we finish making these cookies and then we can hop in the shower?" She bites her lower lip like a sex kitten and drops her eyes to where my now-hard dick strains against my sweats. "I'll take special care cleaning your cock." Her pink tongue snakes out and wets her lips.

Oh, she's good. She's very good.

Unfortunately for Lexi Cross, I have no doubt she'll get naked with me, even if I fill her bra with flour. So, I do.

"Oh, my god!" she screams when the powder fills the lacy red cups. I don't even bother trying to hide my laughter when she gapes up at me with wide eyes. She looks like I just kicked her puppy or something. Grinning, I pull her chest flush with mine and rub against her. Gotta make sure the flour is good and in there.

Lowering my lips to the shell of her ear, I whisper, "Don't start something unless you want to finish it, baby girl." Lexi shivers, and my lips curve into a grin. "Now, let's make these cookies, and we can shower while they cool."

"MY BOOBS ITCH," LEXI WHINES FOR THE TWENTIETH time. She pulls her bra away from her chest and shimmies to dislodge some of the flour. Unfortunately for her, the lace is doing a great job of making sure a decent amount stays embedded in the cups.

"Yeah, well, my balls are covered, and these pants are warm enough that I'm sweating a bit. You do the math."

That has her chuckling as she pulls the final pan of cookies out of the oven. The whole cabin smells sweet and inviting. It smells like Christmas. After we called a truce, mixed the dough, and baked several dozen sugar cookies in various shapes, we worked together to sweep and mop the floors. We had to change the water four times before it stopped looking like glue. Never again. I will never have a flour fight again.

Okay, I would. With Lexi. If it meant making her laugh like that again. But I'd still bitch and moan about the cleanup once we were done.

"These are so good," I say as I take another cookie off the cooling rack and shove it into my mouth. I've had at least three or four. But Lexi doesn't scold me. She just smiles to herself when I hum my appreciation for her baking skills. Because, let's be real, what I've done can hardly be considered helping. There's probably flour stuck to the ceiling, thanks to me.

"If you eat them all, we won't have any left to decorate." Not that it stops her from grabbing her own to nibble.

Surveying the cookies that cover every square inch of counter and island space, I arch an eyebrow. "Pretty sure we'll be okay." Lexi moves the last cookie from the pan to the cooling rack and does another uncomfortable shimmy. It's adorable, but there's no reason for her to stay in those clothes, now that we're done baking. She takes my hand when I extend it, palm up. "Come on, OTG. Let's get cleaned up."

Like Hansel and Gretel, we leave a trail behind us. Flour floats off our bodies, marking our path down the hall and into the main bedroom. The shower in the attached bath is massive, with three shower heads and built-in stone benches, so it only makes sense to clean off in there. We don't speak as I close the door behind us and turn on the water, so it has a chance to heat up before we step in. Then I turn back to Lexi, and we simply stare at each other for a moment as our breathing turns heavy and expectant. My dick grows heavy and expectant, too, which Lexi notices.

The little temptress licks her lips before breaking the spell, crossing the space between us in two steps. She brushes flour off my cheeks with her thumbs before going up on her toes and pressing her lips against mine. It's quick, but heady. Before I can pull her into my arms, she breaks the kiss. Still staring into my eyes, she slips her slim fingers into the waistband of my gray sweats, and then she's dragging them down my hips, over my rock-hard dick and my ass, before letting them puddle at my feet. Those fingers skim along my naked flesh, leaving goose bumps in their wake and making me impossibly harder.

"God, you're beautiful," she murmurs, more to herself than to me.

My voice is rough. "Beautiful?"

"Yeah." She runs her fingers up my abs, tracing the definition of my muscles. "I know it's not the most *manly* way to describe a guy, but it's the most accurate. Your body is art."

I'm completely speechless. Plenty of women have admired my body. I put a lot of work into it, after all. I'm aware it looks good. But I've never, in all my years as an athlete, had a gorgeous woman admire me as though I was a priceless painting or a perfectly carved statue.

I like it.

With heat rising inside of me, I slowly drag Lexi's sweater up her stomach, over her breasts, and off her body. Then I move on to her leggings, peeling them off with the same purposeful slowness. I'm rewarded with hooded eyes and a pretty flush spreading over Lexi's chest. Her lashes flutter when I run a finger up and down her bra strap. I want to tease her. To build up the anticipation until she can't take it any longer. Her breath hitches when I tug the strap off her shoulder and repeat the process with the other. By the time I unhook her bra and let it fall to the floor, Lexi's breathing is ragged.

"Stunning," I say. "You're the most stunning woman I've ever seen."

A breath puffs out of her. "Oh, please. I'm sure you've had models and actresses throw themselves at you."

My fingers skim down her sides. She shivers, and it makes me even harder. She's so responsive. She wants me as much as I want her. "I don't care about models or actresses," I tell her honestly.

"You have so many after you that you're desensitized to it now, huh?" She's teasing, but I'd be blind not to see the insecurities shining out of her eyes. Which is ridiculous. Hasn't she looked in the mirror lately? Doesn't she see herself?

Stepping closer, I thread my injured hand through her hair at the base of her skull and pull her toward me. Leaning down so my nose almost touches hers, I wait until she meets my gaze to speak. "No, baby. I don't care about models or actresses, because they're fake. They look at me and see someone who could help their image. Someone whose presence could grow their social media followers and land them more attention."

Not all of those women are bad. Most of them are upfront about what they hope to get out of a potential relationship with me or the other guys on my team. But I've spent the last four years alone, and there's nothing worse than being in a relationship and still being alone. I want something real. Something deep. Something that makes my heart race and my palms sweat.

Something like the way I feel when I'm with Lexi.

"The thing is, Alexis, I haven't been interested in a woman in over a year. I haven't even entertained the idea of dating. Then you come along with your towel and wine-glass projectiles and accusations of being a hired killer." I apply the slightest bit of pressure and tug her head back. It brings my lips to within millimeters of each hers. "And you're so damned beautiful and ridiculous and a little crazy, and I'm kinda worried no woman will ever live up to you again."

Her breath fans over my lips. Her voice wavers as she simply says, "Oh."

Grinning, I allow my attention to fall to those lips. "Yeah. Oh. See, the problem is that, now that I know no one else will ever measure up, I'm afraid I'm not so sure about this snow-pass thing."

Lexi's eyelids flutter. "Ryder, I—"

"I know," I say, silencing her. "You think this can't go anywhere. I get it. Doesn't mean I have to agree." I rub my nose along hers. "Doesn't mean I won't try to change your mind."

She opens her mouth to protest, but I steal her breath with a desperate kiss. I don't want to hear the reasons this can't work. I don't want her excuses. I know what I'm up against, but I've beaten worse odds. And, after losing both of my parents way too young, I've learned that we're never guaranteed tomorrow. So, if something's important to me

—if I really want something—I shoot my shot. Because you may only get one.

When I break our kiss, it's to drag her panties down her legs before taking her hand and leading her into the hot spray of the shower. "All I'm asking for is a chance, Lexi. Let me prove I'm not like your ex. Let me show you how much I want you."

And with that, I sit her down on one of the stone benches and drop to my knees.

twenty-five

LEXI

Ryder is a god of oral.

My whole body quakes as I ride out my orgasm. I'm slumped on the built-in bench in the shower, and only his arm banded across my belly keeps me from melting onto the floor like an ice cream cone in summer. Watching him eat me out has been an experience. And when he looks up at me with his chin covered in my arousal, I nearly come again.

"Delicious," he purrs, wiping away my juices with one finger, which he then sucks clean. Leaning forward, he kisses me deeply, offering me a taste of myself. "Sweeter than the sugar cookies we made."

God. *He's* sweeter than the sugar cookies we made.

When my body is ready to cooperate, and I'm no longer a boneless sack of pleasure, I decide it's my turn to drop to my knees. I haven't wrapped my mouth around Ryder Hanson's very impressive cock yet, and I refuse to get through this week without the pleasure. This is my only chance, after all.

"Baby, you don't have to do that," he says as he drags his knuckles gently across my cheekbone and down across my lips. "I just wanted to make you feel good."

Looking up at him, I blink away the spray of the shower. "And you did. So, *so* good. But I've been fantasizing about sucking your dick for days now. Do you really want to spoil my fun?"

Ryder chuckles. His hard cock bobs as his upper body shakes. I can't resist. My fingers wrap around the velvety length, and I start to explore. Slowly, I map every ridge and vein and note when Ryder hisses or groans with pleasure, or when his hips buck involuntarily. His attention stays on my face. Even when he grabs the shower wall for support, he still keeps his eyes open and watchful.

When I lean in and lick the drop of pre-cum off the head, his lashes flutter, but he stays strong.

I take it as a personal challenge.

Giving him another long lick as I trace the ridges of his crown with the tip of my tongue, I hum happily. He stares at me, enraptured, and I gaze back at him through the fringe of my lashes. "I can't wait to swallow your cum."

Ryder chokes on air at my sultry words, but I just grin and take him into my mouth. He's big and thick, and I know my jaw is going to ache by the time I make him explode. But I've always enjoyed a challenge, so I focus on what's in front of me.

A very large, very hard dick.

"Shit, baby." Ryder's uninjured hand tangles in my hair as I take him deep into my mouth and swirl my tongue around him. He doesn't push me down his cock, doesn't control my movements; he simply needs the connection. I'm still very much in control of his pleasure.

I've never particularly loved giving head. With every other guy I've been with, it felt like something I had to do. They'd go down on me and I'd go down on them. I always enjoyed making them feel good but derived no pleasure of my own from the act.

With Ryder, I do.

Despite having just come on his face, new arousal floods my core as I savor Ryder's reactions. As I enjoy the salty flavor of him. There's something heady about making this sweet giant of a man fall apart. It makes me feel powerful.

The fingers of one hand dig into the globes of Ryder's ass while I work the base of his shaft with the other. I stroke and tease him with my wet palm as I lick and suck his length. With every bob of my head, I bring him deeper until I'm fighting my gag reflex.

He hisses when his cock nudges the back of my throat.

Well, damn. I never knew I could take a guy this deep. His raspy praise spurs me on, and I ignore the growing ache in my jaw. I want to make him fall apart.

"Lexi," Ryder says through panted breaths. "I'm gonna come, baby."

Looking up at him, I try to grin around his cock but can't quite manage it. I suck him harder. It's sweet that he's warning me. I always appreciate a man who gives me fair warning before he comes, so I can decide if I want to continue working him with my mouth, or if I want to switch to my hands. With Ryder?

I have no intention of pulling away.

"Shit," he says, his hips bucking slightly as he loses

himself to the sensation rippling through his body. "God, Lexi, I'm gonna come."

In response, I take him all the way to the back of my throat and hum my encouragement. His fingers grip my hair tighter as his body goes rigid and hot cum spurts down the back of my throat. I work to swallow it all, but some dribbles out the corner of my mouth. Ryder watches, entranced, as I lick my lips and wipe his cum from my chin. The intensity of his gaze sends pleasant shivers running up and down my spine.

"That was..." Ryder runs his hand over his face. "That was...I mean, damn, Lexi."

Strong hands grip me beneath my arms and lift me to my feet. Ryder tugs me toward him, pressing our naked bodies together. He studies my face as his palms glide up my back and over my shoulder until he cups my cheek with one hand. And then he kisses me.

There's so *much* in the kiss. I'm not sure I want to dissect it. I'm not sure I'm *ready* to dissect it. His words echo in my mind as he owns my mouth.

You're so damned beautiful and ridiculous and a little crazy, and I'm kinda worried no woman will ever live up to you again.

What I don't tell him is that my fears mirror his own. Who knows if what we have could withstand the real world and our real lives, or if we're just enjoying the fragile, temporary high offered by our little bubble? Who knows if Ryder would stay this sweet and attentive and affectionate? None of that matters. From this day forward, he will be the man all others have to measure up to. He'll be the unspoken standard by which all future relationships will be judged.

I'm more than a little worried no one will ever come close.

And when Ryder squirts body wash into his hand and slowly, worshipfully washes every speck of flour and grime off me, I wonder if my plans to keep him at arm's length are worth it. Because these aren't the actions of a man hoping to use me for his own gains. These aren't the actions of a guy who just wants to get laid before he happily walks away without looking back.

Would it be so bad to give this a shot and see where it goes?

Ryder's touches are so gentle and hypnotic that my mind is able to wander. Unfortunately, it wanders to a memory of my dad's reaction when Garrett broke up with me.

"Alexis? Why are you crying?"

We hadn't been close in years, but when Dad had looked at me with concern and actually asked, I let out a little sob and told him the whole story. How Garrett wanted to play hockey. How he'd tried to get close to my dad through me for a chance at an in. How he'd broken up with me when it was clear that was never going to happen.

"I always liked that boy, but he never had what it takes to make it in the NHL."

And that had been it. He gave me a quick hug before telling me he needed to get to the arena for practice. No *I'm so sorry, honey.* Or *What an asshole. I can't believe he hurt my little girl like that. I'll kick his ass.* Just an observation that he'd always liked the fake jerk who'd used me for two years and a no-nonsense assessment of his lack of skills.

Ryder isn't Garrett. I know this. Despite dating me for

two years, Garrett never did anything like this. He never rubbed his fingers through my wet hair and washed the long strands. He never peppered kisses across my shoulders and murmured sweet nothings about how beautiful I was. But that means that Ryder would also have the power to hurt me in a way Garrett couldn't. And if my dad's reaction was lackluster when Garrett broke up with me, I hate to even imagine how he might react when Ryder does.

Ryder, who he likes. Ryder, who he's clearly taken under his wing. Hell, he called Ryder to check on him and wish him a Merry Christmas, while my phone hasn't so much as buzzed with a text message or a stupid Christmas GIF.

Still, do I really want to give my dad any power over who I date? If we give this a try, then break up, who cares what he'd have to say about it? And where Garrett used me to get to my dad, Ryder doesn't need to. He already has his attention. If he thought charming me would get him a bigger in with my father, I'm sure he's realized by now that my dad doesn't care enough about me for that to succeed.

"Tip your head back," Ryder says softly. His large hand cups the back of my head, supporting me as I lean into the warm spray. He uses his other hand to help rinse the suds away. It's sweet and incredibly intimate, and I don't know how to hold him at arm's length after today.

He woke up before the sun to decorate the cabin. He made me breakfast. He ate me out like it was his favorite pastime, and now he's washing my hair and body as though I'm precious.

God, I want to be precious to someone.

No. Not to someone. I want to be precious to *him*.

The realization almost knocks me on my metaphorical

ass. This is crazy. We barely know each other. Though we've been stranded together for less than a week, it feels like I've known him forever. It's that rare connection that feels deep and ancient after only a short time. It transcends all logic and every single self-preservation instinct that has kept my heart from ruin since things blew up with Garrett.

Maybe I don't want things to end after we leave. I'm not ready to admit that to Ryder, but a little seedling of hope has pushed its way out of the hard, cracked soil of my heart. If it keeps growing, perhaps I'll decide that pursuing this thing with him outside of our snow-pass is worth the risk.

Regardless, there's nowhere else I'd rather be as he massages conditioner through my hair.

"You're so beautiful, Lexi." His fingers trail down my spine. The gentle popping of soap suds tickles. "I can't get enough of you."

The feeling is mutual. I can't get enough of him, either.

Once I'm thoroughly clean, it's my turn to take care of him. The problem is, Ryder is significantly taller than me, so when I have to go up on my tiptoes to massage shampoo into his wavy brown hair, I almost slip. Of course, he catches me. I don't even care that he's laughing, because my breasts press against his chest, and I feel every pleasant vibration. I'm lost in the feel of him.

"Here," he says, brushing a wet strand of hair over my shoulder and onto my back. "Let's do it this way." He sits on his perfect ass in the middle of the shower, water spraying down on him. Grinning, I kneel at Ryder's back and wash his hair.

His head falls back as I massage the shampoo into his hair and scalp. Leaning against my chest, he's completely at ease. With closed eyes and a peaceful little smile on his face, Ryder lets me take care of him. Once his hair is shampooed and clean, I lather body wash in my hands and run my palms over his skin. They skim over his shoulder and arms before gliding over his pecs and abs. Back to my chest, Ryder lets out a soft moan as I bring my sudsy hands to his hips before swirling them around his cock. Which is hard. Again.

But this isn't about sex, and he doesn't try to make it about that. No, Ryder is simply content to lean into my warmth and soak up the gentle touches I'm more than happy to provide. I can't help it. My mind conjures scenes of us doing this same thing a year from now, two years from now. I imagine what it would be like to spend my years with a man who is both strong and fierce, and overwhelmingly gentle.

It would be a heady thing, I think—to be loved by him.

All too soon, we're both clean and prune-y. Ryder once again helps me to my feet. But before he turns off the shower heads, he wraps me up in his arms and rests his cheek on the crown of my head.

"I don't want this to end." His words are soft and hesitant, and I know how much he risks every time he's vulnerable like this with me. So, I offer him the only thing I feel able to at this moment in time.

"I don't, either." Pressing a kiss over his heart, I sigh and lose myself in his embrace. "I wish we could stay here forever."

He's silent for a beat, but his breath hitches. It's slight, but I hear it. His arms squeeze me tighter before he releases me and slips his fingers through mine. "Come on, OTG. Let's get you dressed."

twenty-six

LEXI

A SIGH OF RELIEF GUSTS OUT OF MY LUNGS AS I CLOSE the door between Ryder and me. It's the first moment we've been apart all day, and I am feeling *all* the things. My fingers have been twitching with the need to text Rachel since the moment I walked out of my bedroom and found myself in a winter wonderland. So, before I get dressed, I do just that. I flop back onto my bed and open my messaging app.

ME

Merry Christmas, Rach!

Her response is almost instant, just like I knew it would be.

RACHEL

Merry Christmas, Lex! I miss you. How're things with the hockey hottie?

Always right to the point. I love that about her.

ME

Ummmm, things with Ryder are great, actually. Really great. He's... He's great.

RACHEL

LOL. How many times can you use the word great in one text?

Apparently three?

You're falling for him, aren't you?

No!

Yes.

Crap.

LOL! Oh, Alexis. What are you going to do? He plays for your dad.

I know he does. And I have no idea what to do. I really like him, Rach. He's sweet and funny and romantic. He woke up early this morning to decorate the cabin for me and make breakfast. You should see it. It's beautiful.

Really? Wow. That is romantic. Garrett never would have done anything like that.

I know.

God, Garrett was such a dick. I know you were heartbroken when he broke up with you, but I never really liked that guy. He was too full of himself.

Yeah, well, live and learn. And from now on, I'll trust you when you tell me a guy is a douchebag.

Damn straight, you will. Now, what are you going to do about Ryder? Does he want to date you?

Yes.

And you want to date him, but you're scared.

Duh.

What exactly are you scared of?

My dad finding out. Him being pissed. Or him not caring at all. Of getting my heart broken again. Of falling for someone who will choose hockey over me, in the end.

Like your dad always has.

Like my dad always has. Yep.

Look, I don't know Ryder, but from what little you've told me so far, he doesn't seem like the kind of guy who'd hurt you. At least, not on purpose. And hockey's his job, babe. But that doesn't mean you won't be important to him.

I know. I do. I just... I want to come first for once, you know?

I get that. But how do you know he won't put you first unless you give him a shot? You deserve to be happy and loved. But to get that, you have to take risks.

> Dammit. Stop being so logical and wise.

> Can't. It's who I am.

> LOL. I miss you. Next break, I'm coming to Chicago to visit you.

> Please! I miss you so much.

> Talk more soon? I gotta go before Ryder wonders where I disappeared to.

> You know it. Love you, Lex. Merry Christmas.

> Love you too. Merry Christmas.

Clean and dressed, I wander out of my bedroom to find Ryder with another cookie in his hand as he stares out at the snow-covered woods and the lake beyond. For such a large man, there's something so pure and boyish about his expression as he admires the scenery. It's enticing in a way I can't fully articulate. He's not endlessly posturing and pretending to be someone else. He's just *Ryder*. Never once, in the days we've been here, has he made it seem like he thinks he's hot shit or somehow deserving of worship simply because he plays for the Rogues.

My ex-boyfriend was the opposite. He loved being looked at as though he was special. And Garrett was always after adulation and special treatment. Even with me.

God, past Lexi was such a blind fool. Everything was always about Garrett. What he wanted to do that weekend. How he wanted to have sex. What he wanted to talk about. Looking back, I'm not sure he ever really knew me. Which is sad, because we dated for two years. I sloughed off pieces of myself for him the way you peel off dead skin after a particularly brutal sunburn, because there wasn't room for all of me in our relationship. Not when his ego and his desires were so consuming.

But Ryder asks me questions. He watches my face so he can pick up non-verbal cues. It's been less than a week, but I think he actually sees me. Or, at least, he's starting to.

"Ready to decorate some cookies?" I ask him as I wrap my arms around his back. I can't help it. Whenever we're in the same room, I have this compulsion to touch him. To soak up his warmth.

His strong hands run over mine, and I squeeze him tighter. "Heck, yeah. I can't promise they'll look good, but I'm ready."

"Eh," I say, forcing myself to peel my arms off his waist. "As long as they taste yummy, that's all that matters."

I WAS WRONG. TASTE IS NOT ALL THAT MATTERS.

"Oh, my god," I gasp through gut-busting laughter. "It looks like an actual turd."

Ryder's arms cross over his chest, and he rolls his eyes as he peers down his nose at me. "Does not. That is *clearly* Rudolph. See?" He points to the glob of reddish icing that has somehow melted into the poo-brown monstrosity he's calling a reindeer face. "That's his red nose."

"Looks like a popped hemorrhoid," I say under my breath between bouts of giggling.

He sighs deeply, pinching the bridge of his nose. "You know Griffin Wright? On my team?"

I nod, not sure where this is going.

"Yeah, well, one night after an away game, he dropped his pants, stuck his sweaty ass in my face, and asked me if I thought he had hemorrhoids." Ryder's face screws up into an expression of deep disgust. "He did. And they looked nothing like Rudolph's nose."

Tears stream down my face. My sides hurt from how hard I'm laughing. It's impossible not to picture all of that happening, and I don't know if it's from my teasing, or the memory of Griffin's butt issues, but Ryder's suddenly side-eyeing his Rudolph cookie.

"Whatever," he says, shoving his Poodolph cookie away. "Yours can't look that much better. I mean, how are you supposed to make anything look good with this runny icing?"

I try to hold in a laugh, and it just ends up coming out as a snort. Ryder's eyebrows arch at that, but I ignore him. "It's royal icing. It's supposed to be runny. That's how you get such a smooth surface, see?" With a step to the right, I move out of the way, so he can see the cookie I've been working on. It's in the shape of an old-fashioned orna-ment, and I've decorated it with polka dots and little stars that make it look like the light is reflecting off of it. Ryder gapes at it with an open mouth, looks up to gape at me, then returns his attention to the cookie.

"What? How?"

My cheeks hurt from smiling at his adorable sputter-ing. "You just gotta pipe a little border, let it mostly dry, then fill in the empty spaces like I showed you."

"But I did that," Ryder says, his gaze pinging between

my cookie and his. "Why does mine look like poop and yours look so pretty?" He glares at his deformed cookie.

My lips hurt from pressing them together so hard in an effort to stop my laughter. "I thought you said it doesn't look like poop?"

He rolls his eyes. "We both know I'm full of shit."

"Like your cookie," I offer. He shoots daggers at me with his eyes, but then he's laughing.

"Fine, yes. Like my cookie. Ugh." He presses his palms flat against the counter before bringing his head to rest between them. His voice is muffled when he says, "My mom would be horrified."

Chuckling, I rub my hand up and down his spine. "Nah. Moms are great at pretending that whatever art crime you bring home is the next Mona Lisa. She would have told you it was amazing, then locked herself in the bathroom to laugh at you. But you never would have known."

Ryder appears dismayed at this. He straightens and turns to face me with a slack jaw. "Are you trying to tell me she didn't actually love all the drawings I gave her as a kid?"

My nose twitches, and I'm fighting my face to remain neutral. "No, of course not. I'm sure you were an *excellent* artist. One of the few kids with genuine artistic talent."

"I'm questioning my whole childhood," he says with a shake of his head. "Was everything a lie?"

Offering him another pat on the back, I giggle. He's adorable, and fun, and I never want this afternoon to end. I wish his mom was still around to see what kind of man he's become. I'm positive she would be so proud of him. She and her husband raised someone who strikes the right balance between confident and self-deprecating and sweet.

"Makes you wonder, doesn't it?" I tease. "Is your name really even Ryder?"

That has him laughing. I almost don't hear the vibrating of my phone. Picking it up, I see *Mom* flash across the screen. Speaking of mothers.

Ryder notices me staring at the screen. "Do you want some privacy?"

"No, that's okay. Just don't make me laugh. She probably thinks I'm with my best friend, Rachel, or something. She'll ask questions if she hears a guy in the background." And I do *not* want to answer questions about Ryder or this week.

"Got it," he says, pantomiming zipping his lips.

I'm smiling and shaking my head as I press the answer button. "Hey, Mom. Merry Christmas."

"Sweetheart! Merry Christmas. I miss you."

Some of the tightness that's been strangling my chest since my dad called Ryder eases with my mom's words. She's not perfect, but she's a great mom, and I love her. Don't love Jeff, but I love her. "I miss you too, Mom. How's your day been so far?"

"Oh, it's been lovely, just lovely. We got some snow. It's always magical to have a white Christmas, isn't it?"

My eyes move to the windows, where all I can see is white. Despite my annoyance with the power outage and the fact that the roads are impassable, the snow really is beautiful. Even I can't deny that. Plus, it's given me this time with Ryder, so maybe it is a bit magical. "Yeah, it is. We got a lot of snow here too. It was basically a blizzard."

My mom hums a sound of surprise. "Oh, really? I

didn't realize the Twin Cities got hit that hard. I saw that there was supposed to be a decent amount of snow, but a blizzard? Are you safe?"

Shit. "Oh, yeah, I'm totally safe. And I don't know if it was technically a blizzard, but it sure was a lot of snow."

"Well, as long as you're safe and warm, honey, that's all that matters." She pauses as someone speaks in the background. I can't make out what they're saying, but it sounds like a man's voice. Probably Jeff. I resist the urge to roll my eyes. "So, are you with your father today?"

I should have expected the awkward questions to come sooner or later. It's always like this with her, now. She's aware I don't see Dad often, but she still asks every time we talk. I know she's hurting, and I know she's not trying to put me in the middle of things, but it's awkward as hell for me. Especially when it comes to Jeff. I have no idea what to say to her about the guy. I want her to be happy; I do. But I just can't make myself give Jeff a chance.

I glance at Ryder. "Nope. Not with Dad. Haven't even talked to him today."

My mom is silent for a beat, then she lets out a deep sigh. "Oh, honey. I'm sorry. I'm sure he's just busy. He'll call."

Right. He's just busy hanging out with Rogues people and calling the guy I'm crushing on while forgetting I exist. "Yeah, Mom." I steal another look at Ryder. "I'm sure he'll call."

"He will, honey. Yes, your father and I have had our differences, but there's one thing we will always have in common—we both love you so much. He'll call. He loves you."

I know she's trying to be reassuring, but it's awfully

difficult to sound convincing when you know damned well that what you're saying might be a lie. Or, at the very least, wishful thinking. Still, I appreciate the effort.

"I don't want to talk about Dad," I tell her. "Tell me about your day."

"Oh, it's been low key. Jeff and I made breakfast, then we went to an early dinner at his sister's house, and now we're relaxing and watching some movies. He got me this lovely necklace. I can't wait to show you." Jeff says something in the background, and my mother laughs. It's such a girlish sound, it takes me by surprise.

When did my mom start laughing like that?

"That's nice," I tell her.

"Jeff says Merry Christmas, by the way. Do you want to talk to him?"

God, no. "Oh, uh, tell him I said Merry Christmas, too, but I really should get going."

"Oh?" I hate that she sounds disappointed, but come on. Forcing me to talk to a guy I don't know and don't particularly *want* to know over the phone won't do anything but make me feel awkward as hell. "Am I interrupting something?"

A burst of panic shoots down my spine as I turn to Ryder, who's watching this whole interaction with great interest. Like it's another piece of the puzzle that is Lexi Cross, and he's figuring out where this one fits. "No, not interrupting anything. I was just decorating some sugar cookies."

"Oh, I miss doing that with you. Okay, honey, well, I'll let you go. I just wanted to hear your voice and tell you I miss you and love you."

"Miss you and love you too, Mom." My heart gives a

squeeze. I hate that I'm rushing to get off the phone with her, but the longer we talk, the more likely I am to slip up and say something about Ryder. And considering *I* don't even know what's going on with us, I'm certainly not in a place where I feel able to explain it to my mom. My mom, who is waiting for me to call and tell her I've met *the one*.

She's surprisingly romantic for a woman who spent the best years of her life married to a guy more committed to his career than her.

"I'll come by soon, okay? Thanks for calling."

She hums a sound of excitement. "You'd better. Merry Christmas, honey."

"Merry Christmas."

When the line goes silent, I suck in a deep breath. I did it. I spoke to my mom without giving away what I've been up to. She never suspected I'm here at the cabin with a guy. A guy I'd never met before this week. She'd flip about that.

"You okay?" Ryder asks softly.

Am I? I think so. Things with my mom aren't strained in the same way they are with my dad. "Yeah, I'm good. Now, let's decorate some more cookies, and I'll show you the right way to do this again."

His embarrassed smile does funny things to my lower belly. "Sorry, Lex. I really did try."

Hip checking him, I set a cookie down in front of him. "I know you did. And that's what makes it so sad."

Ryder's booming laughter fills the room, chasing away everything that isn't bright and vibrant.

twenty-seven

LEXI

My dad doesn't contact me until after Ryder and I have eaten the fanciest dinner we could muster with our remaining groceries. We're snuggled up on the couch in front of a crackling fire and *The Holiday* when my phone buzzes. Not the buzz of a call, but a text. Thinking it's Rachel again, I grab it with a smile on my face. There's *been* a smile on my face since I woke up this morning, really. And when it has slipped, Ryder's been right there to help me get it back.

So, of course, he notices that smile slip.

"Lexi? You okay?" His voice is so gentle. I know he can read the text—not that he would mean to, but with the way I'm resting with half of my back against half of his chest, he has a direct line of sight—and he's probably worried about how I'll react. Because my dad called him to say Merry Christmas in the beginning of the day, when it was all still fresh and shiny. It's now after nine p.m. and he's finally texting me.

DAD

> Merry Christmas, Lexi. I hope you're having fun with your friends.

That's it. *Merry Christmas*, and *I hope you're having fun with your friends*. What friends? He doesn't know, because he never asked. Once again, I'm nothing more than an afterthought with him. An obligatory text to the obligatory daughter.

Ryder's thumb traces over my hip as he speaks softly again. "Lex? Talk to me, OTG."

I blink dumbly at the screen for another few seconds before locking my phone without sending a reply. Too little, too late. He doesn't deserve one. Pushing a false cheerfulness into my voice, I tell Ryder I'm totally fine. But I can't look at him while I say it. I'm shit at quickly masking my emotions, and one look at me will confirm what he probably already suspects.

I'm not okay.

"Baby." Ryder shifts his position on the couch before grabbing me around the waist and tugging me sideways onto his lap. I don't fight him, because I want the comfort he's offering. In just a few days, Ryder Hanson has begun to feel like my safe place. It's dangerous and probably stupid of me to indulge in these feelings, but I can't deny that I feel them. His knuckles put soft pressure on my chin, silently asking me to look at him. And because I can't seem to resist the man, I do.

His expression is gentle and full of concern when I

meet his gaze, and it cracks me wide open. Despite how desperately I will my eyes to stay dry, tears pool in them before overflowing and dripping down my face. Ryder wipes them away with slow brushes of his thumbs, and I break a little more. My lip quivers, and a sob wrenches itself out of my chest.

"Oh, Lexi." And then Ryder's gathering me in his arms and pressing me into his broad chest, and I'm crying into his hoodie like it's one giant handkerchief. The material and his warm pecs muffle my sobs as he strokes my hair and rubs my back. I should feel embarrassed about falling apart like this, but I don't. Somehow, I don't. Ryder's done his own grieving, hasn't he? It seems unlikely he's a stranger to tears.

"I just don't understand why," I choke out into his chest through my cries. "What did I do to make him not care?"

"Hey," Ryder says, with steel in his voice. His arms band tighter around me. "No. Absolutely not. You didn't do a damned thing, Alexis. You're amazing."

"If that's true, then why does it seem like he forgot about me today? Why does it seem like he *always* forgets about me? Am I not worth the effort?"

It's the first time I've voiced my fears. They've run through my head like lawless rioters, looting and trashing my confidence for years. But I've never said the words aloud. Why now? Why with Ryder? Why do I feel so utterly safe with a man I barely know? Am I that desperate for love and acceptance?

Ryder's muscles bunch and flex against me as he holds me and strokes my hair. So much power coiled within this man, and he's using it to be gentle. To comfort me. Hell, if that doesn't make me fall for him harder.

"I can't pretend I understand Coach," he murmurs close to my ear. "And, frankly, he's pissing me the hell off. If you were my daughter, I'd be so far up your ass, you'd be annoyed with how supportive I was."

I let out a watery laugh.

"Seriously, Lex, you're more than worth the effort. God, baby. I barely know you and I can see that. All I could think about last night as I held you was making you feel special. Giving you a reason to light up the way you always do, and to get even a fraction of that light to shine in my direction. You're worth everything, baby."

He's so earnest when he says it, I believe him. And then I'm sobbing even harder.

"Hey, hey, hey," he says. "It's okay. It's going to be okay. I'm sure your dad knows how amazing you are. He's just distracted right now."

I know the words are meant to be reassuring, but they're not. "He's always distracted, Ryder." I finally give in to the urge to look up at him, despite how much of a mess I am. "He's been distracted since I was a girl. If I told him I never wanted to see or speak to him again, he'd probably feel nothing but relief."

The way Ryder's face screws up into one of disbelief and anger stops up some of the cracks in my heart. "That's bullshit, Lexi. No one who lost you could feel relief."

Oh, sweet man. How wrong he is. And I tell him so.

"You're sweet, Ryder, but wrong. When my ex couldn't get what he wanted out of me, I'm pretty sure he felt relieved to walk away. When I told my dad I wasn't going to spend Christmas with him, I'm pretty sure he was relieved too. I think... I think maybe there's just something wrong with me." More secret fears spilling from my mouth and pooling at his feet.

He growls low in his throat. It's a frustrated sound, and I close my eyes, not wanting to see his annoyance with me. Fingers grip my chin with care. "Alexis, look at me."

I suck in a deep breath, holding it for a count of five before releasing it and blinking my eyes open to meet his.

"Why did you just shut down on me?"

My bottom lip rolls between my teeth. "I'm sorry. I know I'm being annoying. This is so inappropriate. I can't believe I'm crying to you about this."

His blue eyes soften. "Shut up."

My head lurches back and I gape at him. "What?"

"I said, shut up. You're not being annoying or inappropriate. A little ridiculous, maybe, but not because you're upset. It's ridiculous that you believe I'd be annoyed by it." He rolls his eyes again, as if I'm being completely unreasonable and anyone could tell.

"I... I..." I can't seem to get any words out. I'm sitting in his lap, stammering like an idiot.

"If anything, I'm honored. And maybe a little hopeful."

Blinking at him owlishly, I tilt my head to the side. "What? What do you mean?"

"I'm honored that you'd trust me with your emotions and your fears." He tenderly brushes a stray strand of hair out of my face and tucks it behind my ear. "And I'm hopeful this connection means you might give this thing between us a chance once the week is over."

My resolve is crumbling around me with every word he speaks. Because I *do* want that. But I'm still too scared to admit it. And what does he mean by *give this thing between us a chance*? What if we want different things? I realize Ryder is different than most of the hot-shot athletes I've met, but could he really want a *relationship* with me? Not merely something casual, a long-term hookup with no strings attached, but something real?

Because I've done casual a few times, and it's not my thing. I *can* do it, but it's dangerous for me. I'm too prone to feeling rejected, so the few times I've tried to be cool and agreed to a friends-with-benefits kind of situation, I still found myself hurt at the end. Despite having agreed to the terms on the front end, my heart couldn't get on the same page as my mind. When those guys walked away, and that was that, I still felt the sting of rejection. Because if I'd been more interesting or more beautiful, they would have wanted more, right?

God, why is it so hard to simply ask Ryder what he wants with me? To see if we're on the same page?

Because you're scared, dumbass.

After scanning his face for a few thunderous heart-beats, I suck in a deep breath, pull up my big-girl panties, and open myself up to the possibility of being hurt. But also to the possibility of being surprised. After all, aren't they often one and the same?

"Ryder, when you say you want to give this a chance, what, exactly, does that mean to you?"

The way his expression softens eases some of my panic. He smiles—a tentative thing—and cups the side of my neck. His thumb brushes idly over my fluttering pulse. "I know, on paper, we just met. And I'm the first one to admit that I can be a little...intense. But I also think I may not be the only one feeling like we've known each other for years." He pauses, watching my face carefully, waiting for me to spook.

I don't. I don't so much as move.

"Being with you this week—spending time with you—has been... Well, I haven't felt so at ease with anyone in ages. I don't feel like I have to hide anything from you, and I'm sure as hell not worried that you're only laughing at my stupid jokes because you know I'm some hockey player." He gifts me with a lopsided grin as I chuckle.

"No," I agree. "If anything, it makes me less inclined to laugh."

He chuckles and shakes his head. "See? And I love that about you."

I must make some kind of face at the use of the *L-word*, because his eyes grow comically wide, and he shakes his head again, this time more vehemently. "No, no. Don't freak out, Oscar, I'm not saying that I love you or anything." He gives me a guileless smile. "Poor word choice. Sorry."

Taking pity on him, I smirk. "You don't love me? Rude."

"See?" His blue eyes sparkle, crinkling in the corners. "This is what I'm talking about. Don't you feel this? This easiness between us? I don't want this to end. I know you talked about the snow-pass thing, and if that's really all you can give me, then I'll take it because having a tiny piece of you is better than none of you, but I don't think a tiny piece is going to be enough. I want more. I want to take you on dates and hear about your classes and show you off to my friends. I want you to sit near the ice at every game, and I want to win games for you and make you proud to wear my jersey."

Oh, my heart.

Ryder inhales slowly, still watching me intently. Still waiting to see if I'll bolt.

And I probably should. It would be the smart thing to do. Because there's no world where this ends in anything but heartbreak for me. And yet, I find myself wanting all those things too. At least, for as long as they last.

All I can think to say is, "You want to date me?"

"Yeah, Oscar," he says with a laugh. "I want to date you. I want to date you so hard."

Grinning like an idiot, I press my face into his neck. I don't know what to say. And I'm feeling all the things right now. I need a second to collect myself. When I don't immediately say anything, he continues.

"And I know this is terrible timing because the season is underway, and I'll be on the road a lot, and that's not exactly ideal for dating, but with my injury, I'll be out for another couple of weeks. It'll give us some time to spend together and see where this goes before I have to travel with the rest of the team. It will probably be complicated, trying to schedule things around my work schedule and your classes. But I'm willing to try, if you are."

He's so earnest. So hopeful. He's not wrong about our schedules being a hurdle, but I'm used to hockey schedules. I grew up working around my dad's. I know better than most what I'd be getting into. It should be a deterrent. I always hated how much my dad was gone during the season. But I suspect Ryder would put in the effort my dad couldn't—wouldn't. He'd make time for me.

Do I want him to?

Shit. *Yes*, of course, I want him to.

"I'm willing," I say, with my face still pressed against his neck. The words come out muffled.

"Say that again?"

Pulling away from him, I meet Ryder's gaze. "I said, I'm willing to try. I... Well, I've been trying to come up with reasons I shouldn't date you almost since the first moment we met, but none of them seem all that valid at this point."

His cheeks are tight from how broadly he smiles at me. "Oh, yeah? And why's that, OTG?"

"Well," I say, blowing out a breath. "For starters, you're not a serial killer, so my initial reason isn't valid."

He barks out a laugh.

"You're not some self-centered athlete who thinks the world should revolve around him. And you're definitely not trying to get in with my dad, because it seems you're already more in than I am."

Ryder frowns at that, but I make a silly face to let him know I'm only teasing. Mostly.

"But really, I'm just not done spending time with you. I don't want to be. But I don't think it would be wise to show up to your games in your jersey. If we do this, it has to be a secret."

I can tell he doesn't like that idea, but he keeps his mouth shut about it. And I love that he doesn't like the idea of keeping our relationship secret. It means he's not ashamed of me or unsure of me. But I'm not ready to deal with my dad and whatever backlash may come from dating someone on his team.

Besides, if we're going to give dating a try, I want to enjoy the rush of a new relationship without all the pressure that comes along with the weight of others' opinions and expectations. I want to focus on us and what we want. At least, for a time.

Ryder's eyes narrow as he considers it.

"Please, Ryder."

His dark hair bounces as he slowly nods. "All right, Lexi. We'll do it your way for now. But you should know, I won't hide you forever."

And just like that, we step off the edge of a cliff, hurtling toward unknown waters.

twenty-eight

RYDER

I*T'S A CHRISTMAS MIRACLE. SOMEHOW, LEXI CROSS* has agreed to date me. Do I love that she wants to keep it a secret? No. Am I going to let that stop me from winning her over completely and making her mine? Also no. I spent the first few hours with her in my arms last night brainstorming dates she might like to go on once we get out of here.

I'm tempted to bring up New Year's Eve and the invitation from Maddox to hang out with the guys, but I know it's too soon. I still have a few more days to convince her that none of them will tell Coach Cross anything if we ask them not to. Hell, I'm not sure any of them even know Lexi's name—let alone what she looks like—so it's possible we could go to the party and never have to reveal who she is.

But all of this is a problem for future Ryder. Right now, I want to enjoy skinny-dipping in this hot tub with the most beautiful woman in the world and savor the quiet laziness that always accompanies the day after Christmas.

While we soak, I ask her about college and her best friends. She tells me about how she misses a lot of things about going to school in Chicago but that Minnesota is her home. She laments how infrequently she and her best friends see each other, despite only being eight hours apart. And she tells me how freeing it was to live in a city where her dad wasn't a household name, and how much she'd needed space from her parents to figure out who she was and what she wanted in life.

I tell her about my parents. About how they cheered so loudly when I learned how to skate. About the look of pride on their faces when I played my first hockey game, despite neither team scoring, and half of us being unable to skate more than three feet without dropping our sticks. I tell her about all the sacrifices my dad made to keep me in hockey once my mom died. How much I wish he'd gotten to see me play for his favorite team in the NHL.

Our conversation flows so easily, I forget we've only known each other for five days. I don't think about how crazy it will seem to everyone that we're dating after so little time. But with every story we share and every laugh that slips out of Lexi's full lips, I feel more and more certain that we could have something special.

"What made you choose a college in Chicago?" I ask her when the conversation swings back around that way. I can't help but think of Chase Bowen and our rivalry that used to be a friendship, and I rub my sternum. It's a familiar ache, and even though time has dulled it, it's still a wound that hasn't completely healed.

Lexi's lips twist thoughtfully. "I think I liked the idea of being a little fish in a big pond. I know that's not what most people want, but I've always felt so much pressure to prove myself, you know? Going to school in a huge city, where no one knew me, was freeing in a way I can't entirely explain. It let me try new things without worrying about failure."

"Like what?" I want to know everything.

Her emerald eyes glitter as the corners of her lips twitch. "Like, I've always wished I was artistic. I mean, sure, I did some plays in high school, and I think I was pretty decent, but that's the extent of my creative abilities. But I've always had this fantasy of living that tortured artist's life. I thought it would be so cool to walk around the city with an old film camera slung around my neck. I'd take black and white photos of random strangers on the street or a particularly striking sky." She shakes her head. Her cheeks bunch up, even as she presses her lips together to hold back a smile.

"Did you do it, then? Did you take a photography class and start wearing berets around the city while a clove cigarette hung out of your mouth?"

She giggles. "What? Ew. But yes. Yes, I did."

Soaking in the hot water, I wait expectantly for Lexi to continue her story. She covers her face with her hands before peeking out at me through the gaps between her fingers. "I think I managed to take all of five photos the entire semester that were completely in focus. My professor couldn't seem to hide her amusement when it was my turn to show my work. It was... Well, my photos looked like a drunk toddler had taken them."

"They couldn't have been that bad," I say through my laughter.

She shakes her head. "Oh, I promise you they were. At the end of the semester, my professor pulled me aside and told me she was grading me based upon my efforts in the class, and not my work. Then she asked me to please never take another one of her classes, because she couldn't make a habit of doing that."

"No."

"Yes."

"Oh, Lex." I'm shaking with silent laughter as I pull her naked body through the water and onto my lap. The new position has both of us stilling. Our laughter ceases, and we simply stare into each other's eyes. "Was that the first and last art class you ever took?"

She looks away from me and mutters a sardonic, "Nope."

"And what did you take next, Oscar?" I chuckle when she gives me a half-hearted smack to my chest because of the nickname.

"I took a pottery class. With wheels and everything."

"And how did that go?"

She buries her face in my neck. "Not well."

Not well. There are so many ways throwing pottery on a wheel could go *not well*. Grinning, I wrap my arms around her and hold her close. "Care to elaborate?"

She snickers against my skin. "Let's just say that I am now an expert at getting wet clay out of hair."

We both end up laughing at that imagery. When she pulls away from her hiding spot pressed against my neck, I study her. Rosy cheeks that are full and round with her smile, the most beautiful green eyes, that smattering of freckles across her nose. Lexi Cross is beautiful and engaging, and I want to hear all her stories.

I love that she stepped out of her comfort zone in college. I didn't. I stuck to the classes required for my degree and spent the rest of my time training or on the ice. I was always so laser focused on getting into the NHL, especially after my dad died, that I didn't leave room for anything else. Hell, I haven't left room for much else since starting with the Rogues, either.

Maybe it's time to change that. I'm happy with my life. I wish my parents were still here to celebrate my victories with and mourn my losses, but outside of them, I have everything I wanted. I play for one of the best teams in the NHL, I'm developing friendships with my teammates, and I have a swanky apartment downtown. Sure, I share it with one of the other guys on my team because I'm scared to put my name on a lease of my own, for fear it will jinx me, and I'll end up traded to somewhere way too warm to play hockey. Somewhere like Florida. *Shudder.* But I have the kind of place I dreamed about in college. I'm getting more time on the ice, and my prospects are looking good.

Still, after almost a week with Lexi, it's becoming clear that none of that really means my life is full. Not in the way it could be. Because I haven't been sharing all of that with anyone. I've told myself I don't have the time or the emotional bandwidth for a relationship, but maybe that's bullshit.

Maybe I've just been too scared to take a risk and put myself out there.

I'm still scared shitless, but I finally see that putting myself out there may be one of the best decisions I could make. If it means I get to share my days with the beautiful, intelligent, unique woman straddling my lap, I'm all in. I'll put it all on the line. Because Lexi is...

Lexi is someone my parents would have loved.

Lexi is someone who makes me feel alive.

I can't screw this up.

She sighs when I cup her face with my hands, her eyelids fluttering closed. I can't resist. I close the distance between us and press my lips to hers. It's not hungry, like our kisses last night. No, this kiss is the sealing of a silent promise to do whatever is in my power to make Lexi happy. To keep her heart safe. Because it's become very clear to me that Alexis Cross is an expert at protecting her own heart.

I'd like to be the one to take up the mantle now. All I want is to be a safe place for her. A place to fall when she doesn't have the strength to stand on her own. To be someone who will hold her up and protect her.

I'm not dumb enough to say any of that to her, yet. Lexi is fiercely independent. Anyone can see that. If I try to come riding in on a white horse, like some knight in shining armor, she's more likely to kick my ass than swoon. But we'll get there. Probably not to the swooning part, but the letting me protect her part. It may take some time, but I'll show her she can depend on me. That she can lean on me.

"You're beautiful," I whisper between slow, drugging kisses. "I bet you even looked beautiful with clumps of clay in your hair."

She chuckles against my mouth before tugging on my lower lip with her teeth. "Such a charmer, Ryder Hanson. Are you trying to get into my pants?"

I buck up against her. "You're not wearing any pants."

That has her breathing going ragged. "True. I certainly am not."

"Should we head inside? I'll dry you off, grab a condom, and make you scream my name."

"Mm. Yes, please." Lexi wraps her arms tightly around my neck, then hooks her legs around my waist. "To the bedroom, Jeeves."

That devious smirk on her face has me arching one eyebrow, but I give her what she wants. Rising to my feet, I carefully step out of the hot tub, with Lexi clinging to me like a koala, and carry her inside.

"As you wish, madam."

twenty-nine

RYDER

THE PLOWS HAVE THE ROADS CLEARED BY THE 27TH, but the service Coach hired to clear the cabin's drive doesn't come through until the afternoon of the 28th. The tow truck driver arrives shortly after to drag my car out of the ditch and up to the cabin.

"What would you have done if you were alone, and they couldn't pull you out right away?" Lexi asks me. She crosses her arms over her chest and watches me give my car a once-over. One hip is popped out to the side, and she's got a smirk ticking up the corner of her mouth.

"Guess I would have had to live here," I say with a shrug. "Become one with the wilderness or some shit."

She shakes her head at me. "You'd be living off canned beans, since you didn't bring any groceries with you."

I would have. She's not wrong.

"Guess you got lucky, getting snowed in here with me, huh?"

Closing the distance between us, I wrap my arms around her and tug her against my body. She tilts her chin up to look at me, those verdant eyes of hers dancing. Little tease. I press a soft kiss to her lips and whisper, "So lucky. Count my lucky stars, lucky." I kiss her again, our lips soft and pliant as we savor one another. "And not just because you brought enough groceries for both of us."

The way her body softens against mine fills me with a primal satisfaction I can't quite define. Of course, part of it is that Lexi is beautiful. Her body is a work of art, and any man who's attracted to women would puff up his chest if she leaned into him this way. But the main thing is that, in a week, I've earned her trust. I don't think that's a feat too many people can boast.

"Aren't you a charmer?" she teases. Her lips brush against mine with each word.

"Only for you, OTG."

That makes her chuckle. "Yeah. Only for the woman you've nicknamed Oscar The Grouch."

"If the shoe fits..." I offer her a cheeky grin and a shrug. And then I wrap my arms more tightly around her and kiss her again. This time, the kisses aren't soft and pliant; they're hot and demanding. I'm rewarded with soft gasps, which I breathe in. Straight from Lexi's lungs to mine. She shivers. I want to believe it's because I'm just that good at kissing, but more than likely, it's because this garage is cold as hell. "Come on. Let's go inside and get you warmed up."

Linking our fingers, I lead her into the house. My stomach has been tangled in knots ever since the guy came and plowed the driveway. Our time here is coming to a close. Lexi agreed to date me, but we're stepping out of our safe, secluded little snow globe and into the real world. Full of unknowns and obstacles. Part of me worries she'll get home and change her mind about me.

There's also the matter of the New Year's Eve party. The one I still need to tell Lexi about. And then somehow convince her to come, even though the party will be full of Rogues players, and she wants to keep our relationship a secret.

No big deal. Totally fine.

It won't be the end of the world if she doesn't want to go. It really won't be. But if we're going to work, we'll need to figure out how to combine our lives, won't we? And that means meeting each other's friends and coworkers. That means team dinners and dates on the town. And eventually, I hope, games where she's sitting in a seat close to the ice, wearing my jersey, and cheering for me while I play.

But first, baby steps.

We're quieter than we have been as we move around the kitchen, making our last dinner in this cabin together. I want to know what she's thinking, but I'm also scared to ask. I'm not an idiot. I may be all in and ready to give dating a serious try, but she's more hesitant than I am. The longer I put off talking to her about our next steps, the longer I can live in this beautiful delusion that everything will work out between us.

Time to suck it up, grow a pair, and communicate with Lexi, even if it's scary or hard. She deserves that. She deserves someone who won't shy away from the tough conversations. Someone who won't let her slip away with vague excuses. Because she's used to that, isn't she? I don't get the sense that her parents are ones to have tough conversations with her. Hell, it's entirely possible that Lexi has no idea how to deal with confrontation, or even a simple conversation about the future, because she's never seen it in action.

That's one thing I'll give my parents. Even though I don't remember many actual conversations with my mom or what they entailed, I do remember feeling seen and heard. She valued my opinions and feelings. And when she died, my dad got us both into therapy. Sometimes we went together, sometimes separately, but either way, I learned healthy ways to communicate. I won't throw away all those hours of learning and growth just because I'm scared the woman I'm interested in will walk away.

Only one way to find out.

"Do you have plans for New Year's Eve?" I ask, breaking the prolonged silence.

Lexi glances over her shoulder at me. "No. Originally, I was planning to stay through New Year's, but I'm not so sure now. I guess it seems like the cabin will be lonely without you. I'll probably leave tomorrow when you do." She goes back to chopping onions for the chili we're making. "What are your plans?"

I take a break from opening cans of beans and stewed tomatoes to rub my uninjured hand over the back of my neck. "Well, I'm not sure if you're familiar with any of the guys on the team?"

She hums, wobbling her head. It's not a yes, but it's not a no.

"Well, Maddox Graves is our team captain. His girl-friend, Isla, recently moved in with him, and they've invited some guys from the team over for dinner and drinks. I was planning to go to that."

"Oh," she says. Her back is stiffer than it was, and I

don't miss the tension in her shoulders. "That sounds nice."

Dammit. I suck at this. She's not getting it. I drop the can opener on the counter and walk up behind her, wrapping my arms around her waist. "It does. Well, it does if you agree to go with me."

Her silence doesn't surprise me. Rather than pushing her to answer, I sweep her hair away from her neck and pepper it with slow kisses. My hands roam her stomach and brush the undersides of her breasts. After she's had some time to process, I say, "I want to spend New Year's Eve with you. If that means I bail on Maddox and Isla, then that's what I'll do."

"No," she says with a gust of breath. "Don't do that for me."

This woman. "I'll do anything for you, OTG. I'll prove it, eventually."

Her body loosens with those words, and her head falls back onto my shoulder. "I don't want to be the kind of woman who makes you break your plans, Ryder. That would be selfish of me. I just...I'm not ready for my dad to find out about us."

A part of me wonders if she's ashamed to be with me and that's why she doesn't want him to know, but that's an easy fear to squash. I know they have a shitty relationship, so it's probably more that she doesn't want to deal with whatever lecture he'll give us. Because he may be an uninvolved father, but every dad is protective of their daughters when it comes to men, right? I'm sure he'll chew my ass out once he knows. He'll probably threaten me with bodily harm, or he'll threaten my career... But Lexi's worth dealing with all of that. And honestly, I hope he *does* do all of that, so she knows he cares.

"We don't have to tell the guys who you are or how we met," I murmur in her ear. "You can just be Lexi. No last name. No details. Just the beautiful woman who caught my eye and then wrapped her pretty fingers around my heart."

Her body shakes with silent laughter. Then her head turns on my shoulder to look at me out of the corner of her eye. "Won't they recognize my name?"

Ah. This is where it gets tricky. I don't want to hurt Lexi by revealing that her dad doesn't talk about her or have any recent pictures of her up. "Uh, well, Coach keeps his personal life pretty private, baby. I don't think any of the guys would realize by your first name that you're Coach's daughter."

Those big green eyes blink slowly at me. "He's never mentioned me by name at all, has he?"

Blowing out a deep breath, I kiss her forehead. "No. Sorry, Lex."

Her eyes close. "And he doesn't have a picture of me up anywhere in his office, does he?"

"He does," I say, my arms tightening around her midsection. "It's just...you were pretty young in it. I've seen it, and I didn't recognize you."

"Oh." Her brow furrows. "That's more than I expected, honestly, so it shouldn't hurt, but it kind of does."

"I know. I'm sorry, Lexi. He's an idiot."

Lexi only shrugs. "Guess so."

"Will you go with me?" I can't hide the hope in my voice, and I don't really try. I want her to hear how much I crave spending time with her.

She shifts her weight from one foot to the other. "I don't know, Ryder..."

"Come on, baby. I promise you'll have fun. It won't be some wild party or anything. It's supposed to be sophisticated." She snorts. "Okay, well, more sophisticated than it would have been if Maddox didn't have his girlfriend planning it."

I spin her around, press her chest against mine, and tilt her chin up. "If you really don't want to go, that's okay. I'll cancel, and you and I can do whatever you want." And I mean it. I will cancel. She's more important than some party, even if I have been hoping to get closer to the guys. There'll be other opportunities for that.

Lexi blows out a breath. "I don't want you to cancel because of me. I... I'll go. Just, please, can we keep who I am a secret, unless it's unavoidable?"

I kiss her on the forehead. My lips twitch with a huge grin the whole time, making the kiss kind of a strange one. "You sure?"

"Yeah," she says with a little sigh. But there's a smile on her lips too. Not as broad as mine, but it's there. "Yeah, I'm sure."

No doubt, I'm grinning like a total fool, because she starts to laugh. I don't care. I feel like I just won my first, and very important, victory with this woman. Gripping her tightly, I lift her feet off the ground and spin her around in circles. She throws her head back, closes her eyes, and laughs. "We're going to have so much fun. Do you want to come stay at my place until New Year's Eve?" I don't want this time with her to end.

She cocks her head to the side. "I should probably go home. I didn't pack anything I'd feel comfortable wearing to a party." Her fingers tap a staccato rhythm on my chest. "Do you live alone?"

"No." I sure as hell wish I did, now. "I live with another guy on the team. He's on the third line, so he's got his own place but rents out a room, so he doesn't blow all his money. Aaron's a good guy. You'll like him. Especially since he's hardly home." Lexi laughs when I waggle my eyebrows at her suggestively. "I never asked if you have a roommate."

She nods. "Yeah. We're not close or anything. She posted a room for rent on one of the college boards, and it's close to school, so it works out well. We don't really hang out at all, but she's nice enough."

It's far too soon to be thinking about any of this, but my mind instantly conjures images of Lexi and me getting our own place. Of waking up next to her every morning the way I have the last few. I try to imagine how she'd decorate a house. All of it is a fantasy I shouldn't indulge, but this past week has given me a taste of what life could be like living with Lexi Cross, and I want more.

That desire doesn't abate while we orbit each other in the kitchen, working together to make the best damned chili I've ever tasted. It doesn't fade when she welcomes me into her body and falls apart beneath me. And it only grows when she snuggles, naked, into my side with her head on my shoulder and falls asleep within minutes.

And when I wake up with our limbs tangled and her lips pressed against my neck, warm puffs of air tickling my skin, I wish we could skip right past all the adjustments the real world will no doubt require and wake up every morning like this.

But there's no fast-forward button in real life. And in a

couple of hours, we'll leave this cabin and go back to our own beds, where we'll spend the night alone. I can only hope she hates that idea as much as I do.

246

thirty

LEXI

I'VE CHANGED MY DRESS THREE TIMES.

Why am I so nervous? Maybe it's because it's my first time seeing Ryder since we left the cabin. Though we've only spent one night apart, after being snowed in with him for a week, that night felt long and lonely. It was startling to realize how much I've grown used to his presence beside me in bed. How quickly his body heat helped me fall asleep. Alone for the first time in days, I'd tossed and turned last night until my mind finally shut down around two in the morning.

I've been a tangle of knots since waking. I can't wait to see him. To kiss his handsome face and lose myself in one of his all-encompassing hugs. When I really stop to think about how much I'm looking forward to being with him, it's kind of terrifying. The way I crave Ryder Hanson tells me I'll be in big trouble if he decides he doesn't want this. I try to rein myself in and temper my hopes and expectations for the night, but it's like my body has been taken over by my former teenage self. The girl who was endlessly hopeful. The girl who hadn't been used and tossed aside yet.

"You're so screwed if he turns out to be a secret asshole," I tell my reflection. But she's all bright-eyed and oblivious.

As I swipe on another coat of mascara, my body recalls how it felt to be in Ryder's arms. Tingles wash over me. My belly does an anticipatory flip. As nervous as I am to spend the evening surrounded by men who play for my dad, I'm also excited. I've been so focused on my MBA, I haven't made much of an effort to meet people since I moved back home after finishing my undergrad in Chicago. And while I don't expect to find my new bestie at this dinner—not that anyone could replace Rachel—there's a part of me that swells with the hope that I'll be able to carve out a little place for myself in Ryder's life and with his friends.

I want them to like me. I want to fit in. Not because I'm Coach Cross's daughter and they feel obligated to make nice. And not even because I'm Ryder's...not girlfriend. Not yet. Ryder's date? The person Ryder is dating? I want them to like *me*.

It's because of that desire that I've changed so many times. I don't want to dress too formally, but I don't want to be too casual, either. I want to look sexy for Ryder, but I don't want to show so much skin that I end up feeling uncomfortable. And this is the first time Ryder's going to see me in something nicer than leggings and oversized sweaters. I want him to think I'm beautiful.

Running my hands down the sides of my dusky-rose-colored dress, I finally settle. The material is slinky and hugs my curves. It's long-sleeved, so I won't be cold, but it dips down into a deep scoop neckline, showing off just the right amount of cleavage. The bodice is fitted, then it flares out below the waist, the length hitting mid-thigh. Embroidered flowers climb up one side of the dress from the hem of the skirt up to my rib cage, where they end just beneath my breast. A few of the embroidered leaves tickle the underside of one boob.

My hair is mostly down and curled, except for sections at my temples that I've braided and pinned at the back. A few artfully placed pieces of hair escape the confines of the braids and frame my face. I've kept my makeup light. Dewy foundation, a sweep of rosy blush, some winged liner, dark eyelashes, and glossy lip stain complete the romantic look.

My phone buzzes with an incoming text. I grin when I see who it's from.

RYDER

Be there in ten. Is it too much to say that I've missed you? I know I just saw you yesterday morning.

Warmth fills my chest. Some women may like broody, aloof men, but me? I crave Ryder's sweetness and honesty. I love that I know where I stand with him. That he doesn't play games and doesn't want to. It's heady to have a gorgeous man tell you he misses you after less than thirty-six hours apart.

ME

Not too much at all. I've missed you too.

Once I'm pleased with my makeup and my outfit, I

quickly throw some clothes and supplies into an overnight bag and set it by the apartment door. Ryder and I haven't discussed spending the night together after the party, but I'd rather be over prepared than under. I'm pacing the living room floor when another text comes, telling me he's here. I buzz him in, and my heart speeds up a minute later when there's a knock on my door.

"Hi," I say breathlessly when I throw the door open and find Ryder standing there in a perfectly fitted hunter-green suit. His icy eyes melt as they take me in from head to toe. Heat flares in his gaze, and his perfect lips quirk into a pleased grin. My heart does a happy flip when he holds out a bouquet.

"Hey, gorgeous. These are for you."

Sparks fly when our fingers brush as I take the flowers from his hand. The zing of electricity from the contact spreads down to my toes. With a quick sniff of the beautiful buds, I step aside and wave him in. "Thank you. Come in. I'll put these in some water and grab my coat."

The apartment I share with Sarah is a decent size. It has plenty of room for the two of us, especially since neither of us does much, if any, entertaining here. But the minute Ryder Hanson steps inside—all six-foot-whatever of him—the apartment feels decidedly smaller. He takes up so much space as he walks slowly through my home, his head swinging from one side of his broad shoulders to the other while he takes it all in. Not that there's much to see.

This place is temporary for both Sarah and me, and it shows. The living room houses a mismatched sofa and loveseat that were given to us secondhand, and our mid-sized television is the only decoration on the wall facing the couches. There's an Ikea coffee and side table and a couple of ugly lamps Sarah bought at a resale shop. A battered circular dining table fills the space just off the small kitchen, and a narrow hallway sits to the right of it, which leads to our bedrooms and a shared bathroom. The walls are all that bland off-white that comes standard in apartments, and the carpets are a dull beige.

"This is..." Ryder glances back at me. "This is nice."

I laugh as I brush past him and into the kitchen, where I pull a vase from the cabinet. "My roommate and I don't spend much time here," I tell him. "So neither of us has ever really felt the need to do much decorating. It's not much to look at, I know."

Ryder's heat is at my back as I fill the vase. It's so familiar. The firm expanse of muscle pressing against my backside. The warm spread of his fingers across my hips before they skim over my belly. We've known each other for such a short time, and already, this feels familiar. Comforting. A sigh spills from my lips.

"My room is a little more *me*," I tell him as I place the flower stems in the water.

"I'm not sure what I expected," Ryder admits. His fingers play along my lower belly. "I guess you have such a big personality, I was expecting your apartment to match."

Spinning so we're face to face, I lift my fingers to his face and skim the strong line of his jaw, enjoying the scrape of his stubble against my skin. "My roommate and I don't have much in common. We go to the same school, but that's about it. We don't really spend time together, so I guess it's just easier to keep everything the way it was when we moved in."

Ryder nods. His gaze drops from my eyes to my lips. "I

get that. Aaron did some decorating of our apartment, but I didn't even bother doing anything to my room until I'd been with the Rogues for a month. It felt like settling in would jinx things, somehow." His expression shifts from a thoughtful frown to a mischievous smirk. "Speaking of my roommate, he'll be gone all night. Spend the night with me? I'll take you out for breakfast tomorrow and bring you home whenever you want."

Going up on my toes and wrapping my arms around the back of Ryder's neck, I drag his face down so I can kiss the hell out of him. He tastes like mint, and when I sigh against him, his hands go to my hips. A low groan vibrates through his throat as he pulls my hips into his. He's rock hard against my lower belly, and I'm tempted to say *screw it* to the party and drag him into my room. But Ryder Hanson has more self-control than I do, apparently, because a minute later, he separates us with another groan. This time, it's full of regret rather than sex.

"God, Lex. I want nothing more than to bury myself in your tight little pussy right here and now, but I told Maddox and Isla we'd be there." He rests his forehead against mine. Those beautiful, icy-blue eyes of his spear straight through me. "Go pack an overnight bag, baby. We can pick this up later."

"I already did," I admit. My lips twitch when his eyes widen. "It's waiting by the door."

Ryder twists around to look, and his face splits into the most stunning smile when he sees the bag. "That's my girl. You ready to go, then?"

Am I ready? Ready to spend the night with the guy I'm ridiculously infatuated with? Heck, yes. Ready to be surrounded by hockey players who call my dad *Coach*? Not as much.

As always, Ryder doesn't miss a thing. He tilts my chin up with the side of his index finger and presses a kiss to my forehead. "Don't worry, OTG. It's going to be fun, I promise. And if you really end up hating it, we can leave."

My lip gloss is the only reason I resist rolling my bottom lip between my teeth. I stare at Ryder for a moment, noting the sincerity in his blue eyes and the soft smile that plays at his lips. He's not lying. He'll leave if I ask him to. And I know he'd never make me feel bad about it, either. Realizing that eases some of my worry.

"Let's go, hot stuff."

"Hot stuff?" One dark eyebrow lifts.

I make sure he sees my eyes rake down his body before meeting his amused gaze. And then I lick my lips. Sexily. Not weirdly. At least, I hope. "Hot stuff. Because damn, Ryder. You look *really* good in that suit."

His pleased laughter follows me out the door.

thirty-one

LEXI

Maddox Graves lives in a ridiculously swanky apartment. It makes sense, I suppose. He's the captain of the Rogues and the star center. He must make the big bucks, because just the main living area is bigger than my entire apartment.

"Ryder, glad you could make it, man." Maddox clasps hands with Ryder and pulls him in for one of those bro hugs. He's a huge guy. Nearly the same height as Ryder, but he's broad in a way that makes Ryder look almost skinny. Which is ridiculous, because Ryder's all lean muscle and pure strength. Maddox's brown eyes find me over Ryder's shoulder. "Come on in."

"Thanks, Graves," Ryder says with a grin. Then he tugs me to his side and wraps his arm around my waist. "This is Lexi. Lexi, this is Maddox."

The dark-haired man eyes me curiously for only a moment before sticking out his hand and offering me a genuine smile. "Nice to meet you, Lexi. Welcome to our home." Just then, a beautiful redheaded woman sidles up next to Maddox with a roll of her eyes.

"So sorry. Griffin was bugging me about whether we had the ingredients to make him a Shirley Temple." She blows out a breath like she's frustrated, but there's only humor dancing in her blue eyes. "He claims he's not drinking tonight, because he made a bet with your sister that he could get through New Year's entirely sober, but we all know that's never going to happen." Her gaze slides to Ryder and then to me. She greets Ryder with a friendly hello before giving me a huge smile. "I'm Isla. I'm dating this giant over here." She hooks a thumb at Maddox. "Madds told me Ryder might bring a lady friend, but I had no idea he'd bring someone so stunning."

My cheeks heat. "Thank you. I'm Lexi. Your home is beautiful. Thank you for having us."

"And so polite too," she says, smiling wider. "But that makes sense. Ryder always has seemed more polite than any of you." She bumps hips with her boyfriend, who shakes his head and smiles indulgently at her.

Maddox takes our coats, and Isla leads us farther into the apartment, where Rogues players and a few women are spread out, chatting and laughing together. Everyone seems so comfortable. It only highlights how very *un*comfortable I am.

I feel like, any minute now, they'll figure out who my dad is, and things will get awkward.

"So..." Isla offers me a flute filled with bubbly champagne, which I accept. Maddox joins us and wraps his arms around her waist. "How did you two meet?"

I freeze. How did we forget to come up with something

to tell people when they ask us this question? We can't very well explain our naked, serial-killer-adjacent meet-cute without revealing why I was at the cabin, too, and therefore who I am. I force a smile and open my mouth. I have no clue what's about to come out of it, but I'll come up with something, right?

"Lexi and I actually met over a bottle of wine and a shared interest in serial killers." Ryder flashes Isla a megawatt smile while squeezing my hip. "My girl's obsessed with true crime."

I stifle my laughter. That's one way to put it.

Isla clasps her hands in front of her chest. "That's so cute. It seems like everyone meets through dating apps these days. I love a good *we met at a bar* story."

A bar. Right.

Neither Ryder nor I say anything about Isla's bar comment, but Ryder chuckles.

"Yeah, I was just struck by Lexi, you know?"

God, it's almost impossible to hold in my laughter at that one. Resting my head on Ryder's shoulder, I grin. "And I thought Ryder had the most killer smile."

His body shakes with repressed laughter, but Isla doesn't seem to notice. Thank goodness.

"Well, you two are just too cute together—aren't they, babe?"

"Yeah," the big man says with a bemused shake of his head. "So cute."

Sensing her boyfriend's amusement, Isla turns and swats him on the chest. He catches her hand and kisses it. Honestly, they're the cute ones. "Well, please make yourselves at home. There's plenty of food and drinks in the kitchen. The bathroom is down the hall. If you need anything at all, let us know, okay?" She steps away from Maddox to give me a brief hug. "Will you be coming to games once Ryder's back in action?"

I shift my weight from one foot to the other. "Oh, uh, I don't know. We haven't really talked about it."

"Well, I hope you do. I go with Maddox's sister Mira, most games. She's around here somewhere. She's probably hanging out with Griffin. You'll love her."

There's a knock on the apartment door, drawing Isla's attention. "Shoot, sorry. Catch up with you in a bit?"

I nod. "Definitely."

And then she and Maddox are gone. They greet another Rogues player, and I attempt to keep my breathing steady and my heart from racing.

"Breathe, Oscar," Ryder whispers in my ear. "You're doing great. It's just a party. Breathe."

Just a party. Sure.

But I take his words to heart and gulp down a few deep breaths, holding them for a few seconds before slowly blowing them out. I also take a few gulps of champagne, because deep breathing is great for relaxing, but alcohol might be better.

I can do this. It's just a party. And I'm here with the sweetest guy I've ever met.

"Ready to meet the rest of my teammates?" Ryder asks. His voice is still low, and his warm breath tickles the shell of my ear.

Girding myself, I nod. "Yeah. Yes, I am. Let's do this."

His raspy chuckle does funny things to my insides. "That's my girl."

"So, she ran in to make sure I wasn't dying or something and got a full view of my bare ass." Griffin laughs hysterically, Mira rolls her eyes, and Maddox looks like he's ready to kill his best friend.

"Ugh. Last time I check on you when it sounds like you're being murdered." She shudders. "I did *not* need to see you humping the bed in your sleep."

Griffin laughs again. "I can't help it if my wet dream moans sound like murder moans."

"Dude," Maddox says with deep scowl. "I told you not to be gross around my sister. It was a condition of me letting her be your roommate. Do I have to kick your ass?"

"Excuse me?" Mira crosses her arms over her chest and levels her older brother with a glare that would shrivel a lesser man's balls. "*Let me*? In case you've forgotten, you have no say in how I live my life, Maddy-poo."

"Yeah, but I do get to tell my best friend I'll shove a foot up his bare ass if he continues to sleep naked while you're living in the same apartment."

"Come on, man." Griffin leans forward, pleading. "You know the boys need to breathe at night. It's not my fault your sister walked in on me getting some dream lovin'."

Isla wrinkles her nose. "Ew."

"You guys are ridiculous. Help me out, Lexi. You don't think I'm in the wrong, here, right? I was asleep, for crying out loud." Griffin turns his pleading eyes on me, and so does everyone else.

I giggle nervously. "Uh, yeah. I'm not sure what to say about any of this. But you know that cotton is breathable, right? I'm sure your balls would get plenty of oxygen if you slept in some boxers."

Griffin grips his chest dramatically. "Et tu, Brute?

Damn. And I thought you seemed cool." He winks to make it clear he's kidding.

"Don't ask my girl about your balls, Wright. Boundaries," Ryder says. Though he's trying to hide his laughter.

The night is going surprisingly well. Everyone is kind and welcoming, and I'm wondering if judging all hockey players based on my dad and Garrett was a mistake. Would I have met Ryder sooner if I hadn't? Maybe sitting around, laughing my ass off until my stomach aches, could have been a regular occurrence at this point in my life, rather than an experience I'm enjoying for the first time. It's pointless to play the *what-if* game, but it's difficult not to consider it.

Ryder hasn't left my side. He's got an arm around me or a hand on my thigh or massaging the back of my neck at all times. He doesn't seem to notice the covert smirks his teammates are sharing about it, but I do. They're the good-natured looks people give one another when their friend is being sappy and cute. They're happy for him. For us. And it makes me feel all squishy inside.

The Rogues players ask me about myself, and I answer honestly, though I do evade questions that would require me to reveal my status as their coach's daughter. But even that has been less stressful than I worried it would be. All the other wives and girlfriends I meet are kind and funny, and soon, I'm not even thinking about the fact that these guys are hockey players. Or that they play for my dad.

Pressed against Ryder's side on the couch, I can't help grinning. I was so worried about how things would go once Ryder and I left the cabin and took our relationship into the real world. We were so good together in the quiet seclusion of Two Harbors, but there was always the possibility that we'd discover our chemistry was simply proximity and not a genuine connection. But with the way every single one of Ryder's touches fan the flame in my lower belly, and the easy conversation that flows between us, I'm now confident that's not the case.

As the evening goes on, my worries dissipate until I'm simply enjoying our night out together. This could work. We could pull this off. My smile grows, and Ryder matches it as I lean in to press a soft kiss to his lips.

Then the doorbell rings.

thirty-two

RYDER

"I THOUGHT EVERYONE WAS HERE?" GRIFFIN COCKS a brow at Maddox. "Who else did you invite?"

I'm only half listening to their back and forth because I'm so focused on Lexi's warmth at my side. I still can't quite believe she agreed to come with me tonight. Or that she fits in so seamlessly with my teammates. Well, that's not true. I can believe that. Lexi is smart and witty. It's easy to like her, and everyone wants to include her in their conversations. It's as if she was made to fit right into my life.

Maddox rises from the armchair he and Isla have been cuddled up in and checks his phone. "Oh, yeah. I invited Coach to stop by. Didn't think he'd take me up on it, but I guess he's going to dinner nearby, so he said he'd drop in for a beer."

Lexi goes completely stiff beside me as my brain

catches up with what Graves just said. "Wait. Coach is here?"

Maddox nods.

"Shit," Lexi hisses. She's already scrambling out of my hold and rising to her feet. Her eyes ping between the apartment door and the hallway leading to the bedrooms and bathroom. A couple of the guys look at her funny. It's our goalie, Sebastian Navarro, who speaks first.

"Are you okay, Lexi?"

Wide green eyes turn my way. No. Lexi is not okay. She's panicking. And even though I know she doesn't want Coach to find out about us, and I'm going to respect her wishes, I really don't think things would be as dramatic as she believes if he sees us together. But that doesn't matter. Lexi came here trusting me, and I won't squander that trust.

"Wait," I say. It's loud enough that conversation grinds to a halt and all eyes turn my way. I stand and link fingers with Lexi. "This is going to sound batshit crazy, and I don't have time to explain right now, but—" I glance at Lexi. She nods. "—Coach can't know I'm here, and he really can't know that Lexi is here. I need you all to swear not to say anything about either of us. Can you guys do that?"

Every eye in the room bounces between me and Lexi. She can't take her attention away from the door. Maddox runs a hand through his dark hair. "You in some shit, man?"

I shake my head. "It's nothing bad, I swear. It's just... Well, it's complicated. I'll try to explain after Coach leaves."

The Rogues' center blows out a breath through flattened

lips. It's Isla that pipes up and says, "Nobody will say a thing about either of you. Feel free to hang out in one of the guest rooms. I'll come and get you when he's gone." Isla offers Lexi a reassuring smile. And then I'm tugging my girl out of the room, down the hall, and into the farthest empty bedroom.

As soon as the door snicks shut behind us, I hear Maddox's deep voice welcoming Coach into his house. "Well, shit, Oscar. I'm sorry. I never thought your dad would show up here."

Lexi's wide-eyed stare has morphed into something closed off. Something I don't like. She rubs her sternum with her free hand. "It's not your fault. But I should have known better. Coming here was probably a mistake."

Mistake? Bullshit. She's been having fun tonight. I know she has. She's relaxed and charming and she's laughed more times than I can count. Her dad showed up —so what? He won't see us, and I trust the guys not to spill the beans when we've asked them to remain silent. Yeah, we'll have to come up with something to tell all of them, but that's not the end of the world. Right?

Using our intertwined fingers, I tug her forward. She collides with my chest, letting out a soft puff of surprise. With my free hand, I cup the side of her jaw and force her to look up at me. I won't let her shut me out. And I won't let her believe that coming out tonight was a mistake. It wasn't.

"Baby, none of this was a mistake. Are you going to tell me you aren't having fun?" When I rub the pad of my thumb along her jaw, Lexi's eyelids flutter.

"Of course I'm having fun."

"Then, are you saying going out with me was a

mistake?" I'm slightly afraid to hear her answer, but I have to know.

Her mouth falls open and her brow crinkles. "What? No. Of course not."

"Good. Because I don't think it was a mistake, either."

I take a few steps forward, making Lexi shuffle backward.

"I know we'll have to explain now, and that's something you don't want to do, but it's going to be okay."

I take a few more steps forward.

"I get that you're worried about what your dad will say if he finds out we're dating, but I'm willing to take the heat. I don't care if he yells at me or benches me for a few games. You're worth it."

The range of emotions that play across Lexi's beautiful features is truly dizzying. First, her brow wrinkles, and she opens her mouth to speak but thinks better of it. She cocks her head to the side while studying my face. Her perfect lips open and close a few more times. "That's not... You don't understand, he'll..." Frustrated, Lexi shakes her head, and those blonde curls I've been playing with all evening bounce. Frustration hardens her features for another moment, but then it melts away, leaving her looking resigned.

I hate the way her shoulders slump. I press forward two last steps. When the back of Lexi's legs hit the tall bed, she lets out a little squeak and falls on her ass. Hair fanned out around her head like a halo and her mouth opened in surprise, Lexi stares up at me from her back.

"I understand," I rasp as my fingers go to the hem of her dress, which rides up around her thighs. She shivers when I drag it higher. Higher and higher until I can just make out the red lace panties she's wearing. "You're scared, and right now, you're stressed. You need a distraction."

The strangled gasp she makes when my fingers skim along her seam through that thin red lace has my cock standing at attention. I can make Lexi forget that her dad's outside right now, crashing our New Year's Eve. It'll be so very, very easy.

"I'm going to distract you, baby." I slip my index finger beneath the lace. She's soaked for me already. Slick and ready. She lets out a soft moan when I use my thumb to press her clit. I grin. "Shh. Don't want anyone to hear." The look of panic on her face is adorable, and I chuckle. Lexi? Not amused.

"This is a terrible idea. What if my dad walks in?" She looks at the door, then back at me. My girl is torn because I know she's aching for me—her thighs are pressed tightly together—but she's also freaked out about the idea of her dad walking in on us. Which, yeah. That would be bad.

Without a moment of hesitation, I stride over to the door and press the lock. Then I stalk over to Lexi, grab her by the hips, and flip her over so she's on her stomach. She lets out a little squeak of surprise, and I swat her butt playfully. "Quiet, baby. Muffle your cries in the bed, if you have to." And with that, I tug her sexy lace panties off her round ass and down to her ankles. I say a silent thanks to Maddox for being a tall sonofabitch, because it means the bed is taller than most. Between the box frame and the mattress, Lexi's perfect ass and pussy are right where I want them.

"Ryder, we're at a party with your friends. And my *dad* is outside." She hisses the words at me, but her eyes are heavy lidded, and she cuts off with a gasp when I run a finger through her wet slit and press it inside. "Oh, god."

"This may be the first time I take you when other people are around, but I doubt it will be the last. You'd better learn how to come quietly, Alexis."

She squirms as I press another finger inside of her. She whimpers at the intrusion but quickly covers her mouth with her hand.

"That's my good girl." I watch, entranced, as Lexi grows wetter and wetter with every pump of my fingers in her pussy. "Damn, baby. You're turned on by the idea of someone hearing us, aren't you?"

She shakes her head, but the way she presses her ass back into my hand, silently begging me for more, gives her real feelings away. Now I'm imagining fucking her against sinks in bathrooms and eating her out in dark closets. This is...not how I imagined the night going. I'm not mad about it, though.

I play with Lexi for another few minutes until she's writhing and gasping on the bed. Then I grab a condom out of my wallet before unzipping my pants and letting them fall to my ankles. I'm desperate to be inside her. As soon as I roll the latex over my cock, I'm pressing into Lexi's pink, wet heat. With her panties around her ankles, her legs can't spread very far apart, and it makes her impossibly tight. It's my turn to muffle my moans as I bottom out inside of her. I still, breathing heavily and committing the feel of her like this to memory.

"Ryder," she whines. "Please."

That's all I need.

At first, my thrusts are slow and controlled. I want Lexi to feel my cock-head dragging along her inner walls. I want her desperate and needy. Every stroke is a test of my stamina and resolve because she's gripping me so tight, and she's not even coming yet. My pace quickens when pleasure tingles up my spine. Digging my fingers into the globes of her ass, I use Lexi's hips and butt as leverage to thrust into her hot little pussy.

Lexi moans a little too loudly, and I lean over her back and cover her mouth with my hand. She nips at my palm, so I nip her shoulder. That has her back arching and her perfect ass pressing back against me while I pump into her faster and faster. I'm getting close. Fuck, this is hot. I won't last much longer.

Letting go of her ass, I push my hand between Lexi's belly and the mattress until my fingers find her clit. It's an awkward position for me, what with my other hand still covering her mouth, but it lets me fill her deeply. I slam my hips into her ass, my fingers working her clit furiously. My hand barely muffles the sexy-as-hell moans that spill from her lips.

"Come for me, Lexi. Come on my cock." I'm so close. So damned close. But I need her to come first. "Now, baby."

I'm not sure if it's my words, the harsh slap of my hips, or my fingers madly circling her clit, but Lexi comes. Hard. As her body shakes and shudders beneath me, she bites my palm to keep from crying out. Her pussy ripples and clenches around my cock, and I explode. My movements becoming erratic, I press my face between her shoulder blades to muffle my own sounds of pleasure.

We're a twitching, gasping mess as we both come down from our orgasms when there's a soft knock on the door and Isla's muffled voice floats through the wood.

"The coast is clear whenever you two are ready." There's a pause. She clears her throat, and I can almost hear the grin she must be fighting. "Take your time."

Lexi groans, hiding her face in the mattress. I kiss her neck before slowly pulling out. I miss the heat of her immediately. "Let's get cleaned up. Time to face the music."

"That saying is so stupid," she grumbles, turning over and flopping onto her back. Her face is flushed and dewy with sweat. "How in the hell does one *face* the music? You can't *face* a sound." She lets out a little growl. "Doesn't make sense."

I can't help it. I laugh. "You're right, Oscar. It doesn't make sense."

She glares at me. "Shut up."

I lean down and kiss her. "So grouchy for someone who just came all over my dick."

thirty-three

RYDER

We decide to tell them the truth and swear them all to secrecy.

When I lead Lexi out of the guest bedroom, I'm relieved to find that the only people left in the apartment are my teammates and their wives or serious girlfriends. The few casual dates that accompanied some of the guys have been banished to I'm-not-sure-where. It's not that I think any of those women would have ill intentions, but if one of them got pissed at the guy they're seeing and spilled the beans, it would blow up in all our faces. Not just mine or Lexi's, but the guys too. We're about to ask them to keep a secret from Coach.

All eyes are on the two of us as we make our way back to the couch. Lexi's got one hand holding mine, and the other wrapped around my arm like she's scared I'll ditch her to deal with all of this alone. I never would, of course, but she's freaked out. I get it.

"So," Logan Byrne—our first-line right winger—pipes up from his seat on the couch opposite us. He eyes us speculatively. "Why were the two of you hiding from Coach?"

I glance at Lexi. She blows out a deep breath, making her hair flutter around her face. I open my mouth to speak and spare her from having to explain, but she beats me to it. "My name is Alexis Cross. Your coach is my dad."

You could hear ice melt.

Every single guy in the room stares at Lexi like she has two heads. Isla and Mira don't seem all that surprised, but then again, they don't have the kind of relationship with Coach that would make this front-page news.

Griffin narrows his eyes at my girl. "Wait a second. I've seen a picture of you on Coach's desk. Aren't you like fifteen?"

His roommate, Mira, smacks her palm against her forehead. Logan barks out a laugh, Maddox shakes his head, and Sebastian shoots Lexi an apologetic grimace.

"It's an old picture, dumbass," Maddox grumbles. "Obviously."

Lexi shifts uncomfortably beside me. "I'm twenty-three. Not fifteen. Jesus."

"Oh." Griffin nods, like that makes much more sense. Because it does. "Right. Sorry. Carry on."

"How did you two meet?" our goalie, Sebastian Navarro, asks. He poses the question to Lexi, and god bless him for it. His tone is soft and soothing, and it helps Lexi relax beside me.

"Ryder tried to garrote me," my insane girl says with a smirk in my direction and complete deadpan delivery.

Maddox chokes on his beer. "I'm sorry, what?"

Rolling my eyes, I pinch Lexi's thigh. She *yelps*, then

breaks out in a fit of giggles. "She *thought* I was going to murder her," I clarify. Okay, so that's not much better.

"I really feel like we're missing a vital part of the story here," Logan drawls.

"You guys know my dad sent Ryder to his cabin for the week, right?" Lexi asks. The guys all nod. "Okay, well, what my dad didn't know is that I was already there and planning to spend a relaxing week alone."

"During Christmas?" Griffin's brow creases. "Why would you want to be alone during Christmas?"

Lexi sighs. "My parents got a divorce, and it's made holidays a little...awkward. I didn't want to deal with my mom and her boyfriend, and my dad and I don't exactly have a great relationship." She shifts in her seat beside me. "Which is probably obvious because I've never been to a Rogues game and none of you had any clue who I was. My dad's probably never even mentioned me by name, right?"

The guys wince. Because, no, he hasn't.

"Right." Lexi nods, because this is exactly what she expected. "So, I didn't tell my dad I was heading up to the cabin. Didn't think he'd care either way, to be honest, so I didn't see the point." She shakes her head. "Anyway. I was soaking outside in the hot tub when Ryder arrived, so I failed to hear his car or him entering the house. He was standing there like a total creep in all black when I waltzed my oblivious ass inside, and since I had been listening to some true crime podcasts on the drive in, I naturally thought he was there to murder me."

"Naturally," Logan parrots with a smirk in my direction.

"Sooo, I hit him with a wineglass, he saw me naked, and eventually, as we yelled at each other through a closed door, we realized what had happened." Lexi's cheeks are stained pink with the revelation that I saw her naked. I don't think she meant to say that part out loud.

"I have so many questions," Griffin mutters.

"Just let them tell the story," Mira says. She pats him on the head, and Griffin settles in beside her.

"Right," I say, picking up where Lexi left off. "After we talked, I decided to leave. I obviously wasn't planning to crash her week alone. But the weather had other plans. My car couldn't even make it down the driveway. So, we got snowed in together for a week." When I glance at Lexi out of the corner of my eye, she's smiling. I pause the story to give her a kiss on the forehead. The guys let out a collective *awww* sound, which makes her giggle.

"Anyway. I quickly realized that Lexi is amazing and practically begged her to give me a chance. And I don't know if it was all the snow causing a beer-goggle effect, or if she was bored, or what, but we ended up clicking and she agreed to give dating me a try."

"And you don't want to tell Coach?" Sebastian asks me.

"I don't want to tell him," Lexi says. "Ryder would tell him, but I don't want to. My relationship with my dad is...complicated. It's not worth the drama it would cause."

"You think he'd retaliate against Ryder?" Maddox leans forward, his elbows on his knees.

Lexi shifts uncomfortably again. "No, it's not that, but if Ryder doesn't play at the top of his game this season, my dad will blame it on me, and I just..." She sighs deeply, her lips twisting into a frown. "Look, I know it's shitty to ask you guys to keep this from him, but I'm not ready to deal with all of that. So, will you keep it a secret? Please?"

Sebastian's brow furrows as he studies Lexi. "He's your

dad. Why would he blame Ryder's performance issues on you?"

"Yeah," Griffin pipes up. "No way would Coach do that. You're his daughter."

Maddox clears his throat. "Remember that time earlier this year in the locker room and what he said when he ripped me a new one for defending Isla from those asshole fans?"

"Oh." Griffin frowns. "I guess I do."

Shit. I remember. He told Maddox that hockey had to come first. That, when he was coaching, hockey was everything. He didn't have a wife or a daughter. He wasn't a husband or a father. He was just *Coach*. How could I have forgotten that?

"What did he say?" Lexi asks, her tone wary.

Maddox shakes his head. "It's not worth repeating. All you need to know is that, if this is what the two of you want, we'll support you."

"Thank you," Lexi murmurs.

"So, you're not going to come to our games and cheer Hanson on?" Griffin gives me a sad look. He knows there's nothing better than having someone who loves you cheering from the seats. And they all know my parents are both gone.

No one cheers for me from the seats. At least, not anyone that matters.

"I... It wouldn't be a good idea," Lexi says. She looks up at me with a frown. She's smart and perceptive, so I'm sure she doesn't miss the distant look of longing I'm trying to hide.

"And what if things get serious between you two?" Sebastian asks.

Giving Lexi a squeeze, I say, "We'll figure that out when we get there. For now, this is all new. Will you guys agree to keep this quiet?"

"Of course they will," Mira says with a pointed look at Griffin.

"Yeah," Maddox agrees. "We'll keep it a secret."

Logan shakes his head, incredulous. "I'll keep my mouth shut, but watching all of you twist yourselves into pretzels for relationships makes me damned sure of my decision to avoid them. Too much work. Relationships are inconvenient."

Maddox grins at him. "Just wait, Byrne. You'll fall hard one day and change your tune." He runs his fingers through his girlfriend's hair. "Best inconvenience ever."

Logan Byrne, chronic bachelor, doesn't look convinced. Hell, he didn't even have to kick his date out for this conversation. Because he didn't bring one. He *never* brings one. Since I've played with the Rogues, never once have I seen Logan do more than hook up with a woman. And we all know about his one-and-done rule. He never has sex with a woman more than once. He never takes them out for anything more than a few drinks to loosen them both up, and he *never* spends the whole night with them.

We give him so much shit for that one because the guy actually sets an alarm to wake him up in the middle of the night so he's out by the time the poor woman he's spent the night with wakes up. I suppose they know what they're getting into—he's brutally upfront about what he is and isn't willing to give—but it seems so hollow. Especially now, with Lexi snuggled up next to me. Logan has no idea what he's missing.

"Not that you ladies aren't cool," Byrne says to Isla,

Mira, and Lexi between sips of his beer. "But I like my life the way it is. I enjoy plenty of female companionship. And I also enjoy my freedom. Not sure why I'd want the complications a relationship would bring."

"Companionship." Isla snorts. "You can't even remember most of their names the next day. Don't act like you're in it for the *companionship*."

"Oh, come on, Isla," Griffin teases. "Byrne's dick gets lonely. Even if he doesn't."

We all laugh at that. Even Lexi beside me. She was so tense when her dad showed up, but she's back to her normal, charming self now. She piles on the teasing everyone levels at Logan, and I can't help thinking that she fits in so well here with me. With us. And I know she's not ready to go public yet, but I can wait her out. One day, she'll sit in the family box with Isla and Mira, wearing my jersey and cheering me on. It's going to happen. I'll do whatever I have to in order to get us to that point.

"I bet the girls you've slept with have a Facebook group or something," Lexi says between giggles. "Oh, I bet they call it *Feeling The Byrne* or *The Byrne Book* or something. And they all post their pictures and share their stories and compare notes about their sexual encounters with *the* Logan Byrne. And probably their latest STI test results."

Mira laughs so hard, champagne sprays out of her mouth. Griffin howls with laughter, and the rest of the guys join in. Logan gives Lexi the evil eye. He almost looks menacing. Or, at least, he would, if his lips weren't twitching.

"I'll have you know, I'm totally clean."

"You probably single-handedly keep your doctor in business," Maddox teases.

"I wonder if any of the nurses are in your Facebook group?" Isla giggles. "If you signed a waiver, they could probably cut out the middleman and just give your conquests a clean bill of health."

Bash shakes his head. "That would be a HIPAA violation."

"That's why he'd have to sign a waiver," Isla replies.

Logan looks over at Lexi and says, "See what you started?"

"Sorry, not sorry." She rests her head on my shoulder. She's fitting into my world so seamlessly.

We spend the next couple of hours joking and laughing with everyone. And when the live feed on TV starts counting down from ten, I wrap Lexi in my arms and revel in this unexpected turn my life has taken.

Ten.

"I'm glad you're here."

Nine.

Her big green eyes blink up at me.

Eight.

"Me too."

Seven.

"Making you come earlier…"

Six.

"…wasn't nearly enough."

Five.

Lexi flushes and presses her face into my chest.

Four.

"I can't keep my hands off you, OTG."

Three.

My thumb brushes the side of her breast, and Lexi shivers.

Two.

She presses her hips into mine, and I groan.

One.

I cup her face, completely enraptured by her.

Happy New Year!

Leaning down, I take Lexi's plush lips in a slow, sensual kiss that leaves her breathless. Her mouth chases after mine when I pull just far enough away to whisper in her ear. "Happy New Year, Alexis Cross. I can't wait to see what this year brings."

thirty-four

LEXI

"DID YOU HAVE FUN TONIGHT?" RYDER WRAPS HIS arms around me in the middle of his massive king-size bed. It's two in the morning by the time we get to his place, and despite his promise to ravage me as soon as we arrived, we're both way too tired. He gives me a quick tour of the apartment he shares with his teammate, and I'm barely awake enough to snoop. It's decently sized, but nothing as extravagant as Maddox's place. From the little I was awake enough to see, it's the epitome of a bachelor pad.

There are jerseys and team flags on the wall instead of artwork, a massive television with two different gaming systems, and the whole place is fairly monochromatic. Outside of the jerseys, they've decorated everything in varying shades of gray. Ryder's bedroom is much the same, although he has a golden-yellow comforter that reminds

278

me of the gold and gray combination that makes up the Rogues' team colors.

The one thing I do notice is a few framed photos on his dresser. One features a man and a woman with smiling faces hugging an adorable dark-haired toddler. It must be Ryder's mom and dad and a stupidly cute, young Ryder. The other photo is of a teenage Ryder with the same man, only older. His dad. The older man has his arm thrown around Ryder's shoulder. It must have been taken at the end of a game, because Ryder is in full uniform. His dark hair is sweaty and plastered to his face, and a faint bruise shadows his jaw. But they're both smiling widely. It's infectious. My heart pangs for Ryder's loss. And there may be a secondary pang for teenage Lexi, who has no such photos with her dad looking proud and fatherly.

We brush our teeth and fall right into bed. He's cute as hell when he yawns.

"I did have fun," I say with a sigh as I nestle into his arms and rest my head on his chest. More than I was expecting, if I'm being honest. Ryder's teammates were all hilarious and welcoming, and they surprised the heck out of me by agreeing to keep our secret so easily. They even looked pissed off on my behalf when I explained some of my dad's disinterest. Which is a new sensation. To have people other than Rachel in my corner. It's nice.

"I didn't know Graves invited your dad. I wouldn't have suggested we go if I knew." Ryder plays with my hair as he speaks. His long fingers massage my scalp and glide through the curls. He presses a kiss to my forehead, eliciting a happy sigh from me.

"Don't worry," I reassure him. "I know." We both fall silent, and my thoughts turn to my dad. I don't exactly invite him into my life anymore, but there's a reason for that. I've been burned too many times. Waited for him with my eyes on the audience, only to have his seat remain empty too many times. I've cried tears he didn't deserve more times than I can count. Didn't someone say the definition of insanity is doing the same thing over and over again and expecting different results? Well, maybe I expected my dad to show up when I was a kid, but I sure as hell don't anymore.

Yet, there he was, tonight. *Stopping by* one of his player's houses on the way to his plans just because Maddox asked.

God, that stings more than it should.

Ryder's fingers stroke along my collarbone. "You okay?"

"Yeah," I lie. "I'm good."

Fake it 'til you make it. Lie it until you buy it. That's more accurate. Because I'm not just lying to Ryder, I'm lying to myself. I'm good. Or I will be. I don't care that my dad seems to care about everyone else more than he cares about me. Or I won't care, eventually.

"I'm going to go on record and say that I don't believe you," Ryder says softly. "But I get it, so I'll let it slide."

I muffle my chuckle against the naked expanse of his chest. "How magnanimous of you."

"I thought so," he says. The gentle stroke of his fingers down my arm is so comforting, my eyes start to close until Ryder speaks again. "Spend the day with me tomorrow? We can go out for breakfast, then do whatever you want."

I like the idea of going out for breakfast. It's so normal. So mundane. I want those moments with him.

"Sure. That sounds fun." I yawn, and Ryder chuckles.

He pulls the covers up to my chin. "Go to sleep, baby. Sweet Dreams."

IT'S ILLOGICAL, BUT I FEEL LIKE EVERYONE IS staring at us.

We're sitting in a booth at this cute little breakfast place I never knew existed, and we're getting quite a few furtive glances. It's probably all in my head, but I can't help worrying that someone will recognize Ryder, take a picture of the two of us together, and that photo will somehow make its way into my father's hands.

"Relax," Ryder says, reaching across the table and grabbing my hand. His thumb rubs little circles over my skin. "Why do you look like you're freaking out?"

Probably because I am?

"I just...people keep looking at us."

Ryder makes a surreptitious sweep of the room with his eyes and shrugs. "They're probably wondering what a gorgeous woman like you is doing out with a big oaf like me."

"Riiiiight," I drawl. But he's accomplished what he wanted, because I can't stop the grin that overtakes my face. He matches my expression, and those stunning, icy-blue eyes of his crinkle at the corners. "Because you're so unattractive."

Every straight woman in this place checked Ryder out when we walked in. And likely some of the non-straight women too. Everyone can appreciate a beautiful specimen like Ryder Hanson. Objectively speaking, he's near perfection. Tall, muscular, with a strong jaw, a straight nose that he's somehow never broken in all his years playing hockey, and a smile that could melt the frozen panties off an actual ice queen.

I don't blame them for looking, and I certainly don't blame them for appreciating him, but that doesn't mean I particularly like the attention he's getting. Nor do I appreciate the hollow pang of jealousy that clangs in my chest.

But Ryder, bless him, hasn't seemed to notice anyone but me. Even when our server comes by and offers him a flirtatious smile, he simply rattles off his order with barely a glance in her direction. He only has eyes for me.

The problem is that it's not only the women who are doing double takes when they notice my handsome date.

"I think that guy recognizes you," I whisper to Ryder when the man sitting a few booths down with his wife pulls out his phone, leans in close to her, and points at Ryder.

"Maybe. I come here a lot, and some of the staff know who I am. But I don't get recognized very often. Not like Maddox or those guys. I'm still a rookie." Ryder shrugs before taking a sip of his coffee. "I'm not sure I really have fans."

He does, actually. I know because I stalked him on social media that first night we were stuck together in the cabin. His profile was completely clean. No pictures of half-naked women, no drunken videos, nothing even slightly scandalous. Just photos of Ryder working out, photos of him on the ice, and a few videos of his most impressive plays.

It's the fan sites and the hashtags that are scandalous. Ryder's a good-looking man. And the women of Minnesota have noticed. They salivate over shirtless photos, speculate about the size of his dick, and discuss—in raunchy, utterly inappropriate detail—all the things they want to do to him. I felt dirty just reading a few of those comments.

I'm not sure if Ryder is unaware of his female fanbase, or if he's choosing not to mention them, but either way, it's adorable. Plenty of guys in his position would crow like roosters about all the women who want him.

He's down to earth. And even though he doesn't seem put off by the occasional recognition by fans, he also doesn't seek it out.

"So, when do you find out if you're cleared to play?" I ask him once our server drops off our breakfast. I have mixed feelings about Ryder's hand healing. Obviously, I want him to get better quickly, but getting better means getting the go-ahead to play, and then he'll be back on the road. Getting snowed in was its own kind of bubble, but Ryder's injury is another.

I know how demanding an NHL schedule is. Not only watching the effect it had on my parents' marriage, but also experiencing the effect it had on me. Relationships where one person is constantly on the road are difficult. They take commitment and work, not to mention a massive degree of trust and understanding. I'm getting to know Ryder in the middle of the season, but with the rare opportunity to have uninterrupted time together.

Who knows how things will go when he's back on the road?

Ryder flexes his injured hand, staring down at the stitches that cut a gruesome path down his palm. "Not sure yet. I'm supposed to see the doc tomorrow, but I'll probably be out for another week at least."

He misses being on the ice, something that is obvious from his tone. And I think, being a rookie and all, he still doesn't feel like his spot is secure. I'm sure he's itching to get back in the game.

"Do you miss it? It must be frustrating to be benched."

"Yeah." He blows out a breath before shoveling a massive bite of eggs into his mouth. He considers his next words while chewing. "I was having a great start to the season before Chase pulled that shit. I felt like I was making a name for myself on the Rogues, you know?"

I do. I grew up on hockey. Loved it for a long time. Until things with my dad soured it for me. But I still follow along occasionally. Not religiously, or anything, but I keep up with the team's wins and losses. And, even though I didn't recognize Ryder when we first met, and I thought he was a serial killer, I've heard a few people talk about the rookie who has the potential to become a powerhouse star.

"I'm sure you'll pick right back up where you left off," I reassure him.

Ryder stares at me over the rim of his coffee mug. "I sure hope so, OTG."

We fall silent, both of us taking a few bites of food. I consider asking Ryder about Chase. He said they were best friends in college and played on the same team, then had a random falling out, but there must be more to the story. I open my mouth to ask him when a throat clears beside us.

"Um, excuse me. I don't want to be rude, and interrupting your breakfast is practically the definition of rude..." The man from a few tables over who'd been pointing at Ryder shifts his weight from one foot to the other while staring at my date. "But I just have to ask—you're Ryder Hanson, right?"

Ryder glances at me, then smiles at the man. "Yeah, that's me."

The middle-aged man claps and does a little shimmy shake with his hips like a teenage girl who's just found out that the boy she's crushing on likes her back. "I told my wife, but she didn't believe me." He glances back at his table. "See, Sheila? I was right."

His wife, Sheila, apparently, lets loose a long-suffering sigh. "Bill, leave the poor man alone. Can't you see he's having breakfast with a lady friend?"

"Oh." Bill's eyes dart to me. He grimaces. "Uh, sorry." He returns his attention to Ryder. "Do you think we could take a quick photo, and then I'll leave you alone? I'm a huge Rogues fan, and I just know you're going to be a star one day soon. I want to tell my kids I met you."

Sheila groans and shakes her head from their table. "We don't have any kids, Bill."

"We could," he shoots back. "You never know."

"I really do," she replies. "Menopause, remember?"

I can't help it. I giggle. The fan's wife meets my eyes and mouths, *sorry*. Turning to her husband, I smile and say, "Would you like me to take the picture?"

"Oh, would you? That would be amazing. Thank you so much."

"No problem," I reply as he hands me his phone. Ryder's a good sport about the whole thing. He smiles, takes a few photos with Bill-the-superfan, and even signs the guy's polo shirt. When he sits back down at his own table, he regales his wife with a full play-by-play of what just happened, even though she saw the whole thing. She shakes her head but smiles.

If that's not true love, I don't know what is.

"Well, that was entertaining," I whisper, leaning across the table. "And you said people don't recognize you."

Ryder's cheeks flush an adorable shade of pink. He scrubs a hand along his jaw, scratching at the dark stubble growing there. Somehow, he's both incredibly sexy and ridiculously cute with that one motion.

"Yeah, well, it really doesn't happen often." Taking another bite of his eggs, he grins an embarrassed, boyish grin at me. "Sorry about that."

"Are you kidding?" I say. "That was way too cute, and I'm glad I got to witness it."

And I am. I'm thoroughly enjoying every new glimpse behind the curtain.

We finish breakfast and spend the rest of the morning wandering around downtown Minneapolis. We don't have a destination in mind. It doesn't matter where we go or what we do, as long as we can hold hands and flirt shamelessly while we do it.

I wish I didn't need to go back to school in a few days. The temptation to blow off classes is strong, but I can't let myself lose focus. The sooner I get my masters, the sooner I can land a good job. Once I've done that, I can stop relying on my parents and make my own way. Ryder and I will find time to see each other. It'll be fine.

When he asks me to spend another night with him, it takes all of my willpower to decline. I need to get back to the real world. And I also need to do laundry. Which means going back to my place. Even though my bed feels like a lumpy rock compared to Ryder's. And it'll be cold without him beside me.

I'll need to get used to it. Soon, he'll be cleared to play. And sleeping beside him won't be an option when he's on the road for days or a week at a time.

thirty-five

LEXI

"God, I'm so jealous of you right now." Rachel sighs dramatically, and I chuckle. The gusting Chicago wind whips through her long brown hair. Her cute little button nose and her enviously high cheekbones are rosy. But like the winters in the Twin Cities, January in Chicago is no joke. I don't know why she refuses to take the bus or the L to her internship, but she won't. She walks everywhere. Her warm brown eyes focus on me through the phone. "When does he go back to playing?"

It's the million-dollar question. One I've been trying not to dwell on, because I'm not ready for the distance it will put between us. My attention swings between the world in front of me and my best friend's face on the phone screen. Students rush to their next classes all around me. Their pace, like mine, is more urgent in the winter temps than it would be if it was warm out. The frigid weather, combined with my desire to be near Ryder twenty-four-seven, has made the transition back to classes after the break a rough one.

"He should find out this week. His appointment with the doctor is tomorrow. They won't necessarily have a definitive answer then, but his hand is healing well." So well that I constantly have to remind him to take it easy. I can tell he's itching to get back on the ice. If I've discovered one thing about Ryder Hanson, it's that he doesn't like to sit still for long.

Rachel hums. "But you should have another week with him at least, right?"

"I think so. I'm telling myself not to count on it, though." Better to brace for disappointment than hope for the best. I've learned that the hard way over the years.

"I don't know, Lex. It kinda seems like you can count on him." Rachel's holding back on bestowing the full scope of her approval until she meets Ryder, but from the things I've told her, and apparently from the *glow* I'm rocking these days, she's already a fan. "I get that you don't like counting on people, but maybe it's okay to try this time."

"Maybe," I agree. "I just... I don't know, Rach. It's all..."

"Freaking you out how much you trust him already?" Her thin lips curve in an understanding smile.

I wobble my head from side to side noncommittally. "Maybe."

"That's okay. This is still new. Just give it time and a real chance. You deserve to be happy and loved, Lex."

Loved. It's far too early in our relationship to be thinking along those terms. But I also can't deny that I've daydreamed about it. What it would be like to be loved by Ryder Hanson. What it would be like if someone in my life put me first. But that's a dangerous wish to nurture. Ryder is in the first year of a two-year contract. He needs to play well this season and maintain that momentum so he can negotiate an extension. Hockey is his livelihood and his passion. It's understandable if I come second to that. Still, I can't help it. When I'm lying awake in bed at night, I daydream about Ryder telling me that nothing is more important to him than me.

Does that make me selfish? Delusional? Sad? I don't know. Rachel's right, though. I need to give whatever this is time to grow into whatever it could be.

"Is it terrible that I want to look up the guy who injured Ryder and send him a fruit basket while simultaneously wanting to punch him in the dick?" I grin as Rachel chuckles. "He is the reason we met, after all."

"What's his name again?" Rachel asks.

"Chase Bowen."

Her eyes narrow. "Right. He plays here, doesn't he? For the Chicago Blizzard?"

I nod. "Yep. He and Ryder used to be close."

"I'm going to get tickets to one of their games and hold up a mean sign the whole time," my best friend vows. She looks so serious, I can't help laughing. A few students glance my way, but I don't care. Rachel is my ride or die. Her loyalty is unparalleled. I'm lucky as hell to have her in my corner. Apparently, Ryder has her in his now, too.

Laughter spills from my lips as I get closer to the building where my next class is held. "Oh my god, Rach. Please do that. I swear, that would make my whole year."

Her earthen eyes glint with determination. "Oh, I will. I'm going to look up games and ticket prices as soon as I get off the phone with you. I'll get Adam to go with me."

God, I love her. "You're the best, you know that?"

A strand of russet hair whips across her face, making her sputter when it gets stuck to the gloss on her lips. She pushes it out of her mouth with a huff. "I know."

I'm about to commend her modesty when I spot a large crowd gathered near the entryway of the building housing my next class. "What in the world is going on?" I mutter.

"What?" Rachel peers at me through the phone.

"There's a big group of students near the door of Pryor Hall. Which is weird, because it's cold as hell out here." Narrowing my eyes, I try to figure out what's causing the flash mob. It's an eclectic mix of male and female students. Quite a few of the guys look like athletes. They have the build. I can tell, even though they're all wearing heavy coats. The women, though, are what throw me off. They're all chattering excitedly to themselves, giggling, and batting their eyelashes. It seems like they're converging around someone.

And that's when I see a black knit cap pulled over familiar dark hair.

Ryder is significantly taller than most of the surrounding people, except for one or two guys. He's smiling and taking photos with the students, but he looks bemused. Like he can't quite believe these people are even remotely interested in him.

"Oh, my god."

"What?"

"Look." I tap the icon to switch my phone off selfie mode and point the camera at Ryder and his gaggle of giggling fangirls and fawning fanboys. As I get closer, I can see that he's clutching two cups of coffee, and my heart swells, even though a small part of me bristles at the flirtatious looks and touches the women give him. To his credit,

Ryder dodges as many of the touches as he can. It still rankles.

"Is that Ryder?"

I flip the camera back to selfie mode and grin. "Yep. It looks like he brought me coffee. Someone must have recognized him and caused a swarm."

Rachel shakes her head, smiling. "How weird is it that you're dating a guy who gets swarmed with fans?"

"Weird," I say. And it is. I've seen people and reporters swarm my dad after games. At times, it was fun and exciting. Then there were the times when I needed my dad, and he was so preoccupied with the people around him that he didn't even notice I was there. Where it had been exciting and cool when I was younger, it became a source of bitterness and frustration as I got older. Seeing Ryder like this elicits a complex cocktail of emotions.

On the one hand, I'm so freaking proud of him. That he's getting recognized as a first-year player is impressive. It speaks to how well he's been playing so far this season. It's also adorable to watch him interact with people and be so confused by their attention. On the other hand, it makes my insecurities scream. If this is the kind of attention he's getting as a rookie, what will it be like when he really comes into his own? Because I know enough about hockey to recognize that Ryder Hanson will only go up from here. He's skilled and driven, and the way he's gelling with the rest of the Rogues is magical. He's going to be a force to be reckoned with. A household name. The level of attention he receives will only grow.

Can I handle that?

Do I want to?

"Your face is doing something weird, Lex," Rachel says. It pulls me from my spiral. "You okay?"

"What? Of course. I'm good."

My friend only hums. She doesn't completely believe me, but she doesn't call me on it. Rachel is aware of my issues with fame. I vented to her many times during our four years as roommates. "He's not your dad. You know that, right?"

"Yeah," I say. That doesn't mean my logical brain always wins out. As I'm about to reassure Rachel that she doesn't need to worry about me, Ryder's head snaps up and his eyes lock on me. The biggest, broadest smile overtakes his handsome face, and some of my worries ease. An answering smile lifts my lips.

"He just noticed you, didn't he?" Rachel sounds amused, but I'm too busy staring at Ryder to look at her.

"Uh-huh."

"Right," she says with a laugh. "I'll talk to you later. Go have fun with Loverboy."

I offer a distracted *bye* of my own before Rachel disconnects our video call. I shove my phone into my coat pocket as people glance behind them, trying to figure out what's caught the pro hockey player's attention. Ryder doesn't notice any of them. He takes a few steps toward me before one of the guys asks him something.

Ryder's brows pinch. I can tell he's conflicted. He glances at me, then back at the student who says something else. Ryder gives him a short answer. He's too polite to blow his fans off completely. Even if he may want to. I keep walking toward him, and Ryder tries to step around one of the female students. She puts her palm on his chest and says something before glancing back at me. A high-pitched giggle I can hear from fifty feet away grates over my ears. She uses her other hand to touch his bicep, and I feel my smile slip.

Jealousy and annoyance slice through my chest. Who does that woman think she is, touching my man? Ryder tilts his head slightly, and his eyebrows pull together. He shrugs out of the woman's grasp, saying something to her that makes her cheeks flush. She looks pissed when she turns back to glare at me. I glare right back.

I don't like you, either, I silently taunt.

With a few more words and a couple nods of his head, Ryder extricates himself from the crowd and closes the distance between us. The more space he puts between the horde of adoring fans, the more my chest loosens, though I'm still annoyed. I'm annoyed at the flirtatious women who had the nerve to put their hands on Ryder. I'm annoyed at him for not telling them to fuck off the moment he saw me. But most of all, I'm annoyed with myself. My reaction is not logical. I know this. If I had any doubt about how quickly the dark-haired hockey player has wormed his way into my heart, this situation would have made my feelings crystal clear.

I like Ryder Hanson. A hell of a lot more than I should, considering we've only known each other for about two weeks. If I could bitch-slap my overeager heart to snap her out of this and remind her she needs to be more careful, I would. It pisses me off how quickly he's slipped past my defenses. How important he's become in such a very short time.

"Hey, baby," Ryder says softly. He hands me a coffee. It frees up his injured hand, and he wastes no time tangling it in the hair at the nape of my neck and pulling me in for a slow, sensual kiss. Despite my general annoyance, I melt into him and kiss him right back.

Take that, desperate coeds.

I'm immediately pissed at myself again for the ridiculous thought and the simmering jealousy I can't quite shake.

"What are you doing here?" I ask when we finally break apart. Despite my best efforts, the words are sharper than I'd like them to be.

He's doing something sweet. He brought you coffee. Stop being an irrational asshole, Lexi.

One dark eyebrow quirks up. He untangles his hand from my hair and points to the hot cup of coffee in my hand. "Bringing my girl some caffeine." His fingers wrap around my hand and the cup, forcing me to bring it to my lips. A smirk hovers at the corner of his mouth. "Which I think you need, Oscar."

The coffee is hot, sweet, and perfect, but I still glare at him as I take a few sips. "Don't call me that."

"Then don't be such a grouch." The man has the audacity to laugh when I let out a pathetic little growl.

"If I'm such a grouch, why don't you go back to your adoring fans?" *Why? Why did you let that slip past my mouth, brain? What the hell is wrong with you?*

Ryder's second eyebrow joins its compatriot at his hairline, and that stupidly cute smirk blooms into a full-blown smile. "And why would I want to talk to any of them? I happen to find grouchy women sexy."

"You do not."

Even the wind seems to laugh at me. It trills and howls

as it whips through the grounds and tangles my hair. The flirtatious blonde who was all touchy-feely with Ryder watches us, along with a couple of the sporty-looking guys. They're probably laughing at me too. Or wondering why Ryder-Freaking-Hanson is entertaining dirty looks from a woman who looks like the winter version of the Pillsbury Doughboy in her pink puffer coat. I don't look cute today. I look cold and makeup-less. I growl again.

Following my line of sight, Ryder spares only the quickest glance at the crowd behind him. Then those frosted blue eyes that dance and sparkle like unmarred ice in the sun turn back to me. His lips twitch. "Alexis Cross. Are you *jealous*?"

Yes.

"What? No. Of course not." I hide my scowl behind the coffee cup as I take another sip. I can't believe he showed up at my school with a latte for me. He's so stinking sweet and thoughtful. Who does stuff like this? The annoyance I'm feeling with myself only grows. I'm the worst. I'm cranky and grouchy and irrational. Despite wanting to say thank you and tell him how much it means to me that he's done all this, I'm still stewing in emotions that have very little to do with him and almost everything to do with me and my feelings of inadequacy.

Unfortunately, self-awareness doesn't always translate into a corresponding action.

Anyone else would walk away from me right now. Who wants to spend their afternoon doing nice things for a prickly woman who can't seem to just say *thank you*?

But Ryder isn't anyone else. His face softens as he pulls me against his chest and kisses my forehead. "You are totally jealous. It's cute, OTG. I kinda like it."

Ass.

Warm lips brush against my forehead again. "But you should know that you have no reason to be jealous. The whole time those people surrounded me, all I could think about was you. These pouty lips of yours, the way your eyes light up when you see me. I didn't even notice any of their faces. I was too busy looking for yours."

Okay. So maybe he's not an ass.

"You're seriously cute when you're pissed off and jealous, though. Made me hard." He presses his hips forward, and the firm length of him pokes into my hip.

Indignation battles with lust inside me. Focusing on the indignation means I have a smaller chance of combusting into a pool of arousal in the middle of my peers. So, I choose indignation. "I am *not* cute when I'm mad. What the hell, Ryder?"

The damned man simply laughs. He throws his head back, and the deep, melodic sound I'm coming to love pours out of him. More eyes turn our way, but he doesn't notice. Once he's gotten himself under control, Ryder focuses on me. He's not put out by my irrational prickliness. Not at all.

Something tight and scared inside me begins to unfurl.

"Sorry, Oscar, but you are. You're cute when you're mad, you're adorable when you're jealous for no reason, and you're hot as hell when you yell at me." He leans in to whisper in my ear, so only I can hear. "Makes me think of all the times you've screamed my name with my cock buried deep inside your tight little pussy."

Despite the frigid temperature and the wind blowing all around us, my insides turn molten and gooey.

"You can't get rid of me, baby. I don't scare easily."

Plush lips feather across my frozen cheeks, making them tingle. "But if it makes you feel better, go ahead and give me your worst. I can take it."

thirty-six

RYDER

"Rookie! You're here." Logan Byrne slaps me on the back as I enter the weight room. "Does that mean you got good news from the doc today?"

A few of our teammates gather around. They're all good guys, and they've been checking up on me while I've been out with my injury. Everyone is eager for me to get back on the ice. It's been amazing, actually. They're starting to feel like family. I'd forgotten what it was like to have other people worried about you, and I don't hate it. Not at all.

Flexing my injured hand, I grin. "They have me doing some physical therapy, but they said I should be cleared in a week and a half."

It's a bit earlier than they'd recommend in a perfect world, but there's so much on the line right now. I pushed them into clearing me sooner with the promise that I'd keep my damned gloves on when I'm skating. And I will. I have no desire to risk further injury. But I also don't want to risk my place on this team. From the first week playing with them, I knew I wanted to be a Rogue long term. Now, with Lexi in the mix, that has become more important than ever.

Logan grins and claps me on the back again. "That's great news. Have you told Lexi yet?"

Shit. As soon as her name leaves his mouth, I scan the room for Coach. Logan notices my tense expression and grimaces.

"Sorry, man. I wasn't thinking."

"It's okay," I tell him. "But we should probably give her a code name or something. I hate keeping secrets, but I want to be able to talk about her."

Sebastian Navarro nods. "That's a good idea. What should we call her? Do you have a nickname for her or something?"

Chuckling, I shake my head. "She'd be pissed if you guys started calling her by the nickname I gave her."

"Oh?" Navarro chuckles. "Now you have to tell us what it is."

"Yeah," Griffin Wright pipes up. "Spill the beans, Handsome."

Handsome. It's the stupid name the guys gave me the first time I showed up in a game-day suit and the female fans went crazy online. It's ridiculous, but once more than one guy latches on to a nickname, it sticks. Plus, it's close enough to my last name that it doesn't bother me much.

Running my good hand through my hair, I blow out a breath. "You guys have to swear not to call her by this. She'll have my balls if you do."

Griffin starts to say something stupid, but Maddox cuts him off. "No one will call her it."

The rest of the guys nod, so I tell them. "I call her OTG."

Confusion pinches their faces. Navarro cocks his head to the side and asks, "OTG?"

"Yeah," I say, grinning now. She's going to be so pissed if she finds out I told them this. Oh well, there's no getting out of it now. "Stands for Oscar the Grouch. Sometimes I just call her Oscar."

My explanation is met with a beat of silence before the room erupts into laughter.

"Wait, wait, wait." Logan continues to laugh through his words. "You call her Oscar the Grouch, and she still sleeps with you?"

"Um, yeah. But you guys see why you can't call her that, right? She needs a different code name if we're talking about her here."

"Yeah, man," Griffin slaps his thigh as he howls with laughter. "Damned right, we'll need a different code name. Shit, you're lucky she hasn't ditched your ass. Most women would have your head for something like that."

I shrug. "Lexi's cool." Realizing I said her name again, I scan the room for Coach or the assistant coaches. It's just players in here right now, thank god. "I've never met a woman like her."

"Oh, you're fucked," Logan says. He looks amused. And like he can't quite understand why anyone would get into the situation I'm in, let alone a relationship so serious, you do something crazy, like ask your girlfriend to move in the way Maddox has.

One day, he'll understand. And when that day comes, we're all going to give him hell for it.

"Whatever, man. I'll happily be fucked any day by that woman." My double entendre is met with a few chuckles.

"Ooh, I've got an idea," Griffin says, bouncing on the balls of his feet. "Sexy Lexi."

"Dude." Navarro shakes his head. "That literally has her actual name in it."

"Right." Griffin frowns. His eyes unfocus as he tries to come up with another option.

"Blondie?" Logan offers.

"Nah." It's too generic for her. Too boring.

"Wait!" Griffin claps. "I've got the perfect idea. HCB. Like OTG, but this one stands for Hot Cross Buns."

There's a beat of silence as everyone gapes at him.

I clear my throat. "Hot Cross Buns?"

"Yeah, man. Because of her last name. It's like that rhyme. Get it?"

"Are you sure it's not because you think she has a nice ass?" Logan asks.

Griffin looks offended. "Dude, I don't look at my friends' women's asses." His lips twitch. "Just thought it was funny."

"HCB?" Maddox grins. "That good with you, Hanson?"

I shrug. "I guess it's better than Sexy Lexi."

"All right. HCB, it is." Maddox turns to the rest of our teammates. "Got that, guys? I don't want to hear anyone slipping up. We don't want to screw this up for Handsome, here."

A chorus of agreements fill the weight room and I grin at my teammates. I'm lucky to be surrounded by guys who have each other's backs. Most of them go back to racking their weights and working out, but Byrne, Navarro, Wright, and Graves hang around. Logan repeats his earlier question.

"So, have you told her yet?"

"Not yet. I came straight here." And I may be putting it off. I need to figure out how to tell her. Or, more importantly, how to reassure her that things between us won't change when I'm back on the road. After the tidbits I've learned about her childhood—no matter how little, at this point—I'm worried it could be an issue. It just means I'll have to be intentional about our time apart. Lots of phone calls and FaceTime. Lots of romantic gestures. She's going to need reassurance that I'm always thinking about her.

"It'll be fine," Navarro says, accurately reading my worries. "You two seem good together."

"Who's good together?" Coach asks as he strides into the weight room. My stomach twists, but I must not show my discomfort on my face, because Coach flashes a pleased smile. "Heard the good news, son. A week and a half, and you'll be back on the ice where you belong."

"Oh, hey, Coach. Yeah, I'm excited to be back." I exchange a look with Maddox.

"Now, who's good together? You got a girl, Hanson?" Coach waggles his eyebrows in a way he surely wouldn't if he knew my girl was his daughter.

"Uh, yeah. It's new," I say. I'd rather be purposefully vague than outright lie.

Coach nods. "Women are great, as long as they're not a distraction from what matters. Your game's not going to suffer, is it? I'd hate to see you lose your fire over a good lay."

Jesus Christ. What the fuck?

I'm bristling from his crass and, frankly, disgusting words. Even if it wasn't his daughter I was dating, what the hell kind of thinking is that? Are women really just a distraction and a good lay to him? How the hell can he say stuff like that when he was married and has a grown daughter? The rest of my teammates look equally appalled. Even Byrne, who's never had a real relationship in his life. But as far as I can tell, that's because his issues are with relationships themselves, not women in general. He may never sleep with the same woman twice, but he treats them with respect. He and Wright may have joked about sex or made the occasional lewd comment, but somehow, this feels different.

I'm pissed on Lexi's behalf.

Clearing my throat, I try to control my anger. "I'll always play my best, Coach. Regardless of my relationship status."

He must take that as me agreeing with his sexist sentiment, because he nods. "Good man. That's what I like to hear. We've had enough distractions this past season with this one." He hooks his finger in Maddox's direction. Our captain scowls.

Distractions or not, after getting past a preseason slump, Maddox has been on fire so far this year. Everyone has off games. Even the single guys. To blame poor performances on spouses and partners is bullshit. We all agree on that. Coach doesn't seem to have the same qualms.

Maybe he's not the good man I thought he was.

"Right." Coach claps his hands. "Enough talk about women. We're here to work, so let's get to work! Hanson, take it easy on that hand. Only legs for you." He surveys the room, barks out a command to quit dicking around, and strides out of the weight room.

"How is your girl so cool when she was raised by someone with views like that?" Griffin muses.

"Honestly? I'm wondering that myself." I'm practically buzzing with angry energy.

"Well, I guess we all know why his wife left him," Sebastian mutters under his breath. "It can't have been fun being married to a guy like that."

Or being raised by one.

Damn. Now I'm really determined to show Lexi how amazing she is and how much I want her. It'll be hard once I'm back on the road, but I'll work my ass off to show her that not everyone is like her dad. And that, while he may be blind to what an extraordinary woman she is, I'm not.

"Bring your girl around anytime," Maddox says, resting a hand on my shoulder. "Isla loved her, and we all think she's cool."

"Mira loved her too," Griffin pipes up. "I know she's looking for more girlfriends now that she's back in Minnesota. You'd think rooming with me would be enough socializing for her, but she says she needs other women in her life. Whatever."

Emotion creates a lump in my throat, and I swallow thickly before I can reply. "Thanks, guys. We'd love to hang out more. Her best friend is all the way in Chicago, so I'm sure she'd enjoy making a few female friends."

Maddox nods. "We'll plan something else soon. In the meantime, ask HCB if she'd be willing for you to give me her number. I can pass it along to Isla and my sister. They'll make sure she's included."

"Thanks, man." My voice is gruff. They're accepting Lexi, and I appreciate the hell out of them for it. But they're also accepting me. They're making sure we both have people in our corners. "I'll definitely ask her."

"Good," Maddox replies. His expression shifts from protective mode to captain mode in an instant. "Now, go do some leg presses or something. We can't have you out of shape for your first game back."

I grin, giving him a salute.

Nope, we can't have that. I've got a lot to do to prepare for my triumphant return to the ice with the Rogues. For now, I'll focus on my strength training. Tonight, I'll start the more important prep work.

I can't wait.

thirty-seven

LEXI

RYDER SHOWS UP, UNANNOUNCED, AT MY apartment at six p.m. The first thing I notice is the beautiful bouquet of flowers in his hand. The second thing I notice is the way his navy blue Henley hugs every dip and ripple of his muscles. Which is why I just stand there staring, dumbstruck, for a solid fifteen seconds before he clears his throat. His lips twitch with effort as he tries to hold back an amused smile. Even if he'd succeeded, his eyes give him away. They crinkle at the corners, sparkling, even in the crappy fluorescent hellscape that is our apartment building's hallway.

"Gonna let me in, Lex?"

"Huh?" His laughter has me shaking my head to clear away the fog. "Oh, yeah. Sorry."

Stepping aside, I wave Ryder in. Once the door's shut, he hands me the flowers. They smell amazing, and I let myself sniff them for a few seconds. My roommate, Sarah, pops her head out of the hallway.

"Someone here?" She surveys Ryder. Sarah and I don't have much in common, but by the way her eyebrows lift and her jaw goes slack, I'd say we can at least agree that Ryder is hot as hell.

"Ryder, this is my roommate, Sarah." Ryder gives her a little wave, which makes her blush. "Sarah, this is my..." My brow pinches. I realize I don't know what to call him. We haven't really had that conversation yet. "This is Ryder."

"Her boyfriend," he finishes for me with a wink. I turn to look at him, and whatever my face is doing makes him chuckle. But he ignores me for now in favor of saying, "Nice to meet you, Sarah."

She mumbles something unintelligible in response, then ducks her head back into the hallway and leaves us alone.

"Boyfriend, huh?"

Now that we're alone, Ryder sweeps me into his arms, flowers and all, and slants his lips over mine. I can't help it. I moan into his mouth. And when he ends the kiss much sooner than I'd like, I whine. It's not dignified, but he doesn't seem to mind, if the self-satisfied smirk on his face is any indication.

"Yeah. Your boyfriend. I guess we could play it cool for a while longer if you really want, but I figure it's inevitable. Why not call it what it is?"

"Cocky much?" Honestly, he has every right to be cocky. He's sweet and hot, and just showed up at my place with the most beautiful bouquet anyone has ever given me. I could deny that I want him to be my boyfriend, but what would it get me?

A very hard, very impressive bulge presses into me as Ryder replies, "Hell, yeah, OTG. Extremely cocky."

I giggle, but it turns into a soft moan when Ryder presses his thigh between mine and uses his grip on me to grind my pussy along his jean-clad leg. My mind goes to that day at the cabin, when he made me come just like this. "We can't do this out here," I say breathlessly. "Roommate."

"Say you're my girlfriend and I'll stop." He grins wickedly and nips at my lower lip.

"I'm your girlfriend." He draws a gasp out of me when he grinds me along his leg again. "Oh, fuck."

And just like that, Ryder stops. Despite the fact that I'm the one calling for a sexual ceasefire, I can't hide my disappointment. The way lust addles my brain and lights my entire body on fire every time he touches me is insane.

Blue eyes closing, Ryder tips his head back and groans. "Damn, Alexis. It's so hard to keep it together around you." His hands roam over my back. "But I came here to ask you to get food with me. As much as I want to carry you over my shoulder caveman-style into your room so I can ravish you, I was hoping we could talk a bit about how things will go once I'm cleared to play."

The fizzy bubbles of happiness that have been tickling my stomach begin to pop. Every word Ryder has spoken, every gesture he's made runs through my internal processors. He can't be breaking up with me. The man just claimed me as his girlfriend in front of my roommate. Maybe my dad found out about us? No, he looks too calm for that. I suck in a slow breath.

"Lex? Your face is doing something weird right now. Are you okay?" Ryder squints at me. The longer he looks, the more his smile slips.

Get it together, Lexi. I suck in a deep breath and hold it for five seconds before releasing it. "I'm good. Totally fine. Dinner, you say?"

Ryder's head tilts to the side. And then his eyes widen. "Babe, this isn't a bad conversation. When I say I want to talk about things, I mean I want to plan out our schedules so I can see you as much as humanly possible."

Of course, that's what he meant. *Not everyone is champing at the bit to ditch you, Lexi.*

"Sorry," I say, genuinely embarrassed at my reaction. But I suppose it's better to show Ryder my crazy and my issues sooner rather than later. That way, if he sticks around, I'll know he really likes me.

One slow, sweet kiss to my forehead later, Ryder meets my gaze. "You have nothing to be sorry about. Now, let's get those flowers in some water, then grab some food. I didn't do full body training today, but I did enough that I'm hungry again."

That breaks the tension. Pro athletes' appetites are nothing to scoff at. And I had a long day of classes today, so I could eat too.

"What do you have in mind?"

SOMEDAY, I HOPE RYDER LOOKS AS LONGINGLY AT me as he's currently looking at my double cheeseburger.

"God, watching you eat that thing is pure torture." Ryder groans, scrubbing his hand over his face before glaring at his über-healthy dinner of chicken and broccoli. "But I went off plan so many times at the cabin, I really need to buckle down now."

"Poor baby," I coo through a mouthful of burger.

"Watch it," Ryder warns with a twinkle in his eyes. "Or I'll spank that perfect ass later."

Hand over my heart, I gasp for dramatic effect before rolling my eyes. "That supposed to scare me? Don't threaten me with a good time, Hanson."

He laughs at that. Free and loud and with his head thrown back. Ryder's responses to me are always enthusiastic and genuine, and it thaws some deeply frozen part of me that's used to being an obligation, or a stepping stone, or background noise. I'm none of those things with him, and I wish I could take back my panicked reaction earlier. Which is why I draw in a slow breath, suck it up, and start the conversation, so he doesn't have to.

"You had your appointment with the doctor today, right? How'd it go?"

Those stunning blue eyes survey me as he takes a bite of broccoli. "Really good, actually. I should be cleared to play in a week and a half. I have to go in daily for physical therapy, but everything is looking good."

"That's so great," I say. And I mean it. Sure, there's a flutter of worry in my belly about what this will mean for our relationship. But it's like the fluttering of a singular insect's wings, not the frenetic flapping of a whole murder of crows. Manageable. Reasonable. "That means your first game back will be a home game, right?"

Ryder flashes me a mouth full of white teeth as he smiles. "Yeah, it does. You keeping track of my schedule, OTG?"

I shrug. "Maybe." What I don't tell him is that I've been tossing around the idea of going to some of his home games. But incognito, and in seats where my dad would be unlikely to spot me. After New Year's Eve with Ryder's teammates and Isla and Mira, I've been thinking regularly about how much I want to watch my man on the ice. To support him and cheer him on, the way Isla and Mira cheer on Maddox and Griffin. But I'm not ready to commit, yet. And when I do, I want it to be a surprise.

So, yeah, I'm familiar with his schedule. If I'm going to get tickets, I need to do it soon. They're playing well so far this season, which means fans will want to get in on the action.

"So, on the subject of schedules, I know we are both busy and that your classes take up a lot of your time. And obviously, my games can be pretty consuming. I want you to know that I will make time for you." He looks so serious now. Food forgotten, Ryder rests his elbows on the restaurant table and leans forward. "I'm not always great with time management. And I can forget about things if they're outside of my normal routine." He scratches at the stubble along his jaw. He looks like he's working up the courage to say something vulnerable, so I reach across the table and grab his hand.

"We can figure out a system."

"Actually, I think I already have." He swallows a gulp of water while looking at me from beneath the long, dark fringe of his eyelashes. After a few seconds, he reaches into his pocket and pulls out his phone. "There's this shared calendar app I thought we could try. We can both enter our schedules, and it blocks the day out in color-coded squares. That way, it's easy to see when one of us is free, and we can add our dates and plans."

Ryder flips his phone so I can see the screen. There's a colorful weekly calendar. Ryder has physical therapy and practice blocked out, errands he needs to run, even the time between my classes the other day when he surprised me with coffee. He's way more organized than I am. "I know it's kind of lame, but would you be willing to give it a try?"

I give his hand a squeeze. "Actually, I don't think that's lame at all. I'm impressed with your organizational skills."

"It's more of a survival skill than an organizational one, but thanks." The faintest blush colors his cheeks.

"What's the app called?"

He tells me, and I download it immediately. Once it's installed, we set it up so we can share a calendar, and Ryder grins at me. "Thanks, Lex. Obviously, you don't need to put everything on there, just maybe stuff that impacts when we might normally see each other? I swear, I'm not trying to stalk you."

I chuckle. "Are you sure? You could still end up being a serial killer."

An absolutely salacious look overtakes his features. Leaning forward, Ryder whispers, "Baby, the only thing I'm going to murder is your pretty pussy. In the best way, of course."

Well, damn. Now my panties are wet and my face feels hot. Ignoring Ryder's deep laughter, I take an overly large bite of my burger and avoid making eye contact. But all I can think about is Ryder scheduling a time for his big cock to impale my pussy.

Being stabbed may not be the worst way to go.

thirty-eight

LEXI

IT'S BEEN YEARS SINCE I'VE SET FOOT IN AN ARENA. I used to love going to hockey games. What's not to love? The slightly chlorinated scent of the ice, the excited chatter of thousands of fans, the greasy, overpriced concession food, and a fast-paced game full of men on skates. I wish I'd never let my ex and my dad taint the sport for me. I've missed this.

Scanning the arena to make sure I don't spot anyone I know—namely, my dad and his assistant coaches—I get comfortable in my seat. I'm quite a few rows up near the neutral zone, which gives me a great view of the entire rink but also lets me blend in with the crowd. In a perfect world, I'd be down by the boards, cheering on my boyfriend and heckling the other team.

The Rogues are playing the Seattle Leviathans today. They're a good team with an enthusiastic fanbase, but we're better. The arena is a sea of yellow and gray. Only a few specks of Seattle's navy and teal break up the wave of Rogues' colors. Beer is flowing, people shout greetings to their neighbors, and signs wait to be unfurled.

I have one ready too. And since I know my dad and the team will have their backs to me when they're on the player's bench, I plan to use it. It's a drawing of a certain furry green monster in a trashcan with a speech bubble that says, "Take out the trash, Ryder!" I'm no artist, so my Oscar looks a little wonky, but he'll get the point across.

Ryder should know he has someone here cheering him on. That, despite my dad, I'm here for him.

I just hope I don't end up regretting this.

My nerves kick up when the announcer introduces the Leviathans. Every new player that's named makes my heart beat faster. This is the first time I'll get to watch Ryder play in person. It's the first hockey game I've been to in ages. And I'm risking being seen by my dad. I'm also nervous for Ryder. He feels so much pressure to play well and keep his spot on the team. I want that for him. I also don't want him to get injured again or worsen his hand.

I'm a giant ball of nerves by the time the lights in the arena go down, the strobes kick on, and the announcer begins introducing the Rogues. People cheer and scream for each new player. The volume grows louder and louder as they go. When Ryder's name is called out, I join in with the cheering fans around me and scream his name.

Ryder's smile is electric as he takes to the ice and waves at the fans. He's back in his element, and a thrill of pleasure shoots through my belly to see him this way. Happy. Energized. Plus, he looks hot as hell in his uniform. Something the women seated behind me seem to agree with as they comment on how they'd like to sink their teeth into his ass. I laugh and barely resist the urge to turn around and tell them that's my boyfriend they're talking about.

But that would *not* help me remain incognito.

I cheer when they introduce the guys from Maddox's party. And then they announce the coaches. My stomach twists when my dad strides out onto the ice in a crisp, expensive suit. He looks so confident and happy. His sandy blond hair has more gray in it than the last game I watched. His tall, imposing form is still strong, though he's a little softer around the middle than he was when I was younger. But he looks good. Do I want him to look miserable without me? I can't decide. It hits me harder than I thought it would to see him out there like this. But I'm not here for my father. I'm here for my boyfriend.

When my eyes find Ryder again, some of the tightness in my chest eases and my stomach stops roiling. God, how can he have such a profound effect on me already? We've known each other for less than a month. It doesn't make sense, but I also don't want to question it. It's nice having someone in my corner that gives a shit. Someone who centers me and encourages me. The fact that he can bring me to orgasm faster and more times than anyone else ever has isn't a hardship, either.

The Rogues' players skate around the ice for a few minutes to warm up, and when Ryder's facing my direction, I hold up the sign. He's so focused on what he's doing that he doesn't notice right away. But Logan Byrne does. Byrne flashes me a huge smile, then elbows Ryder, prompting him to look up into the seats. When his gaze finds me, I nearly melt from the absolute joy that radiates from him.

He finds my face first. His eyes widen and his lips part.

Like he can't believe I'm actually here. Then his attention wanders to the sign I'm holding above my head, and he doubles over with laughter. Logan joins him, and soon the rest of the guys are chuckling, though they make sure not to look at me all at once, so as not to draw my dad's attention. Ryder stares at me, shaking his head, grinning like a fool. I mouth *good luck* before he skates away. The women behind me wonder loudly who I am.

I'm his girlfriend, I think as affection surges through me. *And I'm in big trouble.*

THE ROGUES ABSOLUTELY KILL IT. LOGAN MANAGES an impressive hat trick, Sebastian only lets one goal through, and Ryder has an assist in the third period that brings the final score to 4-1. The fans go crazy, and I scream my lungs out. I wish my best friend, Rachel, was here to enjoy this with me. Or that I had more friends in Minneapolis. I'm sure Isla and Mira are here in the family box, but I can't sit up there. Not without my dad finding out. And while most dads in his position would be thrilled their daughter came to one of their games, my dad would simply wonder why I was here.

And I don't want to try to come up with a believable lie.

I linger as the rest of the arena clears out, careful to avoid anywhere my dad might appear. Ryder texted me as soon as they hit the locker room, asking me to go out with him and the rest of the team. They're going to a local bar called Chasers, which is their normal post-game hangout. Since I took an Uber to the arena, I'm waiting around for him. But I can't head to the employee lot without risking being seen by my dad.

Fifteen minutes later, Ryder texts that he's waiting outside the main entrance of the arena, and I rush to meet him with a stupid grin on my face.

"Hey, baby," he says, scooping me up in a hug. He twirls me around, kissing me, before setting me back down and opening the passenger door for me. "I can't believe you're here." His blue eyes are crystalline and bright as he scans my face. "Why didn't you tell me you were coming?"

Tucking my blonde hair behind my ear, I shrug. "Wanted to surprise you. And I figured, this way you, wouldn't know if I chickened out and didn't show."

Ryder's head tilts back at that, and he laughs loudly. "Fair enough. God, I can't believe you're here." There is so much affection and joy in his expression. No one has ever been this excited to see me. Except maybe Rachel, but that's how best friends are supposed to act when they see you. None of my previous boyfriends have ever looked at me with quite as much open delight as Ryder does now.

My heart flips pleasantly. He's so different. *I'm* different with him.

I love it.

"I couldn't miss your first game back." Pushing up onto my toes, I grab the lapels of his suit jacket and pull him down for a kiss. Our mouths tangle with fervent need. Ryder pulls away too soon, and his lips quirk against mine when I whine at the loss of them.

"As much as I want to push you up against my car and take everything your hot little body is offering, we should probably go before someone sees us." He pulls back just enough to study my face. "Unless you've changed your mind about keeping us a secret from your dad?"

"No." I groan. "You're right. Let's go." I slide into the leather passenger seat, and Ryder shuts the door behind me.

"You sure you're good with hitting the bar with the guys?" he asks when he gets in beside me. "Isla and Mira should be there too. But if you'd rather be alone, we can go to my place."

"I want to go," I reassure him. As much as I'd love to get Ryder alone and have my wicked way with him, this was his first game back, not to mention a fantastic win. I won't be that selfish girlfriend that keeps him from cele-brating with his guys.

The Rogues cheer when we walk into the bar. They're all holding beer bottles, laughing, joking around with each other. When Ryder and I approach the massive corner booth holding half the team, Isla, Mira, and several hopeful puck bunnies, a few of the guys slide out so I can scoot in and be near the other women.

"To the rookie," Griffin says, plunking bottles in front of us and lifting his own in the air. "That assist was killer, Handsome."

"To Handsome," the guys cheer. Isla chuckles beside me.

"Handsome?" I ask Ryder with an arched eyebrow.

He shakes his head, covering a smile by taking a swig of his beer. "Yeah. It's stupid, but it stuck. Apparently, some of our female fans think I'm attractive."

I laugh, because yeah. The man has fan groups dedi-cated to his ass. A few of the women hanging around the outskirts of the group, hoping for some attention from one of the good-looking hockey players, stare openly at Ryder. He doesn't even seem to notice. Just wraps his arm around my shoulder and kisses my temple.

"Lexi, it's so good to see you again," Isla says when one of Ryder's teammates demands his attention.

"Yeah," Mira agrees. "You should have told us you were coming to the game so we could have sat with you."

I return their warm smiles, grateful for how kind and welcoming they are. "Oh, I'm sure you ladies were sitting in the family box, and I wanted to stay incognito. Don't want my dad to know when I'm at a game."

Mira's smile turns commiserating. "We don't always sit in the box. Sometimes we like sitting down in the stadium seats right by the glass."

"Except for that time we got heckled," Isla says with a grimace. "That sucked."

My brow rises at that. "You got heckled?"

"Yeah," she says. "It was shortly after Maddox and I came out with our relationship and he was having an off game. The fans around us seemed to think that was my fault. He almost started a fight with a few of them."

Barking out a laugh, I glance at Maddox, who steals looks at Isla every few seconds. Like she's the sun, and he's helplessly stuck in her gravitational pull. It's sweet. And after a month of dating Ryder, I can finally admit to myself that I want what they have. They don't question the other's love. They're clearly secure in each other. I want that.

"I heard about that, actually." I suppose I simply hadn't put two and two together that Isla was the woman Maddox had jumped in to defend.

"It's not usually like that," Mira tells her friend with a pat on her hand.

Isla nods. "I know." She turns to me. "Next time, tell us when you're coming. We'll sit with you."

Warmth fills my chest. Ryder gives my shoulder a squeeze, like he somehow knows exactly what I'm thinking and feeling. How much the easy acceptance they've offered means to me. I've been so busy with my master's program that I mistook busyness for happiness. But I've missed having friends around me. Missed sharing nights like this with people who get me and like me.

I need to plan a trip to visit Rachel soon. She's my person, and I miss the hell out of her.

"Okay," I relent. "Next time, I promise to give you ladies a heads-up."

Mira pulls her phone out of her purse and hands it to me. "Put your number in."

I do, and a moment later, my phone buzzes with an incoming text.

HOCKEY HONEYS
MIRA

Isla, this is Lexi's number. Lexi, store our numbers in your phone.

Grinning, I cock an eyebrow as I look up at Mira. "Hockey Honeys?"

"I like alliteration," is her reply. "And I couldn't come up with anything better on the fly."

"I like it." Isla giggles. "It's lame but perfect."

My phone buzzes again. This time, it's a gif with some bees wearing makeup. I store the number with Isla's information, then add Mira's. The three of us laugh.

"Hope you don't mind ongoing and ridiculous text threads," Mira says.

I shake my head, snuggling into Ryder's side. "Not at all. I can't wait."

The night goes by in a blur of drinks and laughter. Ryder can't keep his hands off me, though we're both careful to make sure no one snaps any photos of us together. The last thing I need is a picture of us kissing to show up on some hockey fan site. The other guys help shield us from unwanted attention as well, and I am so thankful. It allows me to relax and enjoy my boyfriend and the friendships developing with the people around this table.

Ryder tugs me out of the booth at the end of the night because I can't seem to keep my eyes open any longer. As we say our goodbyes, the only thing that would make this night better is if we didn't have to keep our relationship a secret.

Not for the first time, resentment for my father curdles in my belly. But then Ryder kisses me before clicking my seat belt into place, and that resentment is replaced by contentment.

This may be more complicated than I'd like, but Ryder Hanson is worth every inconvenience and subterfuge.

thirty-nine

RYDER

"How do you know you've found the one?" I ask the guys as we get ready for an away game against the Boston Renegades. Despite the energetic chatter of the locker room, Maddox, Griffin, Logan, and Sebastian give me their full attention.

"The one?" Logan narrows his eyes. "You've been dating Hot Cross Buns for how long?"

"Dude." I shake my head.

"Apologies," he says with a smirk. "HCB."

Although I agreed to that stupid code name, right now, when he's using it to tease me, it's pissing me off. Noticing my annoyance, Logan grins wider. "And to answer your question, we've been dating just over a month now."

And we've spent every possible minute together. It's been much more difficult to carve out time now that I'm back on the ice, and Lexi's course load isn't anything to scoff at. My woman works hard. So, I show up with coffee or lunch whenever I can to surprise her between classes and steal some moments together.

We're playing the first of a five-game away streak tonight, and even the thought of being away from Lexi for that long has me tense and agitated.

"Dude." Logan shakes his head as he pulls his jersey on. "What's the rush?"

"Ignore him," Maddox says. "Byrne wouldn't know *the one,* even if she lit his hair on fire."

Logan pales and his hand goes to his sandy-blond hair. "Don't even say things like that."

Sebastian's shoulders shake with silent laughter. "I can't wait until you fall so head over heels you can't shut up about her. We'll never let you forget how completely against love you were."

"Not going to happen," Logan replies confidently. "Love is a lie and marriage is just a piece of paper."

"Just because your dad treats it that way doesn't make it the truth." Navarro braces a hand on Logan's shoulder. Logan brushes Bash's words and hand off, but he can't hide the haunted look that overtakes his eyes for a split second before he manages to school his expression.

"You think she may be the one?" Griffin asks, bringing the conversation back around. He grins like a little boy surrounded by puppies. Ever since Maddox and Isla got together, the guy is in love with love. Actually, I'm not sure he wasn't always that way. Some of the things he says make me think the guy's always been a closet romantic.

"Maybe," I say as I bend over to lace up my Bauers. If this isn't love, I don't know what it is. Infatuation? I'm not sure that covers it. Every second of the day, I'm consumed with thoughts of Lexi. I wake up hard as a rock, dreaming of her lips on me, her soft body welcoming mine. Whenever I have a free minute, I'm calling or texting her. I fall asleep with the image of her face painted in vivid colors across my eyelids. Nothing she says bores me. I want to know everything. All the moments of her day. All the thoughts that cross her mind. And I want to tell her everything. Not since my dad passed have I felt so close to another person.

She's *my* person. And I think I'm hers.

"You two are cute as fuck together," Griffin says.

Maddox nods in agreement, even though he'd never use those exact words to describe Lexi and me. "It's different for everyone. I think, for me, it was realizing that I could no longer imagine my life without Isla. There wasn't some huge lightning-strike event that made me see it. More like a thousand little moments that added up to an undeniable truth. Loving Isla became part of my DNA. She burrowed under my skin. And when I thought she was getting back together with her asshole ex-fiancé, it killed me. I was so pissed and so hurt, but even then, I never stopped loving her."

"But is it too soon?" I ask, giving voice to the thought that haunts me.

"You planning on proposing when we get back, Handsome?" Maddox's brow lifts.

"No, of course not." That's not to say I haven't had thoughts of proposing to Lexi *someday*.

Our team captain and star center leans forward in his spot on the locker room bench, resting his elbows on his knees. "There are only two people in the world who can answer if it's too soon to know whether HCB is *the one*. And that's you and her. Anyone else's opinion is just noise,

Rookie." He rises to his feet, grabbing his stick. "But for what it's worth, you're different since you've been with her. You're happier. More focused. Settled in yourself, you know? I can't tell you if she's the one, but I can tell you love her."

I can tell you love her.

Do I? Do I love her? I'm crazy about her, sure. Can't stop thinking about her. But *love*? Do I *love* her?

Shit. I think I love her.

Maddox chuckles. "Admitting it to yourself for the first time, aren't you?" He pats my back a few times, jarring me from my thoughts. "Yeah. It's a mind fuck."

Yeah. It is.

MY RIBS ARE BRUISED, AND I'VE GOT A SPLIT LIP after an altercation on the ice with the Renegades' second-line right winger, but not even my sore body can temper the anticipation I feel when I get to my hotel room and flop onto the queen-size bed. My roommate for the trip is out with the rest of the guys at a bar celebrating a hard-fought win, but I begged off for the night. I need to see Lexi's face. Hear her voice.

My girl picks up on the third ring. Tension melts out of my body when her beautiful face fills my phone's screen. Her green eyes widen when they fall on my split lip. Pushing her golden hair away from her face, she takes the rest of me in. "Oh my god, babe. Are you okay? I can't believe that asshole tried to start shit with Bash."

I can't, either. Everyone knows you don't go after the goalie. That's why I got into a fight. Normally, I stay out of brawls, but the prick with a shitty attitude and straggly lip sweater cross-checked Sebastian into the pipe. All because Navarro was on fire tonight and he'd easily ignored all the right winger's immature chirping.

Shit like that can't stand. So, I went after the guy. Totally worth the time I spent in the sin bin for it too.

"He won't start anything with Bash again," I say with a feral grin. It tugs at my split lip, but I couldn't care less. Lexi's pupils blow wide. Apparently, my girl is a little bloodthirsty. Damn. This woman is perfect for me.

"I miss you," she says, giving words to my own thoughts. "So much. Is that too needy?" She grins. "I don't care."

Chuckling, I unbutton my dress shirt. "Nah, OTG. Not too needy at all. I miss you too. Wish you were here."

"Me too. Stupid school." Lexi blows out a deep breath. Her eyes track my fingers as they undo the next few buttons. Heat fills those beautiful green irises, and her lids lower to half-mast. Her tongue darts out and swipes across her lower lip. "Stupid distance."

"You know, there are plenty of things we can do to feel close to one another, even with thousands of miles between us." I waggle my eyebrows at her and am rewarded with a bright peal of laughter.

"Oh, yeah? And what, exactly, do you have in mind, Handsome?"

My chest warms at her use of my nickname. I like the sound of it on her lips a hell of a lot more than when the guys on my team use it. When I've flicked the last button open, I sit up and shrug out of my dress shirt and jacket. Lexi's greedy emerald eyes track across my now-exposed chest. A pretty pink flush spreads across her cheeks, and I can't help thinking about other pretty pink parts of her body.

"You alone, baby?"

With her lower lip rolled between her teeth, Lexi nods.

"I want to see you. All of you. Would you do that for me?"

Her pupils blow impossibly wide at that, but she looks unsure. Primal satisfaction wells up within me. My girl-friend has never gotten naked over FaceTime. I'll be her first. And her last.

Shit. I can't entertain thoughts like that yet.

"Are you alone?"

"Of course, I am," I reassure her. "I would never let anyone else see you. You're mine, Alexis. Only mine."

Lexi's eyes bounce across my face, assessing me for a few beats, but then she smiles shyly. "And you're mine, Ryder Hanson."

"I am," I agree. "And I'm hard as a rock right now. Because of you. *For* you. I want to come watching you touch yourself." Flicking open my suit pants, I strip down to my boxer briefs and pan the phone down, so she can see exactly what she does to me.

"I've never done this," she whispers when I bring the phone back up to my face.

She needs reassurance that she's safe to take this step with me. She needs to hear that I would never—not *ever*—betray the trust she'd have to put in me to allow herself to be vulnerable like this. And I don't blame her. Revenge porn is a real, and disgusting, reality for women. But even if things between us blew up in spectacular fashion, I would cut off my own hand before allowing anyone to see private images of Lexi. Not that I'd even consider recording what happens between us if she decides to give it a try.

"No one's around to see you, baby. And I would never record you. I need you to know that. Even so, there's no pressure. If you're not comfortable with this, I won't be upset. Or if you'd be more comfortable turning the video off, we could still have plenty of fun together that way."

She considers my words carefully, but I can see how turned on she is. Which is why I'm not surprised a moment later when she squares her jaw and says, "I trust you, Ryder."

I trust you, Ryder. Have I ever heard four sweeter words?

My cock grows rock hard when Lexi chews on her lower lip before setting her phone down and stripping her shirt off. The camera points at her, and I greedily catalog every perfect, smooth inch of her body. Her chest heaves in a simple gray cotton bra, and it's just as sexy as the lacy little numbers I've seen her in. Hell, I don't care what Lexi wears. She's always sexy.

"God," I breathe. "You are so stunning, baby." She glances at me and flushes. "Would you take your bra off for me?"

She only hesitates for a second, and then the cotton garment slips off her shoulders and falls to her bed. Those soft, perfect breasts of hers spill out, and my breath catches in my lungs.

"Beautiful."

Picking her phone back up, Lexi sprawls out on her back. Her free hand skims over her chest, running slowly over her breasts. "Are you going to get naked for me?"

My boxer briefs are off the moment the words fall from

her lips. Lexi chuckles, but when I pan the phone down to give her a view of my hand fisting my cock, she sucks in a ragged breath. "Like what you see?"

"Yes," she gasps. "You have the best cock."

"Well, thank you, beautiful. And you have the prettiest pussy. Is it wet for me? Show me."

Lexi does as I ask. She pushes her simple gray panties down her legs. Her thighs fall open, and I'm greeted with the most beautiful sight. Pink and swollen, she's already so wet for me.

"Oh, fuck." I stroke my cock. "Look at you." I watch, enraptured, as Lexi's slender fingers part her lips. Gathering some of her wetness, she circles her clit and lets out a soft moan.

"Ryder," she murmurs. "I wish it was your fingers on me."

"I know," I say. There is nothing I want more in this moment than to feel Lexi's fingers wrap around my dick. To feel her warm palm gripping me as she strokes me. "Just imagine I'm the one circling that swollen clit, baby. I'm the one spreading your slick juices over that perfect little bud."

Her fingers increase their pace, and her thighs fall farther open. Groaning, I pump myself in time with her self-ministrations. She must be watching me the same way I'm watching her, because she moans when a bead of pre-cum leaks from my slit. I drag my thumb through it, spreading it over my thick head, imagining it's her arousal coating me instead of my own.

"Oh, god, Ryder," she moans. Her hips lift off the bed, and I nearly come when she presses two of her fingers inside her dripping pussy. She fucks herself and I can only stare. My cock is painfully hard now. But I want to watch her come before I give in to the throbbing need of my own body. I'm mesmerized by her.

"That's it, baby," I say. I almost don't recognize my own voice, it's so rough. "Fuck your pretty little pussy. Just like that. Now circle your clit."

She does as I instruct, and I watch her slick fingers withdraw from her body and circle her clit. Her breathing gets faster. Ragged. She's close. I am too. "Ryder," she whines. But her fingers don't stop moving. No, they pick up the pace, pressing on her clit in quicker circles. I stroke my dick faster, too, imagining I'm there with her. Thrusting into her tight heat. Playing her body like a familiar and beloved instrument.

"You're doing so good, baby," I praise through my own panting. "God, look at you. So perfect. So beautiful."

"I'm close," she gasps, rocking against the heel of her palm as she thrusts two fingers back inside of herself. "So close."

"I know you are," I rasp. "Come for me, baby. Come all over your fingers. I'm going to imagine it's my cock your pretty pussy is strangling instead."

"Oh, god," she moans. And then her body is shivering and convulsing. Her stomach tightens and her back arches as desperate sounds pour from her perfect mouth.

I can't hold it back any longer. Two more hard strokes, and I'm coming too. Thick ropes of cum spurt across my lower stomach, and I hear Lexi whisper, "Fuck."

Fuck is right. I've never come so hard by my own hand as I just did. My body buzzes with endorphins as my cock pulses one last time.

Lexi's face comes back into view on my screen. Her

cheeks are flushed and her eyes are wild, hair mussed from thrashing against the bed. She looks beautiful. I wish I was there to hold her.

"Wow," she whispers, smiling wide.

"Yeah," I agree. "Wow is right."

"That was…"

"Incredible?"

She nods. "Yeah."

I want to blurt out that I can't get enough of her. That I think she's it for me. That I'm totally crazy about her and can never see myself feeling this way about anyone else ever again. I want to tell her I'm falling in love with her.

Instead, I say, "Lick your fingers clean for me, Alexis."

She does.

I'm a goner.

LEXI

Ryder has been gone for three days, and I'm grumpy as hell.

My roommate, Sarah, has been blissfully busy with her classes and part-time job, and I almost consider calling and picking up more waitressing shifts. It would give me something to do besides studying and scrubbing the bathroom today.

My phone buzzes, and I pull it out of my jeans pocket as fast as possible. I don't want to miss a text from Ryder.

Except, it's not my boyfriend.

MOM

Sweetheart, are you going to call me back? I've been trying to reach you all week. I miss you.

Guilt gnaws at my gut, but I don't answer. Instead, I stare at the message and try to figure out how to appease my mom without being dragged to a dinner with Jeff. I love my mom. She did her best to make sure I didn't feel my dad's absence throughout my childhood. Every softball game as a small child, every play as a teenager, I could always count on her being right there in the front row, cheering me on. And I don't even blame her for ditching my dad and finding someone who will pay attention to her and be there when she needs him. I just wish she'd left dad and *then* found a replacement. As it is, the awkwardness of how she and Jeff met weirds me the hell out.

I know I need to get over it. I'm just not there yet.

ME

Sorry, Mom. I'm out with some friends right now. Talk soon?

There. Hopefully, that buys me some time.
My phone vibrates again.

MOM

Oh, yeah? What are you girls up to today?

Dammit. I'm not a great liar.

ME

I wanted to see that new rom-com that just came out in the theaters, so I dragged my roommate along with me.

MOM

That sounds like fun, sweetie. Just one question?

What's up?

If you're out at a movie, why is your car here?

Three rapid knocks on my apartment door have me shrieking. I press a palm to my racing heart. "Shit."

A familiar voice cuts through my moment of panic. "Alexis Genevieve Cross, I know you're in there. I heard you scream."

Well played, Mom. Well played.

Head hanging, I shuffle through the apartment and steel myself with one deep breath. And then I open the door to let my mother in.

Kelly Cross sweeps in with her blonde, shoulder-length hair perfectly styled in loose waves, a full face of tastefully done makeup, and her hazel eyes narrowed on me the way only a mother can. She looks good, but she always does. She may be fifty-two, but I swear the woman doesn't look a day over forty. I can only hope I inherit her genes. She dyes her hair to maintain the blonde and ward off the grays she occasionally complains about, but even if she let them grow in, they wouldn't detract from her beauty.

I'm happy to see her. I am. Unfortunately for my mom, I'm also living up to Ryder's nickname for me.

"What are you doing here, Mom?" I stick my head out of the apartment door and into the hallway, looking for Jeff. My shoulders sag with relief when I don't see or hear him. "Where's Jeff?"

Shrugging out of her cherry-red pea coat, my mom rolls her eyes. "He's at home, watching some game. You know how I feel about sports, so I had to get out of the house. And since I haven't seen or heard from my daughter since Christmas, here I am."

Shit. Has it really been that long? Guilt wiggles through my gut like a handful of earthworms. When my mom drapes her coat over the back of the couch, I close the distance between us and pull her into a hug. Her hair muffles my voice when I say, "Sorry, Mom. I've been busy."

"Sure," she says wryly. "And it has nothing to do with my boyfriend?"

I so don't want to talk about Jeff right now. My mom deserves to be loved, and even though I don't like how they met, the man seems to make her happy. I can even admit he's nice. Despite his awkward attempts to play dad. I roll my eyes before pulling away from our hug so she doesn't see.

"Don't roll your eyes at me, young lady."

Jesus. Does she have eyes in the back of her head? Are all moms practitioners of the dark arts, and that's what allows them to know what their children are up to at all times, even when said children are trying to be sneaky? Grinning sheepishly, I pull away. "Sorry."

Mom sighs, her cheeks twitching as she fights a smile. "It's okay, Lexi. I just miss you."

"I know. I miss you too." I move into the kitchen. "Tea?"

"Sure, sweetie."

We fall into silence while I fill the kettle and put it on the stove. Readying two mugs with peppermint tea bags, I turn back to my mom, who has settled in at our little dining table. "So, how was Christmas with Jeff and his family?"

A genuine smile overtakes my mom's face. She practically lights up. "It was great, actually. His sister and her husband were there with their kids. They have a boy and a girl about your age. You'll really like them. And Jeff got me the prettiest little necklace." She gently tugs at a white gold chain around her neck, revealing a diamond pendant tucked beneath the collar of her cream-colored sweater.

"Wow," I say. "It's really pretty, Mom." She beams. "Sorry I wasn't there."

Mom grabs my hand when I sit across from her and smiles ruefully. "No need to apologize. I know it's strange. Though I do hope you give Jeff a chance at some point." Her hazel eyes go distant. "I love him, you know? And he really loves me, Lexi. I forgot what it felt like to have someone love me like that."

My heart squeezes. My mom did a good job putting on a brave face and hiding the worst of her loneliness from me as a kid. But now, as an adult? I no longer see my childhood through rose-colored lenses. For all intents and purposes, my mom was a single parent. Sure, my dad paid the bills and made enough money that we didn't lack for anything, but he was never present. He didn't tuck me in past the age of five or so, didn't kiss boo-boos or make lunches. He didn't do any of the mental and emotional labor. And he neglected my mom in every way, outside of his financial provision.

As annoyed as I get when Jeff calls me *kiddo*, I can tell he adores my mom. And she deserves to be adored.

I suck in a deep breath and chastise myself. I need to do better. It's not my place to judge my mom for how she and Jeff met. He's clearly not going anywhere, so I will make an effort. Mom deserves to be happy. I give her hand a squeeze. "Sorry, Mom. I will, moving forward. Promise."

The way her whole face illuminates at that sends

another pang of guilt through me. Damn. I need to do better.

"You have no idea how happy that makes me. Jeff's family always does a big Valentine's dinner. They serve steak and fancy deserts. I'd love it if you come, honey."

My mind goes to Ryder. I have a boyfriend now. And they don't have a game on Valentine's Day. I know because I checked. But I can't tell my mom that. "Um, is it on the actual date of Valentine's Day? Because I'm not sure I can make that work."

"Why not?" Hazel eyes narrow at me.

"I have plans, Mom."

She stares at me, waiting for me to elaborate. When I don't, she shakes her head. "No, honey, it's not on Valentine's Day itself. Dinner will be the weekend after."

"Oh. I should be able to swing that, then." *Please don't dig into this, Mom.*

"Did you meet some boy at school?"

Not at school, no. "Nope."

"You're being weird, honey."

That makes me laugh. She's not wrong. "It's just a strange situation, that's all. I'll get used to it."

Her face softens. "I know it is. And I'm sorry if you've felt like you have to be in the middle of things between your father and me." She pauses. "Have you seen your dad at all lately?"

If anyone understands the depths of my disappointment with my father, it's the woman sitting across the table from me. The woman whose disappointment forms a deeper chasm than my own.

"No. No, I haven't." Neither of us speaks for a couple of minutes, because what is there to say? Nothing that hasn't been uttered before. And nothing that will alter the state of things.

"You know, Jeff's nephew is an engineer. And he's single." A devious twinkle sparks in my mom's eyes. "He'll be at the Valentine's dinner."

Oh, geez. Here we go. I'm relieved when the tea kettle screams at me from the kitchen so I can give Mom my back and hide my expression. "Mom, no."

"He's cute, Lexi. Blond and tall. Almost six feet, I think."

I try not to chuckle. *Almost six feet* doesn't have the same impact now that it would have had a couple of months ago. Not that she knows that. "I'm not interested, Mom."

"Jeff showed Henry your picture, and he thought you were pretty. Henry is his nephew's name, of course."

"Mom. No." Exasperated, I pour steaming water into the two mugs. Even still, my lips twitch as I repress a smile. "I don't want to be set up."

"Oh, but honey, the two of you would be so cute together. Come on, just give him a chance. One date, and if you don't like him, that's okay."

Laughing, I roll my eyes at my mom over my shoulder. "I'm not going on a date with him. But thank you for telling me it's okay if I don't like someone. I feel so much better now."

"Alexis, really. You're a beautiful woman. You're smart, driven, and fun. Even if you are a little macabre, what with your obsession with murder mysteries." That part, she says more to herself than me. "What's the worst that could happen?"

I grin. "Henry could stab me in the heart while we're

out on some mediocre date, carve it out of my chest, and eat it in lieu of dinner?"

My mom stares flatly at me. It's her *why are you the way you are* look. It makes me laugh so hard that I take a whole minute to calm myself enough to carry the two steaming mugs over to the table without spilling them on my hands and scalding myself.

"Sometimes I worry about you."

"And that's why you're trying to set me up with strangers who could murder me?"

"*Alexis.*" She shakes her head. "Seriously, honey. Henry is a nice man. He's sweet and cute, and I don't see any good reason you can't give him two hours of your life to see if you're compatible."

I love my mom; I do. But annoyance is quickly replacing the humor I found in this situation. Which is why I blurt out, "How about because I have a boyfriend? That's a pretty good reason not to go on a date with a rando, isn't it?"

Oops.

My mother's eyes go wide, her mouth drops open, and her fingers twitch around her mug. A million thoughts per second are flying through her head, and I can practically see them. Excitement that I have a boyfriend, hurt that I didn't tell her about him, worry that he's not good enough, and a brief moment of wondering whether we will choose a spring or summer wedding.

Then her wide eyes narrow and pin me in place. "What do you mean, you have a boyfriend?"

I sink into my chair. "Um, I thought the statement was fairly self-explanatory?"

"Don't sass me, young lady. You have a boyfriend and

didn't tell me? When did you meet this man?" Momterrogation mode initiated.

Oh shit.

My shoulders bunch up to my ears. "Over Christmas break?"

She arches one eyebrow. "Are you asking me or telling me?"

"Telling. I met him over Christmas break."

"Where?"

"Uh, up in Two Harbors."

That has her gaping at me. "You went up to the cabin for Christmas? Alone? Alexis, there was a *blizzard*. You could have been in danger."

Oh, man. This is not going to go over well

"Yeah. It definitely could have gotten hairy. But I wasn't alone." I watch my mom, who is silent, press her lips together in a firm line. "I mean, I went up there alone, but there was someone in the cabin."

"What?" My mom's shout rings out through the apartment.

"It's okay, Mom, it's not a big deal. It's just that Dad had given the keys to one of his players to stay there for the week. And he showed up while I was out in the hot tub."

Mom leans forward, her elbows on the table. "Alexis Cross. Tell me your boyfriend is not a player on your dad's hockey team."

I shrink down in my seat so only my nose and eyes are visible above the surface of the table. Clearing my throat, I say, "Sorry, Mom. Can't. He's one of the players on Dad's hockey team."

Here we go.

forty-one

LEXI

"Does your father know?"

My face screws up in a look of pure *how stupid do you think I am?* "Fuck, no!"

Mom scowls. "Language, Alexis."

Banging my head on the back of the chair, I groan. "Mom. I'm twenty-three. I can say *fuck*."

"Don't try to change the subject, young lady."

I throw my hands in the air. "You started it!"

"Tell me everything," my mom says. A severe frown mars her pretty face. And to think, I was worried about my dad finding out about Ryder and me. This may be worse.

So, I tell her everything. Well, not *everything*. She doesn't need to know that Ryder saw my nips and nub within two minutes of meeting me. Or that I've never orgasmed harder than I do with him. Really, I avoid the topic of sex altogether. But I tell her plenty of other things.

Like how Ryder was the epitome of sweet and respectful. How he never pushed my boundaries or tried to take advantage of our situation. I tell her how he cut down a Christmas tree for me and decorated the cabin. I tell her how pissed he was on my behalf when Dad called him before contacting me on Christmas Day.

My stories soften her, but nothing I say can overcome the one glaring fault that may forever define Ryder in my mother's eyes—he's a hockey player. And on my dad's team, to boot.

"You know what they're like," Mom says. Her tone is gentle, but her body is stiff and unyielding. She thinks I'm an idiot for falling for a hockey player. Especially a pro-hockey player.

I shake my head. "No, Mom. I know what *Dad's* like. Ryder isn't like him."

"You can't really know that yet, can you? It's only been what, a month and a half?" Her shoulders slump, and suddenly, my mom looks tired. "Everything's new, sweetie. He'll be on his best behavior. I'm sure he calls and texts often right now, but a year or two down the road... After you're married and raising a baby on your own and trapped in a life you never thought you'd have to navigate alone, who's to say those calls won't stop? Who's to say he won't just appear and disappear in your life whenever it's convenient for him, like some kind of emotional poltergeist?"

I try not to flinch when she makes the comment about being trapped with a baby, because I know she doesn't mean to hurt me. But damn. It still stings. She loves me and she's always been there for me, but the sensation of being an obligation to *both* parents is like being stabbed in the gut.

But I also feel so sad for her. Sad for the young woman who married a man she was head over heels in love with. Sad for the woman who had big dreams for her life, only to watch them wither away into dry, brittle husks, then break apart on the wind. And maybe, for the first time, I feel a pulse of thankfulness for Jeff in all his awkwardness. Because it's clear that he makes her feel loved and wanted. I can't imagine how my dad's neglect ate at her over the years.

I suppose I don't even blame her for projecting those issues and fears onto me and my relationship with Ryder. But I don't like the way a tiny splinter of doubt lodges into my heart. It's understandable that she's projecting, but it's not fair.

"Oh, Mom."

Blonde hair forms a curtain around her face as she hangs her head, resting it in her palms. "I just don't want to see you hurt by another man who will pick hockey over you."

The splinter digs in deeper.

"He's not Dad."

Her eyes are glassy when she looks up and meets my gaze. "I sure hope not."

"He's not." Rubbing at my chest, I think about all the things Ryder has done to make me comfortable. Although he's not crazy about keeping our relationship quiet, he's never guilt-tripped me or tried to convince me to change my mind. He's sworn his teammates to secrecy. He's reassured me on more than one occasion that I'm important to him. "I actually think you'd really like him."

Even under the scrutiny of my mom's attention, a smile ghosts across my lips when I think about Ryder. I really like him. A lot. And I trust him. Trust doesn't come easily to me. Which apparently runs in the family. Not even that pesky splinter of doubt can erase that trust.

"Does that mean things are serious enough that you want me to meet him?"

Are they? I haven't really let myself go there, but I would like my mom to meet Ryder. I want her to see how *good* he is. "Yeah, Mom. I think they are."

She blows a breath out through her nose. "Okay, then. You tell me when, and I'll meet him."

"Thanks, Mom."

My mother reaches across the table and pats my hand. "Of course, sweetie. I just want you to know that, if things don't work out with this boy, Jeff's nephew is still an option."

Right. Wonderful.

RYDER

God, I've missed her face. Lexi and I have talked and texted, but we got back to the hotel late last night, and she was asleep by the time I tried to video call. Yes, it's only one night, but apparently, I'm addicted to this woman. I need to see her every single day.

"Hey, beautiful." I flop back onto the too-hard hotel mattress and grin widely. It's late, so I'm not surprised to find Lexi in bed, her blonde hair piled on top of her head in a messy bun, her skin bare and glowing from whatever moisturizer she uses. She looks beautiful. Tired, but beautiful. Possibly a little stressed. "How are you?"

"Hi," she murmurs with a hint of a smile. "I'm okay. How are you? That was a close game tonight."

My chest expands. "You watched?"

"Course I did. Gotta cheer on my man."

That Lexi watched the game at home alone is just as surprising to me as the fact that she showed up at our home game last week. It says a lot about her that she's willing to support me and watch a game that evokes negative emotions and memories. And rightfully so. Once again, I think about how badly Coach has to have fucked up with her to get her to pull back from him the way she has. Because it seems like Lexi is the type of woman who shows up for the people she loves.

"What did you do today?" Her brows pinch slightly as soon as the question falls from my tongue. I'm not sure why it has my stomach twisting, but it does. Maybe because I'm hours away. If Lexi had a bad day, there's not much I can do about it. I can't swoop in and pull her into a hug. Reaching through a phone screen isn't possible, so I can't smooth the little furrow between her eyebrows before kissing it better. "You okay?"

"My mom stopped by for a visit. Completely unannounced." Those pretty green eyes of Lexi's roll. "I've kind of been avoiding her."

Lexi hasn't spoken too much about her mom. I get the sense that they've always been relatively close, but her mom's relationship with this new guy seems to have thrown Lexi for a loop. Which I can understand. At the same time—having lost both of my parents—I'd give anything to have my mom show up unannounced at my place.

"How'd it go?"

My girl stares at me through the phone for a moment. A complex cocktail of emotions plays across her features. They're there and gone in an instant. "I told her about you. About us."

It's so hard to keep my face blank. It really is. She told her mom about me? That's good, right? That has to be a good sign.

Except, Lexi looks stressed. So maybe it's not.

"And how did that go?" I ask her carefully.

"She was..." Lexi's gaze dart to the side. As though she's searching for the right word, and she'll find it floating in the air beside her. "She's not a huge fan of hockey players."

Somehow, that doesn't surprise me. It sucks, but it doesn't surprise me. Of course, Coach's ex-wife feels the same sort of hesitation surrounding my sport that his daughter does. Hell, it's likely she has even stronger negative feelings about it. It's not ideal. Coach will probably kick my ass when he finds out I'm dating his daughter. In a perfect world, I'd at least have the support of my girlfriend's mom. I'll just have to do my best to win her over.

"I told her you're a great guy. She thought it was sweet that you woke up early on Christmas morning to decorate the cabin." Lexi worries at her lower lip with her teeth. "She just doesn't want to see me hurt."

Understandable. "I wish I could promise that I'll never hurt you," I say solemnly. "But no relationship is perfect or painless. I'll screw up at some point. It's inevitable. But I can promise I'll do my best to be the man you need. I promise I'll be there for you. The last thing I ever want to do is hurt you or let you down."

"I know," she whispers. She's solemn. Serious. "I don't

want to hurt you or let you down, either." Lexi pauses just long enough to tug her comforter up around her. "My mom doesn't talk much about what it was like being married to my dad. I think she doesn't want to pit me against him or anything, you know?"

I nod.

"But she said some things today that made me realize she was probably much lonelier than I ever realized. And that she felt my dad's neglect well before it ever hit me that he wasn't there most of the time. It's difficult to look past your own personal experiences in a situation like that."

"Don't worry, OTG. I get that." And I do. I don't love it, but I get it.

"You broke past my preconceptions, though." The furrow between Lexi's brown eyebrows smooths out. "I'm sure you'll be able to do the same thing with my mom."

I really hope I can. Some part of me—the orphaned part—always dreamed that when I found the right woman, her parents would love me too. And I am really starting to believe that Lexi is the right woman. It's probably too soon to be thinking that way, but right now, when she's thousands of miles away, it's becoming painfully clear that she's already begun to feel like *home*.

Nowhere has felt like home since my dad died.

The closest I've come is being on the ice with the Rogues, but that's not the same as having a place of rest to call my own. Home sure as hell isn't the apartment I share with my teammate, Aaron. He's a great guy and a solid roommate, but he's got his own friends and family. When I first moved in with him, I had this idealistic fantasy that we'd become best friends and do everything together. But that hasn't come to pass, and it never will. Some of the more senior guys on the team have taken me under their wing, and they're including me more as the season goes on. Still, it's not quite what I've been searching for, even though it comes close.

But Lexi. Something about Lexi feels so familiar. She calls to me. Like her soul holds a missing piece of my own, and the restless, searching thing inside my chest settles in her presence. It's so much more than physical attraction. And yeah, Lexi's beautiful. I'm constantly hard around her. When she welcomes me into her body, it's practically a spiritual experience. And yet, even if something happened and I could never touch her or taste her again, I would still choose to be with her. Because I'm pretty sure she's it for me. She's my person.

So, I want her mom to love me. I want Coach to accept our relationship and support it. The idea of having parents in my life again—even though no one could ever replace my own—is something I long for. Probably more than even I realize. Maybe that's not in the cards with Lexi's parents.

But I'm willing to work for it. Especially since I know how painful it is to lose your parents, and I don't want that for Lexi.

My beautiful girlfriend's lips twist with worry and nerves. "Think you'd be up for having dinner with my mom and Jeff when you're back home?"

I don't even hesitate.

"Of course, OTG. I can't wait to meet them."

forty-two

RYDER

Lexi's mom hates me.

It doesn't matter that I brought her flowers and a bottle of wine, or that Lexi clings to my hand like I'm her lifeline. No matter how many times I make her daughter laugh, the tight scowl is ever present when I catch her looking my way. She hates me on principle and has since the moment I walked into her home.

I stupidly thought I could win her over with some smiles, my best manners, and by treating her daughter like a queen.

I was wrong.

"Sweetheart." Kelly Cross grabs Lexi's hand and gives it a squeeze across the table. "Did I tell you that Jeff's nephew may stop by tonight?"

Jeff, Kelly's boyfriend, shoots me an apologetic grimace from his seat. Despite the unfortunate way he and Lexi's mom got together, the guy actually seems pretty decent.

He clearly loves Kelly, and he's obviously determined to do what he can to build a relationship with Lexi. Plus, despite swearing me to secrecy for obvious reasons, he admitted to being a huge Rogues fan and talked my ear off about our lineup and how we've been playing so far this season while the women were in the other room.

"Mom," Lexi hisses, shooting daggers with her eyes. "I'm sure Jeff's nephew is very nice, but I am here with my *boyfriend*."

Kelly Cross waves a hand dismissively. "Oh, don't get your panties in a bunch. I just want you to meet the man."

"*Mother*."

I'd probably be more upset by the whole nephew thing if Lexi wasn't so adorably disgruntled by it. Am I annoyed? Absolutely. Offended? Sure. But I know where I stand with the beautiful blonde beside me. And while I'd like her mom to accept me, all that really matters is that my girlfriend does.

"I'm looking forward to meeting him," I say with an amused smile. "After all, if Jeff and your mom get married, he'll be your cousin, Lexi. Weren't you just saying the other day how nice it would be to have some cousins?"

Kelly Cross chokes on her wine.

Lexi snorts but quickly schools her features to play along. "Yeah, babe. I was." She turns to her mom with a confused expression. "Sorry, Mom. I realize you're just trying to introduce me to the guy. Obviously, you wouldn't try to set me up with my cousin." Lexi pulls a face. It's the same expression I've seen new parents make when they have to change a particularly rank diaper or their kid has a blowout that spreads runny poop up their back.

"I... No, that's not what I..." Lexi's mom sputters helplessly. She looks at Jeff for backup, but the guy's grinning into his wineglass. At least he's on my side, even if he isn't one of Lexi's parents. I'll take whatever wins I can in this situation.

Recovering, Kelly Cross levels me with a look that practically shrivels my balls. "So, Ryder, what are your intentions with my daughter?"

"Jesus, Mom. What is this, 1950?" Lexi shakes her head, her annoyance back in an instant.

"It's a fair question. A mother has the right to make sure her daughter isn't being taken advantage of." Kelly sniffs.

"Well, ma'am, my intention is to be the best boyfriend I can be for Lexi. To support her and encourage her." I want to tell Lexi's mom that I want to love her daughter for as long as she'll have me, but that would be stupid. Somehow, I doubt telling my girlfriend I love her for the first time in front of her mom is the way to go. But I think I do love Lexi. Being here and sitting through her mom's third degree only makes me more certain that's how I feel. If I didn't, all I'd be able to think about right now is getting the hell out of Dodge. Instead, I grab my girl's hand and meet her gaze so she hears and feels every bit of my truth. "Your daughter is special. I've never met anyone like her."

Kelly narrows her eyes at me. She's still not convinced. "And what do your parents think about this relationship? It's a bit taboo to date your coach's daughter, isn't it?"

Lexi's hand squeezes mine tight, and I see her spine straighten. She opens her mouth, but I beat her to it.

"Well, if my parents were alive, I'm absolutely certain they'd love your daughter." There's no malice or hurt in my voice, even though that familiar pang reverberates through my chest. The one that shakes me a little every time someone brings up my parents. I turn to look at Lexi. "My dad always loved strong women. He'd be proud of me for convincing one I'm worthy of her affection."

Lexi's eyes glitter with emotion as she holds my gaze. She doesn't speak, but I don't need her to. The words are written in the gentle, melancholic upturn of her lips, the soft set of her eyes, and the slight tilt of her head. I've begun sharing more about my parents in the past week or two. In some ways, the time I've spent on the road with the team has been a blessing. Sometimes it's easier to open up about difficult subjects when you can't see the other person's face. And we've spent as much time as we can on the phone or video chatting.

"I'm sorry," Lexi's mom says softly. It's the first time her words haven't carried even the slightest bite of hostility. "I didn't realize."

"There's nothing to apologize for," I answer. And I mean it. Not about my parents and not about being defensive of her daughter. I'm just glad *someone* in Lexi's life is.

"Do you have other family in Minneapolis?" Kelly asks. Gently, this time.

"Unfortunately not. It's just me."

Kelly's face twists with sympathy. "That must be very hard."

I shrug. It is, but it's also not something I can change. "I do all right, most of the time. You get used to it, after a while. But being a part of my team and getting to spend time with my teammates, I've begun to realize that family can be created. It's not limited by blood. We can get second —hell, even third and fourth—chances at it."

Jeff reaches over and squeezes Kelly's hand. Surely, if

anyone understands what I'm saying, it will be the woman who grabbed hold of a second chance for herself. Lexi's mom studies me differently now.

"And I know Lexi and I haven't been together all that long, but she's begun to feel like family too." Any fear I might have that I've just said too much washes away when Lexi's expression grows even softer. "Spending Christmas with her was…" A lump forms in my throat. "Well, it was the best Christmas I've had in years."

"Such a charmer, Handsome."

"It's true, Oscar."

God, she's beautiful.

Jeff chuckles, his brow rising. "Oscar?"

"She was a little grouchy at first when I crashed her quiet Christmas alone." I give my girl a wink. "It was adorable."

Jeff chortles. "She must like you a lot if she hasn't strangled you for a nickname like that."

"He's adequate," Lexi replies breezily. "He does have a really big—"

I cough and plaster my hand to her mouth before she can finish that sentence. I don't think the size of my dick is going to win me any points with her mom.

Lexi pries my hand away. "Heart."

Jeff guffaws at that. Especially when Lexi gives me a cheeky wink after letting her gaze drop to my crotch momentarily.

This woman.

Lexi's mom opens her mouth to say something, but before she can get the words out, the doorbell rings. She exchanges a slightly sheepish look with Jeff before rising from the table. "That'll be Henry. Excuse me a moment."

With a shake of his head, Jeff plucks the open bottle of wine off the table and offers Lexi and me a refill. We both accept. "Sorry 'bout this."

"It's okay," Lexi says, resigned. "I wish I could say I'm surprised, but I'm not."

Jeff's voice takes on a tender note. "She worries about you, and her heart's in the right place."

"You really love her, don't you?" Lexi asks. She watches as the older man across from us gets a goofy, lovesick look on his face.

"Hard not to," is his reply.

It's clear this is the moment Lexi accepts Jeff. Her face lights up as a genuine smile curves her lips. "I'm glad she has you."

"I'm glad to have her." Jeff hesitates for a moment, studying Lexi with a slight twist to his mouth that tells me he's considering something. "Your mother didn't want me to say anything, but you deserve to know. She and your father had been separated for almost six months by the time we met. She didn't want to tell you and ruin your senior year of college."

Lexi's eyes widen, and she looks like she wants to ask a million questions, but Kelly walks into the dining room with Jeff's nephew beside her, stopping this particular line of discussion. By the looks of him, he feels as awkward about this whole setup as Lexi does. But when he notices her hand in mine, I almost feel bad for the guy. Especially when his eyes widen as he takes Alexis in. I know exactly what he must be thinking. She's beautiful. And he'd been dreading this meeting.

Now he's probably wishing he'd agreed to it sooner.

"Sweetheart, this is Henry. Jeff's nephew." Kelly doesn't

look nearly as smug about this introduction as she probably would have before dinner. "Henry, this is my daughter Alexis and her...her boyfriend, Ryder."

Henry shuffles his feet, looking between Lexi and me as Kelly talks. But when she says my name, his eyes widen, and he gives me his full attention. "Wait. Ryder? As in Ryder Hanson? The hockey player?"

"For the love," Kelly mutters under her breath. The poor woman can't seem to escape hockey.

I stand, finding my manners, and extend a hand. "Yeah, man. It's nice to meet you."

"Wow," Henry says. "Same." He glances between me and Lexi and nods. Like he's decided it makes total sense for her to choose a hockey player over her mom's boyfriend's nephew. He's not a bad-looking guy—not that Lexi seems to have noticed one way or another, which does great things for my ego—but my first impression is that he's quiet and likely unsure of himself. And there's no shame in that. But Lexi would eat a guy like this alive. She's too full of spunk and fire. She needs someone who can give it right back to her when she's feeling sassy and spirited.

I'd like to think I'm that someone.

"Hey," Lexi says from her seat. She gives Henry a little wave and pastes an innocent look on her face. "I hear we may be cousins soon."

The poor guy has no idea what to say to that. He sputters, looking between Jeff and Kelly. "Oh, uh, I didn't know you proposed, Uncle Jeff. Congratulations."

Jeff chuckles and shakes his head. "I haven't, kid." Jeff looks Kelly's way. "Yet."

Kelly blushes.

"Well, if everyone's done with dinner, I suppose we should take this in the other room. Anyone want a beer?" Jeff pushes back from the table and claps a hand on his nephew's shoulder.

"A beer would be great," I say.

Henry's gaze bounces between all of us before he shifts his weight and says, "I can't really stay. I have some work I need to catch up on."

To Kelly's credit, she manages to hide any disappointment she may feel that her matchmaking attempt has failed spectacularly. "I'll walk you out."

I've broken down some of her walls, but I haven't fully won her over yet.

But I will.

I'm not going anywhere. Both Cross women will understand that, eventually.

I can be patient.

forty-three

LEXI

I THINK MY MOM ALMOST LIKES HIM.

Jeff gives me a brief hug as we say goodbye, and I give him a little squeeze. The revelation that he and my mom didn't have an affair only helps my feelings for the man change more quickly. It's difficult to dislike a guy who treats my mom like she's the best thing in the world. And even more difficult when my false belief that he was willing to cheat is taken away.

I guess I get why Mom didn't say anything at first, but why has she let me hold on to the false notion that she's a cheater?

"I hope we can do this again," I say to Jeff with a soft smile.

He returns it easily. "I'd like that a lot, kiddo."

The endearment doesn't bother me now. In fact, it makes my chest feel warm in a way it hasn't in years.

When's the last time my dad looked at me like I was precious? Like it would be a pleasure to spend time with me?

When he steps back, my mom wraps me up in a tight hug. Jeff and Ryder shake hands and speak in low voices. My mom sighs. "I'm still worried that he'll put hockey first, but I guess he's not so bad."

Laughing, I pull back from the hug so I can meet her gaze. "Gee, thanks, Mom. High praise, coming from you."

She arches one eyebrow. "It is."

We both chuckle. I can't help glancing Ryder's way. He always draws my eye when we're together, pulling me into his orbit. "Just promise you'll give him a chance. He's not Dad."

"I know," she says, exhaling slowly. "And he's in love with you."

An undignified snort bursts out of me. "He is not. It's way too soon for that."

"Is it?" My mom tilts her face, so she's looking down her nose at me. "I didn't realize love had a specific timeline it has to follow."

"Mom. Come on. He's not in love with me. That's ridiculous."

Her face softens. "That's what I thought. You're in love with him too." She gives my arm a gentle squeeze. "Just be careful, sweetie. You deserve to be loved, and I'm afraid I didn't set a very good example of that for you."

"Mom, no." My chest squeezes painfully. "Don't you dare take that on yourself. That's on Dad." My attention flicks to Jeff. "Besides, you're showing me now."

The rosy glow that lights my mom's face is everything.

She instantly looks younger, and I imagine this is what she looked like when she first fell for my dad. Before he emotionally vampired her and sucked all the joy out of her life. What an asshole.

"I know you're not Jeff's biggest fan, but I do hope you give him a chance, sweetie."

Sucking in a deep breath, I grab my mom's hands. "You could have told me you and Dad were separated. It wouldn't have ruined my college experience."

"He told you that, did he?" She doesn't appear annoyed. There's only affection painted in pinks across her cheeks. "I'm sorry. I shouldn't have kept it from you. It just felt... I was dealing with a lot of shame about the whole thing. I didn't handle it as well as I could have."

"I get it." Emotions are messy. It's easy to look back and clearly see the way you should have done things, but it's a hell of a lot murkier in the moment. "I'm glad I know now."

Mom pulls me in for another hug. Her breath is warm across my neck. "Me too, sweetie. Me too."

Ryder steps up beside me and rests his hand on my lower back. "You ready to go? You've got an early class tomorrow."

For the first time in a long time, everything feels right in the world as I rest my head on his shoulder. "Yeah. I'm ready."

"Thank you for having us over," Ryder says to my mom and Jeff. "It was so nice to meet you. I hope we can do this again."

A genuine smile overtakes my mom's face. "I hope so too."

We say one last goodbye—because Midwesterners can

never say just one—and climb into Ryder's car. Neither of us speaks for the first few minutes as he begins the drive toward my apartment. It's not a tense silence. More that we're both processing the evening. It certainly didn't go the way I expected it to, which is a good thing. But there is a lot to consider. My mom didn't have an affair. Jeff isn't the bad guy. Mom thinks Ryder loves me. She thinks I love him.

She may be right.

When Ryder's large, warm hand covers mine, I turn to look at him. "You okay, OTG?"

"Yeah," I say. "I'm good, actually. Are you? My mom wasn't exactly easy on you most of the night."

My handsome boyfriend shrugs. "I'm good. And I think things with your mom went well. She may not be fully Team Ryder yet, but I'll win her over. Besides, she was just being protective of you. And she's been hurt. By my coach. Can't say I don't understand her reservations."

Sweet, sweet man.

"You don't have to defend her."

"I know. But if she doesn't like me, it's not because of me. It's because of my career. And I'm not my job, you know? I love it, don't get me wrong. Hockey kept me going when my mom died, then again when my dad passed. It's given me something to strive for, something to lose myself in, and a sense of family I desperately needed. But hockey is a brutal sport. No one plays forever. I figure I'll get maybe ten to fifteen years more of this if I'm really lucky."

Ryder flexes his healing hand. "But I could also be done tomorrow. One bad fall, one torn tendon, and that could be it. I'm not putting all my eggs in one icy basket."

"Have you thought about what you want to do after

hockey?" I ask. Because I can't imagine spending so much of my life working toward something that could be taken away from me in an instant like that.

"No idea," he says. Then he squeezes my hand. "But I know that, whatever it is, I want to figure it out with the right woman by my side."

Well, that makes my heart all sorts of fluttery. Because when he says those words and looks at me so meaningfully, my mind flashes back to my mom's words.

He's in love with you.

Oh, boy. Is she right?

I let out a breathy giggle that is extremely undignified and embarrassing. "Well, I believe you can do anything you want."

Thank god Ryder doesn't laugh at my ridiculousness. He smiles softly at me, squeezes my hand, and says, "Thanks, Oscar. You know I feel the same about you. Have you thought more about what you want to use your degree for?"

"Not really," I admit. It's something I need to put some serious thought into, but I have time. And I've been a little distracted lately.

"You'll figure it out."

"Thanks, Handsome."

When we get to my apartment, Ryder walks me to my door. I invite him in, but I'm not the only one with an early morning tomorrow. The Rogues have practice at the butt crack of dawn. Still, it's incredibly difficult to tear myself away from the man. Especially when his kisses are so deep and drugging. I feel like I'm floating when our mouths break apart.

With one palm cupping my cheek and the other hand brushing my hair away from my face, Ryder blinks a few times. He's clearly as affected by our kisses as I am. "God, it's hard walking away from you."

"I know," I say breathlessly. "Are you sure you don't want to come in?"

"Oh, I want to." He presses his forehead against mine. "But I'm going to be the responsible one and go. If I walk in there with you right now, neither of us will get any sleep." To illustrate his point, Ryder presses his hips forward and grinds his very hard dick against my lower belly. When I gasp, he chuckles, low and raspy. "Exactly, baby. Now, get your beautiful ass inside and get some sleep. You'll be pissed at yourself if you can't pay attention in class."

He's right, of course. I still don't like it. My face must show my emotions, because Ryder chuckles again, takes the keys from my hand, and unlocks my apartment door. He gives me one more searing kiss, opens it, turns me around, and pushes me gently inside with a swat to my ass.

"Not fair," I pout. "You distracted me with kisses."

Handing my keys back, he looks adorably smug. "Good night, Alexis. Get some sleep. Maybe dream about me."

Oh, I will. But, first, I need to call my bestie.

"Night, Ryder. Text me when you get home?"

Ryder's smile is sweet. "Course, baby. Night."

When I close the door, it's like I'm in one of those cheesy romance movies, because I lean back against it and melt to the floor in a puddle of lust and emotions.

I am so screwed.

After running through my nighttime routine, I flop into bed and video call Rachel. She picks up on the third ring with a massive smile on her face. It looks like she's still in the office. I can't say I'm surprised. Her internship ends in a few months, and there are several people vying for one opening. My girl's in it to win it.

"Lexi! Hey, girl. How's it going?"

"Ryder met my mom tonight."

There's a pause as Rachel's eyes get wide, and her jaw unhinges. "Was blood shed?"

Throwing my head back, I laugh. Rachel may have only met my mom a few times on breaks, but she's aware of exactly how Kelly Cross feels about hockey and the people involved in the sport.

"No bloodshed. I think she actually kind of likes him."

Rachel sets the phone down and starts typing furiously on her computer's keyboard.

"What are you doing?"

"I need to make sure there have been no crazy natural disasters in the last few hours. If Hell freezes over, it will probably have some kind of blowback here on Earth, right?"

"Oh my god," I get out between giggles. "It's not *that* shocking that she'd end up liking Ryder. He's a great guy."

"I know. At least, I know from all the things you've said. Obviously, I have to reserve my full judgment for when I actually meet him in person." She stares at me expectantly. "Which will happen sooner rather than later, right?"

"There's nothing I want more than for you two to meet, but his schedule is crazy." She's right, though. I want her stamp of approval. I've learned my lesson on that front. If your best friends hate your boyfriend, it's probably because there's something wrong with him. I'd rather know now than later. Before there's any talk of love or futures.

"Does the team have any games coming up in Chicago? Because you could come stay with me, we could go to a game, and then I can meet your boy toy." She waggles her brows suggestively.

Laughing, I roll my eyes. "He's not my boy toy."

"Semantics. Now, seriously. When do they play here next?" She types some more on her computer. Her eyes skim the screen before her face lights up. "Well, look at that. They have a two-game series here in two weeks. And they're weekend games, so you shouldn't even need to miss any classes. And I won't have to miss work." Her lips thin. "Because I'll be damned if I miss work and give that dickhead Karl a chance to appear more dedicated than me."

"Karl?"

"Yeah," Rachel says with a wave of her hand. "I've told you about him. He's that ass-kissing rich boy that thinks he shits rainbows and cotton candy."

"Sounds sticky."

That makes her laugh. "Yeah. He's a sticky little bastard. And even though he couldn't give a shit about this job, and he sure as hell doesn't need the money, because his mommy and daddy pay for everything, he's still trying to knock me out of contention, just so I don't get it." Her hands curl into fists, and I can practically see the fires of retribution glinting in her irises. "But he won't win. I won't let him. I'm getting this damned job for women everywhere."

"Oh, babe." I'm laughing so hard, I'm practically

wheezing. "You are going to love hockey so much. All the checking and fights... Okay, yeah. We'll make it happen."

Her expression shifts instantly to one of pure joy. "Really? Yay! Oh my god, I can't wait to see you. I've missed you so damned much."

"Me too, Rach. Me too."

My best friend studies me. "What else happened at your mom's?"

Startled, I blink rapidly. "Huh? What do you mean?"

"You've got this faraway look in your eyes. You look all dreamy and shit."

"Dreamy and shit?" I snort.

"Don't deflect."

"Ugh." I bang my head back against the mattress. "My mom said she thinks Ryder's in love with me. And that I'm in love with him."

It's Rachel's turn to snort. "That's it? Babe, I could have told you that. You are so gone for that man. And if he's not a complete idiot, of course he's gone for you too."

"I..." My mouth flaps open and closed like a fish out of water. "It's just really inconvenient." That's all I can think to say. It's really inconvenient. Because our situation is complicated. We'll have to tell my dad about us at some point, but the amount of anxiety caused by thinking about it makes me want to pop a few antacids.

Rachel hums. "Love always is. If it's convenient, it's probably not real."

She's right. I know she is. Still doesn't make any of this easier.

"Do you think that Chase guy will be playing? He's on the Chicago Blizzard, isn't he?"

Chase. Ryder's former friend, who almost ended his career. The guy I have to thank for meeting Ryder.

"Probably. I don't know."

Rachel's grin is so evil, I almost feel bad for Chase. "Let's brainstorm mean things to write on some signs. It's been too long since I've made a grown man cry."

forty-four

RYDER

My muscles burn as we run drills on the ice. Chase the rabbit. Fuck, this drill is brutal when you have to do it over and over again. Which is exactly what we're being forced to do. After we lost our last game, Coach is out for blood.

"Pick it up! Do you guys want to win or not?"

Griffin rolls his eyes. "I *want* to go back to bed and sleep for another hour or two."

"Late night?" Logan asks. "I haven't seen you hook up with anyone ever since Mira moved in with you. Strange coincidence, or is there something going on there?"

"Oh, hell, no," Maddox growls. "I will kick your ass, Wright."

Griffin rolls his eyes. "We're just roommates. And friends. There hasn't been any touchy touchy, so you can chill, Madds."

Logan studies Griffin. "So, what's up, then? I need my wingman."

"I don't know, dude. Guess it's lost some of its luster, you know? It feels kinda hollow lately." Griffin shrugs.

Maddox goes to open his mouth, but he doesn't get a word out.

"Am I interrupting your little gossip session, ladies?" Coach shouts. He's in rare form this morning. His bad mood is so profound, I keep waiting for him to call me over and tell me I'm off the team because he found out I'm fucking his daughter.

"He seems more dickish than usual," Sebastian observes. Our goalie's attention swings to me. "Did he find out about you and HCB?"

"God, I hope not." I'm sweating just thinking about it. "Along those lines, I need help with something."

That perks Griffin right up. "Oooh. Is it something sexy and clandestine?"

"Do you even know what that means?" Logan asks with a smirk.

"Shut the hell up. I'm smart." Griffin tries to trip Byrne with the blade of his stick.

Bash rolls his eyes. "Guys. Focus. Ryder needs our help with something."

Sometimes I think this team would fall apart without Sebastian Navarro's steady leadership. Maddox may be the captain, but Bash is like a parent. He keeps us all on the straight and narrow. Well, I don't really need him to do that for me, but some of these other guys sure as hell do.

I give him a nod of thanks. "My girl wants to come to our series in Chicago. She went to college there, and her best friend still lives in the city. It's important to her that we meet."

"Is she planning on trying to stay in the hotel with you?" Logan's expression tells me exactly how stupid he thinks that idea is.

"No, she's going to stay with her friend. She has an apartment in the city." Stealing a glance at Coach, I shudder. "I don't have a death wish."

"You know we'll help with whatever you need," Sebastian says. "You two are good together. I like her."

"She's a hell of a lot cooler than her dad, that's for sure." Byrne winces as Coach shouts out another string of insults to the third stringers.

"So, what do you need us to do?" Griffin asks. He's bouncing on the toes of his skates. For all his fuckboy ways, Griffin Wright is a hopeless romantic.

"Just run interference with Coach when I disappear to meet Oscar's friend. Make sure you give him some kind of excuse."

"We'll tell him you have explosive diarrhea," Griffin says with a completely deadpan delivery.

Maddox shakes his head and scoffs. "I can't believe you get women to sleep with you. How do you do it? Just keep from opening your mouth, unless you're going down on them?"

The rest of us crack up, which earns the ire of Coach, who yells at us to *get your over-inflated heads out of your asses and do the work.*

"Are you going to tell him at some point?" Sebastian glances at Coach. He winces, probably imagining how that conversation would go. Just like I am.

It's the million-dollar question. Because Lexi and I

can't hide our relationship forever. But I get why she's nervous. She's been disappointed by her dad enough. I still haven't completely won her mom over. She has to feel the pressure of it all.

Making sure Coach's attention is elsewhere, I shrug. "I'm following Lexi's lead. It's her dad, you know? And with how rocky their relationship is, I won't push her."

"But you want to tell him." It's not a question. Sebastian knows.

"Of course, I do. I'm crazy about her. Shit, I think she's it for me." It's the first time I've admitted that out loud to anyone but myself. It feels freeing. Which is why I say the next part out loud too. "I'm in love with her."

Griffin pounds the blade of his stick on the ice. The other guys join in. It's like a hockey player's round of applause. "Hell, yeah, man. The girls are going to be so happy to hear that. Mira really likes Hot Cross Buns."

Shaking my head, I chuckle. "Dude. Don't ever call her that to her face."

"You told her yet?" Logan asks.

"No. The timing hasn't been right yet. And I think she feels the same way, but she's kinda skittish, you know?" The last thing I want to do is scare Lexi away. I need to play this right. Maybe I can plan some big romantic gesture while we're away in Chicago and tell her then.

Logan's brow rises. "I still think you guys are all nuts. Relationships are too much work. And they never last."

"Some of them do." I remember the way my dad spoke about my mom. He never even dated after she died. He'd tell me she was the love of his life, and you only ever get one real love. She was it for him, so why settle? That always stuck with me. And I think it kept me from sleeping around the way some guys on the team do. Logan included. I always believed there was one right person out there for me. Lexi's it. I know she is.

Our right winger doesn't look convinced. But I've heard stories about his own father that lead me to believe he was shaped as strongly by his dad's attitude toward love as I was. Logan doesn't talk about his dad much, but we all know about Owen Byrne. The man was a hockey legend in his own day. And from everything I've heard, he's a raging asshole. Honestly, it's probably a miracle Logan turned out as well-adjusted as he has.

"You don't have to believe me," I tell him, "but I've seen it. And my girl and I have that forever love. I know it."

"Quit talking about love like a bunch of teenage girls at a sleepover and *move your asses!*" Coach screams. Realizing he was close enough to overhear parts of our conversation startles me so much that I almost fall on my ass.

The other guys grimace, and we fall silent while Coach watches us. By the time practice is over, we're all sweaty, exhausted messes. We shower, dress, and shuffle out of the locker room, cursing Arthur Cross.

Griffin steps up beside me and nudges me with his elbow. "You should get your girl a jersey with your name on the back. Give it to her before the Chicago games, so she can wear it then." He grins at me and his chest puffs out. "It's like fucking catnip, dude. I swear, seeing your girl with your name on her back is instant foreplay."

I chuckle, but my mind immediately conjures an image of Lexi wearing my jersey. Only my jersey. Hell. Griffin's right. I need to get her one.

He must see the shift of my expression, because he

bursts out laughing. "Yeah, dude. Exactly. I bet there's someone here who can hook you up with one, even if the shop's not open." Pushing me down the hall toward the pro shop, Griffin calls out a goodbye.

And with images of Lexi in my jersey dancing through my head, I go on a wild goose chase to track down someone that can hook me up with one of my own jerseys. It takes me almost an hour before I connect with the correct person, but it's worth it when I watch her bag up a jersey, a Rogues scarf and hat for Lexi, and another set with a blank jersey for her best friend, Rachel. Because I am *going* to win Lexi's best friend over. This is a good place to start.

Mind full of Lexi, I check my phone for the time. She gets out of class in an hour. It's plenty of time to pick up something for lunch and surprise her on campus. And once we're done eating, maybe I can convince her to find an empty classroom so we can enjoy some dessert.

forty-five

LEXI

"YOU'RE HERE," RACHEL SQUEALS AS SHE PULLS ME in for a hug. "Oh my god, I am so excited. I've missed you so much."

Giving her a squeeze, I take a moment to soak up my best friend's attention. "I've missed you more."

"Impossible." She scoffs. "You're running around with a hot boyfriend and I'm here all alone, trying to one-up stupid Karl and busting my ass for an entry-level job opening that probably won't pay all of my rent."

"Dramatic much?"

She tosses her chestnut brown hair over her shoulder and strikes a pose. "Obviously. It's why you love me."

"One of the many reasons," I agree. "Now, where should I put my stuff?"

"Adam is out of town for the week, visiting his sister, so he said you can take his room." Rachel leads me down a short, narrow hallway and into a tidy little room that belongs to one of our other college friends.

"I'm still bummed he's not here." I can't help pouting. Rachel might be my best friend, but add in Adam, and the three of us were thick as thieves since sophomore year of college. If I'd stayed in Chicago, the three of us would have gotten a place together. I don't keep in touch with him as closely as I do with Rachel, but we send each other dumb memes and check in periodically. There's no denying the little twinge of nostalgia that twists in my chest, but I'm glad Rachel has him. I always feel better knowing that she's got Adam to look out for her. Because this isn't the best neighborhood. It's not the *worst*, either, but Rachel walks everywhere. If some idiot had the audacity to follow her home, they'd be greeted by two hundred and fifty pounds of former-football-player, turn right back around, and run the other way.

Rachel stands in the doorway of Adam's room and watches me toss my suitcase next to the bed. "He was really sad to miss you too. I promised him we'd FaceTime and drink margs together, even if we're currently separated by hundreds of miles of cornfields."

"That sounds like a great plan." I twist my neck from side to side, cracking it. "I hate flying."

"I know. Too bad your dad isn't cooler, or you could have flown in with the rest of the team and been way more comfortable."

My stomach lurches at the mention of my dad. "Yeah, that would never happen."

"Maybe he'll surprise you if you tell him." Rachel's expression says even she doesn't believe the words coming out of her mouth. "Be cool about it and glad you're dating a great guy."

"No. You know my dad." Well, she knows of him from the stories I've told. He met Rachel once. The singular time in four years of college that he came to visit me. Even though he had to travel to Chicago regularly for Rogues' games. Even after I offered to meet him wherever he was. He declined every time. Told me he didn't want to *inconvenience me.* As if seeing my dad would have been an inconvenience.

Absently, I rub my chest.

"I know. But I can still hope he'll stop being a selfish, clueless asshole one day." She walks in the room to give me another hug, then grabs my hand. "Now, come on. You need to help me figure out what to wear to the game tonight. I have no idea what to expect."

"Just wear layers," I tell her as she drags me out of Adam's room and toward their small kitchen. "With as cold as it is outside, you don't really need to do anything special. Maybe double up on socks? You'll be fine."

"Okay. I can do that. Come help me make posters. I got two and a bunch of Sharpies. You make one to cheer Ryder on with, and I'll make one that calls Chase's manhood into question."

It's impossible not to laugh, because she does, in fact, have a whole poster-making station set up on the dining table. Along with a list of mean digs at Chase that she asks me to help choose between. Quite a few insult the size of his penis, a few insult his hockey skills, and a couple insinuate he's a little too into his mom.

I veto those.

We're in the middle of making our signs, and I'm telling her all about the last date Ryder took me on, when there's a knock on Rachel's apartment door. I turn to her. "Expecting someone?"

She looks confused. Her brow is furrowed as she looks at the door like it may bite her. "Nope. Do me a favor and grab the bat out of my coat closet."

I laugh but do as she asks.

Rachel glances at the bat in my hand as she opens the door, keeping the chain lock engaged. "Can I help you?"

"Are you Rachel Keller?"

"Yeessss," my friend drawls.

"Great, I've got a package for you. It requires a signature." I edge closer and see the young guy hold up a parcel. He frowns when Rachel doesn't immediately unlock the door. "Uh, you gonna sign for this? I have other deliveries to make."

Rachel winces. "Yep. Sorry. One second." She closes the door just long enough to disengage the chain before reopening it. The delivery guy looks annoyed, but he's never been a woman living alone in a big city, so he can suck it.

As soon as Rachel signs on the dotted line, he hands her a good-sized box and walks away. Once the door's shut and locked again, Rachel brings the mysterious package inside and reads the return address. One eyebrow arches, and then she looks up at me. "It's from your boy toy."

"What?" I grab the box out of her hands. "And he's not my boy toy. Why is he sending you a package?" Curiosity eats at me.

"I don't know, but let's open it and find out."

We tear the tape away and open it together. Inside is a note addressed to me. It reads:

> *Oscar,*
> *Can't wait to see you tonight and meet your best friend. Thought you ladies might like something to wear to the game. The one with my name on the back is for you.*
> *See you soon,*
> *Ryder*

Warmth spreads through my body. It starts at my center and floods through the rest of me. This man. He's so sweet and thoughtful. Rachel squeals with delight as we pull out Rogues jerseys, hats, and scarves. He's even included a fancy hot chocolate kit, with a note that tells us it's for after the game, and a bottle of wine labeled *for girl time.*

Rachel's warm brown eyes meet mine. "Damn, girl. He really is gone for you. This is ridiculously sweet. And to include stuff for me in it?" She holds her jersey up to her chest and looks down at the logo. "Keeper, for sure."

He is. And I'm gone for him too. Maybe it's time to be vulnerable this weekend and admit it to him. Sucking in a deep breath, I lock eyes with my bestie. "I'm in love with him."

Rachel's expression softens. "I know."

"I'm terrified, Rach."

She pulls me into a hug. "I know."

"There are so many people here."

It's impossible not to chuckle at Rachel's wide-eyed expression. She surveys the noisy crowd, easily ignoring the dirty looks being thrown our way for wearing Rogues yellow and gray. My best friend is not one to be intimidated. Every time someone scowls at us, she just smiles and gives them a cheeky little finger wave.

"Oh, these seats are great." After doing a little shimmy, Rachel takes her seat, and I file in after her. I was careful when buying our tickets, once again ensuring that we were outside of my dad's line of sight. Coming to the arena at all is a risk, but my dad is always too focused on the game to care about the crowd.

"This is your first hockey game, right?"

She nods. "Yeah. I can't wait to watch a bunch of hot men skate around and beat each other up."

"That's not exactly what happens," I tell her with a chuckle. "But it's not too far off sometimes."

"So, we're going out with them after?"

Ryder asked us to join him and the guys at a bar after the game. Rachel was thrilled. Especially if it meant that she had a chance to find herself a hot hockey player hookup. She'd gleefully proclaimed that this was her chance to play puck bunny for a night.

"Yeah, they found a place close to the arena, so we can all walk."

She side-eyes me. "Your dad doesn't go out with them after games?"

"God, no," I say with a laugh. "He'll be too busy preparing for the second game in the series. Besides, most coaches don't go out drinking with their team members."

"But aren't you worried he'll see you?"

I shake my head. "Nah. We're going to meet the guys a block or two away from the arena afterward. It'll be fine."

The seats continue to fill with boisterous fans. The atmosphere charges with eager anticipation. And when the announcer's voice booms through the arena to announce the teams, Rachel does a little dance in her seat and claps.

Visiting teams never get the same spectacular introductions as the home team, but Rachel still screams right along with me when he announces Ryder's name and position. Following the sound of our enthusiastic support, my boyfriend's attention lands on us, and the most brilliant smile lights up his face. I blow him a kiss; he rewards me with a wink.

"You know that guy?" a woman two seats down asks. Her expression is curious and a bit hungry. "He's hot."

"He's my bestie's boyfriend," Rachel says with a knowing grin.

The woman studies me and smiles. "Lucky girl."

I really am.

Soon, the announcer is naming the players for the Chicago Blizzard, and when he calls out Chase Bowen's name—the asshole who hurt Ryder—Rachel and I both stand up and boo loudly. She unfurls her poster, waves it above her head and shouts, "You suck, micro-dick!" She's emblazoned the poster with the words *Chase Bowen's dick is so small, he wears unicorn panties so at least he can make **something** horny*. Then she drew a horrible picture of a unicorn with a limp horn and a frown on its face.

A frown that is mirrored by Chase Bowen himself when he notices the sign.

Rachel grins gleefully at his look of displeasure and flips him off.

We're both giggling uncontrollably by the time she sits back down. "Oh god, that was good. Did you see his face?"

"I'm going to have so much fun torturing him today," Rach answers. "I think I'll drag Adam to some games with me when he gets back, so we can both troll that asshole for what he did to Ryder."

I love that I have friends who will give a random jerk a hard time just because he hurt my boyfriend. They're supportive and always have my back. If only we lived closer.

THE GAME IS INTENSE.

The Chicago Blizzard play with just as much determination and intensity as the Rogues do, and it's a constant battle for dominance. The Rogues will score one, then the Blizzard answer with a score of their own. We're tied 4-4 in the middle of the third period, and my nerves are fried.

Stupid Chase Bowen won't leave Ryder alone. He chirps at my boyfriend every chance he gets and never misses an opportunity to slam him into the boards. Ryder looks pissed, but he doesn't instigate any of it. The other guys on the Rogues have responded in kind, though. And it's not just Chase they check whenever they can.

"Holy crap." Rachel winces as one of the Blizzard's defensemen gets smashed into the glass in front of us. "This is freaking awesome."

I can't help but laugh. I knew Rach would love this game. She's fiery and fierce and, man, does my bestie love to shit talk. She's busted Chase's balls every chance she gets. It's wearing on him too. Every time she shouts his name and hurls another insult, the guy's steely gray eyes narrow as he glares at her.

She's throwing off his game, and the Rogues have noticed. Griffin laughs every time he sees her poster. Even the normally stoic Maddox grins when he notices the effect Rach and her sign have on Chase.

And when Chase and Ryder are battling it out for control of the puck right in front of us and Rachel shouts, "Hey, Chase! Did you decide to play hockey so you could handle a stick more than an inch long?" he falters just long enough for Ryder to get the puck, head toward the net, deke, and slap a shot in between the goalie's knees. Ryder does a funny little celly dance before winking at me and Rachel. Chase, though? Chase skates past us and glares hard at my bestie. Good thing the man doesn't have laser eyes, or she'd be toast.

With only thirty seconds left, the Blizzard can't manage to tie the score, and the crowd around us boos when the Rogues win it 5-4. My bestie and I get more than a few dirty looks as people file out of their seats.

"Come on." Grabbing Rachel's hand, I drag her out with the masses. I don't want to be left standing here without the buffer of other people. It would be too easy for my dad to spot us.

"That was so fun," Rachel squeals. "I'm totally a hockey girly now."

"Knew you would be. Now, let's go meet the guys. They're going to want to buy you drinks after the way you got in Chase's head."

One side of Rachel's lips tilt in a sinister grin. "I'm already planning what to put on my sign next time."

God help Chase Bowen. He's made an enemy of Rachel Keller. And she's one of the most determined people I know.

forty-six

LEXI

THE GUYS ALL CHEER WHEN RACHEL AND I MEET UP with them a few blocks away from the arena.

"Dude." Griffin approaches Rachel with his palm up for a high five. "The guys and I are buying you drinks tonight. The way you got in that asshole's head was epic."

Rachel's face splits with a huge smile and, after returning Griffin's high five, she curtsies. "Thank you. Happy to help anytime you guys play here."

"Hell, yeah," Griffin says.

After giving Ryder a kiss hello, I make introductions, then we walk to the bar. We get some looks because it's rare to see so many big guys together like this, and while I personally think Ryder is the hottest guy among them, I can admit that they're all good-looking. But here, they can be relatively anonymous. A few people seem to recognize them, but they're obviously fans leaving the game. And since we're the visiting team, no one says anything or bothers any of the guys. It's nice. Though I am looking out for my dad. My head is on a swivel.

"He's not here, baby," Ryder murmurs in my ear. He's got his arm slung around my shoulder, and he pulls me close so he can kiss the top of my head. "You can relax."

I blow out a deep breath. "I know. I'm being ridiculous. Sorry."

"Don't be sorry. I just want you to relax and have fun. I'm excited to get to know your best friend. It's too bad Adam is out of town. He sounds cool."

"He is," Rachel says, looping her arm through my free one. "I'll bring him to a game the next time you're in town. How great would it be to have a reason to visit us more often?" she asks me. Her eyes are bright and excited, and I have to admit, it is nice that I have another excuse to visit them. Not that I need an excuse.

"I'll try to convince her to come to every away game we have here," Ryder says. "Especially if the two of you make more signs like the ones you made tonight." He chuckles, shaking his head. "You have no idea how fun it was to watch Chase lose his cool over them."

"What's the deal with you two?" Rachel asks. Her curiosity has been piqued, and my best friend loves tea.

"Honestly? I don't even remember what we were fighting about, but we got into it one night a couple months after my dad died. Chase was being a huge dick, and we ended up beating the shit out of each other. I tried to apologize after, but he wouldn't hear it." Ryder's handsome face contorts into a deep frown. "He was one of my housemates. I considered him a brother. It hurt to lose him after I lost my dad, and now we can't stand to be near each other."

"That sucks," Rachel says. "What a dick."

Ryder shrugs, but I know how much it hurts him. "Now I get to call these idiots brothers." He nods in the direction of his teammates. Griffin is trying to convince Logan to give him a piggyback ride, Maddox is scolding Griffin, and Sebastian just watches with a paternal smile. "So, I guess everything turned out all right in the end."

"Still." Rachel's eyes narrow. "I'm going to go to as many games as I can and make Bowen's life a living hell."

That has my boyfriend barking out a laugh. "Remind me never to get on your bad side."

"Don't hurt my girl and you won't."

Ryder's fingers tighten on my hip. "Don't worry. I have no intention of hurting Lexi."

***

"I WISH YOU WERE COMING TO THE GAME tomorrow." Ryder presses me to his body in a long, sweet hug. "But I'm glad you're getting time with Rachel. She seems great."

"She is. And she likes you, so I guess I'll keep you."

He laughs at that, but he doesn't realize how serious I am. If Rachel had hated him, I don't know what I would have done. "Thank god. Because I'm definitely keeping you." Leaning down, Ryder slants his mouth over mine in a slow, sweeping kiss. "Have breakfast with me our last morning here? I'll sneak out of the hotel early and meet you somewhere. There's no way I'll be able to wait until we get home to spend time alone with you."

When I glance at Rachel, she nods. Of course, she's

listening in on our conversation. "Okay," I tell him. "Let's do it. I already miss you."

"You two are disgustingly sweet," Rachel comments.

Logan grunts next to her. "Aren't they? I'm getting a cavity from watching this."

Griffin slaps Logan upside the head, much to Logan's irritation. "Dude. Shut the fuck up. One day, you'll fall in love and we're going to give you so much hell."

His words make my cheeks heat and butterflies alight in my belly. Ryder and I haven't said those three little words to each other. Is that what his friends think? That we're in love? Or did Ryder say something to them? Whatever the case, he doesn't seem nearly as embarrassed as I am by Griffin's casual use of the word. Ryder just shakes his head, rolls his eyes, and cups the back of my head to pull me in for another kiss. This one is teasing and playful.

His eyes dance when he pulls away. "You ladies have fun tomorrow." He lets go of me long enough to give my best friend a hug. "I'm glad we got to hang out, Rachel. We'll have to do it again."

"Agreed," she says.

Ryder turns to give me one last kiss on the forehead. "I'll text you the name of the restaurant. And you can call me whenever, okay?"

God, he's adorable. He clearly doesn't want to leave. Even though I'm desperate for some bestie time, I get it. I don't want to leave him, either. "I'll call you, don't worry. Good luck at tomorrow's game. I'll see you the following morning."

"All right," Sebastian says when Ryder looks like he's going to kiss me again. He grabs the back of Ryder's shirt and gives him a tug. "We need to get back to the hotel, and the ladies need some girl time. It was nice to meet you, Rachel. Lexi, we'll see you later."

Everyone exchanges goodbyes, then Rachel and I hail a cab. Ryder watches us drive away until the car makes a left-hand turn and we lose sight of each other.

"Oh girl, you two have it so bad."

Sighing, I let my head flop back against the headrest. "I know."

"And don't think I missed the fact that he didn't protest when Griffin said you two were in love."

"I know." Butterflies take flight in my stomach again.

Rachel studies me. "Is he the one?"

He could be. But I'm not sure I've let myself go there because my dad complicates things. Even if Ryder is in love with me, I don't expect him to choose me over his career, if push comes to shove. Not that my dad would ever allow that to happen. Still. In those quiet moments before I fall asleep, I picture us together. When my eyes grow heavy and my body relaxes, I can't help imagining what our lives could be like.

A cute house somewhere. A small wedding, surrounded by friends and family. Maybe a kid or two, many years down the line. But when those images try to invade my mind during the day, I push them away. It all feels too fragile and tenuous. And, despite Ryder's sweet words and heart-melting actions, there's a deep part of me that doesn't believe I'm worth choosing. Not when it becomes inconvenient to do so. After all, my dad never has. And he's my dad.

"It's okay to be scared," Rachel murmurs, giving my hand a squeeze. "But I think you owe it to yourself and Ryder to be honest about your feelings."

"I know." I blow a breath out through my closed lips, making them vibrate. "I think he's the one."

The cab pulls up in front of Rachel's building. She pays the driver and aims a blinding smile in my direction. "I think he is too."

We're both laughing as we spill out of the cab and make our way into her building and up to her apartment. Admitting my feelings out loud has me feeling light and free. Like I'm nothing more than a fluffy cloud dancing across the sky.

"Do you have anything hot to wear to breakfast the day after tomorrow?" Rachel asks as we hang our coats.

"Hot? No. I wasn't planning to go on a date while I was here."

My best friend claps her hands. "Then, tomorrow we should grab lunch, do some shopping, and help you figure out how you're going to tell that hot man of yours that you're in love with him."

"Rach…"

"Nope." She shakes her head at me. "There's no talking me out of this. I don't give a crap what your dad thinks, Lex. That man is perfect for you, and he worships the ground you walk on. You're going to take what you want, and your dad will just have to accept it."

Rachel is vastly overestimating my father's ability to accept things he doesn't like, but I can't deny that I want Ryder.

"Fine," I say. "We'll go shopping, and I'll consider telling Ryder how I feel. But you're going to help me think of ways to break it to my dad."

She pulls me into a tight hug. "That, I can do. Now I need to go to bed. Heckling Chase Bowen wore me out."

Laughing, I squeeze Rachel right back. "I think it wore him out too."

We say our good nights as we break apart. My heart is full of gratitude for my amazing friend. And my head is full of all the ways telling Ryder I love him could go perfectly right. Or terribly wrong.

forty-seven

RYDER

THE PIERCING BEEP OF MY ALARM JOLTS ME OUT OF sleep before a pillow hits me in the face. Aaron, my teammate and roommate, groans.

"Dude. What the hell? It's like seven. Our flight isn't for another five hours."

A deep stretch helps my mind wake up, along with my body. "Sorry, man. Secret breakfast date with my girl. Cover for me if Coach comes to the room?"

"Yeah, whatever." Aaron waves his hand at me.

I take the fastest shower ever, throw on some warm clothes, and quietly slip out of my room and down the generic-looking hotel hallway. A quick glance around reveals that the coast is clear, and I stride out of the warmth of the hotel and into the cold Chicago winter. The wind howls as it races between skyscrapers and down city streets before nipping painfully at my exposed face.

I'm practically an icicle by the time I make it to the little breakfast place where Lexi and I agreed to meet at. At least, until I spot her beautiful face. The sight of her wide smile thaws me instantly.

"Hey, gorgeous." I slide into the booth next to her before cupping her cheeks and kissing her silly. We're going to be one of *those* couples this morning. The ones that sit next to each other and can't keep their hands to themselves. The kind of couple other diners roll their eyes at and secretly hate. I don't give a shit.

Lexi hums against my mouth, her body melting into mine. "Hey, Handsome. Is it weird to say I missed you? I just saw you the day before yesterday."

Her words are like a warm hug. "Not weird at all. I've been annoying the guys because I check my phone every five minutes to see if you've texted."

That earns a sweet giggle from my girl. I love the sound of her laughter. Making her happy is practically a drug, at this point. It's one of my favorite things in the world. I open my mouth, the words *I love you* ready to spill out like honey when our server approaches the table. That's okay. I've got plenty of time to tell Lexi how I feel.

"That was a pretty tough game yesterday," she says with a slight wince after our server leaves. "I watched the highlights."

Every minute of the game was a battle. After winning the first game by the skin of our teeth, game two was even more brutal. By the time the third period ended, both teams had seen their share of players sent to the sin bin, there were a few times the game nearly devolved into an all-out brawl, and as the clock ticked down to zero, we were tied 2-2.

The Blizzard won in a hard-fought sudden-death overtime.

It was disappointing as hell, but at least my boys and I kept Chase from scoring any goals. I'll take my wins wherever I can. Coach, though?

"Yeah. Coach was pissed. I swear, the man had literal steam coming out of his ears."

Lexi winces again. "Yeah. I've seen him like that more than a few times. It's not pretty."

Did he yell at her and her mom the way he yells at us? "But he only acted like that toward his team, right? You've seen him yell at his players?"

She shrugs. "For the most part."

"Jesus, OTG. I'm sorry he's such a dick." Pulling her closer to me, I wrap her in a protective hug and kiss her forehead before resting my cheek on her hair. I hate the idea of Coach yelling at Lex. Which is why I suggest the thing I've been thinking about for a couple of weeks now. "I'm going to talk to your dad. Alone. Tell him we're together."

Lexi sucks in a breath, pulls away from me, and looks up at me with wide eyes. "What? No, Ryder. You can't do that."

"I don't want to hide this anymore, baby. I'm proud to be dating you. Hell, I'm the luckiest bastard on the planet. And your dad may be my boss, but he doesn't have any right to tell me who I can and can't see. But I also know just how much of a hothead he is, and I don't want you there when I tell him. If he's going to blow up, I can take it."

"I can't let you do that." She worries at her lower lip, but I see the embers of hope in her eyes. She's been worried about this. If I can convince her I'll be fine telling him alone, maybe that will ease her fears. Still, her face crumples into a frown. "He could mess with your career."

She's right. He could. But crazy as it sounds, I've realized that, as much as I love hockey, it would quickly lose its luster without her in my life. I need to tell her. Lexi needs to understand that I love the hell out of her. And if I'm forced to make a choice between hockey and her? I know which one I'm choosing.

"Baby, you don't need to worry about that. Lexi, I—"

"All right, dears, here we are." Smiling brightly and completely unaware that she has, once again, interrupted my attempt to tell Lexi I'm in love with her, our server sets our breakfast and coffee down in front of us. "Can I get you anything else?"

Yeah. You can rewind time and not choose the exact moment I'm about to spill my guts to drop off our food.

"No, thank you," Lexi replies. She smiles warmly at our server, who cheerily offers to come back and refill our coffees in a bit, then tells us to enjoy our breakfast. When Lexi takes a bite of her French toast and hums her enjoyment, I know the moment is lost. Hopefully, another one will present itself before we part ways this morning. Now that I've decided to tell her how I feel, I don't want to wait.

I also know I'll have to keep working on Lexi to get her to agree with my plan to talk to her dad alone. She's worried about his reaction and what it might mean for my job, but she's an adult. It's not like he can command me to stop seeing his daughter. I'll earn his trust. And not that I need his blessing or whatever other old-fashioned bullshit thing, but I also don't want to drive a deeper wedge between them.

Coach is a hard-ass, and a bastard at times, but he's her dad. I know what it's like to lose a father. That's the last thing I want for her. Hell, my goal is to encourage him to repair the rift between them. Things with her mom are better than they were. I'm hopeful her dad will want to fix things too.

"How was your day with Rachel yesterday?"

That brings a vibrant smile to Lexi's face. "So good. We went out, walked around the Art Institute before lunch, like we always did during college, did some shopping..." She lets out a soft puff of air, her eyes growing wistful. "I miss her."

"Would she ever move to Minneapolis?"

"No." Lexi shakes her head. "She loves it here. And she's trying to get this job with the firm she's interning at. I've tried to convince her to move a bunch of times, but she never takes the bait." A lock of hair shifts, getting in Lexi's way. I brush it away, tuck it behind her ear, and let my fingers linger. Any excuse to touch her.

"Well, then, you'll just have to come with me to all of our Chicago games."

"Yeah," she says, huffing out a laugh. "My dad would *love* that."

"Not really up to him, is it?" I place a quick kiss on her lips before taking a bite of my breakfast.

"Can we talk about anything other than my dad?"

"Course, baby." We need to figure this stuff out, but I get why she doesn't want to talk about him right now. And if it comes right down to it, I can talk to Coach and beg her forgiveness after. "The guys invited us to hang out with them at Maddox's next week. I guess Isla and Mira have been bugging them to have us over. They want to get to know you better."

That banishes the clouds that have begun to hover over Lexi's head. She grins. "I'd like that. They seem really cool."

Warmth fills my chest. When I started with the Rogues, I was in a pretty low place. I'd realized one of my lifelong dreams but had no one to share my excitement with. I was alone, and I hated it. Now, I've got growing friendships with my teammates and a woman I'm falling for. I have people to call when things go to shit and people who celebrate me when things go right.

It's why I'm determined to find a way to tell Coach about my relationship with his daughter. Because nothing in life is guaranteed, and I'll be damned if I let fear hold me back from being with the woman of my dreams. I've been alone long enough. And so has Lexi. But neither of us needs to be alone any longer.

My mind is swirling with plans as we finish eating. I don't want to say goodbye to my girlfriend, even though I'll see her tonight because she's agreed to spend the night at my place. When she insists on walking back to the hotel with me, I know I'm not alone in that. She doesn't want to say goodbye, either.

I text Aaron and ask him to bring my bags down from the room, so I can spend every possible second with Lexi. The wind howls as we huddle against the back of the bus. No one's out yet, and Coach is always the last to board, so we have a few minutes before we need to break apart.

Lexi's back is against the bus as I kiss her. Her little gasps and soft moans have me hard as a rock, and even though I shouldn't, I press my knee between hers. And just like that first time at the cabin, she grinds against my thigh. She drives me wild. If we had time, I'd sneak her into the hotel and up to my room. But we don't.

There are a few whistles as the first couple of my teammates make their way out of the hotel and over to the bus. They make kissing noises as they load their bags into the compartments behind us. It makes Lexi blush the most intoxicating shade of pink as she pulls away.

"I should go." She blinks up at me, her swollen lips tilted in a sexy smile.

"Yeah," I say. But I don't let go of her. "Fuck, OTG, what are you doing to me?"

She giggles. "I'd say sorry, but I'm not. Besides, I don't think I'm doing anything to you that you're not also doing to me."

"Who's doing who?" Griffin waggles his eyebrows at us as he approaches with Maddox, Sebastian, and Logan. "What's up, HCB?"

Lexi rolls her eyes at Griffin. "HCB?"

"Dude," I warn.

Griffin ignores me. "Yeah. We needed a code name for you, and your boy wouldn't let us call you OTG, so we came up with our own acronym."

I laugh when she smacks me on the chest with the back of her hand. "You told them about that nickname?"

"Sorry, Oscar. It just kinda slipped out."

The guys laugh when Lexi pinches the bridge of her nose. "And what, exactly, does HCB stand for?"

"Hot Cross Buns, obviously," Griffin replies. As if that should be completely obvious. The rest of the guys try to hide their laughter. They fail miserably.

"Hot Cross Buns?" Lexi screeches.

"Sorry, Lexi." Bash has the good sense to look apologetic. "If it makes you feel any better, Griffin's first choice was Sexy Lexi, but Ryder vetoed that."

"Oh my god," Lexi says, shaking her head. She's smiling, so I know she's not actually pissed. I'll still hear about this later, I'm sure, but she's more amused than annoyed. "You guys are ridiculous."

"Couldn't have Coach hear us talking about you with the rookie," Maddox offers. He glances over his shoulder, making sure the coast is clear. "And speaking of Coach, you two should probably say goodbye. He'll be out here soon."

I hate this. The sneaking around. I hate that I can't claim my woman in a public way yet. I'm going to talk to Coach this week. Enough is enough.

Lexi's sigh only hardens my resolve. "You're probably right. I'll see you guys this week, right?"

"That's the plan," Maddox says. "Isla and my sister have been bugging us to give them a reason to see you again."

"Well, I'm looking forward to seeing them too." She turns her attention back to me. "I'll head over to your place tonight after I unpack and get a shower. Miss you already."

"God, you two are nauseating," Logan grumbles. I'm pretty sure someone smacks him upside the head, but I don't see it. I'm too busy kissing the woman I'm in love with.

She wraps her arms around my neck and presses her body flush to mine. Our tongues brush and tangle, and by the time I pull away from her, we're both panting. Pressing my forehead to hers, I open my mouth to finally say those three little words. I don't even care that the guys are standing around us.

A deep, booming voice steals the words right out of my mouth. "What the *fuck* is going on here?"

forty-eight

LEXI

Every muscle in my body tenses at my dad's harsh tone.

Shit. Shit, shit, shit.

Ryder's spine straightens, and he shifts, positioning himself in front of me. A buffer to protect me from the red-faced anger of my father. The other guys lose their good-natured goofiness in an instant and take an unconscious step closer. I'm surrounded by a wall of six-foot men and their impressive muscles. It's sweet and comforting, but I know they won't keep my dad from saying what he's going to say.

"I asked a damned question, and I expect an answer," my dad growls, taking another step closer. His gray eyes narrow as he looks between Ryder and me. "What are you doing here, Alexis?"

"Coach," Ryder starts, his palms outstretched. As if he can placate the man shooting lasers out of his eyeballs.

"Don't you fucking *Coach* me, Ryder. I asked my daughter a question, and I expect an answer."

The way my dad glares at me makes me want to shrivel up into a tiny little ball. If I thought for even a second that his anger was because he was worried I was being taken advantage of, that would be one thing. But I know better. I know better, and I'm dreading what he'll say before all of this is over.

I want to curl into a little ball, but I won't. I force my spine straight, push my shoulders back, and step up beside Ryder. "Dad. If you'd like to talk, we can talk. But not like this."

"The hell, we won't, Alexis. You are my daughter and this is my team. You will answer my damned question, and it better not be the answer I think is coming."

I can't help it. I bark out a bitter laugh. "Oh, yeah? And what answer do you think that is, Dad?"

"Coach," Ryder interrupts, drawing my dad's attention back to him. "Look, I get that every dad is protective of his daughter, but I can assure you, I only have the best of intentions with Lexi. Your daughter is an incredible woman, and I know how lucky I am that she ever even gave me a second look."

"When did this start?" My dad ignores Ryder, aiming the question at me. The words are sharp and pointed. An arrow tightly nocked.

Shaking my head, I tell him. "It started when you gave him the keys to the family cabin. Where I was staying for my Christmas break."

My dad is silent for a moment at that. "You said you had plans for Christmas."

"Yeah," I say. "Plans to spend the week alone at the cabin."

Every Rogues player not already on the bus watches us. Their eyes ping back and forth, like they're watching a table tennis match. One with unusually high stakes. My dad serves the ball, and I volley it back.

"I thought you were spending the holiday with friends."

With a sardonic laugh, I roll my eyes. "You assumed I was with friends so you wouldn't have to ask. Because if you'd asked, you would have had to feel bad that you didn't try all that hard to get me to spend it with you."

I can almost feel the pity wafting off the guys around us. The frigid Chicago air is thick with it. But I don't need their pity. This has been my reality for long enough that I've found ways to cope. Ryder wraps his arm around my waist. My dad narrows his eyes at the offered comfort, but Ryder doesn't flinch away. I fucking love him for it. I love him. I love him, and I've never told him.

It may be too late now.

"You know what, Alexis?" My dad crosses his arms over his chest and looks down his nose at me like I'm some petulant child. "I'm sick of your attitude. It was one thing when you were a hormonal teenager, but this?" He shakes his head. "This is something else."

My chest squeezes sharply. I suck in a breath, feeling like I've been slapped. Or shot with the arrow of his words. "Excuse me?"

"Coach," Ryder says, a warning in his tone. My dad ignores it.

"You've never appreciated the responsibility I hold as

the coach of this team. People depend on me, Alexis. These men, their spouses and kids, hell, even the concession workers. You have no idea the weight resting on my shoulders, while you're throwing tantrums about how I don't spend enough time with you or whining about how I missed some silly school thing.

"All you can think about is yourself. Even now. You're a grown woman, and you still don't understand that entire families depend on me to make sure this team is a success."

The world goes utterly still and silent, save for the roaring in my ears.

Tantrums.

Whining.

Families depending on him.

I depended on him. I depended on him, and he was never there. Don't I matter? Don't I count?

"Coach," Ryder growls. His fingers dig into my hip. I'm not sure if he's trying to tether me to him or tether himself to me, so he doesn't lunge at my father.

The bitterest laugh scrapes itself out of my throat. Then another. And another. Soon, I can't stop, and a rogue tear slips down my face. "What, exactly, are you getting at, Dad? Like you said, I'm a big girl now. If you have something to say, fucking say it."

My dad scoffs. "I knew you were desperate for my attention, Alexis, but this?" He points at Ryder. "This is taking things too far. I won't let you distract one of my best players and bring him down, just so you can get back at me for some perceived slight. You won't ruin his career or set this team back. I won't let you."

His words knock the air right out of my lungs. All I can do is gape at the man who was supposed to love and protect me as he finally gives voice to what he really thinks of me. I shouldn't be surprised. This shouldn't hurt.

And yet.

I feel every stupid girlish hope I've held on to that my dad may step up one day and love me the way I deserve turn to ash. I feel the emptiness those childish hopes leave in my chest when they crumble and blow away in the raging violence of his words.

He actually believes I would date Ryder just to get back at him? That I would play with Ryder's heart with the intention of breaking it, so I could fuck with my dad's chance to take the Rogues to the Cup?

I stagger back a step and clutch my chest as Ryder and the rest of the guys start shouting. I don't hear what they're saying. The roaring in my ears is too loud. I should have expected something like this, but to hear the words leave his mouth... I'm lost.

I want to run. I want to find some private place, where I can scream at the unfairness of it all, then cry my eyes out.

"How fucking dare you!" Ryder shouts before he wraps his arms around my shaking form.

"Listen, son, I'm just looking out for you and this team. I love my daughter, but she's not good for you. You're going places, kid, and she'll just try to hold you back. Same way her mother tried to hold me back."

A strangled sob tears out of me. My mom held him back? All she ever did was support him. Love him. Take care of the house and the bills and *me*. But nothing she did was ever good enough for Arthur Cross. How could I have expected to be any different?

Feeling like a wild animal stuck in a trap, I push at Ryder's chest, desperate to get away from here. Thrashing and flailing, I struggle against his hold. But he won't let me go.

I need him to let me go. I need to get out of here.

I knew this would blow up in my face.

How could I have been so stupid? How could I have let myself want this with Ryder? He's either going to destroy his career for me, or he'll realize I'm more trouble than I'm worth. Either way, my dad is right—I'm ruining Ryder's life. Because I am selfish. All I've been able to think about is how much I want to be loved by him. How much I want someone to put me first.

Why would Ryder choose me, when my own father won't? Unless it's out of guilt. I should take the choice out of his hands. Set Ryder free. I should tell him this is over.

Except, I can't seem to make the words come out of my mouth.

I love Ryder. So much. And I don't want to drag him down with me. If the words won't come, I'll just run.

I push against his chest again, needing to escape.

RYDER

Lexi's eyes are wild and filling with tears as she struggles to escape my arms. But I don't let her go. I'll never let her go.

Alexis Genevieve Cross is mine, and I will have her back. Damn the consequences.

"Baby," I murmur, trying to soothe her. "Baby, shh. It's okay. You're okay."

I can't believe the bullshit that just spewed out of Coach's mouth like raw sewage from a busted line. If the shouts and objections from my teammates are any indication, they can't believe it, either.

Here I was, prepared to defend my intentions to the man and reassure him I care deeply about his daughter, and he's more concerned with my career and the team? What the actual fuck?

"Let me go, Ryder," Lexi sobs. "Please let me go."

"Can't do that, Oscar." I'm barely able to push the words past what feels like a boulder in my throat. Her pain threatens to choke me. "Never letting you go."

"Please," she cries. And when she looks up at me with devastation etched into the set of her red-rimmed green eyes, it takes every ounce of my resolve not to haul off and punch Coach straight in his stupid, hateful face.

Cupping her cheek, I press my forehead to hers. "Alexis Cross, don't you understand by now?"

She stills, searching my face.

"I'm never letting you go, because I'm so fucking in love with you, it's ridiculous. So in love that I'm about to get fired for breaking my boss's nose. I have been from nearly the first moment you opened your mouth and accused me of trying to garrote you. You're not going anywhere, Oscar. You're mine."

Lexi sobs again, but this time, she's not trying to push away from me. This time, she sags against my chest as the fight drains out of her. "You love me?"

Tilting her chin up so she's forced to meet my eyes, I nod. "This isn't how I wanted to tell you, but yes. I love you more than I thought possible, baby. And as soon as I'm done yelling at your dad, I'm going to show you just how much."

A watery laugh bubbles out of her. "I love you too. I'm so glad you didn't turn out to be a serial killer."

With a quiet chuckle at her words, I turn to Sebastian and silently ask him to support my girl while I deal with her asshole father. Bash nods and pulls her into a hug. The rest of the guys close ranks around her at my back.

Every last trace of softness falls from my expression as I turn to face Coach Cross. The man shakes his head, like I'm some idiot being taken for a ride. It pisses me off even more.

"Listen, son, I know how tempting a pretty face can be, but—"

"Don't you dare call me son," I growl. "Coming from a father like you, it's a damned insult. Especially after the way you just treated your actual daughter."

Coach's eyes widen with surprise, but I'm not done.

"You know, a part of me feels sorry for you. You've got this incredible daughter who's strong and smart and hilarious, and you don't even know her. It's a travesty, honestly. And I'd say you're missing out on time with the child you raised, but you didn't fucking raise her, did you?"

Coach frowns. "Watch it, rookie. I'm still your boss."

I can't help it. I laugh. "You know what? I don't care."

"Are you really ready to throw a promising career away over a woman?" Coach scoffs, shaking his head. Lexi sniffles behind me as she undoubtedly tries to hide her hurt. God, how can he be such a blind idiot?

A sharp pang of longing and loss for my own father hits me. Not just because I miss him, but because he would have adored Alexis. He would have treated her like his own. He would have happily stepped up and been the father Lexi always deserved. But he's gone, and the only dad Lexi's ever going to have is standing in front of me with utter disdain on his face.

"No," I finally say. "I'm not going to throw my career away for a woman." Lexi gasps behind me, so I hurry to finish my thought. "But I'll throw it away for Lexi, if that's what it takes. Because she's worth it. Something you should understand, but for some unfathomable reason, don't."

Arthur Cross glares at his daughter. "Is this what you wanted?"

"Don't fucking talk to her," I snarl, stepping in front of her and ensuring he can no longer see her. "This isn't her doing. It's yours. No one here is throwing around threats and absolutes, except you."

"I thought this was your dream, kid? The best players don't let themselves get distracted by women and relationships."

It's my turn to scoff. I motion to Maddox. One of our best players and one of the strongest guys in the whole league. "Graves doesn't seem distracted by his relationship. In fact, his stats have improved since entering a committed relationship."

"Sure," Coach says, rolling his eyes. "Until his woman wants more attention than he can give, or he finds himself stuck with a kid who keeps him up all night and takes his focus away from the game."

What. An. Ass.

"All due disrespect, Coach," Griffin says from beside me, "but shut the fuck up. I feel sorry for your ex-wife. And Lexi certainly deserves better."

Coach's face flushes crimson. I can almost see physical steam starting to pour out of his ears. "This doesn't concern you, Wright."

"You're right," I say. "This concerns me and your daughter. And since we're both adults, who are more than capable of making decisions about our own lives and relationships, I'm telling you that it doesn't concern *you* either."

"I'm your coach," Cross splutters.

"You are. And that's why I'm warning you that, as much as I respect you as a coach, if you try to retaliate against me or Lexi, I'll be forced to create the biggest fucking PR nightmare you've ever seen. Can you imagine the headlines?" I stretch my hands out in front of me as though they're a flashing marquee. "*Rogues coach and raging misogynist rejects his own daughter.* Or *Ryder Hanson tells all about retaliatory treatment from head coach.* Or maybe they'll turn us into some Romeo and Juliet love story. That would really get the fans in our corner."

"Hell," Maddox drawls, "we all love your daughter. Maybe we'd give some interviews too."

Pride surges in my chest. Pride and gratitude. Because these guys are in my corner. They're my brothers now. And they won't only have my back, but Lexi's too. I'm not alone anymore. And even if shit hits the fan, I've got a family again. It may look a little different, but family is family. Whatever form it takes.

Coach Cross shifts on his feet, his face drawn into a

harsh scowl. He studies each of the men around me before his eyes land on me. "You sure you want to do this, Hanson?"

It's not my coach I look at when I answer. It's his daughter, with her wide, hopeful eyes that are more beautiful than any emerald.

"I've never been more sure of anything in my life."

forty-nine

LEXI

I can't believe any of that happened.

Throwing my stuff into my room, I pace, replaying every single moment of the confrontation with my dad. My chest hasn't stopped aching. I probably have a red spot over my heart where I keep absently rubbing my skin.

After the *I love you* bombs were dropped in what may be the most romantic gesture anyone has ever made for me —I'm sure it's not how either of us would have planned to say those three words for the first time, but hearing them in the face of my father's scorn and the possibility that Ryder could lose his career? Pretty fucking romantic— Ryder announced that he would fly home on a commercial flight with me. Which set off another round of yelling and threats about *breaching his contract* and other bullshit, until I pulled Ryder into a hug and told him to go with the team. He's going to pick me up on his way back from the arena, where he parked during the series.

He loves me.

Holy shit. He loves me. He's risking his career for me. Which I hate. I don't want him to lose his ability to play the game he adores. But to be someone's priority? That's a heady feeling. It's surreal.

My phone rings, jolting me out of my thoughts. I brace myself before looking at the screen, because there are only a few people this is likely to be, and my dad is one of them.

Except, it's not my dad. It's my mom.

"Hello?" I'm confused about why she's calling me, but I can't deny the relief that floods my body when I hear her voice. Especially now that we've begun repairing our relationship.

"Lexi? Hey, sweetie. Did something happen with your father?" My mom's tone is careful. She's always gone out of her way not to negatively impact my relationship with him. Not that he's ever deserved her consideration. Still, she knows how tense things are.

Sighing, I give up my pacing and flop down onto my bed. "Hey, Mom. Did he call you?"

"Yes." The word is saturated with frustration. "He called and started shouting about how you made a scene in front of the team and disrespected him." My mom huffs out a frustrated sound. "He was being a giant ass. I take it, he found out that you're dating Ryder?"

"Ugh. Yes. Yes, he did."

My mom is silent for a beat. "And how did Ryder react to your father's outburst?" She doesn't come right out and ask me if my boyfriend rose to the occasion or fell to meet her expectations, but I know that's what she's wondering.

"You should have seen him, Mom. He let Dad have it.

Dad asked him if I was worth throwing away his career for, and Ryder said yes. Didn't even hesitate. And a bunch of the guys on the team that I've become friends with stuck up for me too. It was horrible, but also kind of healing, you know?"

My mom hums. "Maybe I was too quick to judge that boy of yours. I just don't want you to live my life, sweetheart."

Oh, Mom.

"I know, Mom. Ryder told me he loves me. Right there in front of everyone. He's not like Dad." I suck in a breath as the true power of my feelings hits me. "I think he's the one."

"I'm glad I was wrong, sweetie. And I'm glad he stuck up for you. Don't listen to your father. He's a colossal ass." I hear Jeff shout a *Hear, hear* in the background and laugh. It's refreshing to hear her be honest about her feelings for my dad. I hope it means she's healing.

"I won't," I promise as a faint knock echoes through the apartment. "Shoot, Ryder's here. He's picking me up so we can talk about everything. Can we do another family dinner soon? I'd like to get to know Jeff better. And I want you guys to get to know Ryder."

"That would make both of us very happy." My mom's voice is thick with emotion.

"Us too," I say. "I love you, Mom. I'm glad you have Jeff. Give him a hug for me, okay?"

"Of course, sweetie. I love you too. Talk soon?"

I nod until I realize she can't see it. "Yeah, we'll talk soon."

We exchange one last goodbye, and I throw a few

necessities into a bag and head for the door. Ryder's got one arm braced on the frame when I throw it open. His dark hair sticks up at chaotic angles. It looks like he's been running his hand through it for the entire trip back from Chicago. Those handsome features I've grown to love are set in a frown. Until he sees me.

"Lexi." Faster than I can register, he wraps his arms around me and tangles one hand in the hair at the nape of my neck. I breathe in the scent of him while squeezing him right back. Ryder peppers kisses across my forehead, my nose, and my cheeks before taking my mouth in a kiss that is so full of emotion, it would knock me on my butt, if not for his arm wrapped around me.

"Hi," I whisper when the kiss ends and I meet his gaze.

Ryder brushes a stray strand of blonde hair behind my ear. "Hi. Ready to go?"

I nod. Ready? I've been ready to jump his bones since he said those three little words. I can't wait to get back to his place, lock ourselves in his room, and kiss every hard inch of his body. Luckily, I don't have school until later in the afternoon tomorrow, and he doesn't have practice until the evening, so we have plenty of time to enjoy one another.

Ryder grins, taking my hand and pulling me out of the apartment. He barely gives me time to lock up before he tows me toward the elevator. We share a few frantic kisses until we hit the ground floor, and then he's dragging me again. Once we're at his car, he leans over me as soon as I'm sitting to buckle my seat belt. I can't stop my laughter.

"In a hurry?"

"Hell, yes." He grins, kisses me on the nose, shuts the door, then runs around the car to his side. As soon as he folds his body inside, I say those three words that have been dancing on the tip of my tongue since he arrived at my apartment.

"I love you, Ryder."

Those icy-blue eyes flutter closed as a smile overtakes his face. He grabs my hand and squeezes before meeting my gaze. "I love you, Alexis. And when we get to my place, I'm going to show you just how much."

My lower belly flips and hollows out. I want nothing more.

We're both quiet as Ryder navigates through the city. There's so much to say, but where do we start?

"Did my dad say anything else to you?" I finally ask, breaking the silence. "Are you in trouble?"

"He can't get me in trouble for dating," Ryder says.

"No," I say, squeezing his hand. "But he can make your life miserable. Find other reasons to bench you."

"You don't need to worry about that. My job is my responsibility. I knew what I was doing this morning. And I don't regret it. So, you'd better not be worrying I am."

"I'm not worried about that at all," I reply. I grin so wide my cheeks hurt. "How could you possibly regret claiming all this?" I motion to my leggings, oversized hoodie, and messy hair, which I'd thrown into a chaotic bun on the top of my head.

"Feeling confident, huh?" He chuckles, squeezing my hand.

"Yep."

"Good." He tries to hold back his smile. "You should."

We're at his apartment building in no time at all, and the moment we stumble into his place, we make a beeline for his room. As soon as the door closes, we're a tangle of limbs and lips and tongues.

Ryder wastes no time tugging off my hoodie. I'm only wearing a lace bralette beneath it, and my nipples pebble in the cool air. Or maybe they tighten because he looks at me like I'm dessert. Dessert he's determined to savor.

"Damn, Alexis. You are so beautiful." His eyes make a slow sweep of my body, and the heat in them is undeniable. So is the love.

"Thank you," I murmur. My cheeks grow warm, and I fight the inclination to look away. "Now it's your turn."

With a grin, Ryder tugs off his shirt and pants. It's my turn to ogle.

Ryder's body will never cease to amaze me. And make me drool. He's muscular, tall, and I love the way he makes me feel small and protected. My primal brain really enjoys it. Though, I hate seeing bruising on his ribs.

"What happened?" I ask, trailing my fingers gently over his body.

"Took a couple rough hits during the game yesterday. It's fine, baby. Hazard of the job." His thumbs drag across my cheek. The look in his eyes makes me wonder when someone last worried about Ryder? I'm sure his friends and the Rogues staff care, but before me, did he have anyone to kiss his bruises or bite their fingernails at games when the play gets rough?

"I don't know if I'll ever get used to that. I hate seeing you hurt." I bend down and kiss each bruise, careful not to hurt him further.

Head falling back with a sigh, Ryder tangles his hands in my hair. "I like that you worry. You don't need to, though."

"Yeah, you say that, but you were just out for almost a month with an injury."

Ryder gently tugs on my hair, silently asking me to stand. As soon as I do, he kisses me again and again, his lips curling into a smile as they meet mine. Then he bends down and sweeps me up into his arms. In three steps, we're at the bed. He lays me down and crawls over me. "I'm always careful, Lexi. But I'll be more careful now. I don't want to worry you."

"You say the sweetest things."

"Hmm." He kisses the column of my throat as his fingers dance and play over my collarbones. "Not nearly as sweet as the way you taste."

And then he positions himself with his shoulders between my thighs, grins up at me, and licks a slow line through my pussy.

"Oh, god." One swipe of his tongue, and I'm a goner. "I need you, Ryder."

"I know, Oscar. I'm going to take care of you." That talented tongue of his circles my clit, and I nearly fly off the bed. He chuckles against my sex. The vibrations are better than any of my toys at home.

Ryder feasts on me until I'm a writhing, whining mess. My arousal covers his chin, and the sounds of him licking and sucking me are obscene.

"I'm close, Ryder. I'm so close. Please."

And then the bastard stops.

"No," I whine. I push my hips up, desperate for more friction. "I need to come. Please, Ryder. Please let me come."

"Don't worry, baby. I'm going to let you come. But I need to be inside of you when you do." Wiping his mouth with the back of his hand, Ryder pushes up off the bed.

"Where the hell are you going?"

He smirks. "Just grabbing a condom, my impatient love."

"Wait." I suck my bottom lip between my teeth. I've never been with a guy without a condom. I have an IUD, so I'm not worried about getting pregnant, but I've never trusted any man enough to go without before. But Ryder? I trust Ryder implicitly. I know he'll do whatever he has to in order to protect me. He proved that this morning. So, I take a deep breath and meet his eyes. "I'm on birth control."

Still. Ryder's body is so still as he stares back at me. "What are you saying, Alexis? I need your words."

"I... You don't need to wear a condom if you don't want to. I'm clear."

"I'm clear too, but it's not just a question of what I want. What do you want?" His fingers skim the insides of my thighs. It muddles my brain for a moment. But just for a moment.

"I want to feel you inside of me. All of you. No barriers." An impish grin tugs at my lips. "Fill me with your cum, Ryder."

"Christ," he hisses. But that's all it takes for Ryder's calm stillness to break. In seconds, I'm pinned beneath his powerful body. Those competent hands of his explore my sides, my ass, my breasts as he claims my mouth with his. There is so much emotion in his kiss. "I love you."

"I love you too," I say on a gasp as one of his hands finds its way between us and he grinds the heel of his palm against my clit. I'm so wet, his hand glides easily over my sex. In no time at all, I'm right back at the edge. "Need you."

"Don't worry, Lexi. I'll never leave you hanging." The promise expands between us. It's about so much more than sex and orgasms.

When Ryder lines the silky head of his cock up to my entrance, we watch each other. His gaze only leaves my eyes to drop to my lips when I open my mouth in a silent cry the moment he pushes inside me. It's so good. To feel him bare, his cock coated in my arousal as he claims my body, is the most exquisite sensation. And if his pained groan is anything to go by, I'm not the only one who thinks so.

"God, baby. You feel so good." Ryder presses his forehead into the crook of my neck as his hips undulate and flex. "You feel like home."

Home. I haven't felt at home in so long. Maybe because I've been thinking of home as this nebulous concept that centered around a house and belongings and all the things I thought made my childhood house feel safe. But home isn't a place. Home is the person who would risk everything for you. Home is the shoulder you rest your head on when life becomes too much.

Home is Ryder Hanson.

A tear slips down my cheek, and Ryder jerks back, his eyes wide and worried.

"Lexi? What's wrong? Am I hurting you?" He tries to pull out of me, but I trap him with my legs.

"You're not hurting me. And nothing's wrong. These are happy tears, dummy. Because you feel like home to me too."

The look of worry on Ryder's face melts into a smile so

devastating I forget to breathe. He slants his mouth over mine and presses into me again. His movements grow faster and our kisses become more frantic.

"Ryder." His name is a plea. A plea for more. A plea for everything.

And he gives it to me.

We both breathe heavily as Ryder snaps his hips into mine harder, faster. Sweat drips down his face and beads across my chest. The sounds of our lovemaking fill his bedroom. It's a rhythmic, primal song. Our gasps are the chorus. Skin slapping against skin forms the beat. Each *I love you* we utter makes up the verses.

Every cell in my body lights up. Pressure builds and my stomach hollows out. I've never felt this kind of anticipation. It's like I'm a bomb ready to detonate. "Ryder, I'm so close. Please."

The man I'm in love with stares at me like I'm everything. Sliding a hand between us, he presses on my swollen clit. "Come for me, Alexis. Come all over my cock as I fill you up."

His dirty words light the fuse, and I finally combust.

Screaming his name, I cling to Ryder as his movements grow erratic and jerky. His hips slam into me. I feel him grow even harder, and then he comes with a roar. His dick jerks and spills inside of me. My pussy clamps around him in pulsing waves as he slows. But he doesn't stop moving. Not until he's drawn every ounce of pleasure out of my body and I'm boneless and panting beneath him.

"That was..." He rests his forehead against mine.

"The best ever?" I supply. My voice is hoarse from all the gasping and crying out.

Ryder kisses me reverently. "Yeah. Exactly that. Best ever. I love you, Alexis Cross."

"Not as much as I love you, Ryder Hanson."

We trade kisses and soft murmurs of love until I squirm as his seed drips down my inner thighs. It tickles.

With a chuckle, Ryder slowly pulls out and gives me one more kiss. "Let's get you cleaned up and fed. You're going to need your strength tonight."

I can't wait.

fifty

RYDER

I'M DREADING PRACTICE TONIGHT. LEXI KNOWS IT, too. It's probably why she hasn't detangled herself from me, even though we both need to shower and get dressed so I can drive her home. I don't want her to miss class because of me. I also don't want her to worry. So, even though I know she's smart enough to infer what's going on in my head, I haven't come out and said it.

I don't regret the things I said to Coach. Not even for a moment. That doesn't mean I'm not freaking out. Hockey has been my life for so long. It was the thing that kept me sane after my mom's death. And what kept me going after my dad's. Who the hell would I even be without the game? And what will I do for a job if all of this implodes?

I make decent money, but a rookie's salary is nothing compared to a player like Maddox, Griffin, Logan, or Sebastian. They've proven themselves to be invaluable. They're stars in their own rights and have the endorsements to validate that. I'm not there. Not yet. Though, this season has been a huge step in that direction. If things keep going the way they have, I could be looking at a huge raise on my next contract and endorsements of my own.

That is, if Arthur Cross doesn't do whatever he can to torpedo my career with the Rogues.

"I'm going to take a shower," Lexi finally murmurs. She gives me a slow kiss before lifting onto her elbows and staring down at me. A crease forms between her eyebrows. "Do you regret it?"

That jars me from my worries. I blink a few times. Cupping her cheek, I shake my head. "Hell, no. I mean, I regret that it went down the way it did. I'm still pissed at your dad for hurting you. But I will never regret choosing you. I need you to know that."

Her brow smooths out, and Lexi gifts me with a sexy smile. "Just wanted to make sure. You going to join me?"

Hell, I want to join her in the shower. But we really do need to get ready, and if I'm in a steamy, enclosed space with the woman I love as water sluices down that perfect body? We won't leave. I groan. "God, I want to say yes, but it's probably not the best idea."

The bed shakes as she giggles. "True. I won't take long."

"Take as long as you need, Oscar."

I watch Lexi's perfect, naked ass sway as she saunters across the room and into the en-suite bathroom. Groaning, I grab my phone. It's been on silent, so I haven't heard if any calls or texts came through. I'm almost nervous to look. The last thing I want to see is a missed call from my agent. He's a good guy, but he's pretty hands off unless we're working on something. If he calls out of the blue, I know I'm fucked.

But there are no calls or texts from my agent. Or from Arthur Cross. Though, it does appear I've been added to a group text with Maddox, Griffin, Sebastian, and Logan. And they've been texting up a storm since six this morning.

I scan the messages, laughing at some of the ridiculous crap they've said, even as my chest tightens with emotion. They're checking up on me. They care. And not just about me, but about Lexi too.

LOGAN

It's almost noon, and no one has heard from Ryder. Should we do a welfare check? Maybe Coach murdered him.

GRIFFIN

He's probably balls-deep in Hot Cross Buns, dude. We'll give him another hour.

SEBASTIAN

SMH. Don't be an ass.

GRIFFIN

What? You'd be balls-deep in your woman, too, if you weren't such a monk.

SEBASTIAN

I'm not a monk.

LOGAN

When's the last time you took a woman home, Navarro?

SEBASTIAN

When's the last time you DIDN'T, Byrne?

MADDOX

Children. Stop fighting.

GRIFFIN

Sorry, Daddy.

MADDOX

Fuck, Wright. I'm your goddamn best friend. If you ever call me daddy again, I'm going to kick your ass.

GRIFFIN

Oooh, kinky.

MADDOX

I can't believe my sister agreed to room with you.

LOGAN

I can't, either. Mira is way too cool to be slumming it with Wright.

SEBASTIAN

There's no accounting for taste.

GRIFFIN

All the women I've been with say I taste incredible. So, ha.

MADDOX

FFS. I'm kicking you out of the chat.

GRIFFIN HAS BEEN REMOVED FROM THE CHAT

MADDOX

Much better.

LOGAN

Great. Now he won't stop blowing up my phone. I'm adding him back.

GRIFFIN HAS JOINED THE CHAT

GRIFFIN

I'm back, bitches.

SEBASTIAN

Dude. Don't be derogatory.

GRIFFIN

Don't be such a bitch.

GRIFFIN HAS BEEN REMOVED FROM
THE CHAT

SEBASTIAN

Why do we love him, again?

I'm shaking with laughter by the time I get to the last
text. I'm still nervous about practice tonight, but the guys
have my back. Everything will be okay. I take a deep breath
and tap out a reply.

ME

I'm alive. You guys can stop worrying.
Just had my phone on silent.

MADDOX

Hey, man. You okay?

LOGAN

I'm adding Griffin back again.

GRIFFIN HAS JOINED THE CHAT

GRIFFIN

STOP KICKING ME OUT OF THE CHAT,
ASSHOLES.

SEBASTIAN

Ryder texted. He's okay. Just had his
phone on silent.

GRIFFIN

Oh, good! Sorry for the balls-deep comment, man.

ME

LOL. All good. Just don't say shit like that in front of Lexi, or she'll kick your ass.

GRIFFIN

Yeah, my roommate would kick my ass too.

MADDOX

How's Lexi?

ME

IDK. Hurt. Worried about how this is going to affect my career.

SEBASTIAN

We're here for both of you. Lexi's cool. I'm sorry she had to hear her dad say all that trash.

ME

Thanks. I'm sorry too. I can't believe he's so blind to how amazing she is.

MADDOX

I told Isla about what happened. She invited Lexi to sit with her and Mira in the family box at the next game. I told her I'd bring it up with you now that the cat's out of the bag and all.

GRIFFIN

Yeah, Mira said to tell her she hopes she comes. The ladies really like Lexi and want to get to know her better.

ME

> Thanks, guys. I'll ask her. I think she'd like that.

LOGAN

> It would certainly send a message to her dad.

SEBASTIAN

> Yeah, and if he tries to throw a fit about it, we'll have your back.

MADDOX

> The ladies want to take her to dinner before the game too. Then we can all go to my place afterward.

A feeling of peace settles over me. There are still so many unknowns with all of this, but I'm not alone anymore. My dad was always there for me. His tireless support pushed me to achieve my dreams. Seeing the proud look on his face after I gave it my all during a game kept me going in a way I couldn't explain.

When he died, I did the only thing I could. I kept pushing myself. Because it's what he would have wanted. He would have hated to see me give up my dreams just because he wasn't there to cheer me on. But each victory felt hollow without him there.

And at the end of every game, when other guys were hugging their girlfriends or wives and embracing their kids, I was alone. I walked out of the locker room alone. Through the family room alone. And out to my car alone. Then I'd go home to an apartment that wasn't really home, and I was alone there.

I'm not alone anymore.

A plume of steam escapes the bathroom as Lexi opens

the door and walks out with wet hair, a pair of tight jeans, and an oversized sweater. My heart squeezes. She's so damned beautiful. The woman is full of light and life. After everything I've witnessed between her and Coach, I wouldn't blame her if Lexi was angry and guarded. But she's not. A little grumpy, maybe, but she's fun and quirky and she embraces life.

And I'm never giving her up.

It's probably too soon to be thinking about forever, but I don't care. Because watching Alexis Cross walk across the room toward me, I know—I'm going to marry this woman. We're going to grow old together. Maybe we'll have a couple of kids or travel the world. I don't know and I don't care. Everything else is a minor detail. We've got time to figure it out.

"Feel better now that you've showered?" I ask her as she towels off her hair.

"Much." Her eyes twinkle. "I was feeling a little sticky."

That has me laughing. She's not wrong. I'm in the same boat. "Before I hop in the shower, I wanted to run something by you. The guys said Isla and Mira invited you to go to dinner with them before the next home game. Then they'd like you to join them in the family box. After the game, Maddox and Isla will have everyone over. What d'you think?"

Lexi's lips twist to the side and she hums. "Are you sure it's a good idea for me to go to the game?"

"Honestly?" I shrug. "I don't see what difference it will make. Your dad knows about us now. Hell, everyone on the team knows. What good is hiding?" Once I've untangled myself from the sheets, I climb out of the bed and wrap Lexi in my arms. She's warm and soft. When she sighs and rests her head on my chest, I'm gone.

I love this woman.

"I guess you're right. It's just... I don't know. I'm still hurt by the things he said."

"I know you are. And I don't want to pressure you. If you don't want to come to the game, I'll completely understand. And so will the ladies." And I would understand. But I can't deny that I hope she'll come. I don't want Coach to think he's won. And if we keep hiding our relationship, he will.

Lexi sighs and wraps her arms around my waist. "I do want to get to know Isla and Mira better. Dinner would be fun. And I love watching you play. Your ass looks great in those pants."

I give her ass a light slap. "You can't even see our butts in those pants."

"It's the mystery of it all." Silent laughter shakes her body against mine.

"You're ridiculous."

"You love it."

"I do." I kiss her head. "So, what do you think?"

"I'm in." She sucks in a deep breath as she meets my gaze. "Your next home game is in two days. That gives me plenty of time to work up my courage."

Courage is something Lexi has in spades, even if she doesn't realize it. Hell, she faced off with me naked and with nothing more than an empty wineglass when she thought I was there to murder her. She's gone after her dreams without the support of her dad. She had the courage to give her mom and Jeff a chance, even when she thought the worst, and a big enough heart to admit when she was wrong and mend those relationships.

I kiss her gently. Lovingly. "You've got this, OTG. And I've got you."

"I know you do," she replies with nothing but trust in her eyes.

"I'll just tell the guys and take a quick shower. Gotta get you home, so you're not late to class."

Grabbing my phone, I shoot off a text, letting the guys know that Lexi's in for all of it. Maddox tells me that Isla will text Lexi that evening to make dinner plans. Then I take the fastest shower of my life, because I can't stand to be away from my girl. Not even for a few minutes.

fifty-one

LEXI

"LEXI! I AM SO GLAD YOU CAME TONIGHT." ISLA'S fiery red hair bounces as she rises from her seat and pulls me into a tight hug, which I return.

"Hey, Lex." Mira stands and gives me a hug too. It's a lot of hugging, but I don't really mind.

"Thanks for inviting me," I say as we all sit. There are already three waters at the table. I take a sip for something to do and because my throat is suddenly dry.

Mira waves her hand dismissively. "We've been wanting to hang out ever since New Year's Eve. I'm just glad you finally agreed."

Mira is wearing a Rogues' jersey with *Graves* on the back for her brother. Her dark hair is curled and tumbles over one shoulder. Isla is wearing a matching jersey with her boyfriend's name. She's pulled her hair into a messy, high ponytail. Both women have minimal makeup on and look completely at ease. It calms my

432

nerves. For once, I feel like I truly fit in. I'm wearing Ryder's jersey with a pair of trendy jeans. I'm not all dolled up—only minimal makeup for me too—but even if I was wearing a full face, I know these two women wouldn't judge me. They're kind and fun, and we've been texting since the morning after we got back from Chicago.

I could be friends with these women. Everything feels like it's falling into place.

Our server stops by the table to take our orders, and once he walks away, I'm pinned in place by a pair of blue and a pair of green eyes. It's Mira who speaks first.

"So, how are you? We heard about how things went down with your dad. It sounded pretty rough."

I deflate, slumping back in my chair. "Um, I'm doing okay, I think. It was not a fun day, and I'm still worried about how my dad may try to retaliate, but things with Ryder are great." We've spent almost every waking moment together, when we're not at school or practice. He never misses a chance to tell me how much he loves me, and I say it just as often.

"He told you he loves you?" Isla's blue eyes sparkle. She leans forward, her attention completely on me. "And in front of your dad and the whole team, right?"

I chuckle. Sounds like Maddox and Griffin have told them the whole story. "He did. It was stupidly romantic, in a way. I mean, I think he would have done it differently if shit hadn't hit the fan, but I won't complain. It left no doubt he meant it."

Isla smiles brightly. "I'm so happy for you two. He seems like a great guy. I know Maddox speaks highly of him."

"Doesn't hurt that he's hot," Mira adds with a wink. Isla and I both laugh.

"Yeah, well, that's practically a prerequisite for that team, isn't it? God, have you ever seen so many massive, sexy men in one place?" Isla fans her face. "Obviously, I'm partial to my grumpy giant, but you'd have to be blind not to recognize the hotness on that bench."

I shrug. "I may have noticed. Even though I tried really hard not to. I dated a hockey player in college. He was a real asshole. It put me off hockey players for a long time. I even tried to ignore Ryder's charms when we got snowed in together, but I'm weak."

They laugh. Isla nods. "I know how that goes. I tried to resist Maddox after our first disastrous date. But he worked hard to prove he's a great guy. And really good in bed. That helped his case."

We laugh throughout dinner. Conversation flows easily, and by the time we're ready for the check, I'm flying high. I have two new friends who understand what it's like being with a professional hockey player, and they're both genuinely awesome people. The laughter doesn't stop as we pile into the back seat of a ride-share. It even *almost* overshadows the buzzing of my nerves as the car pulls up to the arena and we spill out in a tangle of giggles.

Almost.

<hr>

THE ROAR OF THE CROWD IS LESS OVERWHELMING in the semi-enclosed family box. It's still loud enough to vibrate through my bones, but muted enough that I don't have a problem hearing Isla or Mira.

The guys are killing it. Every single one of them is playing like they have something to prove. And maybe they do. I'm not blind to the wild gesticulations of my father or how red his face grows when he's shouting at his players. It doesn't matter that we're up by three at the top of the third period. He's not happy, especially when he notices Ryder's gaze sliding up to the box where I stand, cheering.

"Girl, he cannot keep his eyes off you," Mira says. "It's cute as hell."

It is cute. My stomach somersaults every time he looks my way and grins. Maddox does his share of looking up at Isla, too, but Ryder is way more obvious about it.

Isla clasps her hands beneath her chin. "Ah, new love. It's the sweetest, isn't it?"

Mira snorts. "New love? As if your love is so old?"

"You know what I mean."

The crowd roars as Logan gains control of the puck and the Rogues kick it into high gear. Everyone in the box screams as the Rogues pull off a perfect odd man rush, taking the other team by surprise. Logan passes to Maddox, who passes to Ryder. He's not normally on the first line, but my dad has him there now.

Ryder handles the puck with confidence and ease from the defensive zone, passing it back to Maddox when one of the opposing players gets too close. But instead of staying back by the Rogues' net, Maddox nods at Ryder to head down the ice with them as Griffin gets caught up in a scuffle. Logan checks a defenseman into the boards, and then Ryder is wide open in front of the net. With expert precision, Maddox slaps the puck to Ryder, who lines up his shot and lets it fly.

The scoreboard lights up, the siren blares, and we all hop up and down, cheering right along with the rest of the crowd. Logan and Maddox clap Ryder on the back. Pride fills me. Then Ryder turns toward our box, stares right at me, and points.

"For you, baby," he mouths. I know that's exactly what he says because the camera is on him, and it plays in high definition over the jumbotron. The camera cuts to the box, and I see myself blushing furiously, a big, goofy smile on my face.

"Oh my god," Mira says, clapping. "That's so cute!"

I barely hear her. I'm too busy floating. I can't believe he just did that.

My father turns, craning his neck to see who Ryder is pointing at. As if it would be anyone besides me. As if my face wasn't just plastered, larger than life, on a huge LED screen for everyone in the arena to see. Even from the box, I can tell he's pissed. His face flames red, and he turns, yelling at Ryder and the rest of the team.

"Uh-oh. Daddy Cross looks mad," Mira teases.

I shrug, despite the nerves that begin to churn in my stomach. "What else is new?"

Dad calls for a line change, and Ryder and the guys hop over the boards while the second line surges onto the ice. I watch as my boyfriend squirts water into his mouth, a huge grin on his face as his teammates congratulate him on the goal. They slap his back, and all of them laugh. Until my dad turns their way and points a finger at Ryder.

"What a dick," I grumble, watching. I want to climb out of this box and demand my father stop being such a condescending, retaliatory prick. But I know that wouldn't help. It would probably just get me thrown out of the arena.

I can't tell what Ryder says, but he fires something back at my dad with a roll of his eyes. That doesn't go over well with Arthur Cross. My dad shouts again, wagging that damned finger in Ryder's face. Maddox holds up a hand and tries to defuse the situation, but it doesn't seem to calm my dad down.

There are only four minutes left in the final period of the game, and the Rogues are up by four. It wouldn't be completely impossible for the opposing team to pull off a win, but it's unlikely. That my dad is letting himself be distracted from the game isn't a great sign. He doesn't do distractions. Not when it may mean his team loses a game.

"What's going on down there?" Isla asks. Her eyes are locked on the bench with mine. So are Mira's. My dad gesticulates wildly, and every single player on the bench stares at him like he's grown a second head. He and Ryder exchange more words, and soon, Logan and Maddox join the conversation. If you can even call it that. Argument is more appropriate.

"I don't know," I say. "But I'd guess my dad's not happy at the little goal dedication Ryder did for me."

Mira rolls her eyes. "No offense, but your dad needs to pull the stick out of his ass."

"Oh, I don't take any offense. Unfortunately, I think the stick up his ass has fused with his spine. If he pulled it out now, he may not survive it."

Mira snorts. "I don't get it. You'd think he'd be thrilled his daughter is with someone who loves her the way Ryder loves you."

"It's more about him being pissed that Ryder is with

me, not the other way around. He thinks I'm not good enough for Ryder. That I'll end up ruining his career."

"What bullshit," Isla growls.

I open my mouth to say something else when the crowd roars and my eyes dart back to the bench. The bench where Ryder and my dad are now chest to chest, and every Rogues player not on the ice looks like they're about to jump into a brawl.

"Oh my god," I murmur.

My dad screams something in Ryder's face that causes his body to lock up. Even from up here, I can see Ryder's jaw tick. Ryder says something back to my dad, and then my dad shoves him.

My dad, the coach, shoves his player.

Ryder flies backward. He'd hit his ass if Maddox and Logan didn't catch him. Once he's back on his feet, Ryder shakes his head and says something to my dad. My dad shoves him again, and then Maddox and Logan are holding Ryder back from retaliating.

"Oh my god," Isla says. She covers her mouth with her hand as she turns wide, shocked eyes in my direction.

The crowd roars as my dad and Ryder continue to exchange heated words, but I don't hear them. All I can hear is the pounding of my heart and the ragged intake of each breath I suck into my lungs. I fly out of the box, down the hallway, and make turn after turn until my feet slap against the stairs leading to the main floor.

Ignoring the shouting of security, I barely dodge a few men in uniform and push through the double doors leading to the tunnel. I run as fast as I can toward the Rogues' bench. People shout and scream, the mob mentality desperate for a fight, even if it's between a coach and his players. I want to scream at them. To demand they shut up. But they don't matter. Not really. What matters is getting to Ryder before he does something that could end his career.

I shove past the camera guy who's documenting the argument. He shouts as I push him out of my way, and he almost loses his footing. I don't care.

My heart pounds in my chest and my body feels cold. It's not the normal chill of the arena. It's the icy fingers of dread gripping my spine.

I get to the glass surrounding the bench just in time to hear what my dad shouts at Ryder.

"I made you a star, you ungrateful little shit. I can ruin you just as fast. Is that what you want? I hope that cunt was worth it, because I'm trading your ass to fucking Alaska the first chance I get."

My heart seizes in my chest. I can't breathe.

"That's your *daughter* you're talking about like that," Ryder screams. "What the hell is wrong with you?"

"She was a *mistake*," my dad hisses as my heart shatters. "And she'll ruin your life, just like she ruined mine. Just you fucking wait, Hanson. You'll see. You two deserve each other. Though I doubt she'll still want you when you're down in the minors and barely making enough to pay your bills. Nothing's ever good enough for that brat."

My heart crumbles into a pile of rubble at my feet, and a pained cry slips from my lips. It must just be loud enough for Ryder to hear because his beautiful, sky-blue eyes snap to mine. Tears stream down my cheeks, and I don't even care that this is probably being televised. That the whole world may be watching me break. All that matters at this moment is the pain swimming in my love's eyes. The devastation etched into my face is mirrored in his. My dad looks over his shoulder and sneers at my tears.

"Always with the dramatics, huh, Alexis?"

Ryder lunges for my dad, but his teammates hold him back. "Let me go! Let me out of this fucking bench right now." He strains against Maddox and Logan's hold. "Lexi, baby, don't listen to him. Don't listen to him, sweetheart."

The game has come to a stop at this point. Everyone is watching my humiliation. I cover my mouth with my hands as the first sob rips free.

And then I run.

fifty-two

RYDER

I'M GOING TO KILL HIM. I'M GOING TO GARROTE him. After I break his nose.

That sonofabitch just called his own daughter a vile slur before telling the whole world, and his little girl, that she was a mistake. A. Mistake.

Fuck him. Fuck him and fuck the rest of this game. I don't care if I get suspended or fired or traded to Alaska. Hell, they don't even have an NHL team in Alaska. Whatever. It doesn't matter. All that matters right now is that I get to my girl.

I swear the whole arena is silent as I hop over the boards and fly across the ice. Gameplay has stopped, and there are refs surrounding the Rogues' bench as Coach continues to shout and rant and make threats. For a split second, I think one of them will stop me from getting to Lexi, but he just pats me on the shoulder and tells me to go get her.

She's just approaching the tunnel as I stumble off the ice. Tears stream down her beautiful face and sobs rack her body. I've never seen her so broken. Her dad has hurt Lexi several times since I've known her, but there was always this underlying spark of hope in her eyes. Hope that things would get better. That, someday, Arthur Cross would wake up and realize what a mammoth ass he's been.

That hope is gone. Snuffed out so thoroughly that even Lexi's natural light has dimmed.

I hate it.

"Baby." I drop my gloves and reach for her as she lurches toward the tunnel. At the sound of my voice, she looks up, and my chest constricts. Lexi looks at me like I'm her salvation. The only safe place she has left. And I will *not* let her down. Pulling her into my arms, I shield her from the gawking fans and the flashing cameras. I'll shield her from the whole fucking world if I have to. Her body convulses with sobs against my chest and her knees wobble.

"I've got you," I murmur as I sweep her into my arms bridal style. She presses her face into my sweaty neck, trusting me to get her out of there. Trusting me to take care of her. "I've got you, baby. Everything is going to be okay."

The dull roar of the arena fades as I carry my devastated girlfriend down the tunnel toward the locker room. Her soft cries and the relentless pounding of my heart are the only sounds.

"I'm so sorry," I whisper. "I'm so sorry you had to hear that, Lexi. Your dad is a fucking asshole. And he's the one missing out, not you."

I know that's not really true. Losing a father is something I'm intimately familiar with. And while my loss may differ from Lexi's in its circumstance, it doesn't change the fact that, as of today, both of us are fatherless. Because there's no coming back from this for Arthur Cross. Not even if he wanted to.

So, yeah, I firmly believe that Coach is the one missing out, but Lexi is the one mourning.

The locker room is empty when I carry her in. Heading over to my locker, I sit down on the bench and cradle my crying girlfriend against my chest. My hands smooth up and down her back, my fingers ghosting over my last name embroidered there.

Mine. Alexis Cross is mine. Someday soon, I'm going to marry this incredible woman. And if she wants to ditch the last name that has brought her nothing but pain, she can have mine instead.

"I'm sorry," she chokes out. "I'm so sorry, Ryder."

Gently gripping the hair at the base of her skull, I give it a light tug, silently asking her to look at me. "What the hell are you sorry about, Alexis? What could you possibly have to apologize for?"

"I ruined your career," she cries, new sobs racking her body. "I never wanted you to have to choose between me and hockey, but it happened, anyway. I'm so sorry."

"Oscar." The word rumbles out of my chest like an earthquake. One capable of toppling all these feelings of unworthiness Lexi has been battling since she was a little girl. "I swear to god, if you apologize for something that is not your fault one more time, I'm going to lose my cool and go take a hockey stick to your dad's car."

Lexi's eyes widen, but a watery giggle slips from

between her lips. The moment is short-lived, though. Her face quickly crumples again. "You heard my dad. He's going to ruin your career now. That's my fault."

"No, OTG. It's not. It's Coach's fault. It's his fault he's a raging misogynist. It's his fault he's so fucking selfish that he couldn't see how lucky he was to have your mom as a wife and you as a daughter. He did this, not you. And my career isn't ruined yet. I'm not giving up without a fight."

The sound of voices and the thump of skates heading toward the locker room begin to filter over to us. Lexi tenses in my lap. I hold her tighter.

"I've got you," I tell her again.

Her quiet reply almost undoes me. "I know."

I brace myself for Coach's arrival, but it's our team captain who strides through the locker room doors, looking downright murderous. Maddox's expression softens when he sees Lexi cowering in my arms.

"Coach got kicked out of the game. Don't worry, we won't let him in the locker room."

The guys cluster around Lexi and me, all of them looking concerned.

"Are you okay, Lexi?" Sebastian asks, crouching down, so he's at eye level with her.

She sniffles. "Not really. But I will be."

Our assistant coach, Mike Fry, strides into the locker room, and everyone tenses. His warm brown eyes scan the room before landing on Lexi in my arms. His full lips turn down in a frown, and he runs a hand over his close-cropped black hair.

"All right, team. I know tonight was a shit show, and there are a lot of questions about what happened and how this will affect the rest of our season. I don't have any answers for you yet." Fry sighs. "Unfortunately, everything he said was caught on camera. And it's already on the way to going viral." That has him grimacing as he meets Lexi's gaze. "I'm sorry, Lexi. I can't imagine how you must be feeling right now."

My arms tighten around my girl. She simply offers a half-hearted shrug.

"Unfortunately, that means the press room is packed to the gills. They're going to expect to hear from the first line." Fry looks at me. "And Ryder. Think you guys can handle this without throwing more fuel on the fire?"

"Of course," Maddox says, answering for all of us. "But no one is answering questions about Lexi. This is her fucking personal life being blasted all over right now. Are we agreed?" He looks around the locker room. Every single player nods.

They'll have our backs.

"Is there anything you want me to say, baby?" I ask Lexi.

Her big, green eyes gaze up at me with the utmost faith. "I trust you. Say whatever you feel you need to."

Kissing her nose, I nod. "You got it."

"Good." Coach Fry claps his hands. "Everyone, go get showered and dressed. It's going to be a long night of answering questions."

As our assistant coach heads out of the locker room, and as guys begin tugging off their jerseys, Griffin kneels in front of Lexi, the same way Sebastian did. Meeting her gaze, his voice is soft and comforting. It's a different side of Griffin, and I can see the man he often hides behind his goofy facade.

"The girls are in the family room. How about we form

a wall and take you there? We'll make sure no one sees you or bothers you. You ladies can hang out and have a drink while we talk to the press, then we'll come and get you and head to Madds and Isla's place, like we'd planned. How does that sound?"

"That sounds good," Lexi says. She attempts a smile, but it doesn't even come close to reaching her emerald eyes. She shifts like she's about to get to her feet, but I hold on tighter and pick her up bridal style again.

"Not ready to let you go just yet," I tell her.

She sighs and sags against me.

The guys form a wall in front of us, and a few of our other teammates cover our backs. Lexi buries her face in my neck again, and we make our way out of the locker room and toward the family room, where wives, girl-friends, and other family members can wait for their loved ones as they get showered and speak with the press.

A few people call out Lexi's name and mine, but they're quickly told to move aside by a wall of sweaty muscle. We make it into the family room without anyone really bothering us.

As soon as the door is closed and I set Lexi down, Isla and Mira are there. They wrap her up in a hug and check in with her. She looks back at me every few seconds, but it's clear she feels safe and comfortable with them, which loosens some of the tightness in my chest.

"You good, love?"

"Yeah," Lexi says, closing the space between us and pulling my head down for a kiss. "I'm okay. Hurry up and shower so you can talk to the vultures, then we can get out of here. I need an entire bottle of wine after tonight."

"We can definitely provide that," Isla says. "And food.

Oh, and ice cream. I have plenty of ice cream. Mira and I will help you drown your sorrows in rocky road. Or cookie dough. Or mint chocolate chip."

A watery laugh bubbles out of Lexi. "That sounds perfect."

"Go on," Mira says to me, making a little shooing motion with her hands. "We'll take care of Lexi."

I trust that they will, but I'm finding it difficult to walk away. It feels wrong to leave her side after everything that happened tonight. "You sure you're okay?" I ask her again.

The smile she offers me is real. A little sad, but genuine. "I'm sure. I love you."

"I love you too."

"We love you both," Griffin says. "Now, let's go get showered and get this circus over with."

———

"RYDER, CAN YOU TELL US HOW LONG YOU'VE BEEN dating Coach Cross's daughter?"

It's the third time one of these reporters has asked this question, and I'm getting irritated. I don't want to share the details of my relationship with them. What makes these people think they're entitled to personal information like this?

Pasting a smile on my face, I give her the same answer I gave the last two. "I'm not going to divulge information about my relationship, except to say that Alexis doesn't deserve to be dragged through the mess her father created. Please respect her privacy, and ours. We're real people in a real relationship. This isn't some publicity stunt or a Hollywood movie plot. This is our life."

That same reporter smiles. "So, you love her, then?"

That I will answer. I return the reporter's smile. "I sure as hell do."

People shout over one another, trying to be heard, jockeying for the right to ask the next question. So many cameras flash, I'm getting a headache.

"Do you have any comment on Cross's threat to trade you?" a new reporter asks.

"Listen, that threat was made in the heat of the moment, but I will say this. I don't want to play for anyone else. Minnesota is my home. I've cheered for the Rogues since I was a boy. My dad and I used to dream about me playing here before he died. This is my community, and these guys are my family." I motion to my teammates. "I won't be going anywhere, as long as I have any say in the matter."

I'm aware I may not have a say in this. It's one of the major pitfalls of playing professional sports. You don't always get to choose where you live and play. It's why I haven't bothered buying a house, and why I won't, unless I get a nice long contract extension and hopefully a pay hike. I can't deny I've been thinking about a house a lot more since things with Lexi became serious.

I want to put down roots with her.

"Ryder, what do you have to say to Coach Cross regarding today's altercation?"

I look the reporter dead in the eyes. This one, I have no problem answering. "I'd like to tell him I feel sorry for him. Hockey is the best sport, we all know that." Everyone chuckles. "But like every sport, it can be a fickle lover. We get injured or that perfect lineup doesn't gel the way we'd hoped. When everything's great, sure, hockey may keep you warm at night. But hockey won't hold you when you cry or sit with you in the quiet moments. It can't reassure you that everything's going to be okay or tell you to stop being an idiot when you mess up. It can't grow old with you. It won't look up at you like you've hung the moon."

The room is silent.

"I've found the person who does all of those things for me, and I never want to let her go. And it's crazy to me he'd dismiss and hurt that same person I feel lucky just to *know*. And being *loved* by that person? Well, to be honest, no game—even hockey—could ever come close. I'm sorry he never had the sense to realize that."

There's a single beat of profound silence, and then the cameras are flashing again and reporters are shouting.

I'm tired. All I want is to get back to Lexi and wrap her in my arms. I'm never letting her go.

Coach Fry holds up his hands and says, "That's enough questions about Ryder and his love life. Now, do any of you have anything to ask about the spectacular game these guys played tonight? If not, I know we're all tired and want to get home to our families."

For once, the mention of going home to our families doesn't cut. Because my family is waiting for me.

She makes all of this worth it.

fifty-three

LEXI

My mom calls me while I'm sitting with the girls in the family room.

"Hey, Mom."

"Oh, honey. I saw what happened. Are you okay?" She sounds sad and furious.

Not really.

"I'll be fine."

"Your father is an ass. I can't believe he said any of that. I swear, I'm going to use my alimony to take a hit out on that man." She's silent for a beat. "I should have divorced him sooner. I should have protected you from his bullshit better. I'm so sorry, honey."

"Mom." I love her for everything she's saying, but my dad's behavior isn't her fault. And she did protect me from his negligence as best she could. She always showed up for me. She always cheered me on. Even if they'd divorced when I was a kid, I still would have searched the crowd for

450

him and been disappointed when he didn't show. "This isn't on you. You're a great mom and you always have been. I'm sorry for the times I put his absences on you or took my anger out on you."

"It's okay. I always understood." She pauses, and I hear Jeff say something I can't make out. My mom hums. "Are you watching the press conference right now?"

"No," I admit. "I'm in the family room with my friends. Why?"

"Jeff tells me that boy of yours is doing a good job. He's defending you without giving away any personal information." The hum of the television grows louder in the background.

It's strange to hear Ryder's voice coming through. I can't make out the words, and I'm tempted to ask what he's saying, but I'll wait for him to tell me. I'm emotionally drained, and all I want to do is get off the phone.

"I think I was wrong about that boy. I can tell he really loves you, Alexis. I'm glad you have each other, and I'm looking forward to getting to know him better."

She can't know how much I needed to hear those words. I want her to grow to love Ryder. He doesn't have a mom and hasn't for a long time. Although mine will never replace the woman Ryder lost at such a young age, it would kill me if she always held herself at arm's length.

"Yeah, Mom. I think you were."

"Well, I'm glad for it. Will you two come for dinner soon? Maybe the next weekend Ryder doesn't have a game? I know you're with your friends and probably don't want to talk about things with your father right now. We can talk at dinner?" She sounds so hopeful, my heart does a little squeeze.

"I'm sure we can do that."

"Good. Are you sure you're all right? You can talk to me. Cry, scream, call your dad a miserable bastard. I'm always here for you."

"I know, Mom. I'm just... I think I'm still in shock, you know? Right now, I just need to shut my brain down and be with Ryder."

"I don't blame you. I'll let you go, but call me as soon as you're up for it, okay, sweetie?"

My eyes pool with tears. This time, they're happy ones. Mostly. "Yeah, Mom. I will."

"I love you, Alexis."

"Love you too, Mom."

Isla and Mira watch me as I hang up the phone and shove it in my pocket. But not before silencing it. I'm sure it's about to blow up, and I know Rach will want to talk to me about everything, but I'm not in the mood. I need some time to decompress. For all of this to scab over a bit so I'm not poking at an open wound.

"We're really sorry this happened," Mira says, resting her hand on mine. "This didn't turn out to be the fun game we hoped it would be. I feel like this is our fault for pushing you to come."

"You didn't," I say with a shake of my head. "I wanted to come. And, honestly, this was a long time coming. I knew my dad didn't really love me, but I was holding on to this stupid hope, you know? Now I can move on."

I'm done with my dad. I've given him so many chances. He's shown me who he is, and it's time I believe him. The ache in my chest is intense, but there's also this underlying relief. I don't have to put myself out there anymore, only to be rejected again and again and again. My conscience is clear. I doubt my dad can say the same.

Then again, I'm not sure he has one to begin with.

Footsteps sound in the hall outside of the family room, and the door opens to reveal Ryder and the rest of the guys who participated in the post-game press conference. He doesn't say a word, just strides across the room and pulls me into a crushing hug.

"Baby. Hey. How're you doing?"

"Better now that you're here."

"Fuck. I hated having to leave you." Ryder presses a kiss to my temple. "What do you want to do now? Are you up for going to Maddox's house, or do you need to go home? Tell me what you need, Lexi."

I love that he keeps checking in with me. I love him. "Let's go. It'll help distract me."

"We can definitely be distracting," Griffin agrees with a waggle of his eyebrows. Mira snorts.

"All right, then. Let's roll."

WE'RE AN HOUR INTO OUR NIGHT AND LOTS OF FOOD has been eaten, wine has been drunk, and the ice cream is about to come out. I'm still shattered by everything my dad said, but being here with Ryder and our friends soothes that ache. For the first time since moving back from Chicago, I truly feel like I'm not alone. The man who loves me has his arm wrapped around me, the women I can't wait to get to know better are giggling about something Griffin said, and the guys go out of their way to include me in their conversations and easy banter.

It's nice. Really nice.

Isla has just taken ice cream orders when Ryder's phone rings. I can feel it vibrating in his pocket.

"Whoever it is can call back," he tells me when he catches me looking. The vibrating cuts off, only to start up again immediately. Ryder frowns but ignores it. When the phone rings for the third time, he sighs and digs it out of his pocket. An unfamiliar name flashes across the screen.

"Shit," he says, a frown marring his forehead. "It's my agent. I should probably take this."

The room falls silent as Ryder accepts the call.

"Hey, John."

Knots twist my stomach so brutally that I worry I may be sick. I watch every expression that flits across Ryder's face. I'm not the only one. He's got the full attention of the room.

"Sure. Yes, I understand. No, that won't be necessary. Right. Yep. Sounds good." Ryder runs his hand through his hair but flashes me a reassuring smile when he notices me staring at him and chewing on my lower lip so hard I'm probably drawing blood. "Okay. Yeah, I'll be there. Thanks, John. Talk to you soon."

The air is so thick with tension, you could almost choke on it. Ryder hangs up the phone, blows out a stuttering breath between closed lips, and looks at the guys.

"The bigwigs want to talk to me about what happened tonight. You guys'll probably get similar calls from your agents. Sounds like they're opening up some kind of inquiry into Coach's behavior. Apparently, public reaction has been swift and almost universal." Ryder turns to look at me. "Everyone wants him fired. Especially the female fans. The hashtag *TeamAlexis* is trending. You've already got fan sites."

Shocked, all I can manage is a watery laugh. Fan sites? That's ridiculous. I didn't do anything. I'm not some celebrity or hero.

"We also have a ship name, I guess? It's pretty terrible. Rylexis." Ryder chuckles.

"Ooooh," Griffin claps his hands gleefully. "Rylexis. I love it." He pulls out his phone and begins typing away. Not a minute later, he's laughing hysterically. "Oh my god, they're already making AI mashups of your faces to see what your babies would look like. For the record, they're terrifying. Most of them look like that horrible CGI baby in the *Twilight* movies."

My watery laugh turns into a full-blown belly laugh. "No, they are not." Where would they even find a picture of me? My socials are all set to private. Though, I guess they could have pulled my profile picture and used that.

Griffin holds his phone out for us to see. His eyes crinkle with pent-up laughter.

"Holy shit," Logan says. "That's just not right."

Maddox physically recoils. "I'm not sure you two should procreate. Ow!"

Isla smacks Maddox upside the head. "That's not how their kids would really look. Don't be an idiot."

"That one has six fingers on one hand," Sebastian remarks.

"Okay, okay. Enough with the AI babies." Ryder chuckles. "Anyway, they want to meet with us tomorrow."

"Does that mean your job is safe?" I'm afraid to even ask. If he loses his spot on the team because of me, I'll never forgive myself.

Strong arms wrap around me and squeeze. "I'm not worried. Not with everything he said being caught on camera. My guess is they'll fire him to save face. Which isn't great for the team this far into the season, but then again, maybe we'll all play better without his toxic bullshit."

"We'll be fine no matter what happens," Sebastian says confidently. "We're a solid team. And we've got Coach Fry. He's good at what he does. Good enough to take over, I think." The goalie's eyes land on me. "And Cross deserves to be fired after what he said and how he acted."

I accept the words for what they are. Support. These guys could so easily hate me for throwing their season into potential chaos. But they don't. They don't blame me at all. They're in my corner. In Ryder's corner. It's reassuring because public opinion might be in my favor right now, but if my dad gets fired and the team struggles because of it? That favor could quickly turn to hate. And the internet is a scary place sometimes. Especially for women involved with a sports star.

"Okay!" Mira claps her hands to get everyone's attention. "We can worry about what the big shots say tomorrow. Tonight, I say we binge on ice cream and look at all the scary baby monstrosities. We can even make our own. There are websites for that, right?"

I groan. "As long as no one nicknames our imaginary baby after a cryptid."

fifty-four

LEXI

"Has there been any news about your dad's job?" Rachel stares at me expectantly through my phone's screen. She's checked in with me every day since things imploded.

It's been five days of holing up in Ryder's apartment. I haven't even gone to campus for my classes. My professors all approved online coursework until the media attention dies down. It became very clear my first day back after the game that I couldn't safely walk through campus alone. I was swarmed by reporters the moment I approached the building holding my classroom. Ryder hired a bodyguard to escort me to and from class, but I just couldn't do it. All the attention has nearly given me an ulcer. So now, my bodyguard, Tom, only follows me around when I'm forced to leave Ryder's apartment. Ryder hasn't wanted me to go home to mine since everything went down, and I don't want to be separated from him, either.

I tried to tell Ryder that hiring a bodyguard was overkill, but in private moments, I can admit to myself that Tom's presence helps me feel safer. It's strange to be the source of public curiosity like this, and I don't enjoy having cameras shoved in my face. All this chaos has to die down sometime, but for now, people are still very much interested in me, my relationship with my dad, and my romance with Ryder.

"Earth to Lexi," Rachel sing-songs.

I shake my head, clearing the thoughts away. "Sorry. No news yet. I'm sure he's got clauses in his contract about being fired, so it's not a decision the team would make lightly."

Though I'm looking forward to all of this being resolved, I'm also terrified of how it's going to impact my life. Because make no mistake, it *will* impact my life either way. I've spent way too many sleepless hours mentally flipping through every possible outcome.

Rachel's eyes narrow. "You holding up okay?"

"I don't know. It's been a lot."

Understatement.

"Ryder still being the perfect man?"

My lips twitch up in an anemic smile. "Yeah. He's everything, Rach. I don't know what I'd do without him. I hope I never have to find out."

"I'm happy for you, Lex." Rachel sighs. Her head tilts and her eyes grow dreamy. "Maybe I need to find myself a sexy, protective hockey player."

"Move to Minneapolis, and I'll hook you up with one," I say. The idea of it has my smile widening.

"You know I'm a Chicago-girlie for life. I love this city. Plus, I've worked my ass off to get this junior position at the firm. No way am I letting Karl get the job just so I can pursue a six-foot hottie with a perfect bubble butt." Rachel squeezes the air, imagining a peachy behind. It's ridiculous enough that I laugh.

"Who has a perfect bubble butt?" Ryder strides into his bedroom, where I'm sprawled on my stomach on the bed. He bends down and kisses the crown of my head. He waves at Rachel through my phone. "Hey, Rach."

"Hi, Ryder. Lex was just trying to convince me to move to Minneapolis by enticing me with the prospect of being set up with one of your teammates."

Ryder's forehead crinkles as he considers it. "You might get along with Sebastian. He's a good guy. Though, I get the feeling he's hung up on someone."

"Nah." Rachel chuckles. "I've got plans that involve beating Karl for that job and then rubbing it in his smug, entitled face. I dream about making that brown-nosing idiot cry."

Ryder laughs. "You're kinda scary."

Rachel rolls her eyes. "Only to people who cross me. Like I said before, treat my bestie well and we won't have any issues, Hanson."

"That's my plan. I'm going to treat her like a beautiful, grumpy princess for as long as she lets me." Ryder chuckles as he dodges the half-hearted swat I aim at his stomach.

"Good. All right, well, I gotta get going. Adam and I are going to a Blizzard game tonight. I have the best sign ready for this game."

For the first time all day, I laugh loudly and freely. "I think I've created a monster. Chase Bowen probably cries in the shower after every game you go to."

Rachel's smile is absolutely wicked. "One can only hope. Talk to you soon, Lex. Call me the minute you hear anything about your dad, 'kay?"

I nod. "I will. Have fun at the game tonight. Don't start too much shit."

"Me?" She holds her hand to her chest. "I don't know what you're talking about. Later, Lex. Bye, Ryder."

"Night, Rach."

We wave and exchange one final goodbye. When I hang up the phone, Ryder flops down next to me on the bed and pulls me into his arms. His chest shakes with quiet laughter.

"I wish I could see Chase's face when he sees whatever sign she has planned. Is she really planning to go to games on a regular basis?"

"I think so. At least, as many as she can afford. She really loved going to yours with me. And Adam is always up for watching a game. Doesn't even matter what sport it's for. Except for golf. He hates golf."

"Gotta say I agree with him on that." Ryder shifts our bodies so my head is on his chest and I'm almost lying completely on top of him. He rests his chin on my head and squeezes me tightly in his arms. We fall silent for a few minutes. It's not an uncomfortable silence. Never is, with Ryder. We just soak up each other's warmth and affection.

"I heard from my agent that a rep for the team has a press conference planned for tomorrow afternoon. They're going to announce their decision regarding your dad then."

My heart lurches, skips a beat, then begins to thunder. "Oh."

Ryder shifts us so he's sitting with his back against the headboard and my legs straddle his lap. His icy-blue eyes study my face. I'm sure he can see the panic splashed across it. "Whatever happens, you're going to be okay. *We're* going to be okay. We'll get through this together."

"I know," I whisper. "I just... What if everyone hates me if he gets fired? All the attention has been overwhelming, and it's mostly been supportive. I don't know if I can deal with random strangers talking about how much they hate me on the internet. Yes, that's stupid, because some random Chad's opinion shouldn't matter, but I..."

"Hey." Ryder's fingers gently grip my chin as he silently asks me to look at him. "You don't have to explain. Trust me, all of us know how shitty people can be. And I won't be able to protect you from all of it, but I'll sure as hell try my best to."

My face crumples, and I press my nose into his neck to avoid letting him see the tears pooling in my eyes. "What did I do to deserve you?"

"I ask myself the same thing about you all the time, baby." He holds me in silence as our hearts sync. Despite everything going on around us, in many ways, I've never felt as safe or settled as I have staying here with Ryder. His roommate, Aaron, is rarely home, and when we have the place all to ourselves, I dream about what it would be like to do this every day. To wake up next to him, to come home to each other and share dinners, to stay up way too late each night watching movies or making love.

"My mom asked if we could come over for dinner next Wednesday. You guys don't have a game. Would that work for you?"

Ryder's hands brush up and down my spine. "Yeah,

Oscar. That works. Have you talked to your mom recently?"

"We've been talking and texting a lot more since everything with my dad. It's been nice. I didn't like feeling angry with my mom for having an affair with Jeff, so I'm glad I know the truth now. She was my rock growing up, and I missed her."

It's been such a relief repairing our relationship. I've even talked to Jeff a few times and can admit that he's incredibly kind and so good to my mom. I feel bad about the way I thought of him before. But I can't change the past, so I do my best to make up for it now and get to know him. And honestly? It's been nice. He tells terrible dad jokes and still calls me kiddo, but I'm growing to like it.

Sometimes I wonder if this is what things should have been like with my dad all along.

Ryder kisses me with soft, pliant lips. "I'm glad to hear that. I like your mom. And Jeff."

"They like you too," I tell him. Ever since Ryder defended me on national television, Mom and Jeff have been firmly on Team Ryder. My phone vibrates on the bed by our feet. "That's probably her now. She's been bugging me for an answer about dinner."

Leaning back, I grab my phone and press the green answer button without bothering to glance at the screen. "Calm your tits," I say, chuckling. "I was just about to call you back."

There's a beat of silence, and then a voice that is most definitely not my mother's fills my ear. "Really, Alexis? That's how you answer your phone?"

All the color drains from my face, and Ryder is instantly on alert. He tugs the phone away from my ear, so he can see who's calling, and when he sees *Dad* on the screen, he presses the speaker button. His hands fall to my thighs, keeping me tethered to the earth and him, and his blue eyes are alert and focused on me. "What do you want, Dad?"

A deep, annoyed sigh filters through the speaker. "Look, things got out of hand the other day. It was the heat of the moment, and I said some things I shouldn't have. I want to get things back to the way they were."

The way they were. It doesn't escape me that not once in his little speech does my father say he's sorry or express any real regret. This call isn't about making things right with me.

"And what does that mean to you, exactly?" I ask, my voice wavering slightly before I force myself to harden it. "Getting things back to the way they were. What does that look like?"

My dad sighs again. "Please don't be dramatic, Alexis. This was just a misunderstanding."

A misunderstanding. When I look up at Ryder, a deep scowl mars his face. He stares at the phone like he may reach right through it and strangle my dad. "I fail to see how any of this is a misunderstanding," I say.

"I thought you were using Ryder to punish me," my dad says. As if it's obvious. As if I should have known. He says it like I shouldn't be offended that this is what he thinks of me.

A harsh, cynical bark of laughter spills out of me. "You're unbelievable, you know that?"

"Oh, come on, Alexis. It's not that much of a stretch. You always threw a fit when I couldn't make it to some little thing or other. So, I thought you were getting back at me for canceling dinner with you to attend to Ryder's injuries."

My grip on the phone tightens. "You thought I'd use and manipulate a good man just to get back at my dad for canceling dinner plans?"

"There's no need to be so sensitive. Obviously, I was mistaken. Which is why I'm calling. I want to make things right. I'd like to talk things out and schedule a press conference for tomorrow morning, so we can show a united front."

Stunned silent, I stare at Ryder and mouth, *Is he serious?* My boyfriend's hands grip my thighs a little tighter. There's no missing the rage in his eyes. He's furious on my behalf.

"So, that's what this is about," I finally say. My voice comes out flat and lifeless, but tears pool in my eyes. Just when I thought my father couldn't stoop any lower. "You want me to help you save your job."

My dad scoffs. "You owe me that much, Alexis. I've paid for all of your schooling and the majority of your living expenses. Where do you think that money comes from? A tree in the backyard?"

I want to scream. To throw my phone against the wall. I want to make him feel even a fraction of the pain he's caused me with his rejection over the years. Ryder opens his mouth to tell my dad off, but I shake my head. I need to fight this battle alone.

"No."

Silence. And then, "No? What do you mean, *no*, Alexis?"

"I mean no. No, I don't want to help you sweep this under the rug. No, I will not sit next to you at a press conference and lie to the world. I won't tell them we've patched things up or that you're a great dad or that I think you've learned your lesson. I mean no, I will not help you save your job."

"You *owe* me this, Alexis. It's your fault I'm in this position in the first place!"

The tears in my eyes overflow and drip down my cheeks. But I don't let him hear how much he's hurting me. "No, Arthur. It's your fault you're in this position. It's your fault we don't have a relationship. It's your fault you're a shitty father. I don't *owe you* anything. I'm done."

"Done? I don't think so, Alexis. You do this, and I won't pay for your last year of school. I won't pay for your rent. You do this, and you're on your own. Do you understand?"

I make a strangled sound that's something between a laugh and a sob. "Fine. If that's how you want to play it, Arthur, fine. I appreciate that you've paid for my school and living expenses, I really do. But in every other way, you've been an absent parent for a long, long time."

My dad growls. "You ungrateful little bitch, I—"

"That's enough," Ryder roars. He gently pries the phone from my hand and presses me to his chest with his free hand. "One more word, Arthur, and I will get in my car, drive to your house, and kick your sorry ass. How *dare* you speak to your own daughter like that? You're the worst kind of man. Your ex-wife is a saint for putting up with you as long as she did. And as for Lexi? You're a fucking idiot. You've missed out on years with the most intelligent, beautiful, loyal daughter, and for what? A job you're about to lose, if there's any justice in the world?"

Ryder's chest heaves. "You're pathetic. Pathetic and

selfish and sad." He looks down at me. "Baby, do you want to speak to your father again after this?"

All I can do is shake my head *no*. My throat is tight with the sobs I'm trying desperately to hold in. Ryder presses a soft kiss to my forehead.

"Lexi doesn't want to speak to you again. And if she does, she will contact you. From now on, you will leave her alone. Do you understand?"

"I don't know who you think you are," my dad snarls. "But—"

"I'm the man who loves your daughter," Ryder says, cutting him off. "I'm the luckiest bastard alive. And I'm the man who will kick your pathetic ass if you go against her wishes. Don't fucking try me, Cross. I swear to god, there's nothing I want more."

My dad sputters and coughs, but Ryder ignores him. His mesmerizing eyes are fixed on me. "Do you have anything else you need to say, baby?" I shake my head. "Okay. She has nothing to say to you. Don't fucking call her again, got it?"

And before he can utter another word, Ryder hangs up on my dad. The call ends, and with it, my relationship with my father. Twenty-three years of reaching for his love. Twenty-three years of striving for his acceptance. Done. Just like that. With the touch of a button and the silencing of a call.

"Fuck, baby." Ryder drops the phone and wraps both arms around me, pulling me tight against his chest as the tears fall and the sobs finally break free. "I'm so sorry, sweetheart. I'm so sorry."

I'm breaking because of the things my dad said. All the callous remarks and the awful assumptions. I'm breaking because it's clear he never loved me. My heart hurts because he couldn't even bring himself to apologize for making me feel unwanted. But the thing that pops out of my mouth is, "What am I going to do? I can't afford to pay for school and rent with my shitty part-time job. Fuck, Ryder, what am I going to do?"

"You're going to move in with me," he says. The words are so calm, so sure. Like it's the most obvious answer in the world.

"I can't do that." I press my face into his chest. "You don't have to do that. This is my problem, Ryder. I wasn't trying to guilt you into anything."

"Oscar." He releases me. His hands go to my face, applying gentle pressure to get me to look up at him. "Look at me, OTG."

My vision is blurry from crying, but reluctantly, I obey.

"Move in with me. I'm not asking because you've guilt tripped me into it. I'm not asking because I feel obligated. I'm asking because I fucking love you and I want to fall asleep next to you every night and wake up with you pressed against my chest every morning. I'm asking because I hate being away from you. Move in with me. Because you've become my family. My home. So, please let me provide you with one."

This can't be real. *He* can't be real. Real life doesn't have knights in shining hockey skates. It doesn't have happy endings.

"Please, baby. Move in with me?"

Maybe this isn't real. Maybe this is all some crazy, elaborate dream. The thing is? I'm not sure I care either way. Because Ryder Hanson is my home too.

"Are you sure?"

"More sure than I've ever been about anything." He runs his thumb along my jaw.

"Then, yes. Yes, I'll move in with you."

"Seriously?"

I grin, despite the tears still streaming down my face. They're happy tears, now. "Seriously."

Ryder lets out a resounding *whoop*, then rolls so I'm pinned beneath him on the bed. He kisses me senseless as his fingers fumble to remove our clothes. We're both panting and desperate, and as soon as we're naked, he pushes inside of me. I cry out, needing to feel him in every part of me. I need him to ground me. I'm worried all of this is a dream, and at any moment, it might dissipate and drift away. Ryder pulls out and pushes into me again.

"This is real, baby," he murmurs in my ear. I must have said that out loud. "This is real. I love you so much." His hips snap against mine. "You're my home, Lexi. Let me be yours."

Home.

The word takes on new meaning. It finally feels right. Just like Ryder does as I welcome him into my body.

Home.

fifty-five

LEXI

"You okay, Lexi?" Mira flops down next to me on Maddox's couch. She hands me a wineglass, which I accept gratefully. Isla takes a seat on my other side. The guys are gathered around the kitchen island, talking, drinking beers, and trying not to stress over the future of their team. Ryder looks over at me every few seconds. Always checking to make sure I'm okay. Just like my new friends.

They're all concerned about me and Ryder. But mostly me. It's surreal to have so many people that care after years of it just being me and my mom, then me, Rachel, and Adam.

"I'm okay," I tell Mira. And I mostly mean it. I'm still stressed as hell and worried about what the fans will say if my dad loses his job today, but Ryder and I are going to look at some apartments next week, and he's been amazing. So, yeah, I'm okay. Or I will be.

"Whatever happens, we all have your back," Isla reassures me. "The guys already have a plan for a press conference if needed. They won't let anyone blame you if your dad gets fired."

"I hope he does," Mira mutters. "That bastard deserves to lose his job."

A grin curls the corners of my lips. Yeah. I'll be okay.

The low-level hum of sports recaps and speculation gives way to music and the flash of the Rogues' logo. I freeze in my seat. All the guys move into the living room, abandoning the kitchen and spreading out across the couch and chairs. When Isla moves to perch on Maddox's lap, Ryder takes her place and wraps his arms around me.

"Whatever happens, I've got you."

I offer him a tremulous smile. "I know."

Sportscasters fill the screen. Four of them, sitting behind a studio desk. They begin to talk about the press conference that's about to take place, give a rundown of how we got here, and make their speculations. When footage of my dad's outburst and my escape flash across the massive screen, I flinch. Ryder's right there to soothe me.

"I hate that everyone saw that," I murmur.

"I know. I do too." Ryder squeezes me in his arms. "I do too."

"Chuck LeFevre is live in Minneapolis, where the Rogues are holding a press conference to reveal the future of Head Coach, Arthur Cross. Chuck, what's the mood like there in the Twin Cities?"

The camera cuts to a middle-aged man with dark hair and a navy-blue suit. He taps his ear, then nods once at the camera.

"Yeah, Eddie, the atmosphere here is tense. We all saw the video of Cross blowing up at his defenseman, Ryder Hanson. The footage was shocking enough on its own, but when we learned he was speaking about his own daughter, it took the confrontation to a whole new level.

"We're unsure how long Hanson has been dating Cross's daughter, but it seems pretty serious, given Hanson's replies in the post-game press conference. Public outcry against the coach was swift, with fan pages dedicated to Hanson and Alexis Cross popping up overnight."

"Oh, god." I cover my face with my hands when they show a photo of me. "This is so weird."

"You get used to it," Sebastian reassures me. "Sort of."

"And can you tell us what the local fans think about all of this?" one sportscaster asks Chuck.

"Well, David, the vast majority I've spoken to believe Cross was completely out of line and have expressed doubts that he's capable of bringing this team all the way to the Cup. Others are worried that a change in the coaching staff will ruin that chance altogether. It's hard to say where public opinion will fall when all is said and done."

"They're going to hate me," I groan. "I'll never be able to leave the house alone again."

Ryder chuckles. "I thought you liked Tom?"

"Tom's nice and all," I say, "but I'd like to go back to my classes in person, and he sticks out like a giant, suited, sore thumb. Especially in my morning yoga class."

Isla giggles. "He's not very discreet, is he?"

"Nope."

"Now, Chuck, can you tell me if—Wait, we're just getting word that the Rogues' management has arrived. We're going

live to Minneapolis where a decision has been made about the future of Head Coach Arthur Cross."

My stomach flips and rolls and my hands shake. Ryder pulls me onto his lap and holds me tightly.

"I've got you, baby," he whispers in my ear. "You and me. No matter what. I've got you."

God, I love him.

The room falls silent. Five massive men lean forward, their eyes glued to the screen. This isn't just about me. Whatever the outcome of this announcement, it will affect them too.

"Good afternoon," a representative for the team says into the microphone. *"We all know why we're here, so I won't drag this out. Last week, Head Coach Cross was in an altercation with one of our players, Ryder Hanson. That altercation expanded to involve several of our first-line play-ers, and a good portion of it was caught on camera. After reviewing that footage, as well as statements from the players and witnesses, we have concluded that Coach Cross was the one who instigated the argument."*

My stomach twists.

"Furthermore, we were appalled by the sentiments expressed by Coach Cross toward his own daughter and Hanson. The language and attitudes used by Cross are not reflections of the values held by the Rogues' organization. We would like to extend our sincerest apologies to Alexis Cross and Ryder Hanson. We have decided that allowing Arthur Cross to continue in his position as the head coach of the Rogues would create a hostile environment, which would not be conducive to a winning season and a unified team. It is with those considerations in mind that we have decided to

sever our relationship with Arthur Cross, effective imme-diately."

My heart skips a beat. I gasp, and the rest of the room breaks out in quiet murmurs.

"We know this announcement will worry some of you, as the team has been playing hard and has a real shot at going all the way this year, but we want to assure you we are doing everything in our power to ensure that doesn't change. Assistant Coach Mike Fry will step into the role of interim Head Coach. Mike has been with us for years and is a vital part of the current team's success.

"At the end of the season, we will decide on future steps. For now, we ask that you remain respectful of the parties involved. This decision was made entirely by the team's owners and management, and neither Alexis Cross nor Ryder Hanson were consulted in any way, outside of making witness statements. We have a great team this year, and we are grateful for your continued support. I fully believe these boys will go all the way."

The Rogues' representative concludes his remarks and opens the floor to questions, but none of us listen. We're all too busy processing what just happened.

My dad was fired. He's no longer the Rogues' head coach.

It's done.

The guys talk about Coach Fry and speculate about who they'll call up to replace him as assistant coach. They don't seem all that worried about losing their head coach in the middle of the season. But I am. I think I'll delete all my social media for a while. I don't know if I can handle the potential backlash.

"Breathe, Oscar. Everything is going to be okay. This is a good thing. People will see that."

Will they?

"He's right, Hot Cross Buns," Griffin says. Mira whacks him upside the head. "Ow! That's her nickname, Jesus. Lay off me, woman."

Isla giggles.

Griffin rubs the back of his head. "As I was saying before my roomie assaulted me, you don't need to worry. Fry is good. Really good. Hell, I think he's a better offensive coach than your dad. We won't give the fans reason to blame you for anything."

"That's right," Logan assures me. "We'll be too busy winning for them to be mad."

"Thanks, guys," I say. My heart is full.

"We're here for both of you," Sebastian adds.

Ryder grins. "Along those lines, how do you guys feel about helping move shit?"

"What do you mean, move shit?" Maddox leans forward, one eyebrow raised.

"I mean, I know a great way you guys can be here for Lexi and me. We're getting a place together, so we could use some help moving."

"Oh my god, are you serious?" Isla claps her hands, bouncing on Maddox's lap. The big guy groans but smiles.

I nod. "We're looking at places this week."

"That's really great, you two," Sebastian says. His smile is warm, and I know he means it. "Of course, we'll help."

Logan nods. "That's what family does."

Family.

Yeah. That's exactly what we are now.

PEOPLE DON'T HATE ME AS MUCH AS I FEARED THEY would. Some of them do, don't get me wrong—the internet is a cesspool of trolls and angry men—but overall, I've been pleasantly surprised by the notes of support I've received. The media circus still hasn't died all the way down, but it's significantly less intense than it was right after my dad said those horrible things to me at the game.

I even went back to school in person yesterday. Granted, Tom was with me, and I got more than my fair share of curious looks, whispers, and not-so-subtly taken photographs, but it was fine. I made it through. And Tom didn't even have to beat one person up.

"You almost ready, Oscar?" Ryder sidles up to my back and wraps his arms around my waist as I finish putting on my mascara. "We don't want to be late."

I give myself one last look in the mirror. I don't know why I'm so nervous. It's just dinner with my mom and Jeff. But Ryder and I found an apartment today. One that we love. And it's really close to Maddox and Isla's place. It's not as big and fancy, but it's large enough that it will hold all our friends. I'm already planning the first dinner party.

So, tonight, I'm telling my mom that Ryder and I are moving in together. I guess I'm nervous she won't approve. It won't change my mind, but I want her to be excited for me. For my sake and for Ryder's.

"Okay," I say on an exhalation. "I'm ready. Let's go."

He holds my hand the whole drive, and we make plans for our apartment. Neither of us really has much—most of the furniture in my apartment belongs to my roommate, Sarah, and most of the stuff in his belongs to his roommate, Aaron. Of course, I worry about how I'll pay for all of it, but Ryder won't hear it. He tells me he makes more than enough money for the both of us, and all he wants me to worry about paying for is my schooling. And the only reason he's not paying for that is because I refused. I won't take advantage of him. I don't love him for his money or his rising fame, and I never want him to think I do.

"We're here," Ryder says as he pulls into my mom's driveway. He doesn't let go of my hand or make any move to get out of the car. Just stares at the front door like he's worried it's going to bite him.

Running my thumb over his, I ignore my own worries and try to assuage his. "I've got you." I echo the words he so often says back to him. "My mom's a fan of yours now. They're going to be excited for us."

Ice-blue eyes swing my way. There's a furrow between them. "You sure?"

"Completely. And even if they aren't, it wouldn't make me change my mind about you. I love you, Handsome. We're going to live together, and it's going to be great. We'll pick out furniture, hang so many photos on the wall, and make messes in the kitchen.

"I'll make you bougie grilled cheese when it's cold or homemade chicken noodle soup when you're sick. You'll carry me to bed when I'm too tired to drag my ass there myself. You'll leave the toilet seat up, and we'll argue about it. I'll leave too much makeup all over the bathroom vanity, and it'll drive you nuts.

"We'll fall asleep in each other's arms and wake up tangled together in the sheets. It'll be perfect and hard and wonderful. And I'm going to love every minute of it."

Emotion pools in Ryder's eyes. He blinks at me a few times, his mouth opening and closing. But no words come out. Instead, he wraps his hand around the back of my neck and pulls me in for a kiss that melts my panties and sets fire to my heart. His tongue sweeps across my lips and dances with mine. He kisses me like I'm everything.

When he pulls away, I'm panting. "I love you, Alexis Genevieve Cross. So fucking much, I feel like my heart might explode."

"I love you too, Ryder." Movement out of the corner of my eye draws my attention. My mom leans in the doorway to her house, a wide smile on her face. Jeff peeks at us from behind her. I giggle. "We have an audience."

It takes everything Ryder has to drop his hand from the back of my neck and peel himself away from me. "Come on, then. Let's go have dinner with your family."

We climb out of the car, and Ryder links his fingers through mine. The contact grounds me. Ryder grounds me.

"Hey, you two." My mom's smile is so wide, it makes her eyes crinkle in the corners. "We're so glad you could make it."

"Hey, Mom." I relax into her arms when she wraps me in a tight hug. When she releases me, she turns to Ryder and holds her open arms out to him. He only hesitates for a second before accepting her embrace. He's so much taller than her, it should look comical—the way she's holding him like he's a child in need of comfort. The same way she held me. But it's not comical. It's everything.

Ryder's shoulders are only stiff for a moment, and then his body heaves with a deep sigh. His eyes close, and the softest smile plays at his lips. My mom pats his back and just hugs him for a solid minute. It makes my heart fill with so much love. For my mom and for the giant man who has proven himself to be gentle and kind and loving. He savors the hug, and when he finally pulls away, there are tears in his eyes.

"Thanks, Mrs. Cross."

"Psh," my mom says, waving a hand in his direction. "None of that, now. That's not how you refer to family."

"Family?" His voice is so hopeful, my chest aches.

"Family," my mom replies. "I'm afraid you're stuck with us now, Ryder. And I'm a hugger."

Ryder's smile starts off small but grows with each passing second. His eyes glitter with happiness and love. "It's been a while since I've had mom-hugs. I think I can live with that."

Mom wraps her hand around his and gives it a squeeze. "Well, whenever you need a mom-hug, I'm here, son."

A tear slips down Ryder's cheek. He clears his throat and squeezes my mom's hand back. "Thanks, Kelly. Really."

As Ryder and my mom exchange a look of understanding, Jeff pulls me into a hug. "Hey, kiddo. It's so good to see you again. We've been worried about you."

"You have?"

"Of course," Jeff says. As if it's the most obvious thing in the world that he'd be worried about me, along with my mom. As if all my shitty behavior has been long forgotten.

"Jeff, I—"

"Nope. None of that, Lexi. You have nothing to apologize for. Maybe if we'd been honest with you, things would have started out differently. But none of that matters.

Now, we get to move forward. And eat a really delicious roast. Your mother has outdone herself this time." He gives me a wink, and I chuckle. Then he holds out his hand for my mom. "Come on, Kelly. Let's get these kids something to drink, so they're not parched when we interrogate them."

My mother's bell-like laugh is free and joyous. I'm hit with so much gratitude as she and Jeff walk into the house hand in hand. She's happy. Really happy. Maybe for the first time since I was born. And so am I. The Cross women have finally found their matches.

"You good?" Ryder asks me quietly as he steps up to my back and wraps his arms around my middle.

I sigh, letting myself soak up his heat and his strength. "Yeah. I'm good. Better than good." Turning in his arms, I look up at the man I once thought could be a serial killer and laugh at myself. I should have realized my error right away. No serial killer has eyes as kind as his.

Ryder smiles, and his dimple makes an appearance. "What?"

"Just thinking about the first time we met."

One eyebrow hitches up. "Oh, yeah?"

"Yep. I was so wrong about you. You could never be a killer."

He laughs, and I feel it all the way down to my toes, the comforting vibration of it filling me. "Obviously."

"But you *are* a thief," I say.

His second eyebrow joins the first at his hairline. "A thief? Really? How so?"

"Because." A slow grin tips up one corner of my lips. "You stole my heart."

Ryder laughs again, tugging me into his chest, and I

join in. "Oh, Oscar. That's the cheesiest line I've ever heard."

Pulling away from him, I pretend to pout. "Whatever. You know you love it."

"I do." He bends down, his face centimeters from mine.

"You love me," I whisper.

"So much it hurts, baby," he replies. "Because you've stolen my heart too. Except, I don't want it back. I want you to keep it for me. Keep it safe. Can you do that?"

I nod. "I've got you, Handsome."

His lips feather across mine. "And I've got you, Oscar. Always."

Always.

My heart skips a beat.

I really love the sound of that.

epilogue

THE FOLLOWING CHRISTMAS

RYDER

"ARE YOU SURE EVERYTHING IS ALL SET?" I ASK Sebastian for the tenth time.

His chuckle filters through the phone at my ear. "I promise. It's all exactly as you specified, and we'll be waiting in the bedrooms."

"What about the cars? If she sees them, the whole thing could be ruined."

"Relax, brother." Bash laughs again. "We all crammed into two vehicles, and they're parked off the side of the garage. She won't notice them."

"Okay. Yeah, of course. Sorry, I'm just nervous." Despite the frigid winter temperatures, there's sweat on my brow. I wipe it away with the sleeve of my coat. "Shit, she's coming out of the gas station. We'll be there in half an hour."

"Got it. Take some deep breaths. Relax. You've got this."

Navarro's pep talk almost works. "I've got this. Thanks again, man. See you guys soon."

I hang up just as Lexi makes it to the car. She shivers as she climbs in and wiggles her perfect ass against the heated leather seat. "All good?"

"Yeah." Her nose wrinkles. "That bathroom was gross, though."

I chuckle as I pull out of the gas station and back onto the road. "All gas station bathrooms are." Reaching for her hand, I link our fingers. I need to touch her. She's the only thing that can calm me down. "Are you ready for a weekend away?"

"Yes." Lexi leans across the armrest and lets her head fall to my shoulder. "God, am I ready."

After everything happened with her dad, Lexi never fully escaped the attention and gawking of her peers at school. So, she took extra classes and finished a semester early. She thinks we're heading up to the cabin to celebrate that. And we are, but that's not all we're celebrating.

"I'm so proud of you."

"Thanks, Handsome."

"I, uh, I got some news today."

Lexi sits up and turns those emerald eyes of hers my way. "You did? Is it good news?"

We didn't win the Cup last season, but we did make it through three rounds of the playoffs. After Cross was fired and Coach Fry took his place, we had a couple of fumbled games, but we ended the season better than we started it.

And with Lexi in the family box, cheering me on every game she could, my playing got better and better. Now, I almost have as many fans as Maddox, Griffin, Logan, and Bash. Almost. Which is why my agent was pretty confident he could get me a sweet extension offer. But you never know with these kinds of things.

"I heard from John."

Lexi's hand grips mine. "Did they extend your contract?"

I want to tease her. I want to give her sad puppy dog eyes and make her wonder. But I'm too excited, and I can't banish the smile that curves my lips.

"Ohmygod, they did, didn't they?" She's bouncing up and down in her seat. She's so damned adorable. And mine. All mine. God, I'm a lucky bastard.

"Yeah, baby, they did. Five years. And it's huge. So many zeros that I don't know how to wrap my mind around it."

"Hell, yeah!" Lexi shouts. She's so loud and enthusiastic, I'm sure they can hear her from the next town over. "I'm so fucking proud of you, Ryder. So proud."

The thing I love about Alexis Cross? She'd be just as proud of me if it was only a one-year extension for chump change. She doesn't care about the money or the notoriety. She only cares that I'm happy. And I am.

I'm hoping I'll be even happier by the time the night is over.

"Thanks, Oscar. I'm just glad I don't have to try to convince you to move with me because I got traded."

She waves her free hand in the air in a flippant gesture. "You wouldn't have to convince me. I'd go wherever you go."

So easily. She says it so easily. As if it would be no big deal to uproot her life and follow me to who-knows-where. Of course, I'd do the same for her. If, one day, she finds her dream job in Chicago or California, or hell, even Alaska, I'll happily pack my bags and follow her there. Because Lexi's not only my biggest fan. I'm hers too.

Gravel crunches beneath our tires as I pull up to the cabin. Our cabin. Lexi's mom and Jeff bought Arthur out shortly after he was fired. Lexi doesn't know it yet, but Kelly and Jeff plan to present us with the deed as a wedding present.

The cabin is lit by that one single exterior light. The guys, Mira, and Isla are all hiding in the back rooms of the house with the blinds closed, so it looks like the place is empty.

"I love you, Alexis Cross. You know I'd go wherever you go, too, right?"

She offers me a blinding smile. "Of course."

Sometimes, every once in a blue moon, I still think about Arthur Cross. And when I do, I feel sorry for him. Not because he's miserable and alone, and the only job he could get coaching hockey was a high school team out in the middle-of-nowhere South Dakota, but because he willingly gave up the love of a woman who offers her loyalty so freely and completely that she's utterly ruined me for anyone else.

But I won't make that mistake. I pat the outline of the box in my pocket for the hundredth time since we left our apartment. No, I'm never giving Lexi up. Not for anyone or anything. I'm making her mine.

"Can you believe it's been a year since we were last

here?" she asks as the car comes to a stop in front of the cabin.

"Nope. It feels like just yesterday when you chucked a wineglass at my head and flashed me those perfect tits of yours." I chuckle when she whacks my arm with the back of her hand before climbing out of the car. Almost the very moment she does, massive, fluffy snowflakes begin to drift down from the sky.

"Oh my god, it's snowing." Lexi looks over at me with big, excited eyes before tilting her head back and catching a snowflake on her tongue. I take a mental picture, because this moment is one I want to remember.

"Just like when we met."

"Well." She chuckles. "Hopefully we won't get a blizzard this time."

"Hopefully not," I agree. My stomach twists itself into a pretzel and my heart hammers in my chest. I extend a hand for the woman I'm in love with. "Come on. Let's get inside and get you warmed up."

She takes my hand with such trust. There's no hesitation. Even after a year of being with her, I still marvel at that. At being the one she trusts implicitly. I leave our bags in the car. We won't need them just yet. My hand shakes as I try to slot the key into the lock.

"Looks like I'm not the only one who needs to warm up." Lexi wraps her arms around my left bicep and presses in close to me. "Come on, Handsome. Let's get inside and get naked."

Chuckling, I finally manage to unlock the door. We'll definitely get naked, but not yet. "After you," I say, pushing the door open. The moment Lexi steps inside the cabin, it lights up like the North Pole. There's a massive tree in the same spot where we put it last year. It's meticulously deco-rated, and I know I have Isla and Mira to thank for that. Fairy lights twinkle and shine from every available ledge, doorway, and surface. The fireplace is lit and crackling, and candles line the mantel. It's perfect. Exactly as I hoped it would look.

"Ryder," Lexi says with a shaky breath. "Oh my god. Look at this place. It's beautiful." She takes a few more steps inside, and I close the door behind us. Her eyes glitter as they absorb it all. Curious fingers trail across fresh evergreen garlands and linger on glass baubles. She takes in everything with so much wonder and focus, she doesn't notice me drop to one knee. "It's the most beautiful thing I've ever seen."

"I can think of one thing more beautiful," I say. My voice is rough with all the emotions clawing up my throat.

"Oh, yeah?" she says, her voice light and teasing. She spins around. "And what's tha—"

Lexi's words die on her tongue, and she stands there, silent, mouth open. Tears brim in her eyes, making them look impossibly greener. "Ryder?"

"The most beautiful thing I've ever seen," I say after clearing my throat, "isn't a place or an object. It's not the lights in this room or the snow falling outside. The most beautiful thing I've ever seen is the woman standing in front of me. I thought so from the moment your naked, crazy ass threw a wineglass at my head."

Watery laughter bubbles out of her throat as she takes a step toward me.

"But your beauty is so much more than skin deep, Alexis. It permeates everything you say and do. It's in the way you laugh, your loyalty, your love. It's your heart and your mind and every little quirk and habit that makes you *you*." With a shaking hand, I pull the black velvet box out of my pocket and flip it open.

Lexi gasps, tears dripping down her face. "Oh my god."

"I fell in love with you in this cabin, Lexi. I know that sounds crazy, because we barely knew each other and you were determined to fight the thing between us, but it's true. I fell in love with you here, and I've never stopped loving you. *Will* never stop loving you. I'll love you through sickness, I'll love you through hardships and triumphs and joys. I'll love you through the quiet moments and the ones the whole world sees. If you let me, I'll love you forever."

Lexi's hands cover her mouth. She's shaking like a leaf. I hold the ring box up to her, and her gaze pings between the massive cushion-cut diamond and my face.

"Alexis Genevieve Cross, I'm already yours. I have been since the moment you accused me of being an axe murderer. And I want nothing more than for you to be mine. Would you do me the incredible honor of becoming my wife?"

"Yes," Lexi sobs, throwing herself into my waiting arms. "Hell, yes, I will. I love you so much, Ryder. I'm all yours. I've always been yours."

Our lips crash together, and we get so lost in each other, I don't even notice our friends spilling into the room until they start clapping and cheering. Lexi startles, but then she's laughing against my lips between kisses.

"Congratulations, lovebirds," Griffin shouts.

"Let's see the ring," Isla says.

When Lexi and I stare at each other, we both start

laughing. We went straight to making out, and I didn't even slip the ring on her finger.

"May I?"

She holds her left hand out to me while she wipes tears away with her right. "Please."

It's a perfect fit. I made sure of it. The massive diamond glitters and sparkles under the fairy lights.

"It's beautiful, Ryder."

I hook a finger under her chin. My fiancée's eyes meet mine.

Fiancée.

"It's nothing compared to you."

The room erupts into a chorus of *awww*. Lexi giggles, and I kiss her silly. She's breathless when I pull away, and I have to help her stand because her knees wobble. Turning to face our friends—the people who've become our family over the past year—I'm hit with a deep sense of love and belonging.

This is everything I've ever wanted. *She's* everything I've ever wanted. And I'm never—not ever—letting her go.

acknowledgments

Thank you for reading Ryder and Lexi's story!

I know I'm just a teeny tiny little fish in an enormous pond, but it will never cease to amaze me that people read my books, let alone love them. So first and foremost, thank you, dear reader, for giving The Christmas You Crash and the boys of the Rogues a chance. And for giving me a chance. Your time is valuable and there are a million books on your TBR, so that you picked mine up makes me feel like I've won the lottery.

To my bestie, Kim—thanks for listening to me go on and on and on about these books and always acting interested. What would I do without you? That goes for you too, Ashley W. and my sisters. I have talked your ear off about these books and my dreams.

Jennica and Ashley—I hope every writer has colleagues that turn into best friends the way you two have for me. This business can be lonely, but you two always have my back.

Now for the people who have helped make this book pretty inside and out. Thank you to my awesome beta readers. Raquel, Kim, and Jen, thank you for helping me spit shine these books. Thank you to Andra and Laura for creating the most beautiful covers in the world. You're both so sweet and talented, and I feel privileged to work with you. Finally, thank you, Autumn, for taking away all of my errant commas and adding them back where they belong.

And most importantly, to my babies, who inspire me to do hard things and reach for my dreams. Eisley and Jude, I love you both so much that sometimes I tear up just thinking about how great you both are. Is that weird? Whatever. Your mom's weird. ;) Love you, sweeties.

about the author

Piper Hale is a Midwestern girl who loves golden-retriever heroes, imperfect heroines, and some coffee with her sugar. She lives with her two crazy (but amazing) kids in the middle-of-the-map USA.

Piper grew up listening to her dad's silly stories at bedtime, became a voracious reader as a child, and never forgot her high school creative writing teacher, who told her she had what it took to write romance. Even if she didn't give it a go until the pandemic.

These days, you'll find Piper writing contemporary romance that's sassy, sexy, and chock-full of cinnamon rolls.

also by piper hale

For an up-to date list of Piper's books, please click here or visit
https://linktr.ee/piperhale